Tiny White Lies

Fiona PALMER

Tiny White Lies

hachette
AUSTRALIA

hachette
AUSTRALIA

Published in Australia and New Zealand in 2020
by Hachette Australia
(an imprint of Hachette Australia Pty Limited)
Level 17, 207 Kent Street, Sydney NSW 2000
www.hachette.com.au

10 9 8 7 6 5 4 3 2 1

 A catalogue record for this
book is available from the
National Library of Australia

ISBN: 978 0 7336 4162 6 (paperback)

Cover design by Christabella Designs
Cover photographs courtesy of Shutterstock and Getty
Author photo courtesy of Craig Peihopa
Typeset in 12/17.8 pt Sabon LT Pro by Bookhouse, Sydney
Printed and bound in Australia by McPherson's Printing Group

 The paper this book is printed on is certified against the
Forest Stewardship Council® Standards. McPherson's Printing
Group holds FSC® chain of custody certification SA-COC-005379.
FSC® promotes environmentally responsible, socially beneficial
and economically viable management of the world's forests.

To Dr Sam Cunneen and all the amazing doctors who are changing and saving lives

Mackenzie and Blake. I love you to infinity and beyond

1

Ashley

'U SKANKY BITCH*!!*'

'*Why do u bother coming to school, nobody likes you!!!*'

'*Stupid whore with a munted face like a dropped pie!! Go infect some other school.*'

Ashley's fingers were white as they gripped her daughter's iPad. Waves of nausea hit her like rough seas slapping against the side of a boat as she read message after message on her fifteen-year-old daughter's Instagram account. The more she scrolled through the obscene comments the more her face burned hot with rage.

Emily had begged to have an Instagram account last year and Ashley had allowed it, eventually. It was hard to resist her only child's charms and persistent nagging, but it came with the caveat that the password never be changed so Ashley could keep tabs. Which she did and found it all to be innocent friend chatter. But after a while the checks grew further apart until they stopped altogether. That was until today.

If Ashley Grisham allowed herself to be brutally honest, she had known for a while that something wasn't right with Emily. But they were both coming to terms with overwhelming changes and she was trying to give her daughter time and space to grieve, to heal. She thought Emily would come around in time. But more and more, Emily returned home from school quieter and quieter, moving slowly through life, shoulders drooped, head heavy and her eyes so sad it was breaking her mother's heart. And the distance, as if Em were on a boat drifting out to sea, seemed to grow between them with each passing day.

Of course Ashley had tried to talk with her, to check in, but Emily's reply was always, 'I'm fine, Mum.' Emily would flash her one of those smiles with her naturally red lips and straight teeth, the sort that could make the world believe she was the happiest, luckiest kid ever. Ash had been falling for it for too many years, or maybe she knew but was too scared to see the truth behind that smile. Because that smile was one Ash herself had worn on many occasions.

But it was in Em's eyes that the truth lay. She had Ash's blue centres but her father's large, almost almond shape. They were stunning, lending a pixie look to her narrow face and pointed chin. It was when those eyes sparkled that Ash could believe that Emily was really smiling.

Ash dropped her head against the iPad, ignoring the mess of red waves that got caught up in her fingers. Emily was lucky not to inherit her hair colour and freckles, even though her husband had loved both.

Oh, Owen! Why did you have to leave us?

Maybe Ashley had been leaning on Emily too much? Too much pressure for a fifteen year old? Emily had always been her rock, so much stronger and only still a teenager. Was it all just finally wearing her down?

Yesterday had been a turning point.

Em's brushed but still scraggly blonde hair had hung limp over her shoulders when she came home, but this time there was something stuck in it, smeared through it. Ashley had reached to pluck it out when the wet mess clung to her fingers.

'Oh, ew, Em, what *is* that?'

Emily had shrugged, making her oversized school polo shirt move like a flag in the wind. She hated clingy clothes and made Ash buy the next size up every time. If Ash even tried to buy something that would fit her nicely it would just end up kicked under her bed.

Ash had left her hand on Emily's shoulder until she finally spoke.

'It's banana.'

'How did banana end up in your hair?'

'Don't worry about it, Mum. It's nothing.'

Again she'd given that smile, the one that didn't reach her eyes.

'Emily?' Ash had taken her hand and held it between hers, eyes locked and waiting for the truth.

A huge sigh had escaped Emily's lips. 'It's nothing. Just some mean girls who like throwing food. I just got caught in the crossfire.'

That smile again.

'I'll go and have a shower.' Then Em had pulled away and headed off to her room in that slow, steady crawl.

Ashley knew she had only got a half-truth, just enough to 'Keep Mum Off My Back', and after stewing about it for most of the night and most of this morning she had finally remembered the Instagram account. And suddenly it was all coming together.

Emily was being bullied. Her beautiful, amazing daughter. Abuse was being hurled at her for no reason and she had been hiding it, putting on a brave face for her mum.

Ash lifted her head and touched the iPad again. She scrolled through more of the hurtful messages. Each one worse than the previous.

'If you died, no one would care.'

'Do it, do it, do it!!'

'Just kill yourself already u know u want too just like your daddy!!!!'

Clang!

The iPad smacked against the floor at her feet. Ash felt as if she were teetering on the edge of the cliff again, huge waves licking up the rocks reaching for her, pulling at her feet. The prickling on her skin started; the waves of dizziness.

'Oh god,' she murmured before collapsing back against the chair in the lounge room. It had been hard enough having to tell Emily how her father had died let alone see Owen's suicide being used to taunt her.

Count to five! she tried telling herself. But every time she tried to say 'One', those words raced past her eyes as the room turned dark.

'Just like your daddy!'

'Do it, do it, do it!'

A small part of her brain was trying to clutch onto reality. Ground yourself, the tiny voice whispered.

Ground yourself.

Ash started to move her feet on the floor while her hands searched beside her in the blackness. She could feel the material of the chair and the soft tassels of the yellow throw pillow. Her stomach rolled as she fought off the queasiness.

Focus, Ash! Think of Emily as a baby, holding her in your arms, her sweet baby smell, her gentle coos.

Distracting herself with her favourite memories usually helped, but it was a hard battle to overcome when the panic persisted. It felt like hours that she sat there in her own private hell. To some she probably looked like she was meditating but she could feel the slick sweat coating her skin as on the inside the war raged on.

It was probably ten minutes or more before Ashley felt herself gain control; before the room came into clear view and she could breathe again. She felt as if she had just run a marathon: her breath in heavy pants, her limbs and chest aching, her body frazzled and her brain like mush.

Pulling the black band from her wrist, she tied her auburn hair on top of her head, needing to free her neck from the constricting thickness of her waves. Her eyes caught the black shape of the iPad and she felt the prickle again, but she quickly glanced away, searching for something else to hold her thoughts. Anything.

A light-cedar-coloured acoustic guitar resting against the wall made her feel warm. She went over and picked it up, holding it against her chest as if she were about to play it. Her fingertips pressed against the strings one by one. Owen had taught Emily how to play on this guitar. She was just five when he had first propped her up on his knee, the guitar cradled against her small body while he helped her make her first chord. Then he got her to strum it, and the sound of it made her eyes shine so brightly. It was something they both loved and shared. Since her husband's death it had sat untouched. Hardly looked at. Avoided.

Eight months.

Ashley ran her fingers across the strings, the sound not quite right but still it filtered through her body like vines tethering her to the floor. It was the grounding she needed to bring her back to calm.

She strummed it absentmindedly while she sought out their family portrait that hung on the cream wall above the guitar. Owen with his blond scruffy hair at odd angles and his larger-than-life smile. His arms were around Ashley and Emily and they were all smiling as they watched the colourful butterflies around them. The sun had been out, shining through the butterfly enclosure, but ten-year-old Em had been watching her dad with delight. It had been a good day.

If only they'd had more like it.

With the instrument still clutched to her chest Ashley dared to think about Emily and the abuse she was getting online and at school. She doubted the banana incident had been an accident or a one-off. Kids could be so mean. Emily was a beautiful girl with a big, caring heart. Was that why she was a target? They were jealous of her stunning features? Or did it have more to do with her father's death?

It was common to hear Nirvana or Pearl Jam playing from Emily's room, or indeed her rendition of 'Thunderstruck' on the guitar, her fingertips having callused long ago. On weekends she lived in torn jeans and checked shirts. Anyone would think it was the early nineties and Kurt Cobain was still alive and grunge the in thing. Ashley had wondered if Owen's music influence on Emily had flared more since his death, and if she was finding ways to be closer to him.

Now, a million thoughts rushed through her mind. Should she call the school and make a complaint? Reply to all the messages and scold each child? Talk to Emily about it? Ash felt as if she were on a spinning carousel and didn't know how to get off.

'Oh crap!' Ashley caught sight of the clock on the wall. 'Bloody hell, I'll be late for work.'

She returned the guitar to its usual place and ran to the kitchen to collect her large black handbag and keys, all the while silently cursing her panic attacks and their ability to suck chunks of her life away. If only she could get control of her emotions. The coping techniques her therapist had given her were now her mantra, as well as the natural oils and calming sprays that at least gave her a small sense of control.

Ashley glanced around the house, checking everything was where it should be. Out of habit she adjusted the tea towel hanging on the oven door so it was straight, pushed in the two chairs around the dining table.

The iPad was still on the floor where she'd dropped it but she didn't have the strength to go and move it. The little prickle along her skin warned her to keep moving and leave the house; she couldn't afford another panic attack when she was already late for work. She knew how ridiculous it sounded, a grown woman scared of a square piece of technology, but in her mind it was a snake with fangs. The words it carried were venom. Ashley just couldn't handle thinking about those messages again, not yet. Maybe she was weak, she felt weak and silly most of the time; but Nikki, her best friend, always reassured her that she was none of those things.

Ashley pressed a hand down her navy skirt and checked for stains on her white shirt. When nothing else caught her eye she dashed from the house, locking it behind her, and then reached back to check it.

The morning traffic was in her favour and she arrived, not at work but at Emily's school.

She parked out the front, car running, and scanned the school. It was eerily quiet and empty, everyone inside, not even one kid loitering outside or taking a slow bathroom break. What had she hoped to get out of this visit? Spot the mean kids and go yell at them?

You're too weak for that, Ash.

Her little voice was right, she wasn't the confrontational type, but how she longed to be that strong mum who would stand up for their kid and give those horrible brats a good talking to.

'You're late for work, woman,' she chastised herself and set off for the shopping centre with no minutes to spare.

She parked quickly – at least the parking angel was on her side today – and with her handbag gripped tightly against her chest she walked like a kid wanting to run around the pool but knowing the watchful eyes of the lifeguard weren't far away. Inside the air-conditioned shopping centre music blared from the nearby hair salon, and in front of her four older women talked loudly as they shuffled slower than a wombat, forcing Ashley to weave around them and narrowly miss taking her hip out on the island Puffin Fresh Donut stand. Her eyes were drawn to the fashion boutique Designs on the right; two female mannequins wore stunning evening dresses in blue and lemon, but she couldn't see Nikki, who was the manager. She so desperately wanted to see her friend's face, to hear her reassuring voice, get her thoughts on this cyberbullying. On her break she would send a text to see if they could catch up for lunch.

Ashley felt her bladder swell as she passed the corridor to the public toilets but she tried to suppress it; there was no time to spare, and her boss Margie would give her a weighted stare all day if she was even a minute late.

'I'm here,' she practically shouted as she entered the pharmacy, which, luckily, seemed empty of customers.

Margie, in her pressed white shirt and blue pencil skirt, glanced at her watch before turning back to her task near the counter. 'Did you do your hair this morning, Ashley?' she said without looking up.

Oh, damn! She remembered scraping it up into a mess to cool her neck. Quickly she headed into the small room at the back where they kept their belongings and had their breaks. It doubled as a storage room, but it did have a small mirror on the wall, and as she caught her reflection she cringed. It was like a rather large rat had nested on her head. Her chest started to flutter, not in a good way, so she immediately reached into her bag for her balance oil and smeared it onto her wrists before fixing her hair.

'You okay, Ash?' asked Tim, leaning against the doorframe.

'Yep, nearly done.'

Ashley, happy with how her auburn waves now sat, headed towards Tim. 'It's been a horrible morning.'

He raised an eyebrow. 'Oh honey, you did look a bit dishev-elled when you ran in. Careful, Margie's on the war path, but on the upside she's off in ten minutes for a meeting.'

'Really?'

The little diamond earring in his ear sparkled as his smile lit up his pale face. 'Gone for the rest of the day.' He did his signature 'spirit fingers' celebration. 'Oh, but she wants to see you before she goes,' he added with a grimace. 'Don't shoot the messenger,' he whispered as he left.

Ashley sighed heavily, then plastered on her biggest smile and went to find Margie.

Margie was in the corner at her desk next to the head phar-macist. Ash thought she resembled a stern old headmistress and that underneath her long pencil skirt she hid a cane, one she was dying to use. Margie would get a glint in her eye when she was about to deliver bad news or pain – and today, as she turned towards Ashley, that evil glimmer was there.

Oh, great.

'Ashley, I'm glad you could join us at work today. Please take a seat.'

Ash grinned like an idiot, trying to appease the woman when all she wanted to do was strangle that triumphant look from her face. The 'seat' Margie offered was the tiny stool she used to reach the higher shelves, but Ash sat on it with as much dignity as she could muster.

'I'll cut straight to the point, Ashley. I have been asked to tighten the budget and look at our staffing. I'm sorry to say that we no longer have a position for you here.'

Ash blinked, trying to understand Margie's words. 'Pardon?'

'Consider this your notice.'

Ash's mouth opened but no words came.

'Do you understand?' Margie continued, clearly preventing her lips from curling as if she took great delight in her power. 'We can't justify the extra staff and have made your position redundant, mainly because others have been here longer. Phil will go over your final pay and entitlements this afternoon.'

'I don't have a job?' Ash suddenly realised what this meant. 'I need a job.' Without Owen, there was no one else to pay the bills. Since his death, the cost of his funeral and dropping to one income meant that Ash was hardly making ends meet. She'd sold his ute, but that was only a quick fix. Ash gaped at Margie, then firmly closed her mouth. She would not play the recent-widow card.

'I'm sorry, I know it has been a hard year for you. We thank you for your service with us at the pharmacy. I'm sure someone will organise something for you on your last day.'

Then Margie fluttered her hand impatiently as if Ash were an annoying fly.

'Oh. Yes, okay,' muttered Ash as she tried to get up off the stool gracefully and failed. As she stood she felt a huge weight press against her chest, and in her muddled state of mind she did an awkward bow to Margie, as if she were the Queen of England, and left.

You idiot. She swore internally as she searched for Tim. She found him sorting the condom selection, his favourite task, and rushed almost into him.

'Hey, sweets. What did Hitler's mother want?'

'To fire me,' she huffed.

Tim's mouth and eyes flew open in his usual over-the-top flair but his shock made her feel a little better.

'Shut the front door!'

'I kid you not. Oh, Tim, what am I going to do now?'

Tim pulled her into a hug as a nearby customer watched them. Ashley didn't cry, she couldn't cry, she was in too much shock to muster up any tears.

Instead she felt the heaviness of her mind, like a throbbing volcano waiting to erupt. Visions of Emily and the constant worry of how she was going at school today were hard to ignore, and now the fact that she was jobless had just added to the weight on her shoulders. What *was* she going to do now?

2

Nikki

NIKKI SUMMERSON GENTLY PULLED THE GREEN SILK DRESS over the hard cream mannequin. She paused at the breasts, the material pulling tight, and gently eased it over them. Her hand moved back to the breast, feeling its shape and its odd hardness. Even hard they were still better than hers.

Stop it, Nikki! she scolded herself and yet her gaze lingered on the breasts. At thirty-eight she was ogling breasts on a mannequin like a horny fifteen year old. It was ridiculous, she knew that, and yet here she was unable to stop admiring how perfect they looked and the way the dress moulded around them to show off the designer styling. Nikki would kill to be able to wear this dress.

'That dress is stunning, Nikki. Did it just come in?'

Heat burned up her throat and she took a moment before turning to reply to her assistant, Alice.

'Yes, six came in but I think this is my favourite.' Nikki smiled at twenty-two-year-old Alice, who had the spark of the

13

young and a curvaceous body to match. Alice was a lovely size twelve, and knew how to wear her make-up to highlight her features, but it was her bubbly personality that had won her this position.

'You should try that one on, it's your colour, Nikki. Make those gorgeous emerald eyes of yours pop,' said Alice as she ran her fingers over the silky material.

Nikki would normally have jumped at the chance, but not now. All she felt now was a sense of loss and longing. Like a model past her prime, never to grace the catwalk again.

Lately it had been hard to come to work, to be surrounded by such beauty and still wear a smile when inside she felt like she was slowly rotting like one of her son's half-eaten apples left behind the couch.

'I might take it home one night,' she said, hoping that was enough to stop Alice before she began to insist Nikki try it on.

'Yes, you should. Once Chris sees you in that, look out.' Alice gave a little growl and wiggled her perfect brows.

Nikki's stomach jolted at the thought.

'Hey, were you going to take your lunch break now? Or did you want me to?' asked Alice.

Finally the escape Nikki needed. 'Oh yes, I'll go. Ashley wants to meet up for lunch today. Would you mind finishing up here and then we can start rearranging the front window.'

'Sounds great. I'll get things cleared away.'

While Alice fussed over the dress, Nikki darted to the back room for her bag and then set off into the shopping centre. She tucked her straight blonde hair behind her ear and twitched a bit as her bra rubbed against her skin. She was thankful for her chunky designer jumper, but soon it would be summer. Nikki shuddered at the thought.

The shops weren't especially busy today, so the short walk to the other end was painless. No dodging phone-consumed teens who didn't move or groups of mums with prams employed as battering rams, four abreast and hard to pass. Everything seemed to irritate Nikki these days, even Chris being extra helpful at home. She had a hot husband she couldn't bear to look at lately. And instead of getting better it was getting worse, because she knew he was waiting and wanting. The more he did nice things to try to win her over the more she felt like screaming and running the other way. Which was horrible, because she did love him. Was this what having a mid-life crisis felt like?

'Hi Nikki.'

She looked up as she entered the modern Expresso Bar. 'Hi James,' she said, waving to the owner, who wore a white-and-blue striped apron over his black clothes. His grey hair was always cropped short and tidy.

'Ashley's just arrived. I'll bring you both a coffee and take your orders.'

'Thanks, James.'

Ashley was sitting in the corner booth, staring at the opposite wall. Her shoulders were hunched over as if her gorgeous flaming locks were too heavy. She looked how Nikki felt.

'Hey Ash, you okay?' Nikki slid into the small booth opposite her. The black leather seat was worn but comfy.

Ash sighed heavily. Her face seemed paler than normal, making her freckles stand out. She was so down-to-earth gorgeous against Nikki's higher-maintenance, designer, always-look-amazing self and yet they had been fast friends these past four years since meeting when their girls started high school together.

'No, I don't think I am,' Ash finally replied.

Nikki's concern for her friend drowned out her own issues and she felt a little relieved to have a moment of breathing space; something she didn't seem to get much of these days.

'Is this why you wanted to meet up? What's wrong?'

Ashley's blue eyes, framed by ruby lashes, shone with tears as she looked up. 'It's ah ... um ... Sorry, it's been a shitty day so far.'

Nikki waited as Ash seemed to sort through her emotions and thoughts, all the while wondering what could possibly be wrong. She'd not long ago buried her husband – surely the universe could give her friend a break?

Taking a gulp of air, Ash exhaled her words in a rush. 'It's Emily. She's being bullied and abused.'

'What?' Nikki wasn't sure she'd heard right.

'Oh Nikki, I don't know what to do.'

Ash flung her hands to her wet face while Nikki dug through her bag for her little tissue packet and passed her one. 'Here,' she said, nudging the tissue into her fingers and waiting, letting Ash take the lead.

She pulled her hands from her face and dabbed herself dry. 'I'm sorry. I'm such a mess. But it's so awful. Has Chloe said anything?'

Nikki shook her head. She never got much out of Chloe unless she wanted money for new clothes or a beauty treatment; the rest of the time she was in her room and on her phone. Chloe was convinced she was going to be the next big Instagram sensation or YouTube star giving make-up tips. 'No, she's not mentioned anything about Emily. But I'll ask her tonight, just feel her out. What's been happening?'

Ashley sighed again just as James arrived with their coffees. 'Here you go, lovely ladies. What would you like for lunch?'

Nikki glanced at Ash, who was staring at the wall again. 'Um, can you decide for us today, please, James? Something comforting? One of our usuals.'

He squinted slightly, assessing them. 'I'll sort it, and some hot apple pie for dessert, I think.'

Nikki smiled. Now that did sound good. When James left she touched Ash's hand. 'Tell me everything.'

Ash pulled one of her tiny brown bottles from her bag and rubbed some oil on her wrist before she started from the beginning. She whispered the words she'd read from Emily's Instagram account but she couldn't bring herself to repeat the last one.

'*What?* They were telling her to take her own life?' Nikki sat back, appalled. 'That is disgusting, Ash, what kind of kid would say those things!' Nikki closed her eyes and hoped Chloe wouldn't ever get messages like that. Or even worse, that she wouldn't ever say horrible things like that. 'Were any from Chloe?' she suddenly asked, her heart in her throat.

'Oh no,' Ash said quickly. 'Chloe would never. They don't run in the same circles, but even so, I know Chloe's heart and she wouldn't be capable of that, Nikki, not to Emily. I'm positive.'

Ash smiled weakly and Nikki felt the pressure around her neck release. 'I hope you don't mind but I'll still be having a chat with Chloe regardless. It's just not on. She could be friends with these people for all I know. What are you going to do? Have you spoken to Emily?'

Ash shrugged as she picked up the coffee she'd just spotted in front of her. 'I honestly don't know what to do. I had a panic attack over it and have been in La La Land ever since. Should I go to the school? Are these people even in her school? Kids today have friends from all over the bloody country. How are we supposed to protect them?' She took a sip of her coffee. 'But I'll talk to her tonight. I feel so sick that she's been dealing with this on her own. Why didn't she come to me?'

Ash's blue eyes, rimmed red and glossy, skittered sideways, and Nikki felt like there was more to this story. Or maybe something else on her mind that she wasn't ready to share. 'I wish I knew, Ash. Maybe they don't want to worry us? I didn't tell my parents much either when I was that age. Remember what it was like as a teenager? I thought I was *so* grown up . . . But you don't realise until you really are an adult just how wrong you had it.' Nikki sighed. 'Sometimes I wish I could go back to those days and really enjoy them. They're supposed to be so carefree, but . . . This whole online world, and these phones concern me so much. I mean, Josh is a thirteen-year-old boy who has never climbed a tree. He sits on his phone or his PlayStation playing with other people online and I feel like I'm losing him. He's like a boarder, this boy who eats and sleeps with us, but there's no conversation, no interaction. And don't get me started on Chloe. She thinks she has to have a "presence" on social media to be popular. She wants to be famous. An influencer. I have a full-time job trying to stop her from going to school all made up like she's off to a ball. Sometimes the fights and battles just wear me down until I give in a little. And I hate that.'

'I know. What are we supposed to do? How am I supposed to help Emily? Take all her devices away so they can't touch her?'

They both leaned back as one of James's staff brought over their lunch. A Caesar salad and a creamy pasta dish. Nikki reached for the salad at the same time Ash took the pasta.

'Thank James for us please, Syd. He knows us too well.'

The young man nodded and replied that the dessert would be out in ten.

'I think putting her devices away would be good,' Nikki said. 'So she can't keep reading the messages and letting them consume her. But what about the banana in her hair? Go in and speak to the principal, just make him aware of it at least?'

Ash nodded. 'I think I need to. Surely a teacher has noticed something. Or if not I need to see that they're keeping an eye out.' Ash stabbed at her pasta. 'I feel so awful that I didn't find this out sooner. I'm her mum, I'm supposed to be able to protect her.'

'I don't think we can fully protect them from everything, Ash. Poor Emily. Don't they know she just lost her dad?'

Nikki watched as Ash moved her pasta around her plate, her face still so pale. The poor woman had been through hell, losing Owen the way she had and then trying to sort through the funeral and keep herself and Emily going. Nikki wasn't sure how she'd cope without Chris.

'One of them . . .' She took a breath. 'One of them mentioned Owen, and it implied they knew how he died.'

'Have you spoken with her?' said Nikki gently. 'It was bound to get out and go around the school. Kids love any sort of gossip.'

'No, not yet. She was already at school. We haven't spoken much about Owen's . . . death, except after it happened. Since then it's like neither of us wants to bring it up and open old wounds.'

'I understand. But Emily's a strong girl, Ash, don't forget that.' Nikki had seen firsthand the way Emily watched her mother, looking for signs of her panic attacks and knowing how to divert them or help her through them. Chris had once told her that he thought Emily had the eyes of a wise person who had been here before, mature beyond her age. And Nikki knew what he meant; she had seen Em pick up on emotions in a room, seemingly aware of things going on in the background while other kids were oblivious. Chloe seemed years younger at times in comparison and yet she had been born only four months after Emily.

'I know she is. Though I think that's mainly because I'm *not* strong.'

Nikki reached for her hand and squeezed it. After the funeral Ash had confided her despair at not realising Owen was suicidal and her pain at thinking she could have saved him. Nikki had heard the guilt in her friend's voice and held her while she'd cried and cried. She stayed the first few nights with Ash so she didn't have to be alone. She held her hand while she organised the funeral arrangements, hugged her when she fell to pieces and reassured her every day that she was not responsible.

'You are *not* to blame, Ash. For any of this. I'll keep reminding you of that for as long as I have to.' Nikki straightened up and put on a determined air. 'Now, let's work on how you'll approach Emily. We both know how difficult teenagers are to talk to,' she said, rolling her eyes.

Ash gave her a small smile, and took a bite of her lunch.

'We need to find a way for you to discuss the abuse without putting Emily offside or on the defensive. Especially when it's hard to guess which way she'll go,' said Nikki while filling her fork with salad.

'She'll probably deny the whole lot just so I won't worry. I don't want her to blow this off as nothing.'

'Agreed. It's a serious matter. I hate bullying.'

The apple pie with a side of ice-cream eventually arrived and both women pounced on it while the waiter took their half-eaten lunches away.

Ash brushed her hair back and fanned her face. 'Wow, it's so hot in here. How are you not boiling in that jumper, Nik?'

Nikki shrugged and hoped her red face and clammy skin weren't too noticeable. The truth was, she *was* hot. But they were nearly done and she would soon be back in the air-conditioned bliss.

'I wish I could be more help, Ash,' said Nikki, avoiding the jumper question; it was easier than lying. 'But I don't really know the best way either. This mothering gig is mostly guesswork and fear of getting it wrong. I wish I had the best answers.' She could see the despair written all over Ash's face, her neck tense and shoulders rolled forward, and wished there was some way to ease it.

'Me too. Thank you, Nik; just talking with you has made me feel better.'

'I'll help any way I can, you know that.'

'I know. I wouldn't have made it through Owen's funeral without you by my side and the days after,' Ash said softly. 'It works both ways too, you know.'

Nikki focused on cleaning up the last of the pie on her plate to avoid Ashley's words but it didn't stop them cutting through her. She felt as if she were betraying her closest friend, but she just couldn't confide in her, not yet. Maybe later when she'd got a grip on it herself. She just needed time to wrap her own head around it before she could talk to anyone. It was still too raw.

3

Nikki

NIKKI SAT IN HER CAR, RESTING HER HEAD ON THE STEERING wheel, just for a moment. Work used to be the joy of her life, an escape from the kids and a way to feel like she was more than just a wife and mum. But lately it was sapping her energy, and coming home was no relief. There didn't seem to be a place she could escape to anymore, to leave her muddled mind for some quiet distraction. With a sigh she got out of the car and headed up the front path.

Maybe she should try getting out in the garden more. She glanced at her freshly pruned roses as she stood by the front door. Chris had the place looking shipshape, to the point where she didn't have to lift a finger. Lawns mowed to look like bowling greens, garden beds free of weeds, all the housework done. He was every wife's dream and she should be happy but it only made her feel useless and gave her far too much time to wallow in her own thoughts.

'You okay, Mum?'

Nikki turned to see Chloe walking past their white picket fence, which was the envy of the street. The perks of having a handy husband, although now he was the manager of the building company, his days as a tradie long gone.

'I'm fine, honey. How was school?' she asked.

'The usual.' Chloe wore eye make-up, a little liner and shadow. After an escalating, seemingly unending fight Nikki had relented to allowing this but even now she didn't like seeing her fifteen year old looking much older than she should.

Nikki had to admit (but not aloud) that Chloe did have a deft hand when applying make-up – indeed, Chloe did Nikki's make-up for any events – thanks to all those YouTube clips she watched. She was in awe of her daughter's beauty. Long silky blonde hair, clear milky skin and high cheekbones that Chloe knew how to accentuate. It also worried her, Chloe looking older than she was. Nikki had seen the turned heads, the extra attention directed towards Chloe wherever they went. That's why they had a strict rule that the kids walked home from school together.

Not that Josh was by her side now; instead he trailed behind his sister, head down and eyes glued to the phone held sideways as he walked. No doubt playing some game. He'd probably not even notice if a car stopped and someone abducted his sister.

'Josh,' she called out when he'd walked past the front gate.

He looked up, realised he'd gone too far and turned around, head bent back to his game.

Nikki shook her head. Josh had been such an active kid, out kicking the football with Chris whenever he could, but then his school mates started to get PlayStations and Xboxes and he hounded until they gave him one for his eleventh birthday.

It started out as a novelty and wasn't so bad, but then the whole online gaming part of it took over. Having unlimited data didn't help – it was as if Josh was trying to test the truth of that statement. Chris still tried to get him out to kick the footy every now and then, which was fine in summer but in winter it was darker earlier, and Chris didn't get home until later, and everything just got harder.

She reached out and ran her fingers through his blond mop, brushing it back from his eyes. 'Hey kiddo.'

'Is there any food? I'm starving,' he said by way of greeting.

Chloe had already unlocked the front door and vanished inside but Nikki soon found her in the modern white-and-black kitchen, her school bag dumped by the island bench, with cupboard doors open as if the police had come in for a drug raid. 'Chloe, really?'

'Mum, why don't we have any food in this house?' she grumbled.

Nikki placed her handbag at the end of the black marble bench.

'Have a seat, you two, and I'll whip up some pancakes.'

'Oh yes, thanks, Mum,' Josh said as he went to the fridge to get out the maple syrup.

Chloe sat down, phone in hand. Nikki assumed that meant she was hungry. It was a spur-of-the-moment decision, something she hadn't made the kids for a while, but she also sensed an opportunity.

'So, I was talking with Ashley today about Emily,' she said as she collected the ingredients.

'Oh no, this sounds like a lecture,' moaned Josh, his eyes rolling.

They were both sitting on the stools opposite Nikki as she mixed the ingredients.

'Kids, put the phones down and listen for a minute, please. I want to have a serious talk.'

'I told you it was a lecture,' Josh mumbled.

Nikki ignored him. 'Emily is being bullied,' she stated a little gruffly.

'What?'

The sudden confusion and concern across Chloe's face sent relief flowing through Nikki. Her daughter still had some real emotions left that weren't expressed through emojis.

Josh put his phone down, his face slightly red.

'Who's bullying her?' he asked.

'Lots of people. They're saying horrible things to her on Instagram, things that had Ashley in tears,' said Nikki. 'It's hurt her a lot. Knowing that there are kids out there picking on Emily and telling her . . .' Nikki paused. Should she bring up suicide with her thirteen year old? Her first thought was that he seemed too young for such a conversation, but then she realised with a sickening feeling that Dolly Everett hadn't been much older and that this topic was probably well overdue. She sucked in a breath and said the words that scared her. 'People have been telling Emily to kill herself because no one likes her.'

She let her words sink in, watching Josh's brow crease and Chloe press her lips together.

'Really, Mum? That's horrible,' said Chloe as she tapped her pretty pink nails together. A nervous habit she'd had since she was ten.

'It's deplorable. And I hope that you two will never *ever* send messages like that to anyone, or say such hurtful things to people. We can never know what another person is going through.'

'Like . . . Emily's dad *died*. Don't they know that?' said Josh. He started spinning the maple syrup bottle around on the island bench.

'Some of them are teasing her about it,' said Nikki.

'That sucks,' he said with a frown. 'I like Emily.'

Nikki knew most schools had anti-bullying programs in place but it was something that needed to be reinforced at home also. She wondered if the kids who sent those messages had ever been spoken to by their parents about bullying. The way these kids were with their phones made it so hard to know what they really got up to when they thought they weren't being monitored. Chloe insisted on keeping her phone password private, but at least Josh hadn't changed his.

'Some of these kids find it very easy to say hurtful things in a text but if the person was standing in front of them I doubt they would say any of it. That's what makes this texting generation so oblivious to the pain they can cause. Chloe, you've texted me some nasty messages when you don't get your way but when I talk to you face to face, you can't repeat any of it, can you?'

Chloe shook her head slowly.

'Chloe says horrible stuff to me all the time,' said Josh.

'But you're my brother.' She glanced away as she added, 'I still love you.'

Nikki smiled. As much as they fought she could tell they cared about each other and that's what counted. With the pan hot she poured in some mixture to make five small pancakes.

'Is Emily okay, Mum?'

'I'm not sure, Chloe. Ashley is going to talk to her today. She's hurt that Emily didn't tell her about the abuse.' Nikki turned to face them and was glad to see she had their full attention. 'I want you both to tell me any time there's something that's bothering you, okay? We're your parents and we want to help. Don't worry about upsetting us. Promise me you'll come to us if you ever feel sad, or people are hurting you or you just need someone to talk to? Your dad and I won't get mad.'

Josh and Chloe nodded.

'I want to hear it, guys.'

'We will, Mum,' said Chloe.

'Yeah,' said Josh with a shoulder shrug. He looked like he didn't have a care in the world, and at this moment he probably didn't.

'You may not think you need to talk but even the littlest thing is best shared with a loved one. If you don't want to tell us, then talk to Pop and Nan, or each other.'

Josh screwed his face up and shot a look at his sister.

'You have to look out for each other. We all do – that's being a family.'

Nikki got out two plates and transferred a couple of pancakes onto each before passing them to the kids.

'Chloe, have you noticed Emily getting picked on at school at all?'

Chloe's brow creased as she rested her head on her hand. 'She does spend a lot of time alone. There are some girls in the year above us that go out of their way to trip her and do mean stuff, but no one stands up to them because we're all scared of them,' she said, pulling at her bottom lip with her teeth.

'Why haven't you mentioned this to me before, honey?' Nikki tried to keep the shock from her voice. 'Nothing is too small, because you never know when it will become something huge. Have any of you thought of going to a teacher or the principal?'

Chloe rolled her eyes. 'As if, Mum. We don't want them making our life hell.'

'Can't you make it anonymous? A typed letter outlining what you see and that way they can't find out?'

'Nothing will be done about it,' said Chloe despairingly. 'Without someone to stand up and point the finger what can they do? They would probably never believe an anonymous letter.'

Nikki rubbed a finger between her eyes. This was why bullies got away with so much; it just seemed so hard. 'Don't you kids secretly film stuff?'

'I think that's illegal, Mum,' said Josh.

'There's all sorts of clips that pop up on my Facebook page calling out people who throw rubbish from their cars and stuff. At least it's something to take to the principal.' For all Nikki knew this probably happened already. Kids kicking teachers or teachers wrestling kids – everyone filmed everything these days.

'There's so much for us to try to stay on top of. And it's not just bullying in the schoolyard these days, is it? It's cyber-bullying. There's the fear that a pervert could be contacting you online, pretending to be a kid and you'd never know.'

'Gross, Mum,' said Josh.

'How do you know that those people you play with online aren't old creepy dudes,' said Chloe pointedly to Josh as she ate a pancake.

"Cos I know,' he replied, poking out his tongue. 'You probably have heaps of creepy people as your friends. You don't even know most of them.'

'I do too,' she snapped back.

'Who knows six hundred people?' Josh leaned over and smirked. 'And they send you their privates.'

'*What?!*' Nikki waved the spatula in the air between them.

'They do not,' said Chloe reaching for her phone.

'I saw over your shoulder the other day. A big hairy slug on your phone. It was *so* gross.'

Nikki felt like she was about to faint. The kids kept bickering at each other while she grappled with this new revelation.

'Chloe, you better not be sexting!' Nikki squeaked out. Surely her daughter was too young for all that? It was bad enough when Chris – *her husband* – asked her to send him photos when he was away, but some random horny teenager or worse, a pervert, sending porn to her daughter – that was so much worse. 'You haven't sent anything back, have you?' she shot out. The blood had drained from her face as she started to feel a cold chill spread through her bones.

The house filled with smoke and a charcoal smell.

'Mum, the pancakes,' said Josh pointing behind her.

The kitchen smoke alarm started to shriek, or maybe it was Nikki's head, she couldn't tell. Quickly she pulled the pan off the stove and turned it off, scooping out the blackened remains.

'Josh, can you please go open some windows and then take your bag to your room.'

He shot Chloe a look that said *you're in trouble* and almost skipped off to the nearest window.

Chloe got up to move but Nikki reached for her hand. 'Wait, please.'

She plopped back down with a grunt as the smoke alarm stopped. 'Do we have to?'

Nikki waited until she heard Josh's door click shut. He needed to have this conversation as well but it would probably be better coming from Chris. A man-to-man talk about respect: for himself and for women.

Nikki put the leftover pancake mix in the sink and sat on the stool next to Chloe. She wanted to brush back Chloe's hair, tuck it behind her ear, but she didn't dare. The last time she did that she got into trouble for messing with her styled tresses that had taken 'hours' to do.

'How many boys are sending you photos of their . . . privates?' she asked gently.

'Oh *Mum*.' Chloe cringed. 'It's not like I asked them to send me their junk. I think they do it hoping I'll send something back.'

'Have you?'

'No.' She glanced down at her phone, her fingers holding it like a lion's jaws on its first meal in a week.

Was she afraid Nikki would ask to see her messages?

'Chloe?'

'I swear, Mum.' She bit her lower lip again before dropping her head so her hair fell like a curtain, hiding her face. 'I . . . may have sent a bra shot to Lachy when we were dating but that was it, I promise.'

Nikki cringed. How many juvenile photos were out there in cyberspace? It was a porno of epic proportions, a collage of insecure and feverish teenagers. Snapchat probably gave them false security. Back in her day they had to go looking for the naughty magazines, but now you just switched on your phone and typed 'big dick' into Google and you could see all sorts for free. Nikki had tried. Also a few other things she'd heard but didn't know the meaning of – some images you just couldn't erase.

Chloe was flushed when she lifted her head. 'It's one of the reasons I broke up with him – he kept nagging about it but I didn't want to do it.'

Touching Chloe's shoulder, Nikki took a breath and forced herself to smile. 'Well, I'm pleased to hear that, honey. That's a very grown-up attitude and it makes me very proud.'

Her daughter's eyes bulged. 'Really?'

'Yes, you did the right thing. As well as never forwarding on anything you receive. Just delete it immediately.'

Nikki knew that on the other side of this coin were plenty of girls with low self-esteem sending many photos to boys for approval, to be popular, to be liked. Even to compete with other girls. If only they realised it was for the wrong reasons.

'But they go over this stuff in school, right?' she asked. 'It's been in the newsletter. Telling kids how these photos end up going viral and the whole world ends up seeing them?'

'Yeah, but nobody really listens. Mum, I know girls that let guys do all sorts just so they'll date them.'

Nikki rested her chin on her palm. 'I'm sure it was no different in our day, we just didn't have the technology at our fingertips. It was all said and done in person.' Nikki remembered when she was sixteen, the image appearing suddenly, facing Billy Johnston behind the basketball shed when he'd asked to feel her boobs for a cigarette. Nowadays they'd probably just send a photo. Was that better than having some sweaty-fingered boy with fuzz on his chin feeling your chest? Or was it worse because the boy could then show that photo to the world? Both situations seemed pretty shitty. She shivered; to this day she could still remember that clammy hand.

'Teenage years are really hard. I've been through it too, don't forget. I just hope you keep making the choices you know feel right here,' she said touching her heart. 'Respect yourself and others and don't let anyone make you do anything you're not comfortable with.'

'I'll try, Mum. Thanks for not being mad at me about . . . you know.' Chloe screwed up her face.

This was the first real chat she and Chloe had shared about boys and sexting, and Nikki felt a little bit of relief in the hope that it would help Chloe, and maybe open a doorway to some better communication between them.

'I want you to come to me any time without fear of being told off. I don't care how big or small. If there's a problem we'll deal with it together. Promise?'

Chloe raised her shoulders slightly. 'I promise to try?'

Nikki nodded. 'I'll take it,' she said, leaning over and kissing her daughter's forehead.

'Did you want to see the photo?'

'Good lord, *no*!' she said quickly. Teenage 'junk' was not something she needed to see, ever. 'Just delete it, honey.'

'Can I go now?' Chloe stood up and reached for her school bag.

She waved her off and watched Chloe head to her room, fingers already tapping away on her phone.

The bench was cold against her forehead as she rested her head and contemplated calling Chris. But she didn't want to worry him at work; it could wait until he was home. She let out a sigh of relief but there was a churning sensation in the pit of her stomach; there were still so many unknowns ahead of them. How many more photos would Chloe receive? How many messages begging for images or dirty conversations? The thought was horrifying. She pressed further against the bench, trying to cool the heat in her face. She once thought trying to toilet train and get two kids to sleep was hard work. They passed that milestone only to crash into other, harder things.

'Argh,' she groaned and watched her breath fog up the bench. *Why was life so damn hard?*

4

Ashley

ASH FINISHED WORK AT THE SAME TIME EMILY FINISHED school. Since Owen's death the pharmacy had been accommodating, letting her work shorter days so Em wasn't home alone. Well, they had been until they fired her. Had her change of hours been a thorn in Margie's side? Too hard for her to manage the roster and find staff? Ash wouldn't be surprised; Margie lived and breathed the pharmacy as if it were her spoiled only child.

Her last day of paid work was coming closer, and it made her so anxious she had to pretend it wasn't actually happening. She needed to start looking for another job, but the thought of going through that right now filled her with dread, especially when she didn't want Em to know just yet that things were about to get tough. And what if she couldn't find a job? Would Em think she was a failure? Would it put even more pressure on her when she already had so much to deal with at her tender age?

It was a five-minute drive home and a seven-minute walk for Emily. Ash used to drive by the school to pick her up but when she turned fourteen she'd demanded to be allowed to walk.

'Mum and Dad, *please*! I know nine year olds who walk home further than me.'

They'd really had no choice – they had to cut the apron strings – but it had come with a list of non-negotiables. Text when you leave. Carry a whistle and pepper spray. And learn basic self-defence, which Ashley had found in a special class at a nearby gym.

Owen went to watch one day and hadn't been impressed with the female instructor.

'She's enjoying this too much,' he'd mumbled as she instructed her class how to knee a man's groin.

But Ashley felt reassured that her only child was armed with the tools she hoped she would never need.

'I'm home,' she sang out as she closed the front door with her foot.

They had a nice home, which meant a decent mortgage, one she would struggle to pay without a job. The house was on the slightly less affluent side of the suburb to Nikki and Chris, but the huge money Owen earned on his mine job the past five years had seen their house undergo some renovations. A modern kitchen, Owen insisted, and his special room had been upgraded with sound-proofing. It had been Owen's place to play music and shut the world out.

Literally.

No one had been in his room since his death.

'I'm here,' came Emily's voice from the kitchen.

Ash walked into the bright kitchen, white, almost like a
new piece of paper, where the only colour came from the black
oven and stove top. The floor, walls, countertops and appli-
ances were all white. Some days Ashley felt her hair was too
vibrant for this kitchen, like a wine stain on a wedding dress.
But Owen had insisted on white.

She plonked her bag and the shopping onto the bench,
feeling a tingle of apprehension – not to do with Emily, more
just coming home to this house. It was like that most days,
walking through the door and feeling as if the whole floor
were covered in broken glass.

'Hot chocolate time?' Ash asked Emily as she paused to
study her daughter. No stray banana bits today. Good.

'Yeah, sure. I'll put the kettle on,' Emily said softly.

'I bought Tim Tams,' Ash added as she unloaded the shopping. 'So, how was school?'

'Same–same.'

'Is that a good–good or a bad–bad?' Ash asked.

Emily wouldn't look at her, but instead turned and busied
herself in the cupboard looking for cups.

'Is there anything you want to talk to me about? Anything
at all, about school, about your friends or even about Dad?'
Ash felt as if her head were out the car window and she was
trying to talk into the fast wind, hardly able to catch her breath.

Emily frowned. 'Is that what the hot chocolate and Tim
Tams are about?'

Ash tried to smile. 'Guilty.' She reached for her daughter's
shoulders and held her at arm's length. 'But I do think we
should sit down and have a chat.'

'Whatever.'

The lack of an emphatic 'no' left Ash feeling confident. They remained silent as they went about unpacking and making the drinks.

'Let's take these into the back garden,' she finally said, picking up the pack of chocolate biscuits and her cup.

Ash detected an eye roll but Emily followed her out the white French doors to the timber deck and down onto the lawn towards the white lattice table and chairs sitting under a white painted arbour with a healthy Japanese wisteria. In spring to summer it put on an amazing display of pink but today it was just a green vine.

She relaxed into the hard chair and felt more at ease. Maybe it was being out of the house or maybe just being in the outdoors that she loved so much; either way, this spot was her version of Owen's room. As a kid she'd often slept outside with her dad. They had used a torch to spot birds in the trees and together they'd found shapes in the stars. Emily wouldn't have the chance to make any new memories like that with her dad. A little girl without her dad, it was heart wrenching.

Emily sipped her drink, her eyes anywhere but on her mum.

'I'm sorry we haven't really had a good talk since—' She paused, swallowing the lump that had suddenly appeared in her throat. Ash tried to clear it and started again. 'Since your dad's funeral.'

'It's okay,' Em said quickly, glancing away.

'No, it's not. It's been eight months. I don't know about you but there are days when I still come home expecting him to be here. I still think he's just at the mines and will be home someday soon.'

Emily nodded, her hair shiny with oil, like a young Courtney Love.

'I do too. Sometimes I find myself tiptoeing past his room and then realise that he isn't in there.'

They fell silent as, above, birds tweeted in the afternoon sunlight.

'When did you prune the roses?' Emily asked, suddenly glancing around. 'And weed the garden bed. It looks nice.'

'Last week. You might have noticed if you ever came out of your room. I could always use the help, you know.' Ash smiled.

Emily shrugged.

Ash let it go. 'I tried to give you some space, because you've been dealing with a lot, but it's been long enough. I want to talk about the messages on Instagram.'

Ash was half prepared for an outburst accusing her of snooping, but it didn't come. Instead Emily's eyes welled up with tears as she stared at her cup.

'Oh, Em. Why didn't you tell me?' Ashley pulled her daughter into her arms.

'I didn't want to worry you. You have enough to deal with now Dad's gone.' Her words faltered, the last few coming in splutters like a choke on an old tractor.

'Em, we need to be there for each other, that's what will help us get through this. That means sharing all of it, including the ugly stuff.' But even as she spoke the words Ash felt like a hypocrite; she realised that telling Em about losing her job would only add to her stress, so she tucked it away for another day; tiny white lies to spare Em. 'I don't want you hurting. I'm so angry at what they said but I'm more concerned with how you are.'

Emily half lifted a shoulder and wiped at her eyes. 'I'm trying to ignore them. They just want me to react. They're stupid, Mum, that's all. Most of the kids at school have no clue about the real world. After school everything will be different. None of this will mean anything. Who's popular, who's not.'

Ash was a little relieved at Em's mature response but it still cut her deeply. 'You're right. Some kids just don't have the maturity to see that, or they don't want to. I'm glad you feel that way and don't believe what they said. But I understand it hurts, and you shouldn't have to deal with that alone.'

Ashley opened the Tim Tams and offered them to Em, who took two. One she ate and the other she sucked her hot chocolate through, melted chocolate smearing her top lip. Ash felt a tight knot in her stomach at the thought of Emily one day – soon – being an adult, and no longer being able to watch her smear food on her face. It was one of those adorable moments she loved, like Em in her high chair aged two and eating a peanut butter sandwich. She'd still found nuts in her hair two days later.

'Is there anything I can do? Talk to someone at school about the bullies?'

Em's body stiffened and her eyes flew open. 'No. Please, Mum, no!'

Ashley frowned. 'I don't want them to get away with it. It's just not fair.'

'Life's not fair, Mum. I thought you would have figured that out by now.'

Ash frowned as she stared at Em. 'You're too young to think like that.'

That made Emily grin. 'Mum, promise me you won't go to school! It will just make things worse. They'll move on soon enough.'

'Do you really want them picking on someone else? What if it's Chloe?'

Emily looked away and started picking at her broken nails. 'I'd hate that. But what can we do?'

Ashley sighed and tapped her finger against her lips. Em had a point, but what was the best way to go about taking down bullies without bringing on a shitstorm? Reporting anonymously was the only way to guarantee Emily wasn't dragged into it, but if she was the only kid they were bullying, then they would still figure it out. 'I'm not sure yet, Em. I'll keep thinking and I won't do anything until I've discussed it with you, okay?'

Emily nodded emphatically.

'It's nearly school holidays, maybe the break will help? Maybe we should go somewhere different and make it device-free.' Ash stared at the house. They could both use a break. Maybe even stretch it out to three weeks? Well, that's if she could even afford to take them on a holiday. It would have to be cheap.

Emily leaned back in her chair, surveying the backyard. 'I'm keen to go anywhere. We haven't done any trips, not since Dad started working on the mines.' She sighed. 'Sometimes I wish Dad had never taken that job. He didn't like it, did he?'

The back of Ash's neck suddenly felt clammy, her skin prickled and itched as if they were being attacked by insects in the garden. 'No, he didn't like it much.' That was the understatement of the year.

Maybe if Ash had been able to convince him to find another job he'd still be here? If only he'd listened when she told him to get help, to talk to someone, anyone. Thoughts of Owen raced through her mind, but she knew she couldn't share them with Emily; not these ones. They came with too much shame and guilt.

'If you ever want to go visit your father's grave, just let me know and I'll take you. It might help?'

Em screwed up her nose and dropped her eyes.

'You were the absolute best thing in our lives. You know that, right?'

'Sometimes I felt like Dad wasn't as sure about that as you,' Em whispered.

'We both had our tough days, honey. We were young and inexperienced. Raising a kid is hard work, but underneath all that is love. I know your dad adored you. Sure he stressed about being a good parent. We all do, but I think he worried more than most that he wasn't good enough.'

'I know. I didn't understand when I was little, but the last few years I was old enough to realise he had depression.'

This seemed suddenly harder than dealing with Emily's bullying issues. Especially with Em staring as if she were waiting for Ash to say something. But no words came. She could only nod.

Emily reached for another biscuit. Their cups were now empty on the table.

'The beach.'

Ashley watched crumbs fly from Emily's mouth as she spoke.

'Pardon?'

'The beach,' she repeated after swallowing. 'I'd like to see the ocean and have sand between my toes. For the school holidays.'

'It's winter.'

'So? I'll rug up and we'll have a beach bonfire. I don't have to swim but it would be nice to smell the salty air. I can't remember the last time I was at a beach.'

Ashley frowned. She couldn't remember either. There was a vision of Emily as a baby eating beach sand in her cute spotted bathers and another when she would run to the waves and then scream and run away as they crashed at her feet. She was maybe seven. Had they been at Margaret River or Busselton then?

'Well, I think we have to rectify that, most definitely.'

The beach was free, even better.

Emily jumped up. 'Thanks, Mum. I think it would be awesome.'

Ash watched Emily bound towards the house, her hair flying behind her like a cape. It was the most animated she'd seen her in a while. It felt good, like the warmth of a hot soup on a freezing day. Only a little niggle remained that Em might be hiding just how much the bullying had affected her. After dinner tonight she would bring it up again and together they could do some online research. It might give her another chance to open up more.

Pulling out her phone, she typed into Google: 'Beach destinations in WA'.

5

Nikki

'MORNING, BABE.'

Chris rolled over in their bed and kissed her cheek. His hand found her belly and she tried not to flinch.

'Morning,' she replied.

Chris was smiling, his sleepy eyes, a golden hazel, gazing at her in a way she was all too familiar with.

'I'll go make us coffee,' she said quickly, throwing back the covers and putting on her dressing gown over her blue flannel pyjamas.

He lay on his side, elbow bent with his head resting on his hand as he watched her. He was frowning slightly, more disappointed than angry, but if she tried to look at him objectively she knew he was hot and any woman would crawl back into bed. His brown tousled curls, lean body with a scattering of hair down his chest and a hint of stubble along his jaw, with perfect lips. She knew he was gorgeous but lately she just couldn't feel anything. She was like a broken toy, useless and unworthy.

'I'll come and help, start on breakfast,' he said jumping out of bed buck naked and then began to put the cover back into place as if they'd not been there seconds ago. When he was done he picked up his phone, his fingers scrolling over the screen.

Nikki opened her mouth but didn't know what she was going to say, so she closed it and headed downstairs to the kitchen. The house was still dark except for a glow in the TV room. With a frown she padded to the door knowing full well what she was about to see.

'Joshua Summerson!' she shrieked.

Minecraft filled up the TV screen and Josh was in the beanbag a metre from it with a controller in his hand and earphones on. He hadn't even heard her. Nikki stepped into the room and scoffed when she noticed the open jar of Nutella on the coffee table, a half-eaten bit of bread next to it that was so full of Nutella it had oozed onto the wooden top.

She could feel the steam starting to seep from her ears.

As Nikki ripped the headphones off his head, Josh looked up suddenly, his red bleary eyes wide.

'Mum! You scared me.'

Now she noticed some discarded chip packets beside him.

'Have you been here all night?' she growled.

He had the nerve to still be playing his game while she was talking.

'Josh, if you don't turn that off right now and answer me I swear I'll run it over with my car.'

Josh frowned and put his controller down and turned to face her with a pout and crossed his arms. 'Fine.'

She huffed like a bull to a red flag, and the thought of charging her son did cross her mind. He had no right to be angry at her for interrupting him. This kid had so much attitude when playing games.

'What's going on?' asked Chris.

He stood at the door in his work pants and yellow hi-vis shirt, work socks on his feet. His phone was in his hand and he glanced at it as the screen lit up and dinged.

'Josh snuck out of his room to play all night. Look at this mess!'

'It wasn't all night,' Josh shot back.

Nikki tilted her head at him and he sank back into the beanbag.

'Josh, buddy, we've talked about this. Quick, clean up your mess and go and get dressed for school. Then after school we'll be setting some new rules and consequences.'

The thirteen year old dragged himself out of the black beanbag, its rattly noise filling the room along with the sound of scrunched empty biscuit packets. His bottom lip dropped as he sulked his way from the room. Chris darted forward and scooped up the Nutella and half-eaten sandwich and followed Josh.

Nikki just stood there, feeling a weird sense of disbelief and this niggling feeling that she was losing control of everything. She dropped down into the nearby cream couch while staring at the frozen TV screen.

'You okay, babe?' said Chris on his return with a damp cloth to wipe off the remaining Nutella.

'This is crazy, Chris.'

He stopped what he was doing and kneeled beside her. 'What do you mean?'

'I feel like I'm losing my kids to cyberspace. Life feels so disjointed, unconnected.'

His eyebrow raised. 'Yeah, I'm feeling a bit of that.'

She ignored his double meaning. This was about their kids, not them. 'You know what I mean. First Emily being bullied, Chloe with dick pics and addicted to Instagram, Snapchat, YouTube, TikTok and god knows what else. And then Josh. He's not the bubbly, chatty boy we used to have. He lives and breathes his PlayStation. He'd be on it all day long if we'd let him.' She pointed to the offending device by the TV. 'It worries me so much. We need to do something.'

Chris put his hand on her knee and she reached for it, squeezing it tightly.

'Like what? Get rid of them all? It's the future, I don't think we can exclude them from it.'

His phone dinged again, but he ignored it.

'Oh I know, that's what makes this so hard. But I want my kids back. I want them to experience life for a bit without technology consuming them. I mean, look at us. Can't even have a conversation without our phones in our hands. We eat dinner with them beside us.'

Lately Chris had been as bad as Chloe, his phone always in his hand and making noises. When she queried why he was so popular he said it was just work.

'Yeah, they can be all-consuming without realising it. I hear you. So, what do you suggest we do? I can't see us getting their phones off them that easily.' He pulled a face. 'But we should implement phone-free zones, like the dinner table.'

Nikki closed her eyes, holding her head. Chris was right. It was going to be a big shitstorm but maybe they had to try.

'We could have a technology-free school holiday? Maybe we have to go on a trip somewhere to keep them entertained?' she said with a shrug.

'It would be bloody unbearable stuck in this house with them for that long. I've got three weeks' leave owing and the company has been hounding me to take it.' He turned his golden eyes upwards. 'What do you think? Take a decent holiday somewhere? Maybe we could all use a sea change.'

Nikki adjusted her fluffy robe. She knew what he was thinking. Maybe if she was relaxed on holidays she might be more willing in the bedroom. *God, I'm so mean.* Why couldn't she just do what he wanted? When the kids were little it was a case of help yourself while she was half asleep and yet now she couldn't even bring herself to be that accommodating. If they were away on holidays how would she get around it? There was no work to keep him busy or things she had to get up to do. It would just be long sleep-ins and regular morning glories. Nikki inwardly cringed. She felt so horrible thinking that way but she just wanted more time to herself.

Unless . . . Her finger tapped against her lip.

Unless they went somewhere with others so there was less chance of that, maybe even in tents. An idea was starting to form.

'Hey, Ashley was saying they want to go on a holiday to the ocean and get away from the internet as well. What about your cousin's farm down near Bremer Bay?'

Chris sat back on his heels. 'Yeah.'

When the kids were little they had gone to the farm one year for a family Christmas and Nikki remembered the beach and the bush. It was so isolating; she felt like they'd fallen off the face of the earth. Since then his cousin Luke had set up a rural retreat. 'Does he have internet or a phone signal yet?'

Chris chuckled. 'Nup, I doubt it. Unless a phone tower has been built nearby. Are you thinking we go completely off the grid?'

'It saves taking the kids' phones off them. They just won't work.' It was kind of clever. 'Do you think he'd mind?'

'I haven't spoken to Luke in a while but last I heard he was still trying to make that side of things work. It had all gone to shit a bit when Denise left.'

Denise. Nikki remembered the arty woman with her vibrant smile and flowing clothes. Fingers and neck all adorned with home-made jewellery. Their wedding was in Albany and Denise had been barefoot. Nikki had never thought Luke and Denise were that suited, and it turned out she was right.

'Do you want me to call him and see if we can spend some time there?' said Chris, rubbing his face.

'Please, would you? And if Ashley and Emily could come? That way the kids would have company. Micky is the same age as Chloe, I'm sure Josh would love to hang out with him.'

Two or more years ago Luke had dropped in for a visit when he'd had to come to Perth. He brought Micky; it was just the two of them after Denise up and disappeared. Luke had looked like crap. It had been a rough two years for him and she'd watched over Micky while the boys went out for a few beers. They'd returned home after midnight but it was clear their close cousin bond was as strong as ever.

'You know, I spent many school holidays on that farm when I was Josh's age. Luke and I would build cubbies and catch fish. Some of the best times of my life.' The honey hazel swirled in his eyes. 'I think it would be so good for Josh to experience some of that.' He patted her hand. 'Great idea, Nik. I'll give him a call today. See if he minds us staying for three weeks.'

Chris jumped up, putting his hands on his hips. 'Man, I'm getting excited just thinking about it. One time Luke and I dug this hole and covered it with sticks and branches – it was a trap to catch a fox that had been harassing the chickens. Anyway, we didn't get the fox, but Luke's dad fell in it and boy did we get into trouble. Most of the time we had good harmless fun. We buried some treasure down near the beach one year. I wonder if it's still there?'

His face was bright, like a child excited about an adventure to the zoo. Nikki felt a little stirring of something.

His smile vanished. 'Do you think Chloe will cope?'

Nikki waved her hand. 'You leave her to me. This will do her good, to have some sand between her toes and dirt on her clothes.'

'Mum, what's for breakfast,' came Chloe's cry from the empty kitchen.

'I better get onto that,' he said darting from the room.

Nikki turned off the TV and PlayStation before joining them. Chris was at the stove, cracking eggs into the pan one-handed while the other was holding his phone. Nikki rolled her eyes and went to get the toaster out.

'Oh eggs, can I have two, please?' Josh threw himself onto one of the chairs by the dining table.

He was dressed for school but she could smell him from across the room. 'Josh, after breakfast can you please remember to put some deodorant on and brush your teeth.'

'Yeah, boy. You stink,' added Chloe, screwing her nose up.

'I do not.'

'Buddy, I can smell you from here. I think it's turning the eggs green,' teased Chris.

'You can't smell it because you live in it, like a pig,' Chloe taunted. 'They think they smell lovely too.'

Josh poked his tongue out at his sister. 'At least I don't spend hours in front of the mirror looking for pimples to squish,' he shot back.

They managed to get breakfast done without initiating World War Three but if looks could kill Nikki and Chris would be childless. Some days that thought was appealing.

Chris pointed to the dishes as he pulled his phone from his pocket. 'Don't do them, babe. I'll sort them tonight. I better get to work. I'll call Luke on my way.'

He bent down to kiss her goodbye, a hint of buttery eggs lingering.

'Okay, let me know what he says.' She waved him off and then turned to sort the dishes.

And I'm not an invalid.

She didn't start work for another hour and a half, so there was plenty of time to do the dishes, get dressed and drive the kids to school if they wanted a lift.

Nikki glanced out the back window. They didn't have much of a yard, just enough room for some lawn, a shed and the kids' sandpit and cubby house, which had made way for the trampoline that never got used now along with the basketball hoop and cricket set. She didn't have much in the way of a garden – it had been designed to be maintenance-free and all set up on reticulation – but none of them went outside much these days. Once, Nikki and Chris would sit out on the lawn on the weekends watching the kids play and having picnics. The sun had felt nice on her skin and the kids were always loud and excited.

She missed those moments. Turning on the dishwasher, she closed her eyes and tried to imagine herself sitting on the beach watching the waves roll in. Crashing into the sand and pushing further up to her toes while seagulls cried in the distance. She was smiling when she opened her eyes.

A sea change would indeed be good for them all.

6

Ashley

'DO YOU THINK WE DID THE RIGHT THING?'

There was a frown line on Emily's forehead and something weighted in her eyes. As if sensing Ash's appraisal, she looked up.

Ash glanced back at the school, at the kids milling around in their white shirts with a red school logo on the breast pocket and school bags at their feet or slung over shoulders. Their pants or skirts were black, and only a few had unsanctioned pieces like hoodies and bright shoes. Ash squinted at them all, wondering which ones had been harassing her daughter.

Last night after dinner, their research had led them to many sites on bullying, the best one being the Kids Helpline.

'See, even they suggest informing the school,' Ash had said. 'We can't let this behaviour go, Em, otherwise it just breeds and more innocent people get hurt.'

'Hm, I guess. I'm scared of what they might do when they find out I dobbed them in, though.'

'Most of them are probably all bark with no bite. Once their parents find out, they'll be in hot water.' At least that's what Ash had hoped. 'Let's be brave and report them. The school might even be able to organise for a police representative to speak to the school about cyberbullying. Like this site says, it *is* a crime.'

'Will you come with me?' Em had asked softly.

'Of course. Every step of the way. And if it gets worse we can always move to another school.'

This last bit of information had seemed to please Emily greatly.

'I'll call in the morning and we'll organise a meeting when school is finished.' Ash had taken Em's hand in hers. 'We have to stand up for what's right, Em, even if it hurts. That's being brave and showing courage. We need to protect you and also other kids; one day they might just tip someone over the edge.'

In that moment Ash knew they were both thinking of Owen, wondering what had tipped him over, but knowing they would never have an answer.

'Okay, Mum. Let's be brave,' she'd replied.

And brave she had been.

Em glanced back to the school building.

'Of course we did the right thing. Don't you think so?' Ash asked.

'Yeah, I guess. At least the principal believed me. I was worried no one would.'

'It's a serious situation and I'm glad to see him jump on it. It's good to know they take their anti-bullying policy seriously. I certainly feel better for doing something about it. Don't you?'

Emily rolled her eyes but there was a pull of her lips.

'Yeah, I guess.'

Her smile said more than her words, and it brought Ash immense relief. The principal had been very attentive, as he had been when she met with him after Owen's suicide. The school had offered counselling for Em and for the teachers to keep a close eye on her when she returned to class. They had been very supportive then, and now was no different.

They reached Ash's white Suzuki four-wheel drive and climbed in. She turned in her seat to face Emily, her blue top twisting against her body like it was trying to choke her. That's what she got for trying to dress nicely for the principal instead of sticking to her usual shirt and jeans.

'Right,' she said, finally organised. 'Do I think he can fix it? Truthfully, I don't know, Em. I mean, it would be a nice thought, but bullying is hard to stamp out. But I don't want you stressing about this on your own; we'll sort it out together.'

Em nodded and put on her seatbelt.

'If they say something to you,' Ash continued, 'just reply, "Whatever," or something similar so they know you heard them and it lets them know it doesn't affect you. Then when you get home we can throw tomatoes at enlarged photos of them,' she added with an evil grin.

Emily laughed, which made Ash smile. All she wanted was to see Emily happy, and though she hated the idea of Emily suffering, she knew it was a good thing to have found those messages and to be able to do something about it, even if it was for Emily to share her burden and pain. Already Ash could see her daughter walking straighter and smiling more, and Ash felt closer to Emily than she had since Owen's death. Maybe the distance had been her own doing, not wanting Emily to get too close and see all the guilt, and she needed to do something to make that right.

'So, I have some good news, which I think you'll like.' Ash smiled, drawing out the suspense.

Emily raised her eyebrow as her fingers played with the worn hem of her white uniform.

'Nikki has invited us to join them for a three-week holiday to Bremer Bay.'

Her cute button nose wiggled as she screwed up her face. 'What? Where's that?'

'Um, I'm not really sure, actually. Nikki said it's about six-and-a-half hours from here but totally worth it. It's near the beach and apparently the sand is a gorgeous white.'

Emily beamed at the mention of a beach.

'I thought you'd be pleased. And she said there's no internet.'

'None!' Emily said the word as if she doubted it were possible anywhere.

Ash smiled; Em probably thought Bremer Bay was a third-world country. 'Not a cracker, and no mobile service either. You have to use a land line for phone calls. But don't mention that to Chloe and Josh just yet. I'm not sure they're aware.' Ash pulled a face.

Em mirrored her grimace. 'Oh, that's going to kill Chloe.' She tilted her head, eyes questioning. 'What's a land line?'

Ashley snorted. 'You kids kill me. It's a phone that's connected to a wall plug, goes through cables to work. Don't you remember the one we used to have in the hallway?'

'I know what it is,' said Em between laughs. 'So, this place is a long way away?'

Ash nodded. 'It's Chris's cousin's farm. What do you think? It will be lots of bonfires, beach trips, and bush walks and games. You could bring your guitar.'

Ashley held her breath as she drove through the busy traffic. She really wanted to watch Emily, to try to guess what she was thinking but didn't want to pressure her, so she kept her eyes on the road. When Nikki had called this morning, it had seemed too good to be true. They could stay for free and just had to bring food.

Emily cleared her throat and Ash snuck a glance sideways.

'I think it sounds amazing. Will we see kangaroos? Maybe a whale. When can we go?'

Em shot out questions excitedly as their home came into view. Ash pulled into the driveway and cringed at the height of the lawn.

'Oh man, I'm going to need a machete to reach the front door soon. Best I pull out the lawn mower before we leave.'

She shut off the car and sat for a moment, trying to remember Emily's questions. She held up a finger. 'Yes, we should be able to see kangaroos.' They were going into the country, she heard they were as thick as flies out there. She held up a second finger. 'Whales may even be possible; I think it's the right time of year for them.' She held up a third finger. 'And we're planning to leave tomorrow or the next day . . . depending on how quickly we get organised.'

'Yes!' Em gave a very contained fist pump.

'We'll go over there now and have a chat with Nikki and Chris, work out the finer details, what we need to take. We might even be camping in tents.' Ash had only slept in a tent in winter when she was little on their family camping trips down south. She frowned and made a mental note to pack her ugg boots and extra rugs.

'We don't own a tent, do we?' Emily asked as they got out and headed for the house.

'Hm, no we don't. See, there is a bit to sort out.' Ash took big steps over the overgrown lawn like an astronaut in space.

Emily smiled. 'Did you get the time off work?'

Ash paused at the door, keys at the ready. 'Yes,' she said. It wasn't a complete lie; she did have the time off from work, and more. 'Go and get changed out of your uniform and we'll head over to Nikki's.'

They arrived at the Summersons' home just after 4pm.

'Gosh, I love this house,' Ash said as they stepped out of the car. 'It's what I picture when I think of my dream home. You know, white picket fence, perfect lawns, organised gardens and a big beautiful home in soft greys and bright whites.'

'Great, you're here,' called Nikki as she swung the door open for them.

Ash noted Emily trying to straighten her hair, no doubt feeling a little pressure when confronted by Chloe's Barbie-like finesse. It was hard not to reach out and stop her, even say something nice about just being yourself when Ashley still did the same thing when meeting Nikki. Gorgeously-put-together Nikki who stood there in designer jeans and white Vans that seemed to be what the kids were wearing and yet she, at thirty-eight, could pull off. With her straight blonde hair and light make-up that enhanced her green eyes, she was picture perfect. She was always so well styled, as if she thought long and hard about what she would wear each day, whereas Ashley ended up wearing whatever her hand pulled out first from her wardrobe drawers. If it was torn jeans with a hoodie, so be it. At least today she was still wearing the fancy top she'd picked to impress the principal. She always found it hard to find clothes that complemented her red hair rather than made her look like a human troll doll. Funnily enough, someone had given her a troll doll for her birthday as a child, an ugly thing with bright red hair going in all directions and big blue eyes, and ever since that's how Ash saw herself. Of course the only difference was Ash was tall, almost too tall.

'Hello, Em. Chloe's in her room.' Nikki gave her a quick hug and then moved so they could enter the house.

'Hi, Nikki. Thanks.'

Emily walked off towards Chloe's room, and Ash followed Nikki to the kitchen.

Josh was in the TV room – he was hard to miss as he called out to an empty room: 'Trent, go around the back. Now! Quick, get him, *get him*!'

Ash saw his headphones and speaker and then turned to see the TV turn red with splattered blood.

'You can see why we *also* need this holiday,' said Nikki who flicked on the coffee machine. 'Josh is obsessed. I don't think it's healthy but I can't seem to stop him. It's like trying to fight a grizzly bear over a tiny bit of fish. Seriously, some days I'm too tired to fight him. Grab a seat.'

This was one of the many reasons Ash liked Nikki. Even though she was pretty and stylish and seemed like she had her shit together, she didn't. Coming to her house and watching Nikki yell at her kids and rant about chores not being done or the fact that they didn't listen just made Ash feel normal, that being a parent was the same in any household. Nikki never put on airs or graces, at least not with Ashley around.

'And here I was wanting a son too,' Ash said with a smile.

'You dodged a bullet there. I thought maybe it was just Josh but I've talked to some of his mates' mums and they're just as bad if not worse. He would play that thing all night if I'd let him.'

Ash also liked how Nikki could joke. They both knew that Ash couldn't have any more kids, and Nikki didn't tiptoe around the subject, wasn't afraid to be normal with her. Sure, Ash would have loved another child, but in the end it worked out for the best. It was as if god or the universe knew how hard life would be and made the decision for her. Besides, she had Emily. Some women couldn't have any children. She was lucky.

'I think it's bad enough when I see Em's phone light on at midnight when I've got up to go to the loo.'

'Ha, I can remember sneaking the phone into the hallway cupboard so I could talk to my friends for hours. As long as Mum wasn't expecting a call or didn't need the phone I could usually chat for ages.' Nikki stared off into space. 'I'd be squished in there under the coats, twirling the curly phone cord over and over along my fingers.'

'These kids don't know what they're missing,' Ash laughed.

Nikki smiled and turned to froth the milk she'd just put in the jug.

'Hey Ash, great to see you.'

She glanced around to Chris who walked in behind her. He put his hand on her shoulder, its warmth setting her at ease, as he bent to kiss her cheek.

It was hard not to like Chris. Good-looking, friendly, helpful – really, he was the dream husband. Nikki had struck gold with him. Owen hadn't liked him much, but then Owen preferred to keep to himself. Ash had often wondered if he'd felt threatened by Chris's magnetic personality and the fact that he seemed to tick all the boxes.

She sucked in a deep breath; Chris smelled so good, like lemon-myrtle soap and deodorant.

'Hi Chris. So, where are we going?' she asked, eager to start this trip.

Chris helped Nikki with the coffees, putting them on the table. 'Sit, honey, I'll make mine,' he said.

Ash just stared at him. Owen never would have done that, never offered to help so she could sit and enjoy her friend's company. Most of the time she only had Nikki over when Owen was away working. It was just easier to entertain when she had the house to herself.

Nikki replied over the noise of the coffee machine grinding away. 'To Luke's place. Chris's cousin's farm. He mainly runs some sheep, cattle and crops. He has a son, Micky. Michael, but no one ever calls him that.'

'How old is Micky?'

'Nearly sixteen, and he's handsome like his dad, so Emily may like that,' said Nikki with a grin. 'I know you'll love Luke.'

'Is he a sweetheart?' she asked, imagining a country version of Chris.

'No,' interrupted Chris. 'What she's politely trying to tell you is he's hot. Isn't that what you called him when you first saw him?' He sat with them at the table, coffee steaming in his blue cup.

'Trust you to remember that,' said Nikki. 'Yeah, he is. Like Chris, he's attractive and fit.'

Ash was having a hard time imagining someone hotter than Chris. She saw the adoration when he glanced at Nikki or spoke about her full of praise and wonder; he was a one-woman man, for sure.

Chris cleared his throat, then tried to shift the conversation. 'So, we don't have to sleep in tents, unless you want to. We thought the kids might like to try it. But we can sleep in the cabins. Luke built them: they're quite rustic, romantic sea shanties. There's a toilet block, which he also built. We all have to share it, like a caravan park. Other than that, he says just bring sleeping bags, pillows, toiletries, chairs for sitting around the fire and good shoes for walking.'

Ash was twirling one of her springy red ringlets between her fingers. 'Well, that sounds easy enough. Is he really ready to be invaded for three weeks by us?'

'He'll be fine. I think this will be just as good for him as it will be for us.'

A strange expression passed over Chris's face, as if he were drifting off deep into thought about something quite serious and upsetting. He glanced down, his eyes brimming with a sad reflectiveness. Ash was about to say something when he suddenly slapped his hands together, making her jump.

'So, everyone keen to head off tomorrow morning?' said Chris, beaming smiles again.

'You bet,' said Ash shooting her hand up into the air like an eager student.

She was a little hesitant at not knowing Luke or the area they were going to, but it had a beach and Emily seemed happier – and right now that was all that mattered to her.

7

Nikki

CHRIS WAS UP EARLY, FLINGING THE BEDCOVERS BACK AND bounding out of bed. 'This is going to be great,' he said as he pulled on jocks and jeans. He smiled at her. 'It will be good for us all.'

Nikki swallowed, the intensity of his words and gaze sitting on her skin like forty-degree heat but she tried hard not to shield herself with the covers. When he left the room, bare chested, it was like a wave of refreshing cool water.

It will be good for us all.

She heard his hidden meaning. *It will be good for you.* Chris was delusional if he thought this trip would miraculously fix her. Nothing could fix her. Nikki felt like exposed and broken wires that sometimes worked and other times sparked and smoked, permanent failure just a moment away. She didn't want to be touched. She didn't want sex. She didn't want intimacy.

The coffee grinder started up and she quickly got out of bed, hoping to be dressed before he came back with her drink.

She threw off her pyjamas and dressed in jeans and teamed them with a blue skivvy and a knitted black jumper. Yesterday packing had been easy, mainly jumpers and pants; some designer jeans were probably too good to go camping in, but Nikki wasn't planning to dig around in the dirt. She couldn't imagine Chloe roughing it either, but she hoped Josh might.

Chris still hadn't come back, so Nikki pulled on socks, then did her hair and put on lip gloss before heading to the kitchen, where she found him with the jug of frothed milk in one hand and his phone in the other. She paused by the doorway watching him, a giddy smile across his face as his screen held his attention.

'Something good?' she asked. She'd never known him to use his phone as much as he had the past few months.

Chris startled, sloshing milk over the edge of the jug, and quickly put his phone down to finally start pouring.

'Sorry, I'm getting there. Here, honey.' He slid a coffee across the table to her.

Nikki pulled out a chair and sat down to drink it while Chris poured his and then cleaned up his mess.

'I rattled the kids' cages but I think I'll have to go back again,' he said smiling sheepishly.

He took a big gulp of his coffee and then headed off, reaching out at the last minute to grab up his phone.

'Be back in a tick. I'll cook up some eggs.'

Nikki took a sip of her coffee; it was lukewarm, so she took a few big swigs then got up to start gathering ingredients for breakfast.

The smell of cooking food usually worked better than yelling at the kids, and before long Chloe and Josh surfaced with noses twitching and sleep still in their eyes. Chris wasn't far behind them with a shirt on and shoes.

He buttered the toast that had just popped up and then brought them over to where Nikki stood by the pan so they could load up the scrambled eggs.

'I'm so hungry I could eat a horse,' said Josh. He blew out his breath so hard that his fringe moved like blades of grass in the wind.

'You couldn't even,' said Chloe with an eye roll.

'I could too,' he shot back, scratching at his head and causing his hair to stand up more than it already did. 'Well, I could if it was a Nutella horse.'

Nikki put a loaded plate in front of Josh. 'Now *that* I actually could believe,' she said with a smirk. She'd often thought about buying Nutella shares; it's not like the world was going to ever run out of teenagers. Seemed like a sure bet.

After they'd eaten, Nikki stacked the dishwasher as Chris loaded the car.

'Mum, I can't find my phone charger. Have you seen it?'

Chloe stood with her hands on her hips, hair straightened and silky, wearing jeans folded up at the bottom and a cute white top that was far too short. Her eyes were made up with smoky eyeshadow and her lips glistened with tinted lip cream.

Nikki didn't have the courage to tell the kids their phones wouldn't work where they were going. Her theory was that once they got there and realised, the beach and bush would be a big enough distraction. That or they wouldn't chuck a tantrum in front of Ashley and Luke. Both those options sounded better than dealing with the fallout that would come now if she admitted the truth. There wasn't enough shiraz in the house for the tears and whining she would likely have to endure the whole trip.

'No, I haven't seen it. Did you check in your bed or under your clothes? In your school bag?' Nikki shot out options. She would put a tenner on it being in her room under something.

'Remember the time you lost your phone?' said Chris as he walked through the kitchen to the outside door. 'As I recall, it was in your bed.' He didn't wait for her reply as the French door shut behind him.

Nikki watched through the window as he collected chairs on the back deck to put in the car.

'I'll go check my bed, again,' Chloe said despairingly.

Chris stopped in the kitchen with his arms loaded. 'Did she find it?'

'Who knows?' Nikki put some apples and bananas into a bag for the car.

'And people say having kids is wonderful! Clearly their dementia had kicked in by the time that statement was uttered,' said Chris with a smirk.

Nikki let the joke pass. 'You know, last night I got up to go to the toilet and I thought there was a storm outside. All this lightning was flashing through the house and when I got to Chloe's room it was coming right through her window but her curtains were drawn.' Nikki shook her head. 'Turns out she was just up on her phone sending all these Snapchats with her flash.'

Chris frowned. 'What time was that?'

'About one. Don't worry, I growled at her, then realised she couldn't hear me 'cos she had her earphones in. I had to go touch her and then demanded the phone but she said she needed it for music to get to sleep.' Nikki let out a sigh closely related to a snarl. She'd been too tired to fight Chloe and had staggered back to bed. 'I told her next time I'd take it away for two days.'

He adjusted the chairs in his arms, his black T-shirt pulling tightly across his tanned, muscular arms. Thanks to all that shirtless lawn mowing.

'Good.' He leaned forward and kissed her cheek.

Nikki breathed in his crisp scent, instantly calmed.

'Besides, it's not like they're out stealing cars,' he said as he headed to the front door, his phone dinging again. 'They *are* good kids.'

'You're a popular man,' she called out after him as his phone kept pinging.

'Always the way when you take holidays,' he replied before vanishing.

Half an hour later they were milling around their silver Prado. Chris had wanted to take his work Hilux dual-cab ute, but Nikki had convinced him that nearly seven hours of whingeing kids would require a little more comfort.

'I'm a bit nervous,' said Ashley, who had moments ago pulled up behind their car. 'Excited nervous,' she clarified.

Her red hair was piled up on top of her head in a messy bun that suited her and she looked dressed for the country in worn jeans and a black check shirt. Her fingers were in her mouth as she chewed on her quicks.

Nikki put her hand on her arm. 'I am too.' Maybe she was as naive as Chris, thinking this trip might solve all their problems. There was something fanciful about the small sense of hope it had generated.

Emily and Chloe were standing awkwardly by each other, Em picking at her nails and Chloe on her phone.

'To think, those two were as thick as thieves years ago,' Nikki said sadly.

'I know. A lot can change with schoolyard politics and peer pressure.'

'It's like they let their differences pull them apart instead of bringing them closer. I hope they find each other again. I miss having Em over and listening to the girls laugh and sing.'

'Where's Josh?' Ash asked.

'In the car with his headphones on watching a movie on his iPad.' Nikki sighed. 'I didn't have the heart to tell him he has time to watch three movies on this long trip. My butt's feeling sore just thinking about it.'

Ashley chuckled as Chris, who was standing by the car door, cupped his mouth and hollered, 'All aboard!'

'See you at the first pit stop,' said Nikki, then called to the girls: 'Come on, Chloe. Time to go.'

The girls parted ways without so much as a glance.

It took a good half hour to be clear of the city, driving along the Albany Highway among tall pine trees and bush reserves. 'I feel like we are really on holiday now,' she said to Chris as she stared out the window. 'Just missing playing "I Spy".'

Chris chuckled. 'Yeah, road tripping doesn't seem the same anymore with the kids on devices.'

'And if you were hot you had to wind the window down, or Mum would sometimes give us a wet flannel to take on the boiling trips. I'm worried these kids will get their licence and not actually know where to drive to because they've never looked out the window to see where they're going.'

'They don't have to, love. They have Google maps.'

They shared a smile and then lapsed into comfortable silence. Nikki relaxed back in her seat as The Cure played from their favourite playlist. She could almost imagine it was their first trip away together when they were young, before kids, before marriage. Back when life was exciting and they couldn't wait to get to where they were now.

'Mum, I need a bathroom stop,' said Josh, poking his head between their seats.

'Can you wait ten minutes? We should be at the next town by then,' said Chris.

Josh scrunched his face as he thought about it. 'Yeah, I think so.'

By the time they got to Williams they all needed to go.

The next stop was Katanning, where Chris had been keen to do a quick drive through the town.

'I lived here once, for a few years. See that house, kids, that one? I lived there.'

Chris was excitedly pointing and gaping at the house. Nikki didn't think the kids were particularly excited – they had both looked at the start but now were back on their devices – but Chris was too busy studying the changes around him to notice.

'Wow, some things are the same, some things have changed. I wonder if the All Ages Playground is still here. I heard they did up the old flour mill into a Dôme.'

Of course, Chris had to go and see that too. Nikki craned her neck to see if Ashley was still following them, likely wondering what the heck they were doing.

'I'm going to run in for a look and get a coffee. Want anything?' he asked.

'No, I'm fine, thanks. I'll wait here with the kids.'

'Righto. I'll just let Ash know what I've been up to. Might be a good chance for a toilet break, kids?' Chris eyeballed his children. Josh shrugged and Chloe shook her head. 'Great communication skills they have,' he joked before leaving with wallet in hand.

Chris had left his phone behind on the centre console and it dinged. Again. Nikki picked it up, curious as to which worker was annoying him on his holiday.

Mandy.

'Who the heck is Mandy?' she mumbled. Intrigued, she swiped the screen to see the message but was halted by a request for a PIN or thumb print. 'Since when have you had a locked screen?'

Her heart was being dramatic as it pounded in her chest, making it hard to think rationally. Without her even thinking, her finger reached out and tried a pattern, just a square. Denied. She felt a little audacious and guilty. Nikki glanced out the window and watched Chris leave Ashley's car window as he headed for the old brick mill, which was three storeys high and full of windows. It had charm and character and she wanted to go and look inside but . . . Mandy. The mystery of it played on her mind like an addiction she couldn't quite give up.

'That's not it!'

Nikki jumped, the phone slipping from her hands into her lap.

'Jesus, Josh. You scared me.' She picked the phone back up again and then frowned as she turned to her son. 'What do you mean, *that's not it?*'

Josh pulled a face like a teacher who had just asked what one plus one was and no one knew the answer.

'It's a Z, like Zorro.' He waved his finger in the air as if slashing it with a blade.

'How do you know?'

His shoulders lifted and dropped just as fast. 'I've seen Dad do it.' Josh slunk back into his seat and riffled through the snacks bag.

Huh, she thought. So he does pay attention to some things. Wonders will never cease.

She glanced at the building further up the road – no sign of Chris – before entering the Z pattern.

Bingo.

His screen lit up: a family photo of them together at the zoo with half a giraffe in the background and Josh giving Chloe bunny ears. Nikki pressed open his messages, hoping to read the latest from Mandy without showing it had been read.

You should see what I'm wearing. I found this gorgeous black lace—

This was all she could read without actually opening the message. Nikki wanted to shake the phone to make more words fall out. What if she just opened it and then deleted it so Chris would never know?

She felt languorous, as if the world had stopped, frozen in time, and yet her body was racing as if she were high on drugs. Her temples pulsed, her blood sprinted through her pounding heart and she felt like she might pass out. Was she even breathing?

Mandy. Had Nikki heard that name before? Was she a co-worker? Maybe it was just a work joke? Maybe she had lace over her yellow hi-vis shirt? Nikki knew she shouldn't jump to conclusions.

And yet . . .

He had been receiving a lot of messages lately. And there was the new lock on his phone.

She had been distant towards him of late, but . . .

Chris wouldn't cheat. He wouldn't.

Would he?

She used to be dead certain of that fact, but lately Nikki couldn't even figure herself out. Was she really qualified to know what her husband had been thinking?

Maybe she should read the message, and any others he had there. If only to set her mind at ease.

A tap at the window had her dropping the phone again, like a cat on a hot tin roof.

'Sorry, didn't mean to scare you,' said Ashley after Nikki wound down the window.

She switched off Chris's phone and slid it back to where he'd left it.

'That's okay,' Nikki replied, trying to keep the annoyance from her voice.

Ash's eye twitched slightly. 'You all right?'

Okay, so she hadn't done a very good job. And now Chris was on his way back with a takeaway coffee in his hand.

Shit.

'Yep, ready to get back on the road and to our destination.' Nikki forced down the weird panic that bounced in her throat. She felt like she had just run the Stawell Gift.

'Hey, does Chloe want to ride with us for a bit?' asked Ash.

Nikki twisted so she could see Chloe and half expected to have to tap her leg to get her attention but Chloe had one earpiece out and had been listening.

'No, I'm okay here,' she replied.

'That's fine,' said Ash and stopped Nikki from muttering her apology. 'We're having a bit of a singalong – probably not fit for anyone else's ears,' she added with a smile. 'Righto, I'll see you at the next stop. Nearly there.'

She left and Nikki wound up her window, a bit of jealousy churning in her lower belly. It would be nice if Chloe would want a singalong, some mother/daughter bonding.

Chris climbed back in, putting his coffee in the holder on the centre console and clicking his seatbelt.

Nikki tried hard not to stare at his phone, wondering if he would notice it flashing with a new message. What would his reaction be when he read the message? Should she ask who it was from? Or would that start a fight over nothing? She couldn't risk the kids overhearing, so she let it go. For now.

'Let's get this convoy on the road,' he said, shooting her one of his perfect smiles.

Then he started the car and pulled out of the parking spot.

Blink. Blink. Blink.

It accosted her eye like a bad twitch and it was all she could think about for the rest of the trip.

8

Ashley

'WE MUST BE CLOSE,' SAID ASH AS THEY FOLLOWED CHRIS and Nikki. Already the landscape felt coastal as they passed banksias and hakeas, and the blue milky sky seemed to stretch over them like a cocoon.

It had been an easy trip, not having to think about where she was going, instead just following.

At the start they'd been excited and sang songs and played 'I Spy' but the momentum wore off quickly and then they put music on and sat in silence for most of the last leg.

'Good, because my legs have gone to sleep,' said Emily, rubbing her hand along her black skinny jeans. 'And I think that roadhouse sausage roll has given me wind.' She frowned and let out a burp.

Ashley had packed boxes of food for the holiday even though Chris had said that Luke's farm wasn't far from Bremer Bay if they needed supplies. They were counting on not making that trip often, or the lure of the internet might be too much.

'Mum, they're turning.' Emily sat up straighter and pointed ahead where the Prado disappeared off to the right between some scraggly trees.

'Oh wow. Finally. I could really use a toilet,' said Ash as she squeezed her legs together. 'I knew I should have gone at the last stop.'

'Is that even a road?' Emily frowned as they turned onto a narrow track, barely wide enough to fit their car, that disappeared into dense foliage. Grass grew up between the wheel marks and the bush seemed to hug the car as they drove.

'They could use a hedge trimmer on this,' she muttered. 'We better not get a flat tyre.'

'Think Nikki will spit it if her car gets scratched?' Emily asked.

'Right now I'm just worried about our car.' Though Ash *was* a little concerned about Nikki; she did seem a little distracted earlier.

'This is kinda cool.'

Emily sat forward with her nose almost pressed against the window. Her eyes were wide and beautiful.

'Oh my god, Mum! I just saw a kangaroo, it was *so* cute.'

The track seemed to go on forever, or maybe it was just the slow, steady pace that made it seem long. Soon they came around a tight corner and the land opened up before them.

'A paddock, with sheep!'

Ash couldn't help but smile; clearly they needed to get out more if Emily was excited about seeing sheep in a paddock. It was actually quite sad to think she'd not seen a farm before. Ash was lucky to have spent a bit of time on her schoolfriend's farm when she was a kid. She was a boarder and on long weekends Ash sometimes went back to their farm in Corrigin. It had been the best time: riding bikes, driving utes, feeding lambs and puppies. There was so much sky and openness. Emily would have loved it. It made going to Luke's farm that much more important. Looking at Em's face now, Ash knew they had made the right decision.

There were more paddocks and more cattle, then more bush, but before long they came to a sign overhanging the track.

Hakea Hollow.

'That's a cool name for a farm,' Ash said. Underneath, it said, *Summerson and Son.*

'Oh, is that his house?' said Emily.

They slowed to a crawling speed as they tried to take in the sight of the land that opened up before them. It was cleared, with some lawn around the home with big bush poles supporting a verandah. There were sheds off to one side in the scrub; Ash could see their large silver shapes. But to the left, as they kept driving, was a sleeper-edged track that veered away from the house towards a parking area. Beyond that she could see little rustic huts and an ablution block. It had a wildness about it, no grass was mowed and nothing looked new.

Chris stopped, so Ash pulled up alongside them and they all got out.

'Oh, I can smell the ocean, the salty air.' Em stretched her arms out and breathed as if the car had been full of stale air.

Ash had to agree, the air smelled wonderful: sweet and crisp like a recent rain had enhanced the native bush around them.

Nikki stood by the car door glancing around, but the smile was missing from her face, and her kids didn't look pleased either.

'Everything okay?' she asked her as she stepped closer.

'Kids hit the no signal after the turn-off. It's been nonstop whining since.' She was watching Chris with a faraway expression on her face. 'You think you prepare yourself for such events but even then they can still get to you.'

Ash chuckled. 'Yeah, kids are like sneaky SAS soldiers. They know how to beat you into submission.'

'I'm hungry,' complained Josh.

'Where's our hotel room?' asked Chloe as she glanced at the main house hopefully.

'How far is the beach?' asked Emily.

Just then the sound of a ute made them all turn as it arrived from the direction of the sheds and pulled up behind both their cars.

'Luke!' Chris said as he bounced on the balls of his feet.

Ash shielded her eyes with her hand to try to get a good look at the man getting out of the white LandCruiser. Long legs, clad in denim, and a broad upper torso covered with a blue work shirt rolled up at the sleeves. She couldn't see much of his face under the red cap that cast it in shadows, but he was a fraction taller than Chris and had short hair. After Nikki's rave review, Ash had to admit she was a little curious to see what all the fuss was about.

The cousins shook hands then ended in a hug that sounded like two bodies colliding on a football field.

'It's so bloody good to finally have you back here.' Luke's voice was low and husky.

'Thanks for having us,' said Nikki as she walked up and hugged him.

'Hey, Nikki. Looking great as always. I can't believe how much the kids have grown. Hey, Chloe! Josh!' Luke raised his hand, giving them a half wave, which the kids returned.

'This is our friend Ashley and her daughter Emily,' said Nikki turning towards her.

Ash started forward to shake his hand, but then her foot caught on one of the little grass clumps that were dotted around the place and she found herself face-first in the dirt staring at his black boots. *Oh shit.*

'Ash, are you okay?' squeaked Nikki.

A strong pair of arms helped her up and then suddenly she was staring at a mesmerising set of winter-grey eyes, like the snow-dusted coat of a grey husky.

'Wow.'

'*Mum*,' came Emily's horrified cry.

'Sorry, call me Ash,' she said holding out her hand. But she couldn't take her eyes off this man. He had the same chiselled features as Chris, but Luke had a 'man of the land' look about him, a ruggedness, from his short-clipped hair to the stubble across his chin, and he smelled like hard work and sea water with a hint of mint.

'Hi Ash. Oh, are you okay? You're hurt.'

She was struggling to think past his voice and those eyes.

Instead of shaking her hand he cupped it in his, and the warmth made her look down. It took her a moment to realise he'd whipped out a handkerchief and pressed it against a bleeding wound at her wrist. She'd been gouged by a stick she'd landed on. Red seeped through the material.

'Sorry, not the best introduction.'

'Ya think,' muttered Emily.

'Luke, nice to meet you. This is my daughter Emily. Thanks for letting us stay,' said Ash and gave Em the mum nod that demanded politeness.

'Hi,' she said with an awkward wave.

'My son, Mick, will be along shortly, he's just out feeding sheep. Come on, I'll show you to your rooms and then let you get settled in.'

Luke let her hand go and strode towards the first hut. After a moment of delay, during which Ash tried to find the go button on her body, she followed the group to the hut.

They were all similar: rusty tin peaked roof with a small front verandah; walls made of old reused wood; doors and windows like antiques picked up at a salvage yard. But they were cute and quaint and fitted into the bush scene.

'Chris, you and Nikki can have this one. There's room for the kids with the bunks on the side,' said Luke as he opened the door and they all filed in.

'Oh, no tent?' said Josh.

Nikki frowned.

'I'm not sleeping in a tent,' Chloe said.

'I didn't want to share my tent with you anyway,' Josh shot back.

'The girls can share a spare hut together if they like, give the adults some space?' Luke suggested.

'This will be great, thanks, Luke,' Nikki said quickly. 'They've held up well over the years – if anything they're cuter than I remember.' She walked in and touched the pine panelled walls.

Ash loved the jarrah floorboards, and the bed was an old metal frame that looked like something her grandad would have slept on when he was a kid. The bunks on the side wall were a hand-built pine creation with a ladder up the side and ample space. There were old lace curtains on the two windows and in one corner a little black pot-belly fireplace with a neat pile of cut and stacked wood ready to burn. Considering the lack of insulation in the cabin, Ash imagined that the fire would be handy, along with the pile of folded rugs sitting on an old wooden side table.

'It's amazing. Did you do all this yourself?' Ash asked Luke.

She smiled when he nodded and turned away uncomfortably. 'It was a bit of fun at the time, creating something from discarded bits.'

He led them to the next hut, which was the same size but differently configured. A metal double bed sat along one wall, with a single metal bed opposite, and two sets of French doors led to the front deck. Ash had got a better room, she decided. She could lie in bed and watch the sun come up through the glass doors. Probably freeze her butt off, but it would be worth it. She would have to get good at lighting the fire. No reverse cycle in here.

There were five huts forming a semi-circle, about ten metres between each, and a sixth that was halfway built. Luke led the way on narrow paved paths made with old bricks to a building in the middle of the huts. This was the most modern of them all with a new tin roof and a rain tank on the side.

'There are four showers inside and two outside; great in summer but a little chilly in winter,' he said as he walked them to the back wall.

It was a zigzag walk through sleepers and mini orb tin onto pebbled floors that opened up into the outdoor shower. Ash looked up at the sky and vowed she would try to take a shower in the open while she was here. The water just better be hot.

'So much work and detail has gone into this, it's incredible,' she said.

'Yeah, I just did what I was told there,' he said pointing to the patterned pebbles. 'Denise was the creator and I was the maker.'

The inside showers were just as nice, where natural woods and mini orb tin came together to create a simple yet functional area. Handmade wooden shelves that held deep basins and rustic towel hooks made from horseshoes were some of her favourite details.

On the side of the ablutions block was the camp kitchen, which was open on one side while the other two walls were a collection of windows and doors.

'That's cool,' said Em as she ran her hand over the many types of wooden window frames. 'Where did you get all these?'

'Hunted out salvage yards. They all come from old homes that were knocked down at some point. Lots of nice things to be found there,' he said, giving her a wink. 'So, there are fridges here, plenty of gas for the barbecue and the Weber if you want to do a roast. Microwave, plus utensils and plates in the cupboards. Just have a hunt around, you should find everything you need.'

'Is there any internet here at all?' asked Josh.

His face was so hopeful, Ash felt a little bit sorry for him.

'Sorry, kid. Not a cracker out here. But we have motorbikes you can ride, plus pushbikes, and Micky has his own ute. He can teach you to drive.'

Suddenly Josh was listening intently. 'Really? Cool.'

'Um,' said Nikki.

'It's okay, love. Luke taught me to drive when I was nine,' said Chris.

'Yeah, and as I recall it earned you the nickname "bunny" for a while.' Luke laughed.

'Bunny?' said Chloe.

'Maybe when Micky gives you a lesson you'll understand,' said Luke.

'Someone say my name?'

A tall, strapping lad strolled in, shoulders square and walk purposeful. Not a name Ash would have put with a teenage boy but it suited this one. His hair was a tousled blond and he wore a red check shirt, a bit like Ashley's but his had holes and dirt and he smelled like fresh straw.

'Hey Micky, good to see you, mate,' said Chris, shaking his hand and slapping him on the back.

Nikki gave him a smile. 'Wow, you've grown into quite a young man since we last saw you.'

'Thanks, Aunty Nikki. Hi Josh, hi Chlo,' he said casually.

Josh and Chloe remained quite reserved.

'You got big,' said Josh eventually. 'Are you shaving?'

Micky laughed. 'You haven't changed a bit.'

'I have. I'm nearly as tall as Chloe.' And to prove his point Josh stood alongside Chloe and used his hand to measure out from the top of his head to hers.

'Go away,' said Chloe, slapping his hand.

'Micky,' Nikki said with a laugh, 'these are our friends Ashley and her daughter Emily.'

'Nice to meet you both,' he said.

'You too, Micky,' Ash replied. He was handsome and well mannered.

'All right,' said Chris, 'let's start unpacking. We've got a car full of food to sort too. Come on, kids.' He led the way back to the car, his kids dragging their feet behind him.

'Let me know if you need any help,' said Luke. 'There's a two-way in the corner, just call. I'm going to head back to the shed and finish working on my tractor.' He dipped his cap at them and headed out with Micky striding beside him.

Nikki stepped towards her and whispered, 'Well, what do you think?'

'I think the place is great,' said Ash, dodging her friend's loaded question. A few surfaces were a little dusty and cobwebs lurked in corners but Ash would get to work on them soon. 'But right now I have a more pressing matter,' she said gritting her teeth and ducking off back into the toilets.

When she was free from feeling like an over-filled water balloon, she washed her hands and then marvelled at the little handkerchief that was tied around her wrist. When had Luke done that? She remembered it being pressed against her wrist but the rest was a blur of frosty grey. Lucky she had brought a Band-Aid for every occasion, and a spray for every bite.

Ash stared at herself in the small mirror and tucked a loose red wavy strand behind her ear. Her eyes were large and bright. 'Don't go making a fool of yourself, woman.' She pointed at herself and pulled a stern expression.

'Mum, did you fall down the loo?'

'Ha ha, very funny. I'm on my way,' she yelled out.

She gave the redhead in the mirror one last warning look, then headed off to unpack.

9

Nikki

IT WAS A WAITING GAME.

A game of endurance.

And it was driving Nikki nuts. She needed to see the rest of the messages so she could decide if she should be worried. Until then, she was worrying anyway. She had to wait for the right moment, and now they were all busy carting stuff from the car to the camp kitchen and their little hut. But Chris's phone throbbed in her mind's eye like a cigarette for someone who was trying to quit.

She reached into the back of the Prado for the last camp chair and almost had it in her arms when it was whisked away.

'I've got that, hon. I'll light the fire in our room too,' said Chris.

'Oh, okay. Um, I'll make a start on dinner, then.'

He nodded, giving her one of his gorgeous smiles and headed off to the hut. Where his phone was. Sitting on small table along with his wallet. She'd checked.

Slamming the back of the car she headed to the camp kitchen where she found Ashley, her sleeves rolled up as she wiped down the bench with a frantic pace as if she were on a timer.

'Wow, you don't have to clean the place,' she said.

Ashley looked up, her blue eyes wide. 'Oh, it's okay. I just thought I'd give everything a freshen up. I don't think Luke's had time,' she said and went back to wiping.

Nikki raised an eyebrow. Ash's house was always spotless. Maybe that's what it was like to have one kid, but there was never anything out of place, never any dishes on the sink or clothes on the floor. Nikki would quite happily put the ten-second rule to the test on her floors.

'Did you clean the rafters?' she said suddenly realising the cobwebs were gone.

Ash shrugged. 'Habit, sorry. Owen had a spider phobia.'

Nikki nearly asked her if she maybe had OCD as well.

'I was just going to make a start on dinner. I was thinking something quick and easy for the first night. I made a salad yesterday and have some sausages ready to go.'

'That sounds good. I have a potato salad too,' Ash replied without stopping her Sadie-the-cleaning-lady work.

'Chris has gone to light our fire. Did you want yours lit while he's at it?'

'I've lit ours already. Em is keeping an eye on it.' Ash paused and turned to Nikki. 'I really think this will be good for Em. I've noticed a little change already.'

'Oh, that's great to hear, Ash. I think I still have a long way to go before my kids start enjoying their phone-free time.' Nikki pressed her lips together, remembering the last agonising minutes of the car ride.

'What! There's no internet *at all*!' Chloe's voice had reached a fever pitch like a boiling kettle.

Just the thought of it made her head start to throb. Both kids were in their hut lying on the beds, no doubt still complaining to whoever would listen.

Nikki heard movement behind them and turned to find Micky carrying an armful of wood to a metal ring that looked like a rim from a big tractor. He set the wood down and waved to her before setting it up and lighting it.

'I hope some of Micky rubs off on Josh while we're here. He's such a capable young man.'

'He looks so grown up,' said Ash as she rinsed her cloth in the sink. 'Will we meet his mum?'

Nikki turned back to Ash. 'Ah, no,' she said softly and moved closer to her. 'Denise went AWOL a few years back. Just been these two ever since.' She shook her head sadly.

'Went AWOL? How could she leave Luke and her son?'

Ash looked horrified and Nikki knew she'd been affected by Luke. She did practically fall at his feet, Nikki thought with amusement. 'I'll tell you about it later,' she whispered. 'It's a long one.'

'That would explain why this place is missing a woman's touch,' she muttered as she went back to cleaning.

Nikki almost laughed. 'Denise wasn't a big cleaner, nor your mainstream wife. "Hippy" was Chris's word for her; he never liked her much. Not since the time she made him eat a vegan burger.'

'If I wanted to be preached to I would have gone to a church!' he'd complained after a long night eating vegan food and hearing about how meat was bad. 'She does realise she's marrying a farmer?'

When they'd got home the first thing he asked Nikki to cook was a steak, and he'd savoured every bite like he'd been starved for a month.

'Oh, right,' said Ash, her face a little amused.

Chris appeared with two chairs under his arms and set them up around the fire. The orange–red flames were small, licking over the wood like a tongue to an ice-cream. A light smidge of smoke curled up above the flames into the darkening sky.

'Nice job, Mick. Have you got any spare chairs about?' asked Chris.

'Sure, Uncle Chris. We have some Dad made that can stay out while you're here.'

The two figures disappeared to a small shed not far from a vegetable garden near Luke's house, which was a hundred metres away from the camp area, and carted back the long wooden bench seats.

'I'm just going to see what the kids are up to,' said Nikki after she got the sausages out of the fridge. 'Chris, can you please start cooking the sausages?' she yelled before heading back to the hut.

Inside, her two kids were exactly where she'd left them, lying on beds with their phones. 'Haven't the batteries died yet?' she asked.

'I brought my charger,' said Josh. 'I can still play games.'

His tone was rather boastful.

'Well, sorry to disappoint but there are no power points in here, so maybe you should turn it off and go sit by the fire Micky just started.'

Josh sat up and glanced out the window. The flames of the fire were higher, and she could see the spark of interest. Like a wet fish, Josh slid off the bed and, leaving his phone behind, stuck his head out the door for a better look. Then he disappeared.

'Why don't you go and have a look too, Chloe. It's got to be better than just sitting in here. Dinner will be ready soon.'

Chloe grunted and slapped the bed with her hands. 'I guess I have to. Can't be any worse than this,' she said with a pitiful whine.

Chloe rolled to the edge of their double bed and poured herself onto the floor before righting herself and stomping to the door while shooting Nikki a look that could have killed a duck mid-flight.

Feeling even worse than usual, Nikki sat on the corner of the bed and sighed, hoping to expel all the weight she felt. The hut was silent, just the crackle of the pot-belly fire in the corner. Ah, peace.

It only lasted a few seconds before she felt the potent pull of Chris's phone. The black shape was like a line of cocaine and she was craving her next hit. Without thinking she pounced on it, her heart suddenly racing. With a quick glance out the window she spotted Chris with the kids and then, satisfied she had a few minutes, she opened his phone.

With shaking fingers she opened his messages and then blinked. She shook the phone hoping it would make the missing messages appear but there was nothing from Mandy. Nothing at all. She scrolled down the list. There was her name, the kids, his parents, his work colleagues. But no Mandy.

She sank back down on the bed, her body still buzzing from adrenaline.

Had he deleted all the messages? Why? Because he knew they were wrong? How would she know now?

Trying to think, she went into his contacts and found, after *Mum*, a number for *Mandy*. She opened it but it didn't reveal anything and no messages were to be found.

She whimpered like a cornered dog, panic pumping through her veins.

Photos! Maybe he'd kept some . . . if there were any to keep.

Her finger was shaking so badly it took two attempts to open his gallery. Her heart sank like an anchor to the bottom of the ocean when she saw photos of Chris. Chris smiling in the sun. Chris with his shirt off. Chris posing at work. Chris in his underwear – obviously a selfie, because he'd cut off his legs. Her mind raced.

Not one of these photos had come to her phone.

Not one.

And these weren't the kind you sent to your work colleagues or your mates or your parents.

At least she hadn't come across a dick pic yet. She quickly scrolled to the bottom and was relieved to see no porn, besides the odd photo of Nikki he'd managed to hang onto from a few years ago. Then she spotted the Albums.

There were three.

Camera.

Kids.

And the last one labelled *M*.

In this one she found three photos. One of legs in the sunshine. One of a tanned body in a red bikini; the head was cropped out

but she could make out a tattoo of something on the wrist . . .
a name, maybe. And then one of a set of boobs in a black lace
bra. A sexy one, too, with little silver diamonds on it.

But the real pain came from the ample breasts straining at
the lace.

'Oh Chris.'

Her belly dropped. She could try to pretend they were photos
from a porn site that he had taken a shine to, but she didn't
want to be naive – there was too much evidence to ignore.

Nikki wanted to scream but she didn't, instead she wiped
at the tear that had rolled down her cheek.

She gritted her teeth, trying to take control before she became
a mess, and cleared her tracks from his phone before putting
it back on the table.

Then she sat staring at it.

Now, what was she to do? Call him on it? Make a scene?
She didn't want to own up to snooping on his phone, nor did
she want the kids to witness any of this.

She had to be smart about it.

Don't rush into anything stupid, Nikki, she told herself. *Think.*

Maybe there was a way to mention her name, say she saw it
on his phone. But Nikki shook her head – as if he would own
up to it. *Damn it.* She might just have to confess to looking
on his phone and break that trust.

Oh, she felt sick. The food-poisoning sort.

Mandy. Who was she? Where was she from? How long had
this been going on? How far had it gone?

The thoughts spun her off her axis as she fell back onto the
bed, flopping her arm across her eyes. *Don't cry. Don't cry!
Fuck you, Chris!*

Damn it, how could he do this, especially when he knew she wasn't in a happy place.

The door flung open. 'Mum, are you coming? Dad's started on the snags,' said Chloe. Then her tone changed. 'Are you okay? Mum?'

Chloe's concern had Nikki biting her lip to stop the onslaught of tears that threatened. 'I've just got a bit of a headache. I'll be out in a tick.' It came out as a hoarse whisper.

'Oh, okay.' She paused. 'Do you want me to get Dad?'

Nikki shook her head quickly. 'I'll be okay in a minute.'

Chloe waited a moment and Nikki felt a little bit of pride at her daughter's concern. She would have loved a hug from her right now but she didn't want to scare her. She would probably think her mum had lost the plot.

'If you're sure. Call me if you need anything,' Chloe said before closing the door softly.

Nikki relaxed and put her arm down. She had to be strong for her kids.

Sitting up, she made herself walk outside, sneaking like a quiet mouse when really she wanted to slam doors and stomp down to the camp kitchen like an ogre swinging an axe.

But that wasn't Nikki. A confrontation-avoider and peace-maker was all she'd ever been.

The kids were walking around the fire with plates, making their way back to seats while Ash and Chris were getting their meals.

'Sorry, I meant to come back and help you,' she said, touching Ashley's arm.

'Don't worry about it, Nik, we're on holiday. Just go with the flow,' Ash said, blowing back red strands that hung over her eyes. 'Dig in, plenty here.'

Just go with the flow.

Nikki flinched as a hand touched her shoulder.

'You okay? Chloe said you had a headache?' whispered Chris.

How could he look at her with such concern, as if it really did hurt him to think she was suffering? Little did he know he was the reason. Nikki couldn't trust herself to speak, so she just nodded and headed to a spare seat by the fire.

She stared into the flames, eating salad but not tasting it. Not much talking was happening, which suited her fine. The kids were probably still sulking. Her eyeballs felt like they were burning, but she didn't blink. Instead she wondered when exactly it was that Chris's touch had started to make her cringe.

Sometimes when she saw his hand coming towards her she felt a moment of flight, and if gravity didn't keep her on the ground she would fly far away from him. Was that what was making him fly away from her?

Nikki wasn't one for outbursts, she was more a procrastinator. She would stew over something and roll it around in her mind until she was ready to deal with it. This *thing* with Mandy, whatever it was, needed much thought. She needed time. Time to process. Time to build up courage to confront Chris. And more courage to face the truth of it all.

10

Nikki – The Past

'OH, TRY THIS ONE ON, NIKKI.'

Nikki took the dress from Alice and held it up. 'Hm, I think I might. It's a stunning cut.'

'Go on, I've just locked up. The shop is ours.' Alice adjusted her mushroom-pink jacket, pulling it over her ample chest. 'I'm going to try on this black one.'

The soft blue material glided over her skin and she could feel its firmness, it was going to be a snug fit. She glanced down as the folds fell to the floor in gentle moving waves. Nikki pressed the material over her hips, it was fitted but comfortable. Alice had got her the right size. Another reason Alice was ticking all the boxes before her three-month trial was up.

Nikki reached back and did up the clasp at the back of her neck; no zips in this dress, just a gaping hole showing off her back. 'Wow, that is *gorgeous*.'

She turned to face the mirror and her heart sank.

Nikki stood there, not even seeing the beautiful cut of the dress or the pin tucks that emphasised her hips. She thought the high neck might have worked in her favour, not needing cleavage to hold the dress in place, but this was almost worse than having no cleavage.

Nikki tilted her head, as she always did when gazing at her breasts, as if it would right her uneven boobs. They had always been small, but Chris had loved them regardless. Then when the kids came along she was overjoyed at the size they grew to; so was Chris, even though they were more a *look don't touch* sort. But two kids, with both favouring one side more than the other – well, that's what she put it down to – had left her with one side barely an A cup while the other would fill a C if scooped up but instead just hung, drooped.

One side was as flat as a man's chest, the other a saggy long sack. Together, they were wrong. Nikki had to cut and paste her own bras because normal ones wouldn't fit her. At least with a bra she could hide their unevenness, but in a dress like this that was worn without a bra ... well ... she had a blue smartie up near her heart and then the other nipple near her belly. It was ridiculous. There was no way she could wear something like this in public.

'What's it like?' called Alice. 'Parade, please!'

Nikki frowned. Was it just all in her head? Made worse by how she thought she looked?

She opened the curtain.

'Wow,' gasped Alice, standing there in a high-necked black cotton dress. 'You fit it perfectly.'

Then her eyes dropped and her head tilted slightly.

'My boobs ruin it!' Nikki said, heavy-hearted.

'No, no,' Alice started to say and then paused.

Nikki put her *don't lie to me* face firmly in place. 'Alice?' she warned.

'Well, have you tried those sticky boob-holder things? They might pick that one back up to the same level,' she said.

'Thanks, Alice, I love your honesty,' she said with a grin. 'But that's not going to solve this one,' she said pointing to her left nipple.

'What about those silicone breast holders but cutting two sizes and joining them?'

Nikki nodded. 'Oh, I wonder if that would work? I already do that to my bras.'

'Do you?' Alice screwed her face up as she glanced at Nikki's breasts again. 'Kids?'

'Yeah, the joys they don't tell you about. I mean, they weren't great to start with but now ... well, they're just hard work. Under clothes I can kind of make them look even, but poor Chris gets this.' She pointed to her boobs. 'This dress would be killer if I had your breasts, Alice. Gosh, I envy them so.'

Nikki couldn't help but admire the strained material around Alice's plump breasts. They were the sort that epitomised the female form, the sort boys wanted to touch and men wanted to devour. The sort Nikki dreamed about constantly. She glanced away from Alice. Lately she'd become a breast gazer, and if she didn't keep it in check women would start to think she was interested. But Nikki just appreciated what she didn't have.

'I still think Chris would love to see you in that dress. Take it home and show him,' she said warmly.

'I'll think about it,' she said before closing the curtain to change.

The dress had stayed at the shop.

Nikki didn't want to wear it for Chris, because she knew he wouldn't care how it looked, he'd just want to strip her out of it. But she did tell him about it as she was putting on her pyjamas before bed.

'Stunning, you say?' Chris pulled off his shirt and tugged down his track pants. 'Why didn't you bring it home?'

He stood before her in his black trunks, a cross between an underwear model and an Olympic swimmer. Nikki turned her back to him and yanked off her shirt and threw on her bedtime singlet then made a deal out of folding her shirt to put on the chair by her bed. When she turned around Chris was on her side of the bed kneeling, and he reached for her.

'Were you too scared I'd tear it off you?' he said, wiggling his eyebrows as his hands snaked around her backside and tugged her closer.

'It's too expensive for you to do that,' she said, rolling her eyes.

He lifted up her shirt and kissed her belly, which she worked hard to keep relatively flat. It was what Nikki liked to call 'I've-had-kids flat'. A few rolls, some saggy skin but eating right and walking to the park on occasions helped it be as flat as she could hope for without being some fitness fanatic, diet-obsessed, stick-figure mum.

She smiled and sank her fingers into his damp hair. His hands moved to her waist and then up her shirt. She pushed down the need to clench and pull away. She tried not to notice the fact that his hand went straight to her biggest boob and it was only that nipple his mouth kissed and teased. It was hard to begrudge him when there really wasn't much on the other side for him to play with, but his fingers did roll over her other nipple. Maybe he was just checking she still had two?

Chris pulled her down and around so she fell onto the bed. Her mind went blank as he cupped her face in his hands and kissed her. His breath was minty fresh and his skin smelled clean like their lavender soap wash. Nikki moaned as his moist lips worked their way to her ear and to her favourite spot that made her whole body tingle. Then he was making his way back down to her navel. Lower and lower, dragging her under-wear down as he went before he teased her with his tongue.

She closed her eyes, forgetting about her wonky boobs and any uncomfortable feelings she had, as Chris made her body levitate off the bed.

Afterwards, Chris lay against her chest while she played with the hair around his ear and listened to him breathing, almost asleep. His large hand was resting on her belly just below her breast.

'I've been thinking about my boobs again,' she said softly, feeling relaxed but not as sleepy as Chris.

'Hm.'

'I really want to get them fixed. I think it will be money well spent if it means every single day I can look in the mirror and get dressed without feeling inadequate.'

She didn't think Chris had been listening but he moved, lifting his head and leaning on his elbow so he could see her.

'You sure? I don't think you need to, you know I love you just the way you are,' he said.

His golden eyes shone with the truth of his words. She knew he was happy but what he didn't really understand was that Nikki wasn't. And deep down she knew that Chris would be excited if she had two lovely plump boobs. She wasn't stupid, she'd seen the way he'd turned his head at women with nice chests, even commented. Nikki wanted to be able to give him that, as well as feel like a woman again rather than some half-chewed and spat out mum who didn't feel sexy at all anymore.

'I know,' she replied. 'But I want to be able to wear a gorgeous dress without being self-conscious. I want to feel whole again. And for a thousand, even less, a year, I could have that. It would be less than a coffee a day. I've been saving more than that each week and I have five grand put away already.'

Chris sat up, his face serious. 'Wow. You really want this.'

Nikki nodded. 'I really do.'

Chris reached for her hand. 'Who am I to deny the woman I love.'

She smiled and he leaned over and kissed her.

'Go and book an appointment tomorrow,' he said.

'What?'

'I'm sure you've already researched a great plastic surgeon. Knowing you, Nik, you've got it all worked out. Especially if you have five grand saved up already. You've been planning this a while?'

She pressed her lips together and nodded.

'Go and get it done, we can use the extra money in the house loan to cover the rest.'

'Really, Chris?'

'Really, *really*. I just want you to be happy.'

Nikki threw her arms around her husband and cried. 'This makes me deliriously happy. Thank you.'

Nikki couldn't believe it. She'd brought up getting her boobs fixed over the years but Chris had always told her that he loved

her as she was. He didn't want fake. She was the making of
two beautiful kids and he wouldn't change her for anything.
But all the sweet words in the world could never take away
her feelings of inadequacy.

'I wasn't sure you'd ever agree to this,' she whispered as tears
rolled down her face. 'I know you don't like plastic women.'

Chris pulled back and brushed the tears away with his
thumbs. 'Honey, I don't want to ever stand in the way of your
dreams. I just wish I'd realised how much you want this.'

He looked distraught, watching her cry. But she couldn't stop
the tears. Relief washed over her. After years, the thought that
she might finally be happy to see herself in the mirror. To not
want to hide herself from Chris because she was embarrassed.
God, her own husband and she was embarrassed! It seemed
ridiculous and yet, she couldn't help it.

'Oh, baby.'

Chris held her tightly and stroked her back.

'It's okay. These are happy tears,' she sniffled.

'I just feel awful I couldn't make you this happier sooner.'

With a shaky hand, Nikki wiped her face. 'Will you come
to the appointment with me? Please?'

'Of course. You let me know when and I'll get the time off.'

They snuggled back into bed, arms wrapped around each
other as if they were clinging to the edge of a life raft in a
never-ending ocean. Chris brushed her blonde hair back from
her face, his eyes shining like gold flecks in the sun as he
drank her in.

'I love you so much,' he whispered.

'I love you too,' she replied.

Nikki couldn't wipe the smile from her face.

11

Ashley

IT WAS QUIET EXCEPT FOR THE CRACKLE OF THE FIRE AS THEY sat scattered in their camp chairs and on Luke's hand-crafted bench seats. The sky above had turned black and a million stars twinkled like fairy lights on invisible strands. The firelight flickered over the nearby huts, windows alight like eyes, while the boards resembled wrinkle lines. The dirt at their feet was a fine sand, almost grey in colour, and it circled around the fire before turning to unkempt lawn that was spasmodic and patchy with weeds and other grasses. The camp kitchen light was on, small bugs flitting around it, while the toilet block was dark except for two outside lights above the doors.

'It feels like ages since I've seen the night sky like this. It's so big – and all those stars,' Ashley said. She felt small, like a speck of dust as she gazed up into the Milky Way. 'It's breathtaking.'

She wasn't sure who was listening to her rambling; the kids seemed intent on eating their sausages as they stared into the fire like zombies and Nikki was just coming out of the camp kitchen after fetching some dinner.

'You don't really appreciate what the sky has to offer until you see it out in the country, away from city lights. It's impressive,' said Chris, his head tilted back.

Nikki sat in the spare chair next to Ash, instead of next to Chris on the bench seat.

Chris righted his head. 'Are you okay, hon?'

Ash adored Chris for the way he was so attentive to Nikki. His whole focus was on her, across the fire his gaze was heavy with concern and Ash knew that if Nikki even hinted, Chris would jump up and fetch anything she needed. Owen wasn't like that. Or hadn't been like that, she reminded herself. How long would it take for her to get that right in her head? Owen was never going to walk back into their house.

'It's okay,' replied Nikki as she stabbed at her salad on the plate that rested precariously on her knees.

'I have Panadol, Nurofen and some oils if you need any.' Ash reached over and touched her shoulder.

'Mum brought the whole chemist, as usual,' muttered Emily, who sat between Chloe and Ashley. Ash couldn't see her eye roll but Emily's tone implied it. Em was buried under her big black hoodie and blended easily with the night.

'Owen often had migraines. I'm so used to carrying supplies for every occasion.'

Nikki smiled back at Ash but her eyes were glassy and filled with a heaviness, and Ashley felt a prick of concern. It was more than a headache. She was about to ask if she really was okay when approaching footsteps distracted her.

'Hey guys, mind if we join you?'

Ash looked up as that gravelly voice warmed her more than the fire. Luke came to a standstill by the edge of the fire pit, the flames flickering light across his handsome face. He was still in his earlier clothes but with a big thick blue jacket that was open at the front. Micky stood beside him for a moment before taking a seat next to Josh.

'By all means, pull up a chair. There's some tossed salad and sausages left over if you're hungry,' said Chris.

Chloe burst out laughing.

All eyes turned to her and her face reddened, or maybe that was the fire glow.

'Sorry,' she said while covering her smile with her hand, her shoulders shaking with silent giggles.

'What's so funny?' Emily asked.

'Tossed salad,' she whispered back and pulled a face.

Nikki sat up, her breath catching in her throat. 'Chloe Sue! Do you know what that means?'

Chloe's mouth dropped open. 'Oh my god, Mum. Do you?' Chloe replied in a horrified tone.

They stared at each other wide-eyed.

'Who told you?' Nikki demanded.

Ash was having trouble keeping up, but she was starting to think a tossed salad didn't meant the lettuce kind. One glance at Luke and she knew he was none the wiser. He shrugged and sat next to Chris on the bench seat.

Luke leaned towards Chris. 'What did I miss?'

Chris cleared his throat and murmured back, 'I'll tell you later.'

'You may as well say it,' said Josh. 'I'll just Google it.' He started feeling around in his pockets for his phone, then realised he didn't have it. He sighed heavily. 'When I get signal,' he grumbled.

'Who told you about this, Chloe?' Nikki demanded again.

Chloe shrugged. 'I don't know. Someone at school probably mentioned it and so I Googled it.'

'And Google told you what it meant?'

'Yeah. Google tells you everything.'

'That's true,' said Ash. 'At work Tim mentioned a Blue . . . um, something,' Ash quickly deleted the last word, realising the teenage little ears around them were always switched on. 'But he refused to tell me what it was, so I Googled it on my phone.' Ash screwed her face up and put her fork down, no longer hungry. 'Let's just say I wish I hadn't. You can never un-see stuff!'

Chloe leaned forward. 'It's revolting, isn't it?'

Ash felt the blood rush from her face at the thought that Chloe had seen that too. Technology had exposed it all. *What happened to ignorance being bliss?* Ash was scratching at her wrist and stopped it, realising this whole scenario was spiking her anxiety. And she was an adult. How did kids with anxiety cope? Was this part of the reason more and more were being diagnosed – because they had access to all the bad stuff in the world and it overloaded them?

'Jesus. The internet has a lot to answer for. Chris?' Nikki shot to him.

He shrugged. 'What do we do? Ban them?' He paused, glancing at the younger eyes watching him carefully. He cleared his throat. 'Back in our day if we heard something we had to wait to ask an adult we trusted to fill us in – and that's only if they deemed us ready to know it. Now kids have a way to access it all,' he said turning to Luke.

Luke put up his hands. 'Hey, I hate technology. I'm still fighting with my computer to do the bookwork.'

Nikki was rubbing her temples. 'How are we supposed to keep our children innocent for as long as possible when they have everything at their fingertips.' She turned back to Chloe. 'What else have you seen?'

Emily cleared her throat. 'I've seen guys at school watching porn on their phones.' She paused for a moment, her eyes down on her lap. 'And . . . and sometimes I'd get sent photos of men with elephantiasis dicks,' she said quietly. She let her hair drop across her face.

Ash frowned. 'Real penis photos with elephantiasis? What kind of person would send that!' She felt her frustration grow but got a grip on it when she saw the concern on Em's face. She couldn't afford to scare her off. It was brave of her to mention this. Ash reached for her hand and gave it a squeeze and held it until Em lifted her head.

'That's awful,' said Nikki. 'What else have they sent you?' She turned to Ash. 'If I could get my hands on those horrible kids . . . I'd love to teach them a lesson in respect.'

'Get in line,' said Ash. 'I hate cyberbullying more than the face-to-face sort. Faceless keyboard warriors who think they can say and do whatever they like. You should see some of the comments customers have left about Tim on our website. So rude.'

'What is this elephant thingy?' piped up Josh from the other side of the fire. 'Damn, I wish I had my phone,' he mumbled.

Chris glanced at Nikki. 'I'd rather Josh hear it from us.' She nodded, so he continued. 'It's a parasite infection, I think; it swells up body parts – so, a leg may end up three sizes bigger than normal.'

Josh tilted his head, taking it all in. 'And what about the other one?' asked Josh. 'Something blue?'

'No!' All the adults chorused.

Josh frowned then glanced at Chloe and gave her a nod as if to say, *You'll tell me later.*

'You should be more concerned with what Josh watches. He sees people getting shot,' said Chloe. 'Those stupid war videos on YouTube.'

'It's better than watching some silly girl put make-up on five different ways. How boring,' he replied, pulling a face.

'What do you mean, war videos?' said Chris, leaning towards Josh. 'Real ones? Or video-game stuff?'

'Oh, they're real,' said Chloe. 'A boy I know at school loves watching soldiers shooting people. He's obsessed with army stuff, he showed Josh how to find them.'

'What soldiers?'

'Whatever ones he can find. He said some of it's off their helmet cameras from missions,' Chloe replied to her dad.

Josh shrugged and said to Micky. 'It's just like watching a movie.'

'No, Josh, it's not. It's real and I don't want you to watch anything like that again, understand?' said Chris firmly.

'I wouldn't know,' said Micky. 'I don't get enough signal to even use my phone most of the time. Only at school at lunch-time, but I'm usually playing sports with my mates. I think kids get a bit obsessed with stuff that's not relevant. I'd rather be out helping Dad than wasting time on the internet.'

'You sound just like your dad,' said Chris, who seemed a little green around the gills. Which was how Ash felt.

'It was bad enough when Josh was eight or nine and all his mates were playing "Grand Theft Auto". I don't think they even knew how bad the game was, or cared. They thought it was a driving game. It's rated eighteen years and over for a reason. I refused to let him play it,' said Nikki.

'My friends paid out on me for that,' said Josh, clearly still harbouring a little resentment. 'None of them have grown up crazy.'

'Josh,' growled Chris.

Josh sank back into his chair.

Ash knew there would be a private chat later. 'I've only used YouTube to see how to cook something or fix things,' she said. 'I saw a news article about kids' cartoons being edited for violent things. One minute it's a harmless cartoon, the next it's a hanging?'

'Why do people do a lot of things?' said Luke. 'The world is full of mixed-up, crazy, desperate, evil humans. Another reason I prefer to live out here where I just have to worry about snakes.'

'Wait, *what*?' Em reached out and gripped Ashley's knee. 'There's snakes,' she hissed.

Ash shook her head and hoped Luke was just joking. *Please be joking!*

'My dad never jokes,' said Micky with a grin.

'I think both your phones need an overhaul when we get home. It will be text messages and phone calls only, I'm thinking,' said Nikki grimly.

The kids' complaints came thick and fast.

'Mum!'

'That's not fair!'

'All the other kids have it.'

'This sucks,' said Josh, as he folded his arms and kicked at the ground. A spray of dirt hit the fire pit, causing it to shoot sparks. 'This is your fault,' he shot at his sister. 'You ruin everything!' His face said he was mowing her down with his imaginary Uzi.

'Josh, that's enough,' barked Chris. 'The fact that you see nothing wrong with what you're watching worries me.' He frowned. 'Your attitude is atrocious.'

Ash could see the weight of the world on Chris's shoulders. With each kid it no doubt intensified. Trying to do what was best for them, keeping them safe, raising them with respect . . . it was a massive job that didn't have an instruction manual.

'Why don't you yell at Chloe? She's just as bad!'

'She's not chucking a plonka and kicking dirt like a two year old,' Nikki growled.

Ash wasn't game to open her mouth, giving the parents time to do their jobs. But she felt their pain, and frustration.

Josh glanced at Micky, who was poking the fire with a stick. He stood up. 'I'm going to bed.' And he walked off to the hut with his hands shoved deep into his jeans.

'I'll go,' Nikki said to Chris. She stood up, her plate of food hardly touched as she walked to the camp kitchen before following Josh.

'I might go and have a shower,' said Em.

'Me too.'

Chloe and Em headed off together, leaving Ash with the men and Micky. After a few minutes the awkward silence around the fire made her skin itch, so she got up and collected the leftover plates and headed to the kitchen to clean up. Cleaning gave her purpose and less time to scratch and chew nails.

'Here, I found another one.'

Ash had just started filling the sink and jumped at Luke's voice. She turned and was struck by the liquid silver of his eyes under the bright fluoro light. Up close he was even better, the fine laughter lines and the distinguished bits of grey she could see in his hair making him even more appealing.

Suddenly she realised she'd just been staring while he was there holding the plate.

'Oh. Thanks.' She turned off the tap and plunged the plate into the soapy water.

'Did you do this?' Luke asked, looking around, then up and down. 'I've never seen this kitchen so clean. It looks great.' He cleared his throat. 'I'm sorry it wasn't up to scratch. I don't have the time to run a farm, look after Micky and our own house let alone this bit.' He stood beside her and picked up a tea towel. His body warmth was welcome in the cold night air.

Ash flung her hands out of the bubbles and ended up flinging Luke with the suds as she waved at him. 'That's okay, I've got this.'

'I don't mind. Everyone else has bailed.'

Ash turned to the fire and saw that it was indeed circled with empty chairs. *What a waste of a good fire.*

She watched Luke dry a plate before getting back to the task. 'And this place is fine, seriously. I just have this compulsive cleaning disorder.'

He gave her a questioning look.

'Well, I never used to have it. I think my husband somehow projected it onto me.'

'Is he working?'

'Huh?'

'Your husband. He's not here?'

'Oh.' Ash stared at Luke open mouthed. She hadn't had to answer one of these questions in a long time. 'Um, no. He . . . Owen . . . died. About eight months ago.'

Luke's eyebrows shot up. 'Oh shit, I'm sorry, Ashley. I didn't know. I wish Chris had mentioned it, but this trip was kind of spur of the moment and we haven't had much chance to talk yet. I feel like a goose.'

Ash smiled. 'Sorry, I shouldn't smile. But I've only ever heard my nanna say that. *I feel like a goose.*'

'Well, I do. Put my foot right in it.'

'Don't feel bad. I'm bound to do the same thing about your wife at some point. Aren't I?'

Luke chuckled. 'Yeah, well, she left me by choice.'

'So did Owen,' Ash said sadly.

Luke's head tilted slightly. Confusion made him striking and Ash didn't want to burden him with her sob story. And yet his silent manner felt welcoming and open. The next moment she was blurting it out. 'Owen took his own life, so he chose to leave us too.'

He swallowed as he watched her. 'I'm not sure what's worse. Your husband's way or my wife's – she's still out there but has nothing to do with us. Me, I can understand,' he said touching his chest with his hand. 'But Micky finds it hard that she left him, and I almost hate her for it.'

She stared at him. The fact that he hadn't offered the usual sympathy, shock and pity was refreshing, but no less than the fact that he'd offloaded some of his own baggage.

'I can't imagine it,' said Ash. 'Either way seems wrong. I couldn't bear to be apart from Em. At least Em can mourn her father, but poor Micky . . . Does he want to see her?'

Luke shrugged. 'I think he used to. Maybe he still does but he doesn't want to disappoint me by telling me. I don't know. I couldn't leave Micky either. Never.' Luke glanced around before picking up the last plate to dry. 'I hate that Mick puts on a brave face around me because she left me too. He wants to show me he's on my side even though he misses his mum.'

'He wants to know she still loves him.'

'She does, I'm sure. She just can't face what comes with it.'

'Owen couldn't face anything,' said Ash. A slight harshness lined her voice, some of the pain she'd kept hidden, the bit that hated Owen for being so selfish. But she always felt horrible when these thoughts appeared.

Luke just held her gaze. No words were needed, but she felt his compassion and appreciated its silence.

'Well, I think we've done all our dirty dishes tonight.' Luke smiled as he hung the wet tea towel on the rail by the wall. 'Can't say I've talked about Denise like that in a long time.'

Ash pulled the plug and then wiped her damp hands on her jeans. 'Me either.'

'I think it's going to be nice having you guys around for a few weeks. It's been a bit quiet out here with just me and Micky. We'll take you up to the lookout and down to the beach tomorrow.'

'Oh, that I'm looking forward to.' Ash tilted her head back slightly. She was tall but Luke still had a few inches on her. 'Thanks, Luke – and not just for helping with the dishes. It wasn't the greatest first night, was it?' she said with a chuckle.

He smiled. 'Yeah. Well, it can only get better. Anyway, I'm going to hit the sack. Early to bed, early to rise. Night, Ashley.'

His voice was lulling her into serenity. 'Night, Luke. And call me Ash.'

He nodded his head before turning and heading to his home. 'Night, Ash.'

12

Nikki

THERE WERE FORTY-FIVE PINE PANELS ON THE CEILING.

Each was unique, with patterns and knots that swirled in yellows, creams and browns. Nikki blinked. Her hands sat across her belly as she lay in the soft-spring bed. She could see daylight filtering through the curtain yet both her kids were sleeping like the dead. Josh was face down with his pillow over his head, and Chloe was curled up into a ball with her rugs wrapped around her like she'd been through the washing machine.

Chris was snoring softly beside her and had been for the past two hours. Not that it normally worried her. Nikki usually slept well, but last night she'd gone to bed in knots, her mind refusing to stop, and this morning when she woke it started up again.

The kids had been grumpy and Josh had crawled into bed in his clothes, avoiding eye contact and conversation. She'd had no luck talking with him after he'd stomped off, and in the end she'd let him be. When he got a head of steam up he shut her out and there was no way to get through to him.

Chloe had got back from her shower and gone straight to sleep. Chris had also been on edge. Well, they both were, but Nikki was doubly pissed because of Mandy. She'd gone for a long hot shower, hoping Chris would be asleep when she got back. And he was, mainly because of the sheer boredom factor: no TV, no conversation, no games on his phone. The relief Nikki felt being able to sneak into bed, in her thick black pyjamas, was immense. She didn't dare move once she'd got in, in case she woke Chris and he wanted to cuddle.

Thinking about that now, she snuck out of the covers, hoping to get up and ready before anyone woke. She thought about dressing in the bathroom but it was so far away and it would be freezing out. Better to dress in the warm hut then brave the cold morning in search of coffee.

She'd been relieved to find a pod machine in the camp kitchen along with a selection of pods. Nikki chose a strong one and fired up the machine. Its loud groan echoed through the quiet morning. Tucking her fingers deep into her pockets, she glanced around.

The huts stood like silent statues, worn down by the years but determined to stay put. In the bush behind them she noticed two kangaroos, moving slowly as they looked for food. Nikki was surprised she hadn't scared them off when she'd exited the hut. Even now they seemed unfazed by the loud coffee machine. The biggest leaned back on its strong tail, nose twitching and paws hanging out the front.

'They've been there all morning.'

Nikki jumped. 'Jesus!' she exclaimed. 'Ash, where did you come from?' She turned to face her friend.

Ash stood there in jeans, a thick blue hoodie and a black beanie pushed over her red hair. Her cheeks were pink from the cold yet her eyes were bright.

'I've just been for a walk around Luke's sheds and paddocks. Said hello to some sheep and a very friendly cow. I'm sure I've had more conversation with them than my own child this morning. Just a grunt from Em and something about it being *way* too early,' she said with a chuckle.

Nikki rolled her eyes. 'Sounds like our hut. All dead to the world. How long have you been up?'

Ash looked at her watch. 'Since six. But the sound of the coffee machine brought me running.' She smiled. 'It smells so good.'

Nikki got her cup and pulled out another one for Ash as she set about inserting another pod. The kitchen was spotless again. 'Did you clean up this morning?'

'No, Luke helped me do the dishes last night.'

Nikki's eyebrow shot up. 'Oh. And?' She sipped her coffee and nearly melted on the spot from the caffeine hit. 'Let's go sit by the fire, there might be hot coals left.'

Morning dew coated the buildings and chairs, but there was heat coming from the coals. Nikki picked up one of the big sticks Micky had left stacked beside it and gave the coals a poke, causing smoke to rise. Ashley sat beside her, coffee clutched in her hands.

Nikki threw some small sticks onto the smoking coals and was surprised to see them catch alight. Ash added a few more until the fire stopped smoking and came to life.

'I'm still waiting to hear about last night,' said Nikki. She shot Ash a smile.

Ash glanced around.

They were the only two about, besides the kangaroos and trees filled with chattering birds and, further back, the paddock animals baaing and mooing. Smoky clouds cast the day in grey, it felt like it might even rain later. When the morning sun did appear from behind a cloud it made all the dewdrops hanging from blades of grass sparkle.

'It was nice. I told Luke about Owen, and he mentioned Denise, so introductions were well and truly done.' Ash took a sip of her coffee.

Nikki didn't miss her smile, hidden behind her cup. 'You did get right to it, didn't you? It will probably do you both good to have someone different to talk to. I know Luke can look a bit gruff at times but he's a lot like Chris with the gooey inside.' Chris had told her many stories of his favourite cousin. The time he saved all his pocket money to buy flowers for a girl he liked, the elaborate picnic setting he arranged to propose to Denise and then the massive flower-and-balloon display that had filled their house when she'd come home with their new baby. 'In a way they're like brothers. It's a shame they've lost touch over the years.'

'How were you last night? The headache?' Ash asked softly. 'Was that all?'

Nikki felt like she'd just stepped into a rabbit trap. Ash's eyes pinned her to the spot and she knew her friend had sensed something more last night.

'No.' Nikki stared at the small flames. 'There's more, but I'm not sure how to talk about it just yet. I'm still getting my head around it myself.'

'That's okay, but I'm here if you ever do want to talk. I can tell it's weighing you down, and I'm concerned but I won't push.' And to prove it she changed the subject. 'I think this trip might be good for me, as well as Em.'

The relief on her friend's face was instant, her smile small but grateful.

'Because of Owen?' Nikki asked softly. 'You have to live your best life, for you and Em.'

'Oh, I know. Really I do, but I'm just unsure how to go about it. How to let go. It's like he's still here, I still do the same things.' Ash was picking at her quicks, her eyes resigned.

Nikki touched one of Ashley's red curls and watched it spring back. She really was a striking woman; like a red-breasted scarlet robin in a flock of pink and grey galahs. Nikki felt like one of those galahs.

'Just give it time, Ash. I'm sure Owen would want you both to be happy. Maybe some sand and salty waves will help.' She sighed heavily. 'God, I hope the kids improve.'

Ash put her arm around Nikki. 'They will. Shall we start on some bacon and eggs this morning? The smell will get them all up.'

Nikki laughed. 'Yes, seems to work every time.'

Sure enough, Chris was the first out of the huts, followed by Josh and then Em – all sleepy eyed, hair tousled and following their noses to the kitchen. Five minutes later Chloe emerged bright eyed – literally, with a full face of make-up.

'Honey, do you really need make-up today?' Nikki asked.

'It's the holidays, you said I was allowed,' Chloe said with a rumble that dared Nikki to dispute it.

'I know, but . . . out here?' Nikki gestured to the bush.

Chloe rolled her eyes as she continued past her to the kitchen, her chin tilted up.

Nikki wondered if she would have been much the same at that age in today's environment. She had always loved fashion and her *Girlfriend* and *Dolly* magazine subscriptions. Was that their version of today's YouTube? Her mum was always telling her not to wear her lip gloss and eyeshadow, but Nikki didn't have the access to social media that Chloe was submerged in. She shuddered at the thought of having all her teen years on display on the internet for a lifetime to come. The eighties and nineties hair and make-up, and a gazillion photos she couldn't delete. How did she explain that to Chloe – that in twenty years' time all her photos, that she thought were amazing, would be outdated and funny and available for bosses and children to witness. It was bad enough that Nikki's mum had albums of her growing years, but at least they weren't on public display.

After breakfast, while the kids were grudgingly doing the dishes, two utes pulled up on a track just beyond the camp.

'Looks like everyone's up,' Luke said as he and Micky climbed out. 'Who's ready for a ride to the beach?'

'Oh, me!' Em said, throwing down the tea towel.

'Can we ride on the back of the ute?' asked Josh.

'For sure,' said Chris. 'But it'll be cold, so go get a jumper on. And your beanie.'

Josh took off to the hut like he'd just been told that his phone was fully charged.

'Well, that's the fastest I've seen him move in a while.' Nikki turned to Luke. 'I suppose you've been up for hours?'

Luke grinned, his lips parting to reveal white teeth that looked at odds with his tanned features. They weren't perfectly straight teeth – one had a slight twist to it and another was crooked at the bottom – but it didn't detract from his handsome face. If anything, Nikki thought it added a little character, made him approachable.

'Do I smell?' Luke lifted an arm and sniffed his sleeve. 'I was moving sheep.'

Nikki pulled his arm down. 'You're fine. Did you have breakfast?'

'Yep, we've packed some flasks and snacks for the beach. It'll be good to show you the track and then you can come and go as you please and use Micky's ute.' Luke pointed to the white LandCruiser with rust along its window edge and at the bottom of the door. 'It has a two-way if you ever need it. Otherwise you can walk to the beach, it's only about four kilometres away.'

'Won't you need the ute?' Ash asked.

'I've got mine, but you'll want to take the ute instead of scratching your cars, and the sand can get soft in sections.' Luke clapped his hands together. 'All right, who's coming with me?'

Chris smiled. 'I'd be happy to ride in the red beast. I'd take a throaty V8 any day. I can't believe this Patrol is still going.'

Luke looked at his ute like a man might look upon his wife of seventy years.

'She's had my back this, girl,' he said. 'Just can't seem to part with it.'

'Ash and I will ride with Micky,' said Nikki. 'But I think maybe the kids should be on the back of your ute, Luke.'

Ash was watching Nikki, eyes assessing, like a seagull waiting for a morsel of dropped food.

'Sounds good to me. I'll just get my water bottle.'

Ash headed off to the hut while Nikki made her way to the white ute where Micky waited patiently.

'So, you're a good driver, your dad says?'

'Been driving this track and the beaches since I could reach the pedals,' he said proudly.

Micky dressed the same as his dad, in jeans and flannel work shirts. No brand names. Chloe wouldn't be caught dead in Target socks, they had to have the right logo for her to wear them. But then Nikki noticed the Billabong hat and wondered if maybe Micky was susceptible to a few brands after all.

'Do you surf, Micky?'

His grin was huge, teeth perfectly straight and Nikki had a memory of him in braces. She'd been lucky so far but she had a feeling Josh was going to need braces.

'Yeah, Dad and I try to catch some waves. Sometimes we can get a nice little set come through when the wind is right. Otherwise we'll try Fosters; you can get some massive waves there. And sharks,' he said.

'Sharks!'

'Yeah, they only come in if the salmon are around. Sometimes when I'm sitting on my board I can see the dark shapes underneath. Pretty freaky,' he said.

'From sharks?'

'No, the salmon. It's okay, Aunty Nik, we're careful,' he added in a tone that suggested he had been around oversensitive mums before.

'Yeah, well, I hope so. You should have someone watching out for you both.' Nikki cringed, realising what her words implied. 'I can be your eyes while I'm here,' she added quickly, but he didn't seem fazed.

'That would be cool. Do you mind if I teach Josh how to surf?' Nikki's eyes must have bulged because Micky smiled. 'Just in the white wash on our beach, nothing out deep,' he added.

'Oh, right,' she said with a relieved sigh. 'Won't he freeze?' Josh was a lanky kid, she pictured him snap freezing and turning blue the moment he touched the water.

'I have plenty of old wetsuits that will fit him. And the girls if they're keen too?'

Nikki nodded, unsure if Chloe would like to learn to surf. Besides watching make-up videos and movies Chloe's only other interest was playing netball. But maybe Micky might help them all try new things? He certainly seemed keen to show them.

'You're such a good lad, Mick. So grown up,' she said. His face turned slightly pink but his proud smile warmed her heart, so much that she wanted to scoop him up in her arms and hold him tight and tell him he was loved. Had he even been hugged by a woman in the past two years since his mother left? It was a gut-wrenching thought. It seemed to have made him grow into a man so much quicker, taking on adult roles to help keep the farm and house going. 'You still go to school in Jerry?'

'Yeah. But it only goes to year ten. Dad says I might have to board in Albany. I'd rather leave school and help Dad, though. He needs me here.'

Nikki was about to tell Micky he should feel free to do something *he* wanted, but he must have read her expression.

'I want to be here,' he stressed. 'I love this place. I want to help farm with my dad and build this camp business up. I think it could be a real earner. But Dad still wants me to finish school,' he said with a sigh. 'It's crap. Dad can teach me more than my last two years at school could and it would at least be relevant.'

Nikki couldn't help but smile at Micky's openness, and the fact that these days he and Luke seemed more like best mates than father and son. As Ash headed towards them the kids all climbed onto the back of Luke's red Nissan Patrol, the roar of which Nikki could hear as she stepped into Micky's ute.

'Let's go,' said Ashley, climbing in after her and closing the door.

It was a bit squishy in the cab but it beat the cold breeze outside. Micky followed Luke's ute as they headed down a two-wheeled track into the surrounding bush. The eucalyptus tallerack, with their smooth grey bark, edged the track along with small black paperbark trees and shrubs of banksia. Soon the ute-height shrubbery grew tightly together like a hedge, the hard branches scraping the sides of the vehicle like witches' fingernails.

The track turned to a cream sand with tree roots and big sticks mixed in. A few times Micky slowed so they could roll over some of the bigger roots like a boat in big sea swell.

'You're very good at this,' said Ashley.

'Plenty of practice. Take note so you can drive the ute up to the beach and the lookout any time you want. Or there are the two four-wheel motorbikes you can use. Most guests find that easier,' he said, with his eyes on the track.

'There's just something about the coastal flora,' Nikki said. 'There's nothing else quite like it.'

'So beautiful,' said Ash, her head turning to watch the bushes that went past her window. Hard waxy leaves of all shapes and sizes, made to endure the coastal winds and Aussie summers.

They started to climb up, bouncing through large holes in the track until they finally hit the summit. Micky pulled up next to Luke where the track had widened for a small passing lane or a parking spot.

'Oh wow.'

Ash gaped and so did Nikki even though she had seen this view a long time ago. In front of them the green shades of vegetation fell away until it hit the ocean edge and then for miles nothing but the dark blue of water to the horizon.

There were a few plump white clouds in the soft blue sky and even the sun was trying to warm up the winter day. A splash of white sand dissected the sea from the land and white caps frothed on the waves below.

Ash was leaning out the window, breathing in the air and staring as if in a trance. Nikki glanced at the rosy cheeks of the kids on the back; they were all smiles as they chatted excitedly.

'Let's get to the beach,' Em called out.

Luke shot a smile across to them. 'See you down there.'

He drove off with Josh yelling, 'Woo-hoo!' at the top of his lungs with both hands in the air. Nikki closed her eyes and shook her head as Micky took off behind them. They headed off, and where the track split into two they took the right one and weaved down towards the water. The shrubs got smaller, the sand whiter and the sea air stronger.

Closer to the bottom they came out onto small sand dunes covered with tufts of coastal grasses. They drove over them at speed, and it was like being on a rollercoaster. Nikki could hear Josh's laughter peppered by the girls' occasional screams.

Soon enough, the dunes flattened out and they were on the beach. Utes were stopped, doors flung open and footprints marked the sand to where it became damp. Josh had ripped off his shoes and continued on to the water.

'Josh, don't get . . . Ah, never mind,' she said waving him on. The girls were standing together and chatting, the most relaxed she had seen them together in a long time.

'It's amazing. Do you think there are shells?' Emily asked Chloe.

'Let's go look.' Chloe pulled a band off her wrist. 'Just let me tie my hair back, this wind is going to mess it up.'

The sand was so white beneath Nikki's shoes, it almost squeaked as she walked along the beach away from the rest of them. The breeze blew her hair all over her face and her skin broke out in goosebumps, but she found the cold invigorating.

She needed this time, this moment to clear her head, to feel nothing but alive and to take joy in her surroundings.

Maybe Ash had been right, maybe this trip was going to be good for them all.

13

Ashley

ASH SAT IN THE SOFT SAND AMONG THE HAIRY SPINIFEX THAT
grew in clumps around her. She brought her knees up and
hugged them. It kept her warmer and allowed her chin to rest
on her knees as she watched the waves roll in.

'So, what do you think?' asked Luke. 'Do you mind?' He
motioned to the sand beside her.

She smiled and shook her head. Luke sat, not miles away
but not overly close either. But he made a good wind block,
so that was a bonus.

'This is magic. I can't believe you have your own little beach.'

The sand stretched maybe five hundred metres, maybe more,
and was encased at each end by granite headlands that looked
like big rocky cliffs covered with shrubs.

'Can you walk up to the end?' she asked, pointing to the
bigger cliff edge on the left.

'The other track takes you up to the top of that one – it's
our lookout spot. And there are some walk trails around it and

one down to the beach at that end. I want to make some more
on the other side too, to give future guests places to explore.
Actually, that was Micky's idea. He says we need to provide
lots more.'

'Clever kid,' she replied. 'Makes sense. I could just spend
my whole time walking around here and drinking in this view.'
But it wasn't just the view. It was the salty mist on her skin,
the smell of the air and the smart of her eyes in the breeze.
Her hair was jiggling on her shoulders, like Medusa's snakes
wanting to be free, but she kept her beanie on because she
didn't fancy trying to brush the knots out.

'So, what do you do, Ash?'

He sat cross-legged and arms relaxed at his sides. How he
got those long legs folded up like that she'd never know.

'I work at a pharmacy in the same shopping centre as Nikki's
shop,' she said automatically and then grimaced. 'Oh, actually
I don't anymore. I just got fired.'

'Far out, really? I'm sorry.'

'I know, I'm still a little shell-shocked.' Ash shrugged. 'There
I go again, telling you all my dirty secrets. I haven't told a soul
yet. I'm still trying to process it, figure out what I'm going to
do. I'm the sole provider now.'

She wished this topic hadn't come up, she'd been trying
so hard to not think about how she was going to solve this
problem. But it was there as she went to sleep, eating at her
mind until midnight or waking her in the early hours.

'You'll find another job, Ash. I've seen the after effects of
your elbow grease, I can tell you're a hard worker. I'm sure
you'll figure it out.'

'Thanks. I hope you're right. I'm trying not to think about it, I want to enjoy this time with Em, and it's not like I have internet access to be able to start trawling for jobs. But I'm going to have to get onto it when I get home. I just don't know where to start.'

What if she wasn't qualified for anything else? Could she find another pharmacy job close to home? Would working a cleaning job pay all the bills? There were so many questions and no answers. And she had to figure out how to tell Emily.

Ash plucked at the grass. 'It's a shame though, because it was great working close to Nikki. We could catch up for lunch sometimes. Nik and I met when Em and Chlo started school together.' Ash glanced at the girls now. 'They were really close once but then . . . school happened.'

'They'll get there by the end of this holiday, don't you worry about that. Having nothing else to do but hang out and talk really lets you connect.'

'Good. That's the plan. And what's yours?' she asked him.

His eyebrows shot up. 'I'm meant to have a plan?'

Ash laughed. 'Yeah. Are you half-arsing this camp retreat or going legit?' Ash had been trying to work it out – all the buildings were there but they didn't have that well-used feel. It was too good a set-up to be left to rot.

His lips curled in a smile. 'I can't say I've ever heard it put quite like that before.' He thought for a moment, then sighed. 'The farm's okay. We had a big bushfire come through, so I had to rebuild fences but we managed to save the stock.'

'A fire?'

'Yeah, it started from lightning and took out over eight thousand hectares. You can see the effects of it still, especially heading to Reef Beach. I was lucky it only took out the back paddocks and never reached the house. Lots of great neighbours and volunteer firefighters to thank for that.'

Ash couldn't imagine how frightening that would be, but the recent fires all over the country gave her a fair idea of what he'd been through.

'But another income is needed,' said Luke. 'Especially because Micky wants to stay. And he has grand ideas about getting the camp retreat back to a decent business.'

'Well, that sounds good.'

His large shoulders rose and dropped. 'I don't know. The farm's more my thing. I like meeting people and running the camp but if I have a choice the farm comes first. I don't know,' he said again. 'Denise was good at running it. I guess I could get a person in to help with the washing and cleaning and organising. Micky will help, of course, but I sometimes think a woman's touch goes a little bit further than a bloke's.' He gave her a knowing smile. 'You seem to be pretty good at it. You looking for a new job?'

Ash threw her head back and laughed. Em turned and stared at her, face full of conflict. Before Ash could assess it, Em turned back to Chloe. That face was one she was getting a lot of lately.

'Is that a no? I can offer free surf lessons,' he added.

'It sounds too good,' she said and then wondered why she'd laughed. Was it that ridiculous? Could Ash move house, move Em and come live out here? It seemed outrageous and yet deep down she felt as though it were the stuff of dreams. A sea change. She would love to imagine it. But do it for real . . . it wouldn't be possible.

'Really though, I have no idea where to start. The website has been dormant for years. I was hoping Mick would come back from school and handle all that stuff. You guys are the first campers in ages. We have friends come, and family, but no real business customers anymore. You really have to have marketing to get your name out there.'

'Oh, that's a shame because you have everything here. Was it too hard after Denise left?' Ash clenched her teeth. 'Sorry. I speak before thinking. If that's too personal just say so. I'm a—'

'It's okay,' Luke said brightly. 'I don't mind.'

Ash remained silent, watching him from the corner of her eye. Nearby, Chris was chasing Josh up the sand trying to rugby tackle him while the girls were now picking up shells and Nikki had walked the length of the beach and was nearly at the cliffs.

'It was more before Denise left,' he eventually said. 'She left because it was all too hard.'

Ash wasn't game to ask if he meant their marriage or the business.

His Adam's apple bounced as he swallowed. 'You know, I've been thinking about building a little pergola, nothing fancy just something rustic that would blend in with the surroundings down here, just back off the beach. A place to run to if it starts to rain or to hide in the glaring heat. It can get quite hot here in summer.'

The topic change wasn't missed but Ash let the conversation roll onward to new territory.

'That would be handy. I'm surprised you haven't got one here already.'

'I don't want to spoil this natural beauty with manmade things.'

Ash tilted her head and stared at him. He was a deep thinker, she decided. 'I'm sure if you tuck it back a bit and make it similar to the huts it will fit in nicely. It'll also give you a place to put a bin so people won't leave rubbish here.'

'Hey, now you're thinking. Good idea. That has been a problem in the past.'

'Maybe you should rope Chris into helping. I hear he's pretty handy at building.'

Luke chuckled. 'Yes, true. I'll think on it.'

They sat and watched the waves roll up the beach. Chris and Josh were now digging a big hole with their hands and the girls had taken a seat on the dryer part and made patterns in the sand with their fingers. Em's hair moved in the breeze like a silk shirt on the washing line – she wouldn't have knots to worry about with her fine straight hair.

'How is your daughter coping?' Luke suddenly asked.

Had he noticed Ash watching her? 'With her dad gone or the bullying?'

He frowned. 'Her dad. I didn't realise she was being bullied.'

'Yeah. Cyberbullying as well.' Ash was smoothing the sand with her hand; it felt so soothing, so pleasant against her palm. 'I was devastated. Maybe more so than Emily, I think. She didn't want to tell me about it. So I wouldn't worry.' She glanced over at him. 'It's the worst feeling ever.'

'Do you know what you're going to do about it?'

Ash was now playing with one of her red strands, winding it around her fingertip as if it were an old-school phone cord. 'We went to the principal at her school, and we have some plans in place. Coming here seemed like a good start, away from it all.' She sighed. 'I'm finding this single parenting a bit hard.'

'I hear you. Now the pressure's twice as great.'

Luke had hit the nail on the head. Ash felt like she lived in that pressure constantly.

'And as for her father, well . . . she seems to be handling it better than me.'

'You think? Kids are good at putting on a brave face but I wonder what really goes on inside.'

'Yeah, I know.' She looked down at her feet. She wore thick socks and her running shoes but was tempted to rip them off and bury her toes in the sand. 'Em has always seemed more grown-up than other kids. Maybe it's being an only child, I don't know, but she's got an old soul, I reckon.'

'She doesn't dress like I thought a city kid would, she kinda suits this place,' he said with a smile. 'So do you.'

Ash felt her cheeks heat up. 'Do you mind if I take Em to see your animals? I must admit I went for a stroll this morning and found myself chatting to a very friendly cow.'

'Ah,' said Luke with a chuckle. 'You met Gertie. She was Micky's pet calf when he was little. She thinks she runs the joint.'

'I like her.' Ash grinned, remembering how the cow put her head over the fence and sniffed her jumper like she was used to getting treats. 'And the sheep with her?'

'Also pets. Ramsay and Lambert.' He picked at some of the tussock-forming grass beside him.

'Any more pets we should know about?'

'Um, there's a kangaroo we call Mia who hangs around the huts with her young one. She's quite friendly but the little one isn't so sure of us. Then just the chooks. We just recently lost our border collie, Dan.'

'Oh, I'm sorry. We never had any pets, although I had a cat when I was little and when she died I was devastated. Must be nice to have so many animals. Poor Em has always wanted anything, a cat, a dog or even a fish. She would always try to befriend bugs or snails in the backyard and one time brought in a pet rock. I think she was having a go at us even at the age of eight.'

'Kids, they're a clever bunch. Micky's known how to push all our buttons since he was born. He was a handful.'

'You wouldn't think that now. Seems like a nice, mature young man.'

Luke smiled. 'Thanks. You never know if you're raising them right. But I think he's got his head switched on. For now at least,' he added.

'Uncle Luke, come and look at our hole!' yelled Josh. He then bent over into the hole and half his body disappeared.

'I better go check this out,' he said popping up onto his feet easily as if he were on his surfboard.

As Luke headed towards the boys Nikki was nearly back to where Ash was sitting.

'Nice walk?' she asked.

Nikki's face was flushed but bright. 'It was lovely. I want to do that every day.' She dropped down right where Luke had been. 'You and Luke seem chatty?'

'Yeah, he's easy to talk to. I feel at ease around him too, which is weird considering how good-looking he is. I'm normally a blubbering idiot. Maybe because he reminds me so much of Chris.'

Nikki chuckled. 'They're so similar. That must be it. I'm glad you're relaxed.'

'And you? How are you going?'

'You've already asked me that this morning.' Nikki's forehead creased a little.

'Just checking in. I do worry. I hope it's nothing serious.' Ash couldn't say why but what she saw in Nikki's eyes sent a familiar nervousness tingling through her body. It wasn't a feeling she ever enjoyed.

Nikki remained silent.

'I have a feeling it's to do with Chris,' Ash gently prodded. 'He loves you to bits, you know.' Ash gave her what she hoped was a supportive smile.

'Hmmph. I used to believe that to my very core. I even used to think he loved me more than I loved him, if that was even possible, but now I'm not so sure.' Nikki turned to Ash and dropped her voice. 'Strange question, but did you ever look at Owen's phone? Ever get jealous of who he might be texting?'

Ash chewed on her bottom lip for a moment. This was not what she'd been thinking and she now tried hard to stop her mind from reading too much into it. 'No. I didn't. But I never felt I had to look.'

'But do you think you would if you thought he was having an affair?'

Her eyes bulged. Chris having an affair? Never. Never ever. Nope. It couldn't be possible. Ash swallowed her gazillion questions and focused on her reply. 'That's a hard one.'

'I know, right. Do you break the trust and ruin a relationship or do you trust and risk getting your heart broken?'

'Faark, Nikki. That's some hard stuff to comprehend without a drink.' Ash tried to lighten the mood but Nikki's eyes were heavy and sad. 'Oh honey, I wish I knew the answer but I think it becomes an individual choice. What about discussing your concerns before searching his phone?'

'What if you were, say, seventy percent sure something was happening due to what you found on his locked phone? Which had never been locked before. How would you discuss that without saying you'd broken his trust?'

Ash was staring at Nikki, while Nikki stared at the sand at her feet. Ash was struggling to believe the words from her friend's mouth, but she had to cut to the chase. 'Are you that sure he's having an affair?'

'Yes. No.' Nikki's voice cracked. 'Maybe. I'm not sure about anything anymore.'

Nikki had tears in her eyes as she turned to Ash.

Ash put her arm around her shoulder and pulled her close. 'Shit.' It was the only word she could muster. Never did she imagine being in this situation with Nikki. 'Try talking to him, Nik. Don't do anything rash. Maybe he's not? Maybe he locked his phone for work or to stop the kids using his data.'

Nikki didn't reply but Ash felt the slight nod and heard her sniff.

'How long have you been feeling like this?' she asked softly. 'Since yesterday.'

It was less than a whisper and her words nearly got carried away on the coastal breeze but Ash heard them and felt a little relief that this was so new. She'd hate to think Nikki had been stressing over this for ages and hadn't mentioned it. That was a lot to struggle with on your own.

Ash then realised her hypocrisy. She had been struggling with her own problems and had never confided in anyone, not even Nikki. Suddenly she felt ashamed. Nikki had shared a huge issue with her and what had Ash shared? *Nothing*. But was there anything really to share? Not anymore. So, did that not count? Either way, she had a heavy heart, and it felt a bit, like disloyalty.

'I got fired,' she said suddenly.

'Oh, *what*? Really?'

She nodded.

'Ash, I'm so sorry. What happened?' Nikki wiped at her eyes, her concern growing as Ash gave her the rundown on how Margie ruined her day.

'What will you do?'

'I don't know. At this point I don't want to think about it.' Which was a lie; it was all she could think about.

They sat together watching the boys dig the hole and the girls make a shell sandcastle while beyond them the waves continued to swell before crashing and rolling up the beach, over and over. There was a pulse about it, a continued monotony that was soothing and reassuring. The frothy remnants were like a tongue licking at a wound until it was healed. Surely if they sat here long enough their problems would be washed away?

Ash sighed. One could only dream that the ocean could heal that much.

14

Nikki – The Past

NIKKI OPENED THE DOOR AND GLANCED BACK TO MAKE SURE Chris was right behind her. Her nerves were fluttering and she felt like she might float up into the sky if she didn't keep a tight hold on the door handle.

'Are you going to go in?' Chris asked.

She swallowed and stepped inside.

A receptionist smiled from behind a high counter. 'Good morning,' she said before confirming Nikki's appointment time and asking her to take a seat.

Off to the left was the waiting area, sectioned off by an open bookshelf that had books, of course, and row upon row of cards. Curious, Nikki read one.

'Thank you, Doctor Sam. The girls are amazing!'

The next card read something similar. Well, that was a good sign. Of course Nikki hadn't just walked into the first plastic surgeon she'd found. No, for years she'd been on-and-off looking at who was in Perth, stalking their Instagram accounts or scrolling through their websites of 'before and after' photos and the reviews. This plastic surgeon was at the top of her list.

Before she could even sit down a tall, handsome man came in and called her name. He wore lovely-fitting blue pants, a leather belt and a crisp white shirt but it was his smile that had her forgetting her own name.

'Mrs Summerson?' he said again.

She nodded.

'Come this way.'

Nikki went to follow and then remembered Chris, but he was two steps behind her. She reached out for his hand and he returned her nervous smile.

'Grab a seat. I'm Sam,' he said, shaking their hands before they sat down.

Nikki tried to relax in the chair but her eyes were taking in his neat office desk and the black privacy screen off to one side.

'So, tell me, what are you hoping for?'

Nikki took a deep breath and rattled off her requirements. 'I would like my breasts to be even. That's really it. One is much smaller. I don't want them huge but I'd like them to have the same fullness and for them to look as natural as possible.'

'Do you play any sport?' he asked. He took some notes and then continued. 'We have the round shape and the teardrop. The teardrops are textured so they don't flip around after surgery.'

He gave her an implant to feel. It was firm but squishy and felt how she expected a breast to feel. She passed it to Chris, who gave it a few squeezes before passing it back quickly.

The doctor gestured to the screen. 'If I could get you to pop behind the screen and take your top off I'll have a look and take some measurements.'

Nikki felt her nerves ramp up as she removed her shirt. Chris cleared his throat as he waited on the other side of the screen.

Nikki kept her eyes on the window as the doctor approached, a tape measure in hand.

'Right, I see what you mean. I'll just measure your chest to see how much volume is possible for your breast width and skin.'

He took all sorts of measurements and then handed her a sports top.

'Put this on and we'll try some breast sizes so you can feel the weight of the extra volume and see the different shape that it creates.'

Doctor Sam came back with a soft round implant in each hand. They looked like oversized marshmallows but in an anaemic cream colour.

'Is that a C cup?' she asked of the first one she tucked in.

'We don't work in cup sizes. Instead we use the cubic centimetre volume or cc's. This one is 350cc, and 300cc for the other. What do you think?'

Nikki walked out to show Chris while glancing down at the new bumps.

'How do they feel?' asked the doctor.

'Great,' said Nikki as she tried to curb her sheer delight at what she saw. She glanced to Chris, who was smiling, but he wasn't looking at her chest. He was watching her. 'What do you think?' she said.

'I'm happy with what makes you happy. Is the size okay?' Chris asked.

Nikki nodded. 'I'm happy with either.'

Doctor Sam then ran her through the sizes that would work with her measurements.

'Right, get dressed and I'll go through the surgery that's required. Then we'll take you to the 3D imaging so you can see what they'll look like.'

When she was back in her chair beside Chris he reached over and held her hand, which helped ease her racing mind as the doctor talked her through the process.

The 3D imaging was the best part. Nikki saw her own body with round, even breasts. It looked magnificent and she couldn't stop smiling.

'So, we're going with a teardrop, under the muscle and 350cc high profile,' Doctor Sam said.

Nikki nodded emphatically. It was like being told she could eat all the cheeses in the world and none would settle on her hips, ever.

'How do you feel?' said Chris as they walked back to the car hand in hand.

'Overloaded with boob jargon but excited. Did you see that 3D image, wow. I can't wait. Thank you for coming,' she added. 'You won't mind the scars?'

'No, not at all. Scars are sexy,' he said, winking.

Nikki laughed.

Chris stopped walking and pulled her to him. He stared down at her with golden eyes. 'I love seeing you so happy.'

He'd often said he hoped he would never have to live without her, and moments like this she truly felt it. Finding Chris that day when she walked past the construction site on her way to work at the young age of nineteen and a half had been a stroke of luck. He'd been carrying tools and boxes of nails when one had fallen and Nikki had picked it up for him. The moment she put the box back on top of his armful she'd met his honey-coloured eyes and that was it. She had fallen.

He'd thanked her and moved on when his boss called out but on the way back from work she made sure to walk slowly past the site, trying to spot him. Except they had all looked the same in their matching KingGee sand-colour uniforms. It wasn't until the next day he'd spotted her and come over to introduce himself, and the rest was history.

'Are you going to tell the kids?' he asked suddenly.

Nikki had already thought about this. 'No. It's only day surgery, I'll be fine. No need to worry them, and I don't want Chloe or Josh to get the wrong idea about body image.'

'Yep. I'd doubt they'd even notice. Your friends might,' he added.

'Maybe. But if they ask I'll tell them the truth. Until then, I'd rather it stay between us.'

'Done.'

Five months later she had shipped the kids off to her mother's for a few nights with the excuse that Chris was taking her on a romantic trip. Instead, she headed to the day hospital in West Perth. She'd told her mum, who thankfully told her dad so she didn't have to. She was glad that her mum was supportive, even if she didn't really understand why Nikki wanted to have it done.

The West Perth hospital didn't feel like a hospital, more like a small health centre.

'I'll see you on the other side, honey,' Chris said as he kissed her goodbye as she stood in her gown, ready for the surgery, her torso marked in Texta by Doctor Sam like a preschooler's road map.

'You'll love them,' Sam had reassured her.

'See you soon,' Chris said.

Nikki didn't remember going to sleep, she didn't even remember feeling drowsy. One minute she was chatting to the anaesthetist and then she was waking up in another room in a bed where Chris sat nearby waiting.

'There you go. How do you feel?' asked one of the nurses.

This bit also became a blur. Nikki remembered the wonderful feeling of drowsiness and the thought that she could happily nod back off to sleep. Somewhere in there she had an icy pole and they helped her get dressed. She looked down at her chest to find the surgical bra firmly in place around two swollen mounds.

'I have boobs,' she mumbled as she glanced at Chris.

He was wearing a bemused expression and would later go on to tell her she was still a bit out of it and was waffling all sorts of things about her new breasts.

The next day she felt much better and had a shower. It was the only time the surgical bra came off and she could finally have a look. White bandages covered the stitching on her bigger breast that had needed the additional work to lift it, but her small breast was no longer small – it was huge. Nikki knew it was mostly to do with swelling, but still. It made her eyes pop. Suddenly she was excited about trying on a new dress.

All in good time.

'What do you think?' she asked Chris as he came in to check on her.

'Wow, they look big and sore. Do they hurt?'

She shook her head. 'No. Meds must be helping. I can't wait to see them when they've settled.'

'Patience, my dear. They're not going anywhere,' he said with a smile. 'For real, I don't think they will head south ever.'

Nikki smiled. 'For the price of them they wouldn't want to.' Then she reached out and took his arm. 'Thank you,' she said seriously. 'For understanding and supporting me on this. I know you were happy enough, but I wasn't and it was affecting how I saw myself.'

He bent and kissed her forehead. 'I just wish I'd realised sooner how you felt. All those times you wouldn't go swimming or wear bathers. Just so you know, I'm really looking forward to some skinny dipping.' He waggled his eyebrows, kissed her again and left.

Nikki glanced back in the mirror at her over-ripe melons, and the smile on her face was one she hadn't seen in a while. She had avoided catching sight of herself naked in the mirror for so long, but not anymore.

She turned, admiring her profile. 'Marilyn Monroe, eat your heart out.'

15

Nikki

'I'M BORED,' SAID JOSH IN A WHINE THAT IMPLIED IT WAS all Nikki's fault. He shot her a stare to reinforce his displeasure.

'Well, go play a board game. I saw a pile in the camp kitchen in that end cupboard.'

They were sitting around the fire after lunch.

'Or you could read a book. There are some in that same cupboard,' she added.

Nikki had found them while the kids did the lunch dishes. Although considering the half-arsed effort Chloe put in, taking minutes to dry off one fork, it was a miracle anything got done. Emily had dried half the dishes in the time it took Chloe to do one. But it had been a start, at least. They'd told the kids that they were to help with each prep and clean-up.

'Why?' Josh had asked when the duty roster had gone up.

'Um, because this is our holiday too and why should we have to do all the work?' she'd replied.

Josh had looked to the sky and pouted, not game to do a proper eye roll while she was watching him.

Now he sat, draped over his camp chair and swinging his leg as if it were his only source of entertainment.

'Well, *I'm* going to read a book,' said Nikki, getting up.

'Sounds like a plan.' Ash pulled herself up out of the chair and followed her.

'There should be something worth reading.' Nikki opened the cupboard and moved to the side so they could both look. There were a dozen books; some were old and worn, others looked new but had been sitting in the cupboard a while. She needed something engaging, something to take her mind off Mandy and Chris. Talking with Ash made her feel a little better, but she knew she needed to talk to Chris. But when and how to do it was her problem, so for now all she wanted was to escape into a book.

'Oh, I like this one. *The Six Sacred Stones*. I like Jack West Junior, that's me for the next few days,' Ash said as she tucked it under her arm. 'Looks like there's another one too. Awesome.'

'I think this must be Luke's library,' Nikki said with a smile as she fingered through the books, listing the authors as she went. 'Markus Zusak, Tony Park, Bryce Courtenay, Michael Robotham, David Lagercrantz.' She grabbed a Tony Park.

'Why don't you go and read a book?' Ash asked Em.

She and Chloe were sitting side by side and staring at the sky watching the clouds go past. 'I think it's an elephant,' she mumbled before sitting up. 'Actually I think I might go and play my guitar.' Em got up and headed to the hut.

'I'm going to go and have a sleep,' said Chloe and shuffled off to their hut.

'Why don't you go and see Dad?' Nikki said to Josh as she opened the book. 'He's over at the sheds with Uncle Luke.'

Josh grunted. 'Urgh, may as well. Nothing else to do.' He rolled off the chair onto his knees in the dirt, his chair falling over backwards. Josh got up and walked off, dragging his feet and leaving the chair where it lay.

Nikki sucked in a deep breath and let it go. She would not get up and fix the chair nor hound Josh. Not this time. Instead she lifted the book and sniffed it, and with a smile she started to read.

They got maybe an hour of blissful reading in before the kids reappeared and descended on them like hungry mosquitoes. If only they could swat them away.

The usual cries were heard.

'I'm hungry.'

'I'm bored.'

'Something bit me, see?' said Chloe lifting her leg up and shoving it almost across the front of Nikki's book.

Nikki glanced at it. 'Just a mozzie bite or maybe an ant.'

'Could be a spider bite,' added Josh.

Chloe squealed. 'Will I die?' Her painted lips twisted in alarm.

'Not helpful, Josh,' Nikki growled. He snickered.

'It's itchy, do spider bites itch?' Chloe dropped her leg and scratched it again.

'There're a few mozzies about. I remember Luke mentioning there were coils in the camp kitchen,' said Ash. She picked up a yellow leaf and used it to mark her page before closing the book and setting it down on her chair as she rose. 'Josh, you wanna help me light some up?'

'Sure,' he said, following Ash.

Nikki smiled, happy to leave Josh in Ash's care as she got further and further into the story set in Africa. Every now and then she would glance up and see them setting up smoking mozzie coils around the campfire, the huts and the toilet block and kitchen. The smell wasn't great but out in the open it made her feel like they were really camping. It was funny the way scents triggered certain memories. For Nikki, the smell of freshly cut timber reminded her of Chris. When they first met he'd been cutting up wood for a house renovation and it oozed from him like a freshly squeezed orange. It was one of the things that had attracted her to him. A hard-working man using his hands building homes had an allure to it. Maybe that came from having a dad who was a mechanic and his brothers a cabinetmaker and plumber. Chris had worked his way up into a large building company and earned big bucks, but he didn't come home smelling like timber anymore. She missed it. Seeing Luke reminded her of the younger Chris, and she hoped he had fun getting his hands dirty once again.

As Josh headed back to the fire Nikki could tell he was brewing up another 'I'm bored.' But she was saved when Micky came roaring around his house on a red four-wheel motorbike. He stopped it not far from them in a small sideways skid that made Josh run to him in awe.

Micky was grinning. 'Who wants to learn how to ride?'

'Me!' said Josh. Then he glanced at the girls quickly before turning to Micky. 'Me *first*!'

This time Nikki put her book down as they all headed over to the bike. Micky was a great teacher, showing them the basics before letting them all have a go doing a lap of the outer perimeter.

'Now, the rule with the bike is, you can ride it solo to the beach but you must have this two-way at all times,' he clarified and touched the portable hand-held that was strapped to the handle in a carry case. 'It's for safety, and it would pay to let someone know you've gone too. We have a few bike tracks you can ride over that side of the house,' he said pointing. 'Just don't go silly and scare the animals.' Micky directed his gaze at Josh.

The kids all piled on, with Josh behind the controls.

'Thanks, Micky,' Nikki said as Josh took them off. 'That will keep them entertained for a while.'

'Until they run out of fuel, I'd say,' he said with a chuckle.

'What are the men up to?' she asked.

'Dad's roped Chris into fixing the chook pen, and then he mentioned something about collecting bits to build a hut at the beach,' said Micky.

'Oh really?' said Ash, who was comfortable back in her chair with her book. She glanced up at them with a strange expression on her face and a small smile.

'Yeah. I think Uncle Chris is having fun helping him source materials for it. It's like they're on a treasure hunt sifting through all the old bits Dad's collected over the years. He never throws anything out, says the old stuff makes the best things.'

Nikki was suddenly keen to go and watch them hunt around, keen to see Chris in his element. But then she remembered she was angry and sad and confused. It was better to let him be.

'I might get back to my book, then,' she said. 'What are you going to do?' she asked Micky.

'I'm going to go get the other bike and show Josh the tracks.' Micky then turned and jogged towards the sheds.

'He's so grown up, and then you see glimpses of the boy,' said Ash as Nikki sat beside her.

'Yeah. It's nice to see both sides. I could also give him a hug for keeping the kids occupied,' she said, opening her book with zest.

'Same. This book is great.'

'I hope they're prepared to get their own dinner tonight.'

Nikki lifted her book, but her eyes didn't take in any of the words. Instead her mind wandered. Over and over she ran different scenarios, trying to work out the best way to broach the subject of Mandy with Chris. She imagined how the conversations would go, what she would say and what he would say. The more she thought about it the more she could feel her emotions getting out of control, as if these scenarios were real moments.

A panic began to rise, and she hated the sensation. It felt like a loss of control. She breathed deeply and forced herself to focus on her book.

It took three goes before she could retain the paragraph she'd read and move on to the next. By two pages she was pushing the world out of her mind and moving into the one Tony Park had created.

A calm settled over her and she relaxed into the camp chair. Chris could wait.

16

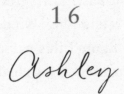

Ashley

IF ASH HEARD 'I'M BORED' UTTERED FROM ANY TEENAGER'S lips she was going to beat them with her book or rip her ears off.

'Right, I'm going for a stroll. Anyone want to come with me?' she asked as she used a dead leaf to mark her page and sat the book on the ground by her chair. She glanced at the kids, each one arranged over their camp chairs like they did on the couches at home – Josh, almost upside down; Chloe and Em with legs draped over the ends like they were being carried – and each with an expression that would have curdled milk.

Chloe was filing her nails while Emily cleaned hers with a tiny twig. Josh drew patterns in the black sandy dirt by his chair with his eyes shut, but his heavy sighs were as constant as a heartbeat.

'I guess that's a no,' mumbled Ash. Nikki was engrossed in her book, so she headed off around the house to the other paddocks she was yet to explore.

Ash had always felt restless. Like a child with ADHD, she couldn't sit still for long. Even watching a movie was a stretch for her, not that she ever had time for one, unless Owen had felt like it. But even then she was sometimes on edge, a feeling like ants crawling around under her skin waiting to be released.

A white blur flapped past. Lifting her head, Ash watched the seagull fly a circle around her. No doubt it was searching for dropped food and figured this camp would cater. It had probably smelled the bits of food Josh had dropped off his plate at lunch. There was a knack to eating off a plate balanced on your knees.

She neared Luke's house with interest and studied the rammed-earth structure with its wooden-framed windows. It was a romantic-looking home, full of warmth, or maybe that was just the earthy blocks and the wide span of the paved verandah. The garden was neat, mainly lawn and native plants that grew well in this area. To one side, the leaves of a huge peppermint tree shook in the breeze like pompoms, and an old wooden swing on ancient ropes hung unloved from a lower branch. She was keen to see the inside of his house and what he had used to accentuate the rammed-earth walls. It was very Luke. Warm, earthy and rustic. Suddenly feeling a little silly, she veered away, afraid of being caught with her thoughts.

She walked the tree line along the driveway, knowing there was a fence and paddock behind them. It was cool, and as the afternoon wore on the chill in the air grew. Maybe she shouldn't have left the warmth of the fire with only her flannel shirt and puffer vest, but the constant moaning . . . being cold was worth the quiet. It did feel soundless and yet it wasn't dead silent. The nearby leaves rustled in the breeze, birds chirped and flew around, interrupted occasionally by calls from the animals in the paddock, combining in a harmonious soft sound of background music. She drank it all in, the sounds and sights, and before she knew it she'd reached the end of the paddock and turned to head back.

If she'd hoped the walk would be head clearing, she was wrong. At first it had been distracting, the beauty of the bush, but then over time her mind wandered freely and then landed on Owen again, as it usually did. It was hard not to analyse his death. Had she been the cause? Had she not done something right? Could she have done more to save him? How had she missed the signs?

'That's a pretty serious frown.'

Ash squeaked and jumped as if a mouse had just run up her arm. Clutching her chest she shot a look at Luke. 'Geez, warn a person next time,' she gasped, her breath catching.

'I've been standing here for a good minute watching you walk down here. How far did you go?' he asked.

A whole minute? She must have been deep in thought not to have noticed him. As she glanced around she realised she was near the shed where Gertie and the pet sheep lived.

'Oh, um, I went right up to the end paddock along the fence line.'

He nodded his head. 'Hm, you're brave. No snake or kangaroo attacks?'

Ash felt the blood drain from her face. 'You weren't joking about the snakes?' she asked, her voice a high-pitched wobble. 'And kangaroos don't attack . . . do they?'

'I don't joke. Not about snakes. And some big boys who feel threatened don't mind throwing a few kicks, especially if you get too close.'

She could understand that about the kangaroos and had seen some video clips of massive males that looked ripped like boxing champions or Chris Hemsworth in *Thor*. 'Are the snakes dangerous?'

'Tiger snakes and dugites – yes, highly venomous.'

He was watching her with a calm, almost serious expression. It did nothing to settle her twitching nerves.

Then Luke cracked a smile. 'Don't stress, they don't get about too much in winter, and if you make enough noise when you walk they'll move away. It's when you surprise them that they can get nasty. Tiger snakes especially, I find them feisty and aggressive sometimes. I would rather come across a dugite any day.'

His smile had her feeling a little flushed. 'Um, so I need to be wary but not super freaked out.' *Oh my god, the kids!* She would give them a serious warning when she got back to camp.

'Yep. Look, we've lived here for ages and Micky has been all through the bush-building cubbies and sleeping outside and he's never been bitten. The key is not to startle them. If you see one, just slowly back away.'

Ash sighed and felt some blood rush back to where it was needed. But she was seriously thinking they should have a first-aid lesson on snake bites at camp, just to be sure.

A *moo* from her right caught her attention and she saw Gertie standing near a bit of straw a few metres inside the fence. Her odds of dying from a cow bite were about the same as her chance of winning the Nobel Prize. 'Hey, Gertie,' she crooned.

The cow tipped her head as if listening and then shook it and mooed again.

'She's a bossy girl. Wants you to go to her. She's as lazy as they come.'

'Can I?' she asked.

Luke held out an apple for her. 'Take her this and she'll love you forever.'

'Oh cool.' Ash took the red apple and headed for the fence. Lifting her long legs she bent the wire a bit and hopped over the top, but when she was nearly over, the barbed wire snagged on her flannel shirt and yanked her back and into a heap on the ground to the sound of material tearing.

'You okay?' asked Luke, who was now over the fence and holding out a hand. She was relieved to his see face was filled with concern rather than laughter. Probably thought she was a complete dingbat.

'Yeah, I'm okay. Don't think my shirt is, though.' She took his hand and let him pull her up with ease.

Luke held out his own shirt, showing a small tear at the bottom. 'You're not the only one to get caught by the barbs.' Then he chuckled.

It felt good to laugh. For a while she had wondered if she would ever remember how, but this place was making it easy. A smidge of guilt tried to ruin her mood but she pushed it aside. It was too good a day to feel down.

'I'm not normally this . . .' Ash searched for the best word that would describe her.

'Vertically challenged?' Luke offered.

Ash laughed. 'Yeah, that.'

'Maybe I should get you out surfing and work on your balance. Might help,' he said with a shrug. 'Always happy to teach.'

She smiled and nodded, noting that it was the second time he'd mentioned surf lessons. Before she could say more, her hand grew suddenly wet as a big slimy tongue sucked the apple from her hand. She almost yelped but upon seeing Gertie, realised the poor cow had got sick of waiting for her treat.

'She must like you,' Luke mused.

Ash gave her a pat, and seconds later Ramsay and Lambert were pushing against her legs wanting attention.

'These guys are pretty cool. I need to get Em out here to meet them.'

'How about we take one to meet her,' said Luke picking up Lambert with ease.

They weren't really pet lambs anymore; Ramsay was fully grown and huge, and though Lambert was half the size he was far from being a baby. Still, Luke somehow got back over the fence with the big lamb in his arms before putting it down.

'Will he follow us?' she asked but had her answer as they headed back to camp.

Lambert trotted along quickly to keep up with their long strides.

'I've got babies out in the paddocks and a few mums yet to give birth, since a ram got out after they were tucked away.'

Ash frowned; she'd never thought about the logistics of having sheep before. Imagine keeping men locked up until it was time to go and make babies. 'So, we might be able to see some being born?'

'Sure. Why don't we get the kids and jump in the ute and go check on them now?'

'That sounds fantastic,' she replied, smiling at him as they walked side by side with Lambert, who was, she decided, the coolest woolly pet she'd ever seen.

'What's Chris up to?'

'Josh wanted to take him for a ride on the motorbike, so they've gone to the beach.'

So, it was just the girls and Nikki waiting for them back at the fire. All as she'd left them nearly an hour ago. Nikki would finish that book tonight by the looks.

'Oh Mum, who's that?' said Em jumping off her chair and jogging over to meet them.

'This is Lambert. He came to say hi.'

Ash smiled as Em bent to Lambert's height while he sniffed her jumper for food.

'Looks like he's trying to nibble me,' Em laughed. 'Chloe, check it out, he's so soft.'

Chloe had already moved off her chair and soon both girls were patting and cuddling him.

'He smells funny.' Chloe's nose wriggled as she wiped her hand on her jeans.

'That's the lanoline in the wool. They all smell like that,' Luke explained.

Nikki looked over her book, a smile on her face. 'He's a bit cute.'

'Thought we'd bring him over to say hi. Do you girls want to come for a drive and see if any lambs are being born?' Luke turned to them, waiting for their answer.

'Oh, yes please,' said Em. 'Tiny little ones. Cool.'

Chloe screwed up her face. 'Like, are we going to see blood and gunk?'

Luke shrugged. 'It's a possibility. We may even have to help some mums out, but there are lots of cute lambs, snowy white with wriggling tails.'

Chloe weighed up her options. 'Okay. It's better than sitting here.'

'Nikki?' Luke asked.

'I'll pass, thanks. Can't put this down,' she said and promptly returned to her page.

'Right,' he said, 'that leaves us. Come on. We'll walk back to the ute and put Lambert back in his yard or else Gertie will get pissy at me for playing favourites. You don't want to fall out of favour with Gert – she can hold a grudge.'

'Yeah, right,' said Chloe in disbelief. 'She's just a cow.'

'I'll tell her you said that,' he teased.

Ash couldn't hide the grin that formed, and it stayed there for most of the drive. The girls were happy to ride on the back, seemingly a new-found love. At one point she heard the girls singing songs as they hung on, and Ash pictured their hair streaming out behind them.

'Thanks, Luke, this was a great idea,' she said as she got back in after opening and closing another gate. 'Although I'm starting to see why I was invited,' she teased.

He shot her a cheesy grin and she felt her heart lurch. It was a weird sensation. Sure, she'd been attracted to men before, but this was like a jolt of more than just liking what she saw. This was liking the man, liking how she felt in his company. It was strange and new and it was followed by anxious responsiveness.

So much so she had to look out the side window until she could settle her body. She tucked her hands under her legs so she wouldn't scratch or pick. Beside her Luke was totally comfortable in his own skin, so utterly calm that she was soon relaxed. Was this part of the attraction?

'There's one,' Luke said.

He seemed none the wiser to the turmoil crashing around in Ash, and the distraction of his pointed finger was welcome.

'Oh, I see.' A white skinny-legged lamb was unsteadily walking beside its mum.

Luke brought the ute closer and then stopped so they could watch. There were more off in the distance but this little cute one was nice and close. The lamb kneeled and started to suckle milk from its mother – and it was at that moment Ash heard the girls gasp and coo as its tail wiggled and flicked about.

A head appeared in her window as Emily hung down, her eyes wide. 'Mum, it's *soooooo* cute. Can we have one?'

'This one needs to stay with its mum,' she said. And was a little relieved, but for a moment she couldn't help but picture a lamb in their backyard.

'Oh,' said Em, with disappointment.

They watched it for a while, its tail wriggling like a kite string in a strong wind, and none of them could help but smile. Luke eventually moved further along, edging the mob, and they saw a ewe with a pair of twins close by and a group of lambs huddling together like schoolgirls discussing boys in the playground.

'Do you check them often?' she asked.

'I look every day while they're lambing, just in case a ewe's in trouble and needs my help.'

Ash's eyes went wide. 'Help?'

'Yeah, that's what that box of gloves is for,' he said gesturing to the one by her feet. 'They get stuck and the mum's worn out and they can die, so we help pull them out. It's a bit messy but better than dealing with dead ones.'

'Wow, I never realised they would need help.'

'You're welcome to come with me each time while you're here. I'd happily have an apprentice lamb birther,' he said with a grin.

Ash thought for a moment. Could she handle that? She wanted to. The young Ashley, the teenage Ashley, had been up for anything like that. Keen to give experiences a go and push herself to learn new things. Then she met Owen, a sweet and deeply affectionate man who swept her off her feet. Falling pregnant and getting married had changed her, and as time wore on she felt herself taking on Owen's caution, his fear of stepping outside his comfort zone. She wasn't sure who she was now. Life had been the three of them for so long she didn't know how this new Ash should act or be. Maybe it was time to try some things for herself?

Sucking in a deep breath and watching the lambs hop and skip, she nodded before turning to Luke. 'Yes, thanks. I think I'd like that.'

He gave her a nod in return and went back to watching his sheep. Had she imagined the small smile she'd seen grace his lips?

Suddenly Luke stopped the ute, then opened the glove box and pulled out a pair of binoculars.

'What's up?'

'I can see a ewe down over there. I don't want to get too close unless she needs help.'

'Why did we stop?' said Chloe, now bent over Luke's side window.

He got out and held up the binoculars for her. 'See that ewe over there? You can see her giving birth.'

Chloe put them up to her eyes.

'Turn the little wheel if you need them to focus more.'

'I can't see where she is,' she said pulling away and then trying again. 'Oh, there. Oh, wow, I can see its head. Oh, *gross.*'

'Let me see,' said Emily, who had moved to Chloe's side and had her hand up ready for the binoculars.

Chloe eventually passed them over.

'See, when they get stuck you have to grab their little legs and pull, sometimes quite firmly, to get them out,' Luke explained.

'How do you know if they're stuck?' asked Em, the binoculars still positioned at her eyes.

'Well, if nothing is happening. And sometimes the ewe is already dead and the lamb could be half out. You usually get the feel that something isn't right.'

'So, you just hang onto the lamb and pull. Sounds gross,' said Chloe.

'Oh, the lamb is out,' said Em.

'My turn.' Chloe practically pulled the binoculars from Emily's face. 'Oh, it's so little.'

'You girls could take the bikes around the mob each day and keep a lookout for me, would be a huge help,' suggested Luke.

He took the binoculars back, wiped some make-up off the end of them and passed them to Ash. She glanced at Chloe, wondering if she had circles around her eyes; it would be rather funny. But the girls had quickly got back on the ute as Luke climbed in.

Luke waited for her to spot the lamb, which was now standing beside its mum. She could see its little pink tongue as it bleated. It was just how Em had come into the world, crying.

17

Nikki – The Past

ALICE WAVED THE SHIMMERING DRESS IN FRONT OF HER. 'This one.'

Nikki quickly walked over to where Alice was unpacking the order. She glanced at the array of new items hanging up on the nearby rack.

'Don't bother, nothing else comes close to this dress. It's the pick, believe me.'

And Nikki did. She'd quickly grown to trust Alice's opinion. She'd proven her eye for sizing up a customer and knowing what would work to suit their shape and colour tones. Alice was made for this business and she'd been the first person to notice Nikki's change in shape.

'Your boobs look great. Did you make a new bra?' she'd asked one morning.

'No.'

She had new bras! That had been a delight in itself. A real

bra she didn't need to modify in the dark of night like a spy writing out intel on a coded message.

Of course she didn't want to lie to Alice, she'd become such a good friend and work colleague, so Nikki had told her the truth.

'Oh wow, good on you. I've noticed the change, Nik. You're more confident,' Alice had said.

'I feel more confident. Actually I'm way more confident. I can wear clothes without feeling anxious and I don't avoid the mirror anymore.' Nikki had laughed. 'If anything I can't stop looking.'

They'd laughed and it had felt good to share it with someone who understood and wasn't judging her. A Kardashian she wasn't, and this procedure hadn't been done with becoming an Instagram sensation in mind. It was purely personal. Nikki still had fears of being judged by other people, be it friends and family or Joe Bloggs off the street. But she couldn't fault how amazing she now felt.

'Don't work your sales magic on me, if you say it's good I believe you.' Nikki took the dress and went to try it on while Alice clapped her hands excitedly. The Italian-made piece started with a plunging bodice, fitted at the waist, and fell gracefully with a tiered, floor-sweeping skirt. But the best bit was the glimmering gold lame finish that caught the light like her diamond ring in the sunlight.

Nikki took off her pink bra, one Chris had picked as part of a matching set. She smiled, remembering how she'd let him take it off just last week, something she never used to allow. She hadn't wanted anyone to see her old mismatched bras, let alone touch them.

The dress looked even better on.

'Alice, it's gorgeous.'

'Get out here, woman,' Alice demanded.

Nikki stepped out and watched Alice's mouth drop.

'Oh my god, stunning. And those boobs look *ah-mazing*!'

That had been Nikki's thought too. The plunging bodice had revealed the curve of each breast just a little and it made her feel like a young fashion model. She was tempted to send Chris a photo. Bugger it, she would.

'Alice, can you take a photo for me, please? I want to show Chris.' She grinned like a schoolgirl.

'You don't want to take it home?'

'Alice, I saw the price tag. It's a pass,' she said with a chuckle. 'This one isn't leaving the shop until it's sold.'

'Fair enough. Well, let's get a few good photos, then.' Alice brought her phone up close. 'And I think a cleavage shot is in order.' After a few seconds she smiled. 'There. That should be enough teasing.'

She handed the phone over to Nikki to check the photos. 'Wow.'

'I know, right. I wish you had somewhere to wear this dress.'

'Me too. Chris is going to love these.'

She texted the photos, and Chris's reply came through before she'd got the dress off, leaving her to stand in the change room like a giddy teenager staring at her phone with a goofy smile.

OMG HOT! with a few flame emojis and the big eyeballs. *I'm knocking off work now!* followed by a winking face, a drooling one and the purple eggplant.

Nikki had floated through the rest of the afternoon happy and excited about getting home to see Chris. It was like when they were first dating, exploring each other all over again, and she was loving it. For so long her lack of confidence had killed their bedroom antics, her embarrassment and unease quickly overtaking her libido.

Nikki was in the kitchen peeling carrots when he arrived home and snuck up behind her.

'Feel that,' he said as he wrapped her up in his arms and pressed against her. 'I've had it all afternoon,' he mumbled, voice husky and deep.

Nikki pushed back against him just to confirm, and smiled.

'Can we sneak off now? The kids won't even know we're gone,' he said against her neck, kissing her skin.

He smelled good, a hint of that fresh-cut timber that lingered on his clothes and made her knees tremble.

'Were you out on site today?' she asked, tilting her head so she could smell more of him.

'How did you know?' he asked, puzzled.

'I can tell,' she said before pressing her lips against his ear. 'You can help me with dinner if you like. Feel like cooking the meat on the barbecue?'

Chris groaned. 'You're going to make me wait, aren't you?'

He flipped her around and pressed her against the bench before taking her face in his hands and kissing her.

The peeler dropped from her hands, hitting the floor with a clatter. She managed to keep hold of the carrot.

'Oh gross, get a room.'

'Chloe,' she said breathlessly pulling away from her husband. 'Dinner's not ready yet.'

Chris moved to the sink and picked up the peeler and took his time washing it.

'Not sure I want what you two are serving up,' Chloe said with a giggle and then snatched the phone charger off the side table and promptly left.

Nikki glanced at Chris, who was trying hard not to laugh.

'That is why you can wait a little longer,' she said teasingly and then slapped his backside.

Dinner had been wonderful, Chris's legs stretched out so they rested against hers as he sent her hot, lingering looks over their dinner plates.

Time dragged slowly, doing the dishes and then getting the kids sorted and into their rooms. They were allowed an hour to relax and read before bedtime but she knew that it wasn't adhered to, that their phones came back out for god knows how long. She could usually tell by how tired they were in the mornings. Nikki would take the phones off them at night and the uproar was worse than an umpire making a wrong decision at the football. The kids would swear black and blue that they wouldn't use them past nine o'clock and she'd relent and it would all work well for a while and then the signs would be there and the cycle would begin again.

'Are we alone yet?' Chris whispered as he stuck his head into the laundry.

'Honey, we won't be alone for years yet,' she said with a smirk.

He rolled his eyes as he held out his hand. Nikki switched on the washing machine before taking Chris's hand and letting herself be led to their bedroom.

Chris closed the door behind them and continued to pull her towards their ensuite. He turned on the shower then faced Nikki, a smile curling his lips and his eyes locked on to hers with an intensity that made sweat break out along her neck in anticipation.

'It's been a long, *long* day,' he growled as he tugged at the bottom of her shirt.

Obligingly Nikki lifted her arms and let him pull her shirt off. She loved the feel of his eyes on her, devouring her body as if he'd just spent a week crossing the desert and she was an oasis of water. Of course he had always looked at her like that, but Nikki truly didn't feel like she was that oasis until now.

Chris crushed his hands against her breasts, his thumbs brushing over the plump skin that her black bra didn't cover. His lips then kissed the same section of skin while he expertly unclipped her bra. A groan escaped his mouth, or was it hers, Nikki wasn't sure as she arched back. Then she heard a wet reverberating sound as he pushed her breasts together.

She laughed and looked down at him. 'Are you motor boating me?'

He looked up, cheeky smile on his face. 'Just wanted to see if it was possible.' He winked then went back to devouring her nipples.

It was true the only time that had been possible was when she'd had the kids, but her breasts were usually sore and leaking milk. Nikki was surprised at how good her boobs felt now; no pain, no numbness and she felt all the sensations through her nipples that were now hard. Chris spent plenty of time on both breasts, neither one favoured over the other. And it was nice not to be thinking about it, instead Nikki was grappling at his pants, undoing his button and zipper in between running her hand along his length. Minutes later they were undressed, and Chris pulled her under the water as he kissed her. There was some more teasing with soap wash but it didn't last long as neither of them could wait any longer. Chris lifted her up, pressing her back against the white tiles. Nikki wrapped her legs around him, holding on as she sucked on his ear and clung to his strong shoulders.

'I love you so much,' he murmured.

Chris said the same words ten minutes later as they lay naked and dry on their bed, snuggled and sated.

'I love you too, honey.'

Nikki glanced at her chest, still surprised to see two wonderful, even mounds. Normally the boob with the most would have run and hidden in her armpit like an egg cracked into a lopsided pan. But now . . . Nikki couldn't stop the smile that tugged at her lips. She loved what she saw.

'Hey, don't touch – they're mine,' mumbled Chris as he flicked her hand away and put his in its place.

'They just feel so real and plump.' The scars didn't worry Nikki at all. A small price to pay to feel this amazing. She only wished she'd done it years ago.

Chris was still massaging her breast but then paused. He tilted his head towards her, frowning. 'Is that supposed to be there?' he asked.

Nikki felt where he was indicating. 'Might be just some scar tissue,' she said. One breast had a scar around her areola and down underneath but she knew over time it would be less red and turn white like her stretch marks.

She stretched out, enjoying their combined nakedness, like a cat in the sunlight, her fingers playing in her husband's soft hair.

Life was pretty great.

18

Nikki

NIKKI WOKE UP WITH THE SUN AND STRETCHED AS SHE glanced around the room at everyone else asleep still. She tried her stealth moves again, slipping from the bed and dressing like a woman escaping a strange bed after a wild drunken night out.

'Where're you going?'

Nikki froze. She was sitting on the bed doing up her shirt buttons.

Chris's hand found her waist then felt her clothes. 'What's going on?' he said a little more clearly as he tried to wake up.

'Nothing, go back to sleep,' she crooned. 'I'm just going for a walk to the beach.'

Then she stood and left the hut before he could mutter anything else. Outside the air was almost painfully crisp, icing up her lungs as she breathed, but once she started walking along the track she forgot about the chill, especially as the sun came up and warmed her skin.

Leaving the camp, she was soon absorbed by the bush track, aware of the morning birds and the trails in the sand left by lizards or snakes. She shuddered at the thought of snakes. For good measure she kept her focus on the ground in front of her, not just for snakes but the tree roots that made it a tricky walk at times. Her breathing was laboured as she started the climb to the small summit and at the top she paused to take in the view and calm her breath. The sea breeze was stronger up here, blowing her hair about. She pulled her jacket tighter and flipped up her fluffy hoodie over her head and buried her hands in her pockets before starting the descent to the beach.

In no time she reached the bottom small dunes and felt the burn on her thighs and back of her calves. God knows how long she stood there just staring at the view, watching the waves crash rhythmically against the shore. Indigo blues and opaque bubbles churned together over white sands. The sun glinting across the water and bouncing off the granite headland on her right made it look like a child had taken browns, reds, greys and black plasticine and merged them all together in a mash of colours. Some of it shone like flecks of gold. Yet it was the smell that put her at ease, salty and clean.

'I found you!'

Nikki spun around to see Chris walking towards her, long strides and a wide smile on his face as if he'd been watching her in a happy moment.

'Chris, what are you doing here?' It came out a little accusingly and she cringed. 'I thought you'd gone back to sleep,' she added quickly.

'No point with you not next to me. And an early morning walk to the beach sounded good.'

He came up behind her and went to put his arms around her but she stepped away.

He frowned. 'What's wrong?' Chris watched her for a moment before continuing. 'I didn't mean I've come for sex. I just want to spend some time with you.'

Nikki hoped her relief wasn't visible.

She could see the yellow in his eyes turn golden in the morning sun and the hint of confusion along with it.

'Nikki, what's going on? I feel like you've been avoiding me.'

He went to step closer but she flinched, so he remained still.

Before Nikki could even gather her thoughts her vision went blurry as tears started pooling and rolling down her cheeks like a monsoonal rain in the tropics.

'Honey, what is it?'

She could tell he wanted to hold her but she thrust out her hands like an angry lollipop man facing an impatient car at a school crossing. Through her tears she saw his distress; he wanted to help her – if he only knew he was the cause.

'Please, talk to me,' he begged.

Nikki wiped at her face angrily until she could see him clearly. She needed to watch his reaction. 'This is about Mandy,' she spat.

Chris baulked as if she'd punched him in the stomach. His breath left his lips with a rush and his face crumpled.

She could see he was genuinely shocked and wondered if his heart was racing as madly as hers.

His mouth moved, like a goldfish searching for food, but no words came out, not straightaway.

Nikki used her sleeve to dab at her cheeks again.

Finally Chris found his voice. 'How did you . . .'

The wind carried away the last of his words or maybe he never spoke them but what he had said confirmed her suspicions.

'How long, Chris?' she cried. It was a despairing moan that followed her words as if her heart had begun to crack, a fault line appearing through its middle and the effect of it caused her body to shake.

His eyes were wide, tears brimming on his lower lashes as his lips twisted and his hands went to his head. 'Nikki ... I ... please, it's not what you think.'

'How long?' she growled.

Chris closed his eyes and spun around, almost pulling at his hair. Then he opened them and took a step closer. 'Please, hear me out. Mandy means nothing.'

Nikki backed closer to the ocean, the breeze taking her sobs the moment they erupted. She felt sick, her heart was racing so fast she thought she might pass out and the only thing that probably stopped her was the crisp air.

Never, ever did she imagine this would happen to them. This was what she'd always wanted to avoid, this gut-wrenching pain of two souls being torn apart. But it couldn't be stopped now. She wanted answers.

'How did you find out?' he asked in the tiniest voice. Like a scared child who was offered a treat but was afraid it was a trap.

'It's not important how I found out, Chris, your face alone is enough proof.' What irritated her the most was that she loved Chris so much and still wanted him, his handsome face and strong arms and his reassuring words. He had always been her confidant but not now; no, in this she'd had to turn to Ash and it felt wrong and strange. It just made his deceit burn all the more painfully.

'Tell me.'

Chris's shoulders dropped but his eyes remained on her.

'Two weeks,' he said dejectedly.

Her eyebrow shot up. 'Two weeks? Two weeks for a lifetime of marriage?' she said. Part of her was relieved, two weeks seemed better than two months or two years. But it didn't hurt any less. Her heart was still having its own mini earthquake.

'Please, Nik, just hear me out. Let me explain. It's been hard—'

'Hard?' she cut him off quickly. 'It's been *hard*? It's been fucking hard for me, Chris, and you don't see me off with someone else,' she spat as she turned and screamed in frustration. Her life had been utter hell this past year and yet she was supposed to cut him some slack?

'It's not what you think with Mandy. I don't love her,' he said, his voice breaking. 'I'm sorry, Nikki. I love you. I never wanted to hurt you.'

She spun back to face him, her finger already pointing in his direction. 'Well, you should have bloody thought of that sooner.' Nikki wanted to hit him, to poke her finger into his shoulder until he was crippled with the pain she was feeling. But she didn't. Instead she gritted her teeth and ran off back up the path while fresh tears stung her cold but flushed cheeks.

She ran like her arse was on fire, amid sobs and angry grunts as she steamed up the hill then turned on the track that led to the lookout on the other headland. Nikki wanted to be lost. She didn't want to go back to camp, she couldn't.

When she was sure Chris hadn't followed her she slowed to a walk. Her mouth was full of saliva and she wiped angrily at her runny nose as if it were an annoying fly. It made sucking in much-needed air hard but soon her blood stopped pumping and by the time she reached the end of the path her chest no longer ached from the burning pain of running.

The view at the edge nearly sucked her breath away again. Below her the dark blue ocean surged up the cliff face and a wave of vertigo struck her as if the water wanted to pull her down to its depths.

Taking a quick step back Nikki took in her surroundings. Behind her sat a wooden chair and as she got closer she noticed the plaque on it.

Rebecca – Always in our hearts.

Nikki sat down and traced the words with her finger before turning to look at the view from this special spot.

With the granite headland like the bow of a big ship she almost felt like Rose on the *Titanic*, looking out over the ocean. The bush around her was low, none of it obstructing the 180-degree view nor providing shelter against the wind off the water.

It dried her eyes, and the salt from her tears and maybe the air crystallising on her skin made it feel dry and crisp.

She sat there for a long time, staring ahead with her hands in her lap, thinking about Chris, their kids; and every now and then she would retrace the inscription and think of Rebecca.

19

Ashley – The Past

'GOOD MORNING, MRS KING. TAKE A SEAT, DOCTOR BENTON will be with you shortly.'

The friendly receptionist's voice rang out in the small waiting room. Mrs King took a seat against the far wall, about four seats up from Ashley. Her name seemed at odds with the blue-tracksuit-wearing lady in her late twenties who looked like she hadn't brushed her hair in a while. But Ash wasn't here to judge; for all she knew, Mrs King had four babies at home and was suffering postnatal depression. This was not a place to assume you knew what was going on based on someone's exterior. Just last month she was sitting in here with a well-dressed woman who looked as if she'd just stepped out of a hair salon, oozing expensive perfume and wearing a shiny gold watch and matching gold sparkly jewellery. But mental illness wasn't selective, it didn't go after a certain race or age group and it didn't care what you had in your bank account. It was like a disorientated bull ant that would crawl up the nearest leg of a passing person and sink its teeth in. People who looked like they had all their shit together could sometimes be the ones struggling the most.

Ash had learned a lot over the years and her understanding of the illness was much better, yet the cure seemed a distant goal. Constant visits to doctors to change medications or adjust doses or try different techniques and therapists proved that there was no simple fix. It wasn't like cutting out your appendix or tonsils. God, she only wished it could be that simple.

The clock ticked loudly above her head on the white wall, echoing as if they sat in a bright cavern. She always took this seat, it stopped her from being able to stare at the clock, watching the second hand tick its way slowly around while Owen was inside with Doctor Benton. It hadn't always been this doctor's surgery, with its slightly ridged blue chairs and collection of beach photos on the wall. No, there had been a few others and yet the chairs always seemed to be the same. Never completely comfortable and yet better than a church pew. And the wall art, even though different, was still the same bright, peppy pictures, as if their aim was to make your day better. But did they really work or was it just another reminder that your life wasn't as great as those depicted on the wall?

Sometimes Ash felt like this was her church, sitting in this chair and silently pleading and praying that this time they could find the right mix of medications. That maybe this time Owen would last longer before throwing away his medications or finding the dosage was too strong or weak and ending up on this rollercoaster of waiting rooms.

'Oh love, would you like a tissue?'

Ash glanced up, realising she'd been staring into the beach photo but not seeing the sand or water, to find the receptionist, Nancy, standing before her with a box of tissues.

Had she been crying again? She blinked, her eyes feeling dry and scratchy. At the same time she felt wetness in her hands. Blood was smeared over them. She frowned and tilted her head as she tried to clear the fogginess from her mind. She'd been picking again, without realising.

'Oh, thank you, Nancy.'

Ash took two tissues from the box and wiped her hands. Her torn quicks were suddenly stinging now she was aware of them.

'No worries. The bathroom is just around the corner if you need to clean up.'

Nancy gave her a smile and went back to work as if that had been a normal occurrence; in her line of work it probably was.

Did that mean Ash should check herself in with Doctor Benton too?

The blood stained the bathroom sink pink before the water cleared it back to its porcelain white. But the red stuck in the edges of her nails like chipped nail polish. Not that she had any nails to paint. She knew she had to stop chewing them back till they bled, but she couldn't stop herself.

When she came out from the bathroom she headed back to her usual chair but Nancy called out before she could park her backside.

'Mrs Grisham, Owen is out and has gone to the car.'

'Oh, okay. Thanks,' she said in her half-squat position. She stood upright as Doctor Benton appeared beside Nancy.

'Mrs Grisham, have you got a moment?' he said and then headed to his office, not giving her a chance to reply.

She started towards his room but glanced back to the door.

'It will be quick,' Nancy reassured her with a smile.

Ash swallowed as she entered Doctor Benton's office, feeling like a child heading in to see the principal.

'Ashley, take a seat, please,' he said as he sat behind his desk and folded up a file.

His hair was greying at the edges but his face and hands were quite smooth. Not much in his office gave away personal information. Just one photo frame that faced towards him that she could only assume would be his family. Or maybe a pet; there was no wedding ring on his hand.

The seat was warm and she realised Owen had been sitting in this exact spot just moments ago. She clasped her hands nervously into her lap but couldn't stop her foot from bouncing. Was this how Owen felt every time he came to see the doctor? Did he feel just as apprehensive and tired of the merry-go-round of treatments? It was no wonder he sometimes got sick of being sick and would stop taking his pills. Ash saw how hard it was for him, the constant battle he waged inside let alone adding the problems of the outside world.

Finally the doctor finished what he was doing and exhaled as he smiled at her.

'Is Owen okay?' she asked, desperately hoping he wasn't about to break bad news.

'He's fine,' he reassured her. 'He will no doubt tell you about our meeting.'

Doctor–patient confidentiality, she knew. But if she wasn't here to discuss Owen, then why?

Before she could ask, he spoke.

'How are you coping, Ashley?'

She leaned back and frowned, wondering where this had come from. 'I'm fine,' she replied automatically.

He let out a deep breath that said he didn't believe her. 'Hm.'

Ash felt the wetness on her fingers and the tang of blood in the air. *Damn it.*

'Ashley, I'll be frank. I'm here to help Owen but you as well. I know it's not easy living with someone with mental illness, but you don't have to do it alone. How are you really? Tell me, are you showing signs of anxiety?'

The way his green eyes drilled into her told her he already knew the answers to his questions. A tightness rose up her throat and she felt backed into a corner. She wanted to fob off his concerns but his eyes had her pinned like a cornered animal.

She sighed and held up her hands for him to see, the quicks still weeping little drops of blood. She felt like she had just bared her soul to him. Her innermost secret. The thoughts and feelings she kept buried and never told a soul because, well, who was she to complain when it was Owen who was struggling with a real illness.

Heat burned in her cheeks as his eyes studied her hands.

'It's nothing to be ashamed of, Ashley. It's not just Owen who is living with a mental illness, you do too. I can't imagine it's easy, his mood swings, the stress, the anxiety, wondering how he's feeling, what he's thinking.'

Her breath rushed between her teeth as she teetered on the verge of tears.

'It is a bit hard,' she murmured. 'Wondering, trying to guess his mood so I can accommodate it and not set him off, tiptoeing around as if I'm on eggshells, trying to protect Emily and then save Owen from himself. Some days it's very hard.'

'Do you have a support group?'

She stared at him blankly.

'A network of friends and relatives who can help you, or a group of other partners who are going through similar things?' he asked.

Ash shook her head slowly. Owen didn't like people knowing their business, in particular about his mental health, so that meant she couldn't go running to friends or family. She spent her days telling little lies to all those she loved. *No, Owen is sorry he couldn't come – he had to work.* Or, *Owen's off visiting his parents.* Or, *Owen's fixing the sink in the bathroom. It's been leaking again!*

Lies made up to explain why he couldn't attend parties or dinners or school events. He didn't like going and yet she wasn't allowed to use the real reason so was left making up lie after lie. Her mum knew he suffered depression but not the extent of it, and Ash knew that if she told the truth her mum would be around all the time and that would set Owen off and he would know she'd blabbed. It was easier just to deal with it on her own. As Owen said, it was their private business, not anyone else's.

Ash only had to imagine herself in Owen's position and knew she wouldn't want the whole world to know either.

'Owen is very private,' she said to Doctor Benton by way of explanation.

'Yes, I understand that. But a support group means no one else has to know. It stays in the group. I think it would help you immensely, Ash. I could even put you on some medication to help with your anxiety.'

'No!' she said quickly.

His eyebrows shot up and she realised how harsh it had come out.

'I don't want two parents on medication. I need to stay clear-headed while I have a child to care for,' she added, her neck corded and back hard.

She couldn't afford to spend days sorting out dosages, waiting to identify any reactions or adverse effects. Ash couldn't risk any disruptions. Maybe it was her need to be in control or fear of depending on pills, but there was no way she was going to take anything stronger than a Panadol.

'Hm.' Doctor Benton gave her the faintest nod before he jotted something down on his notepad.

'This is the name of a friend of mine who works in alternative areas. I would love you to go to see her. I think she can offer you help and advice on how to handle your anxiety through oils, tapping and meditation.'

He held it out and Ash took the corner but when she pulled he didn't let go, instead he waited until she met his eyes.

'I will let Nina know to expect your call,' he warned.

Was she that easy to read? Her shoulders sagged a little as she nodded. 'I will call her. I promise.'

And she meant it. Doctor Benton let the paper go and smiled.

'Good. You need to look after yourself, Ashley, because if you're not well, then how are you going to look after Owen and Emily? They need you fit and healthy. I really hope you do see Nina; I guarantee it will help. It's okay to get help. It doesn't mean you are weak. Do you understand?'

Ash felt like a child being spoken to, but gently. She knew he was just worried and trying to help. She was listening, even though she didn't want to. Her body wanted to fight against the news of seeing someone; it felt like defeat, giving up and acknowledging she had issues. It did make her feel weak. And she hated that.

'I know you're right, Doctor Benton.' Ash stood up, her whole body leaning towards his door, aching to escape.

'You'd be amazed at what the right natural oils can do. So many people are using them for everyday ailments.'

She smiled; maybe she was being a bit melodramatic. 'Thank you. Bye, Doc.'

'Take care, Ashley. I'll see you next visit.'

In other words he would be checking up on her. It was kind of irritating and yet she felt a tiny bit of relief that someone had taken notice and that they cared. Because she was feeling like crap, even if she hated to admit it.

She glanced at Nina's number as she left. Yes, she would book an appointment once Owen's new dosage had settled. She would do it for herself and for Owen and Emily.

Besides, if the oils didn't work at least she would smell nice.

20

Ashley

'WHO WOULD LIKE SOME MORE PANCAKES?' SAID ASH, WAVING one in the tongs she was holding. 'I have three left.'

'Me!' All three kids chorused.

Ash glanced over at Luke's house as she dished up the fluffy pancakes. This morning the fire wasn't lit, so they were all sitting in the camp kitchen.

'So, what have you kids got planned today?' she asked.

'More boredom,' said Josh with a pout.

'Sleep,' said Chloe, as she ran her fingers through her hair looking for split ends. 'God, all my friends will think I'm dead! I must have a million unchecked Snapchats.' She moaned. 'All my streaks. I was up to four hundred and sixty-eight with Natalie. This sucks soooo bad. I'll have no friends left by the time we get home.'

Chloe's face was made up again, this time with a sparkly blue eyeshadow and blue-tinted mascara. She was the last to breakfast, as if she couldn't be seen without something on her face. It made Ash feel sad for her. One thing she noticed when looking on Instagram was the difference between Emily's account and Chloe's: Emily's profile picture was of her guitar, and the only photos she'd posted were memes or of things she was looking at, never images of herself. But Chloe's was the opposite: only selfies, and hundreds of them. Different make-up faces, photos of her in nice tops, in the sunlight, with her hair different ways, full of self-gratification. All the comments, hundreds of them – did Chloe even know half these people, Ash wondered – all saying how gorgeous she looked, and Chloe had taken time to reply to each of them. Ash was so glad that Em didn't seem to need the approval of others to make her feel good about herself. But Ash remembered her own teenage years and the need to be accepted and included, and she doubted that Em was as together as she made out. A brave face could hide a lot, and for the time being she would keep a close eye on her daughter.

'I'm sure your friends will still be there, Chloe. If they are real friends they will be,' said Ash, making a point.

Chloe rolled her eyes. 'I'm having a massive case of FOMO. I have no idea what my friends are doing right now . . . none!' she shouted.

A loud squeal nearly made Ash drop the pancake bowl she was washing. It was so loud she thought one of the kids must have cut a leg off.

'Get it off me, get it off. Aaaaagh!'

Chloe had shot up off the chair and was jumping around the kitchen area and shaking her arms as if she were hanging onto live wires.

Josh, who at first appeared shocked, quickly realised why Chloe was screaming and began to laugh.

'Where?'

Ash went to her, but remained a safe distance from her flapping arms lest she end up with an elbow to the nose.

'It was on my jumper,' she sobbed, tears starting to roll down her face, leaving blue streaks on her cheeks.

'It's here,' said Em. 'You flung it onto the table.'

Emily pointed to it before she put her cup on the spider and squished it.

'All gone.'

Josh was still laughing, rocking back on his chair as if this were the best show he'd ever seen.

'Your face,' he said between bursts. 'You look like a panda.'

Chloe screamed again in frustration and barged past Ash and hit Josh in the head on her way to the bathroom.

'That was totally worth the pain,' he said rubbing his head. He stood up and put his plate in the sink. 'Thanks. I'm going to go ride the motorbike.'

'Okay,' said Ash, still trying to digest what had happened. 'Lucky we have the best spider-killer here at camp,' she said giving Em a wink. 'Remember when your dad made you that certificate after you relocated that huntsman outside? Gosh, he hated spiders. About as much as Chloe does, I'd say.' Ash smiled.

Emily got up suddenly and walked out without a word or even a glance in Ash's direction.

What did I say?

But even as she thought the words she knew that whatever was bothering Emily had to do with her father.

'Morning.'

Chris wandered in past Em, his greeting short and lifeless. What was with people today, she wondered. Chris ran a hand through his ruffled hair. His face was pale but his hollow eyes said more than his appearance and greeting.

'Sorry, there's none left. I wasn't sure if you or Nikki had eaten yet.' said Ash. She wasn't really trying to pry but if he wanted to clear up where they'd been she wouldn't stop him.

But Chris gave nothing away. 'Thanks for sorting the kids, Ash.' Then he gave her a sad smile and walked off. The usual bounce in his step was gone and it resembled Josh's bored, lethargic walk more than ever.

She could feel the tension in Chris's body and it transferred onto her, into her muscles that were slowly tightening and she felt that churn in her stomach like an ocean of acid. Ash didn't like confrontation, nor was she comfortable when people were upset or emotional or showed too much of their feelings. So, pretty much life in general. Her life was one big rollercoaster of fear, panic and anxiety. After the dishes she would go and roll on some of her calming oil mix, take the Bach flower drops Nina had prepared and then she would clean.

Ash started in the camp kitchen and bathrooms, then she weeded and tidied around the outside showers and found a rake by Luke's garden shed to run over the whole camp area. It felt good, all of it. This she could control; this she knew how to do. It was weird how soothing it was. A little OCD maybe, but it was what worked for her.

And the best bit, by the time she was done it was past midday and the kids had regrouped for lunch.

'This place looks great. You've been busy,' said Nikki as she walked into the camp kitchen. Her red-rimmed eyes and swollen lids stuck out like a massive teenage pimple.

Ash rushed to her side. 'Hey you, all okay?' she whispered softly, so Chloe and Em wouldn't hear them from their place at the far table. They'd found some old kids' colouring-in books and a handful of coloured pencils and seemed to be having fun as they concentrated on making their pictures beautiful. Chloe had cleaned her face but hadn't reapplied her make-up.

Nikki closed her eyes and breathed out slowly. 'Been better,' she replied. 'Let me help with lunch. Sorry I've been AWOL.'

'Think nothing of it. We are all capable of looking after ourselves, kids included. You take whatever time you need and don't worry.' Ash rubbed her back but didn't press her for details.

Chris cleared his throat, appearing behind them. 'I'm just going to help Luke, and then Josh and I will be back for lunch.'

Nikki's back stiffened but she turned to face her husband. 'Yep, sure.'

Ash could feel an underlying current but they were playing it cool with company around. She was familiar with this sensation, often with Owen when they were in mixed company and even more so in front of Emily.

'Right, what shall we make?' Nikki opened the fridge with purpose, and even though her voice sounded strong the slight quiver of her hand gave her away.

'Can I have a have a spaghetti-and-cheese toastie?' asked Chloe.

Ash watched Nikki power on through lunch, looking anywhere but at Chris, who sat slumped as he tried to speak normally to the kids while sending devastated glances his wife's way. Things were much quieter than usual but the kids didn't seem to notice. Just Ash, who knew what to look for and could do nothing but watch from the sidelines as her two best friends tore their hearts to shreds.

'Can I have that?' asked Em as she eyed off Ashley's remaining half toastie.

Ash handed it over. It was hard to feel hungry when her belly was churning with the hurt filling the air around them.

She still found it so hard to imagine Chris cheating on Nikki. Ash would have thought Owen more likely to cheat before Chris; it was so unbelievable, and yet here they were. Guilt and despair dripped from Chris like hot wax from a candle and she wanted nothing more than to shout at him, 'Why?' He was supposed to be one of the good ones, so how could this happen?

Again Ash gritted her teeth and swallowed her own feelings, reminding herself that this wasn't her battle. She was so lost in her thoughts she didn't notice Luke approach. But the distraction was very welcome.

'Hey, gang,' he said.

'Are you hungry? The jaffle maker's still warm,' said Nikki.

'No, I'm good thanks. I'm just going to light the fire so it's cranking for tonight. It will be a cool one.'

Luke always seemed to know what the weather was going to do, reeling off the day's temperature and conditions like a part-time meteorologist. But, she guessed, having animals and crops meant you had to pay attention to Mother Nature to ensure they didn't suffer.

'And I was thinking we could make damper,' he added. 'I have marshmallows as well and stuff for s'mores.'

Josh screwed up his nose. 'What's damper and s'mores?'

Chris was staring off into space, so Luke explained.

'Damper is a traditional Aussie bread that stockmen and swaggies baked in the coals of a campfire,' he said seriously, sounding like David Attenborough. He smiled before reverting back to his own husky casual voice. 'We had it all the time growing up. We put our own spin on it and added cheese and herbs, and Nutella and golden syrup.'

Josh perked up at the mention of Nutella.

'And s'mores are an American campfire treat where you roast a big marshmallow and stick it with some chocolate in between two crackers. But we cheat and use chocolate biscuits and just add the marshmallow. You'll see. After one, you'll understand.'

Luke smiled, and Ash was caught by the way he made the space around him glow like a sunset hue.

'Sounds amazing,' said Chloe.

Both girls were staring at Luke as if he were a big block of chocolate, licking their lips and dreaming about how good these s'mores would taste. Ash was staring too, but her thoughts were on how good Luke would taste. She frowned, her cheeks suddenly burning at the thought. It felt like cheating and yet her husband was gone, and Luke's wife was AWOL. How long was a reasonable time to wait before allowing herself to admire another man after Owen's death? It was different before, when Nikki first mentioned how handsome Luke was – it was as if they were talking about a young Brad Pitt. Just a man to admire. But now that she knew Luke better and liked him as a person, well, that threw it into a different area. One she wasn't used to or prepared for. The realisation that she like-liked this man made her feel weird and uncertain.

Nikki and Chris were still quiet, so Ash stood up. 'I can help you with the damper.'

What are you doing?!

More time with Luke, was that a bad thing? She wasn't sure how she should be playing this. Avoid the man or punish herself more by enjoying his company?

'Cheers,' said Luke. 'That would be great.'

Ash watched him glance at Chris, his face clouding over. He looked back to Ash; he had questions but she shook her head slightly and he got the hint that now was not the time to ask them.

'Right, who's going to help me with the fire? We need some small sticks.'

'Do we have to?' complained Chloe.

'Do you want to have s'mores later?' Luke asked her pointedly.

Chloe nodded and headed towards the bush. Josh and Em were already halfway there.

Ash nearly called out for them to watch out for snakes but then closed her mouth. Chloe didn't need an excuse to get out of collecting sticks.

When Nikki began to clean up, Chris moved to grab some plates but she held up a hand.

'It's okay, I've got this,' she said flatly.

Luke raised an eyebrow at her tone, but he merely glanced again at Ash and then went outside to the fire pit.

'Need a hand to carry some logs over?' she said as she followed him, trying not to glance back at the camp kitchen and the feuding couple.

'That would be great, thanks.'

Side by side they headed to the large woodpile stacked at his house. While loading their arms up they both snuck glances to Nikki and Chris.

'Am I missing something?' he whispered to Ash.

Ash winced, her face screwing up. She wasn't about to betray Nikki but she didn't want to lie to Luke, so she said nothing.

'That bad, hey?'

Luke's face fell and she had the urge to reach out and squeeze his hand. Instead she collected the wood.

When they reached the fire they heard Nikki, a tremor in her voice.

'Just give me some space, Chris. I'm not ready to hear you out.'

It was said with a force that propelled Chris from the kitchen and had him stalking towards the sheds, hands in his pockets and head down.

'If you need me I'll be in the hut reading,' said Nikki as she left the kitchen with an armful of books.

Ash gave her a small nod and a reassuring smile. When she turned back to Luke to hand him her pile of wood, she found him studying her.

'What?' she said, for a moment wondering if she had food on her face. But then she realised he was concerned. She opened her mouth to say something when Josh appeared, running with an armful of dead sticks.

'Don't run, Josh. If you trip you might skewer yourself.' Ash cringed as the mental picture formed in her mind.

'It's not pretty, I've had that happen,' said Luke.

'No way, true?' said Josh in awe as he dumped the sticks by the fire pit.

Chloe and Em followed not far behind him with smaller handfuls.

'Yep, but I was riding the motorbike and came a cropper and a stick went through my arm here,' he said pointing to a spot above his elbow.

'Gross,' said Chloe. 'Where's Micky?'

'He's over at the house. Why don't you go find him, he has a movie collection if you want to go watch something,' said Luke. He looked to Ash for permission.

'Fine by me. One movie won't hurt,' she said and the kids cheered and took off towards the house.

'That's the most animated I've seen them,' said Luke with a chuckle as he set the fire and ignited it.

'Same. I'm hoping that they relax a bit and start to entertain themselves.'

'It's still early days yet. Micky's going to take Josh into the bush and show him how to make a cubby house. Still a few old ones in there and plenty of tracks. They'll get there,' he reassured her.

Luke spun around, taking in the campsite, quiet and still except for the crackle of the fire. His eyes finished their search and rested on Ash. 'So, any chance you know what's going on?' he whispered, nodding his head towards Nikki and Chris's hut.

She pressed her lips together as she thought. 'I can tell you that something is going on but I can't tell you what I know.' Ash sighed. 'I just hope they can sort it out.'

Luke narrowed his silver eyes and nodded. 'Should I be concerned?'

She leaned her head closer to Luke. 'I think Chris may need someone to talk to, so if you get a moment with him . . .' She let her words drift off.

'Gotcha. Thanks.' He sighed. 'I've never seen him look so bad.' He stood with his hands on his hips watching the flames grow. 'I kinda knew Denise and I weren't suited but I loved her and was willing to try. But these two, they've been soul mates from the get-go. I think to some degree I rushed into our marriage because I wanted what they had.'

'Owen and I rushed into ours because I got pregnant with Emily. I often wonder if she hadn't come along if we would have made it that far.' It had crossed her mind over the years, wondering where life would have taken her. 'But then I wouldn't change anything because Em is the best thing in my life.'

'Yeah, that I agree on too.'

Luke's eyes drank her in and she couldn't look away, the connection of understanding holding them together like a rope. 'Right, well, this fire is set for a while. Shall we make the damper? I . . . have all the ingredients, I can bring them over?' he asked.

A slight hesitation in his voice and she realised that this strong man was also a little unsure and vulnerable. He stood, waiting for her reply, his chest heaving with each breath.

'Um . . . sure,' she said smiling, trying to reassure him. Just cooking together and yet she felt her belly flip.

'Right. Cool.' Luke darted back to his home and returned with arms full of flour, butter, cheese, spices and Nutella.

Her fingers brushed his arms as she helped him unload them onto the bench and she tried to ignore the tingles that shot through her.

'Thanks,' he murmured.

He watched her as if he could see the electricity running along her skin, then cleared his throat. 'Right, let's make a mess. Bit of self-raising, salt, butter and some milk.'

Ash took the milk from the fridge and then washed her hands after Luke. Again they bumped arms because the sink was small and the bench made for one, but she liked the close working quarters. There was something nice and warm about being in close proximity to a man that made her feel a little like a teenager again.

Before long, dough coated her hands like gardening gloves and flour was all over the place as if Josh had thrown a few flour bombs. 'Sorry, I'm a messy cook.' She chuckled, feeling young and joyful.

'Wait, hold still,' said Luke.

He leaned over and plucked something from her hair, her face heating as his breath caressed her. It didn't help that he smelled amazing, a hard-working, masculine scent that blended farm work and coastal proximity.

He held his large flour-dusted hand out flat with the offending dough on his palm, showing her.

Ash smiled. 'Now, how did that get there?'

'How did it not, your hair is half white with flour,' he said chuckling.

'Might help hide all the red.'

Luke frowned. 'I love the red. And the freckles.'

She had a feeling he didn't really know the effect he could have on women, had probably been on his farm for so long he had no idea that he'd be prime steak in the city, gobbled up by every single woman around. If he wasn't so easy to chat with and down to earth Ash would be a nervous mess, but over the past couple of days she felt like she'd gained a good friend. She constantly had to remind herself that she was not a married woman, she was single and it was completely fine to be attracted to Luke, but it was hard to adjust fifteen years of thinking. She didn't want to keep feeling guilty every time she gazed upon Luke.

His eyes latched onto her face as if he were indeed counting her freckles. She resisted the urge to bury her face in her hands. 'Stop, now you're embarrassing me,' she said with a laugh.

Smiling, he resumed cleaning up their mess and the silence that followed was a comfortable one.

'I hope Nikki and Chris work it out,' he said suddenly.

'So do I. Thanks for not asking me to break Nikki's confidence.' She gave him a smile.

'I understand. I think it shows just how great a friend you are to Nik.'

Her face flushed at his words, or maybe it was the way he studied her.

'Will you have a chance to talk with Chris?'

'I plan to try. He was there for me through the hardest time of my life. Right now he looks like I did back then. I want to be there for him.'

Ash rested her hand on his tanned forearm. 'I'm sure they'll work it out,' she said reassuringly, though she wasn't sure if her words were for Luke or herself.

That night after dinner the damper was pulled from the fire and eaten smothered in butter. As Luke had predicted, it was a cold night, so they were rugged up in jumpers and long pants but the fire threw out warmth and made them all glow orange.

'So, what's the verdict, Josh?' asked Luke.

Josh was sitting next to Micky on the bench seat, his jeans with a fresh tear at the knee. The girls were huddled close on the camp chairs and Chris was next to Luke and Josh while Ash and Nikki were opposite them. Ash had to give Nikki points for sitting out by the fire, keeping up the family appearance for the kids when she was clearly struggling. Ash knew her well enough to see through her façade.

'It's okay,' Josh replied eating the damper slowly, tossing it around on his tongue.

Chloe cleared her throat. 'So, what about these s'mores?' she asked Luke hopefully.

He laughed and produced a packet of digestive biscuits that were coated in chocolate on one side.

The girls licked their lips as Luke roasted a big marshmallow and squished it between the biscuits then passed it to Chloe. 'The hot marshmallow melts the choc, perfect combo.'

Chloe took the offered treat and didn't waste time taking a bite. 'Oh my god,' she mumbled, 'it's amazing.'

There was chocolate and white gooey marshmallow stuck on her lips but she didn't care as she devoured it.

'Me next,' said Josh, jumping up to grab his roasting stick.

'This is great, Luke, thanks,' said Ash as she watched the kids excitedly roasting marshmallows. 'We might all be sick later,' she chuckled.

'All we're missing now is music,' he said.

Ash smiled and leaned towards her daughter. 'Emily, why don't you go get your guitar? Play some background music for us.'

Emily's eyes were wide in the firelight, making her look more like a pixie than ever.

'Wow, you can play?' asked Micky. 'I wish I could.'

Suddenly Emily perked up a bit. 'You might not like the songs I play,' she said frowning. 'It's a bit old school. Nirvana, Metallica, AC/DC, Van Morrison, Red Hot Chili Peppers.'

Luke slapped his leg. 'Now that sounds even better. Micky's grown up on my old CDs, we'll be in our element.' He gave her a smile. 'Please, Emily.'

'Yeah, please?' added Micky. 'It's not a true campfire if someone's not playing music.'

'Okay,' she said shyly and got up to fetch her guitar.

When she came back she sat and strummed a few notes nervously before starting on 'Summer of 69'. Her head was down, focusing on the notes, but it jerked up when Luke and Chris started singing the words. Em smiled shyly at first but when the men picked up their voices and got stuck into the song she beamed and began to play with more energy. Her head remained up and she started moving along with the melody, her lips forming the words but her sound was non-existent against the exuberant men.

Chloe and Josh had no clue but Micky was singing along, tapping his hands against his knees keeping the drum beat for the song.

'Sweet, that's awesome, Em,' he said after the song.

Ash was glowing with pride, the fire and the way Emily was thriving on the attention for once. She had only ever played with her dad at home, and now she had a crowd who loved her playing. It was new for her, a big step, and already Ash could see her confidence soaring.

The crowd went wild when she started 'Thunderstruck' –
even Josh knew that one thanks to a movie called *Battleships*.

'This is mint,' said Micky before requesting a few songs.

Emily grinned.

'Do you know any Taylor Swift songs?' asked Chloe.

Emily tried to indulge them all in their requests, but some
songs she didn't know. She laughed, 'If I had internet I could
Google the music sheets,' she said giving Ash an ironic shrug.

Even Nikki and Chris seemed to relax and enjoy the music.
They were still avoiding each other, but the night was so much
fun they seemed to have called a ceasefire. But for how long?
And what would happen afterwards – would they sleep in the
same hut, or would one take the spare?

Em beamed as she finished another song and everyone
clapped.

'Your dad would have loved this,' Ash said. 'He loved
watching you play. He'd be so proud.' She turned to Luke.
'Owen could play so beautifully. He wrote songs too.'

'I didn't know that,' said Chris. 'I wish I could have seen
him play.'

Ash sucked on her bottom lip as she realised Owen wouldn't
have played in public. It was only ever Ash and Emily who got
to hear his songs, and that depended on how he was feeling.
She was sure there were plenty of songs even they never heard.

Emily opened her mouth, but then frowned before looking
down at her guitar and playing another Taylor Swift song
for Chloe.

'Oh my god, oh my god, I love this song. I know all the
words.' Chloe cleared her throat, flicked her hair back and sat
up straight as she sang.

Luke caught her eye and smiled. 'She's good,' he mouthed, his head nodding in time with the song.

Ash sank back into her chair and watched the glowing embers rise into the black night sky. It felt wonderful to be with friends, having a great time and enjoying the outdoors. There was something special about this kind of quality time that invigorated one's soul.

Josh let out a massive yawn, which then rolled around the group like a pass-the-parcel.

'I think it's time to hit the hay,' said Luke. 'Thanks, Emily. Can we book you in for another night? You were brilliant.'

Em grinned and nodded. 'Sure.'

'I'll come help you shift that cupboard first,' said Chris, moving towards Luke.

Luke nodded, though Ash had a feeling this was news to him.

'Night all.' Luke waved as he walked towards the house with Chris and Micky while Chloe and Josh were already headed to their hut.

Ash had her answer about the sleeping arrangements.

'You were amazing, my girl,' Ash said, draping her arm around Emily's shoulders as they headed to their hut. 'I know your dad would be so proud. He would have loved to witness that.'

Em shrugged and then stepped out of her embrace to reach the door first. As she disappeared inside, Ash glanced back at the fire pit. Flames were low but the coals still glowed red. It seemed such a shame to leave it. What was it about a fire that was so alluring? She smiled. Tonight had been just what she'd needed.

21

Nikki – The Past

'I'M SORRY, YOU HAVE BREAST CANCER.'

'Pardon?' Nikki blinked rapidly as she focused on the doctor's lips as he repeated himself.

Chris was holding her hand but she couldn't feel him, she couldn't feel anything. It was like her body didn't exist, as if she were a ghost.

'It's breast cancer,' he confirmed again, slightly slower.

Nikki had thought she'd prepared for this moment. There had been plenty of time from when Chris found the lump. It wasn't until she felt what he'd pointed out the next day that she realised it might not be scar tissue, and booked a doctor's appointment just to be sure. With cancer in the family, she wasn't going to delay.

At first it was thought to be a calcification and she had to go through the ultrasound and needle biopsy and the dreaded few days' wait for a diagnosis. Just last night she'd cuddled up to Chris and they'd discussed the worst-case scenario. 'Try not to stress, we can work through anything they throw at us, step by step,' Chris had said. She'd believed him, they were so strong together.

And yet now . . . it felt like she was already dying. Her kids' faces flashed through her mind. From their birth, to their first steps and starting school. What she wouldn't see hurt the most; the weddings and grandkids.

It was something you couldn't really prepare yourself for, the dreaded diagnosis. Cancer didn't mean instant death. She knew that. People survived cancer all the time. Yet it didn't make her feel any better right now. There was something earthshattering about hearing that C word.

'What does this mean?'

It was Chris who'd spoken. Nikki wasn't sure she could find any words, her mouth was dry. She sat frozen in the padded chair in her doctor's office just staring at him. His room had been quite inviting when they first came in, nice grey carpet and black furniture and bright white walls with tasteful art. Now it felt like a cell.

Dr Kirby rested his arms on his desk and laced his fingers together. His hair was thin and greying slightly but it was the mole on his left cheek that Nikki stared at now. Anywhere but his eyes, so full of understanding. He'd probably been in this situation a million times, but it was a first for Nikki. She'd hardly seen a doctor since she'd had her children.

'Well, you have a few options,' said Dr Kirby addressing them both. 'A lumpectomy followed by some radiation, or a mastectomy.' He handed over pamphlets on both.

Nikki took the pamphlets and stared at them, not really seeing any words as her mind raced. It came down to two options: have a dissected boob or no boobs at all. She almost laughed but managed to turn it into a cough. Finally she had the breasts she'd always wanted and now they had to go. Was it some form of Karma? The universe's way of making her appreciate what she had? It kind of felt like a cruel joke.

'What do you recommend?' asked Chris. 'Will the lumpectomy keep Nikki's breast shape?'

He squeezed her hand and she knew he was asking for her and for that she was thankful. Words still escaped her but she wanted to know the answer to his question.

'I can't recommend the right treatment for you – both will work but it's what suits you. The lumpectomy will alter the shape of your breast but I can't give you specifics. They will want to take as much tissue as possible for a clear margin.'

'Will it come back or end up in the other breast?'

Nikki sagged in her chair a little. *Thank god Chris is here.*

No one knew about this appointment. Nikki couldn't tell her mum – she had already had a scare when her dad had bowel cancer, and Nikki couldn't bring herself to add to the burden before she was even sure. With surgery and chemotherapy her dad had come out the other end of it and was doing fine, but the ordeal had been devastating for her mum. There was no way Nikki was going to cause more upset.

'Look, let me run you through the advantages and disadvantages of each and then take some time to think on it. But the sooner we get onto it the better.'

Nikki nodded. 'Thank you,' she managed to mutter and tried hard to focus on his explanation of each.

Later they left his room, pamphlets in hand and her head hurting. They walked hand in hand without a word; Nikki didn't remember leaving the building yet somehow she was standing by their car. Chris opened her door and she climbed into the familiar area that smelled like her kids' leftover food scraps and stinky feet with the faint hint of strawberry from the car tree air freshner that was nearly spent. Something about being in her own space made her mind flip out, and by the time Chris got in the other side a river of tears was rolling down her face.

'Oh baby,' he crooned and reached across the car to scoop her into his arms.

Nikki sobbed against his chest, drenching his shirt as his hands rubbed her back. He smelled so good and his arms were so strong, it only made her cry more. This man was her everything. The moments in between her sobs she could feel his body shaking and looked up to see tears streaming down his cheeks, his eyes red and face contorted. Never had she seen him so distraught but when he saw her watching he quickly wiped his eyes and cleared his throat.

'I'm sorry, honey. I'm trying to be strong, but seeing you like this is killing me,' he croaked and swiped at his face with the back of his hand again.

Nikki put her palm against his cheek and blinked her own tears away so she could see him clearly. 'It's okay. We both need time to process this. Better to get it out here than at home with the kids.'

He nodded and bent to kiss her. It was a tender kiss, mixed with salty tears and it was a moment Nikki knew she would never forget. It was like all her senses were heightened and her body alert to every sensation.

'I love you,' he said between kisses, his lips trembling a little. 'We'll get through this together.'

They gripped each other tightly until both their tears had dried and their breathing became more even.

'Do we go home and tell the kids?' he asked.

Nikki stiffened. 'No.' She sat up to face him. 'I don't want to worry them, Chris. In fact, I don't want anyone to know, especially Mum. She's already gone through this and I don't want to worry them until I have to, okay?'

'But you'll need support.'

'I have you,' she said, running her hand through his hair and letting it rest at the nape of his neck. 'I won't have the kids thinking I'm about to die when I'm not,' she said strongly.

It made Chris smile. 'You're the boss.'

'Indeed I am.'

Chris started the car, but it wasn't until five minutes later that she realised they weren't going home. She shot him a glance.

'You'll see,' he said with a small smile.

As they pulled into a parking spot in Cottesloe Nikki found she was looking straight at the ocean.

'Come on,' said Chris getting out of the car.

He took her hand and led her down to the grassed area and found a spot under a tree not far from the iconic Indiana Tea House. Framed with tall green pine trees that blended with its soft mint roof, the Tea House with its romantic arches and many paned white windows stood proud against the blue of the ocean that lapped at the sand by its foundations. It was a special place for them. It was here, as they enjoyed a summer afternoon, that Nikki first told Chris they were having a baby. It was a place that always filled her with energy, love and inspiration.

'I just think we need to end this day better,' said Chris as he sat down, using the tree as a back rest and helped Nikki to sit between his legs so she could lean back on him.

Nikki sighed and relaxed against him, feeling the rise and fall of his chest which was as rhythmic as the waves before them. She interlaced her fingers with his.

'I like your thinking,' she said, smiling.

They didn't talk, about the kids or her diagnosis, instead they people-watched and enjoyed the afternoon sun. It had been a while since they'd just taken a moment out for them in a special place, with no kids and no distractions.

'We better go, it's nearly time to get the kids,' said Chris.

They got up and she hugged him. 'Thank you.'

'Best day of my life was meeting you.' Chris kissed the tip of her nose and smiled.

Later that night, after forcing themselves to maintain a sense of normalcy over dinner for the kids, they lay in bed reading the pamphlets.

'There's so much to get our heads around,' Chris murmured.

'I know. I figure the more we understand the better.' She sighed. 'It was nice tonight at dinner, but hard too. Nice to have that slice of normal life where I could pretend it wasn't about to change.' She adjusted the bed sheet over her legs. She was wearing her favourite black silk nightie. She had a feeling it was Chris's favourite too. 'Don't worry, I won't stick my head in the sand either. I know the quicker we move on this the better.'

'I know, babe. You found it really early, like the doctor said.'

She nodded, and picked up her phone. There were some great sites focusing on breast cancer, with not just the fact sheets but stories from women who'd been through it. Chris had ditched the pamphlets and was reading from sites on his phone as well.

'Look at the disadvantages of having a lumpectomy compared to a mastectomy,' said Chris passing his phone over. 'But compared to losing your breast maybe it's still better?'

'I'd rather have no breasts if it means surviving,' she replied. 'Besides, I can always have breast reconstruction.'

'So, what are you thinking?' asked Chris. His gaze was neutral but supportive.

Nikki screwed her lips as she bit the inside of her cheek. 'Well, I'm thinking of a full mastectomy.'

His eyebrows raised slightly. 'Really? You don't want to try to keep some form of breast?' he asked gently.

She shook her head. 'I love these breasts but I'm not about to die for them.' And love them she really did. She put her hands over them. 'I want to see my babies grow up, Chris. I don't want to go through radiation and keep half a breast only for the other one to get it down the track. Why take that chance? If I just get them both removed now I can feel safer that any cancer and any future cancer is gone. And the recovery is quicker, I can get back to the kids without worrying them and no one needs to know.'

His reply came a few breaths later. 'Are you sure?'

'I know it may sound strange after all the fuss I made over my breasts but this is cancer, Chris.'

He nodded but he didn't look quite convinced. If he thought otherwise he kept it to himself.

'So, we're keeping this between us?' he asked again.

'Yes. I can do this with your help. Are you with me?'

Chris smiled but it was filled with a sadness that tugged at her heart. She knew he wanted more help for her but he wouldn't go against her wishes.

'I've always been with you. You and me, babe.'

Nikki hoped he was right.

22

Nikki

NIKKI STRETCHED OUT IN THE BED, RELIEVED THAT CHRIS hadn't come back to the hut. Rolling over, she watched her kids sleep for a moment. They wouldn't even know their dad was missing, which was a good thing. Nikki didn't want to be fielding questions, but at the back of her mind, cowering in the deep recesses, was the thought of answering questions that filled her with dread.

'Why is dad leaving?'

'Are you getting a divorce?'

'We hate you!'

Okay, so the last one was more a statement but it still scared her. The thought that this could blow up and cause not only Nikki but her children so much hurt was almost too awful to contemplate. Did she believe this 'affair' would be the end of their marriage?

Nikki sat up. The prospect of not having Chris in her life had never crossed her mind. It would be like living without her legs. Even now she couldn't fathom it. She had always been proud of their marriage, and others always commented how perfect they were as a couple. Chris had said he'd found his soul mate and she'd believed him, so how could he ever cheat?

But two weeks? Was that worth ending a seventeen-year marriage over? *Depends if he's telling the truth.*

Nikki didn't like where her thoughts were going, so she threw back the covers and quickly got dressed. As she power walked along the track towards the beach, her mind kept coming back to Chris. She loved him with every fibre of her body and didn't want to throw away what they had built together. But could she trust him? Did everyone deserve a second chance? Lord knows she had been hard to live with lately, she was sensible enough to admit that, and yet . . . surely she didn't deserve this? Nikki was so twisted into knots she couldn't bring herself to have the conversation they needed to have. Was she too scared of his answer? *Hell, yes.* She didn't want to lose her husband and she was too weak to face the truth.

How was she going to get through the next two weeks? Should they pack up and go home?

When Nikki reached the summit along the track she paused to catch her breath and take in the small private beach in the shape of an easy smile. It was then that she had her answer. They would stay. This trip was mainly for the kids and she could use this view to get through the murky waters ahead. Taking a lungful of salty air, she smiled. At least here she had places to escape to. Invigorating places. If they went home they would all be stuck in the house together while anger and resentment festered and the kids went nuts.

You're just going to have to suck it up, Nik. Be a rational adult. Face whatever's coming.

On her way back up the track she heard a vehicle and waved as Luke came into view.

'Morning, Nik,' he said as she leaned on the ute window.

'Hey, Luke. What you up to?' she asked, taking in the load of wood and tin on the back.

'Thought I'd make a start on this little lean-to. Chris is just getting breakfast sorted then he and Josh and Micky are going to head down to give us a hand.'

He shot her a smile and then put his hand on top of hers. He didn't say anything, but he didn't have to. He gave her a nod, just a slight one but it portrayed a whole wealth of thoughts and emotions.

'So, you ladies should have a nice quiet camp for a while,' he added with a wink.

'Thanks, Luke. I'm sure the boys will get a kick out of helping you. We'll have to have a barbecue lunch at the beach when it's done.'

'I'd like that,' he said.

Back at camp, Nikki found Ash with the girls cutting up carrots and potatoes.

'What's going on here?' she asked. 'Need any help?'

Breakfast was all done, it seemed, and they'd cleaned up and made a new mess.

'We're putting a stew on the fire for dinner. Bit of diced steak and some gravy and we'll have a campfire meal fit for a king.' Ash smiled. 'Did you bring any green vegies we can put in it?' she asked.

'Oh no, please don't,' said Chloe, pulling a face.

Nikki noticed her daughter's make-up was a little different today, a little lighter: eyeshadow and mascara; the full foundation and blush were missing. 'There are some tinned peas, I think.' Nik bent down to search the cupboard by the fridge. 'Bingo.'

'Don't worry, Chloe,' said Ash. 'You won't even taste them when they've been simmering in meat juices all day.'

'She's right,' chimed in Em. 'We used to have this kind of stew all the time and I could never taste them – and I hate peas.' Em put her finger in her mouth and pretended to gag.

Chloe pointed her carrot at Em. 'You better be right,' she said.

'Owen loved this stew too,' said Ash. 'He'd sometimes add new things and we'd have to try to guess what it was.'

'I'm done,' said Em slapping down the potato peeler a little harder than necessary. 'Chloe, wanna go see Gertie?'

Em grabbed her arm and started dragging her away from the kitchen.

Nikki watched them go, amused and pleased at the way they chatted so much more easily now.

'Have you seen Chris?' Nikki whispered to Ash as she cleaned up the girls' vegetable peels.

Ash shook her head. 'No, not since we finished breakfast. He said something about helping Luke. I haven't seen the boys either.'

'Yep, I saw Luke and he said they'd be off helping him today,' Nikki said. 'So, it's just us at the moment.'

'Nice. More reading?' Ash suggested with a smirk. 'Too early for a glass of bubbly? Or maybe we should stick to chocolate for now.'

'We have chocolate?'

'I brought a stash of Tim Tams for a special occasion. This seems fitting.'

With renewed enthusiasm they finished the stew and tucked it aside ready to put in the coals before grabbing their books and a freshly made coffee and settling by the fire.

'Are things a bit better?' Ash asked as she handed over the Tim Tam packet.

Nikki tried to hide her cringe. She knew Ash was just trying to be a good friend, but still she didn't want to talk about it. 'Not really. But I do need to talk to him and sort it out.' She shrugged.

'Well, let's enjoy the quiet while we have some.'

Nikki could have kissed her. 'Agreed.'

The building project down at the beach took the boys all day, and it wasn't until four o'clock that they arrived back looking worn out but satisfied.

'You look like you had fun, Josh?' Nikki put her arm around him. His shirt was torn and grimy but his smile was huge.

'It was cool. I got to hammer in some nails and climb up top. Micky and I are going to start work on our own cubby tomorrow,' he said excitedly. 'Oh, and he's going to help me set up a tent to sleep in.'

'Come on, we'll go get it,' said Micky.

Nikki smiled as she watched the boys head off towards the house. One tall, one short but both were animated and happy. In Josh she saw glimpses of the outdoorsy kid he had once been. At seven she'd had to practically drag him inside for dinner, and he'd be up to his elbows in sand making a tunnel for his

Matchbox car racetrack. Or he'd be perched on the side fence, watching all the neighbours with his homemade spyglass and pretending to be Captain Jack Sparrow.

Nikki turned to focus on the men. Chris looked tired but happy, it felt strange watching him. 'Go get cleaned up; dinner's nearly ready,' she muttered quickly.

'It smells wonderful,' said Chris just before his stomach rumbled. Luke laughed as Chris held his belly.

'That includes you and Micky,' she said to Luke. 'We have plenty. And Ash baked some bread to soak up the gravy.'

'Gee, how could we refuse?' Luke shot Ash a smile. 'Thanks, that would be great.'

And then it was just the girls left, sitting by the fire talking.

'Oh, have you seen *Riverdale*, I love that show. I have Netflix on my phone. You must get it. And *Sex Education*, that show was *so* funny,' said Chloe, whose voice then dropped to a whisper as she described a few scenes in the show. 'You would love *Stranger Things*, it's set in the eighties and the clothes are epic.'

'Oh, I've heard about that one. Is it scary? I don't mind a bit of gore,' said Em.

Nikki helped Ash carry over a table to set up with the bread and plates.

'We could have a games night. I'm itching to play some of those games with the kids,' said Ash. 'We don't do enough of that at home.'

Nikki nodded. 'I don't think our games have come out of the cupboard since our last holiday up north two years ago. Bit sad,' she agreed. Chloe had been thirteen and Josh eleven, and she and Chris had fun teaching them Greed and Sequence.

Josh had loved it, feeling like an adult playing with them, and he always wanted to win. He'd have his serious face on at all times, clearly not realising how cute he looked with creases between his eyes. And Chloe had laughed until she'd snorted when Chris blew all his turn on Greed. They hadn't had any other family moments as good as that trip.

The men came back clean, with the heady scent of deodorant wafting around the smoky fire, just as Josh and Micky finished erecting the small two-man tent next to their hut.

'Here, let me help with that,' said Luke, taking the gloves to lift the pot from the coals for Ash.

Nikki watched Ashley's eyes flutter closed and her nose twitch as Luke moved past her. She knew how easily scents could change your mood, like the salty air or the tang of cut timber. Chris was wearing her favourite deodorant tonight and it just made her want to hug him. But she wouldn't let herself, couldn't let her natural instinct kick in.

'This smells soooo good,' Luke purred as he held the plates for Ash to load up.

Suddenly there was a queue behind Luke of kids, all twitching noses and licking lips.

'It was Owen's favourite. One of his mother's recipes, I think.'

'He liked to cook?' asked Luke.

'Sometimes,' Ash replied.

Nikki caught the frown that flickered across Emily's face in the firelight as she stood staring at the ground waiting her turn for a plate of stew. Nikki's heart tore for her; it must still be hard for her to hear her dad mentioned. Nikki suddenly wondered how her kids would manage without Chris. God, they'd be devastated. She shook her head; it wasn't even a thought she could attempt to fathom, it made her feel sick just thinking it. Then she remembered just how close she'd been to having to leave them. She drank in her children's faces, so glad the outcome had been in her favour.

Dinner was a quiet affair as everyone focused on devouring their food. All the bread disappeared and bowls were wiped clean with it, or in Micky's case, with fingers.

'Em, can you play some more songs for us, please?' said Micky. 'Nothing beats a campfire with tunes.'

'Even better when it's from someone who can play,' said Luke. 'Remember old Uncle Rob?' he asked Chris.

Chris smirked. 'Uncle Rob thought he was the best guitar player since Slim Dusty. His singing was so bad that the dogs would go and hide.'

Josh was smiling. 'Have we ever met him?' he asked.

'Nah, mate. He died before you were born. But besides his bad singing and missing tooth he was a lot of fun to be with.'

He and Luke shared a sad glance.

'What was his favourite song he used to sing?' asked Em. 'If I know it I'll play that one first.'

'"Waltzing Matilda",' Luke said softly.

Em smiled and stood up to fetch her guitar. 'I might be a bit rusty but I reckon I can get most of it.'

She was true to her word, and as Nikki watched Emily play, she was overwhelmed by the talented, beautiful young woman. She wished Chloe was a bit more down to earth like Em, less worried about what everyone thought and what was popular. Some days she could cry for missing her daughter, her little chatterbox who loved her pink elephant teddy bear and would talk her ear off after school about everything that had happened.

'Owen would have loved this. His famous stew and Em playing,' said Ash.

Suddenly the guitar stopped mid strum, the last notes ripped away like an angry snarl.

'Why do you say that, Mum?' Em's tone was accusing and loud.

Ash wasn't the only one caught off guard. Nikki and the rest turned to Emily with confusion at her sudden outburst.

Em was staring at her mum, eyes wide and glistening with tears. 'Why do you say those things about Dad? He would have *hated* this!' Her voice trembled. 'I'm so glad he's not here. He would have messed all this up. Some days I hate him,' she almost yelled. 'I mean . . . hated him,' she corrected.

Nikki glanced to Ash, she was focused on her daughter, whose face had crumpled.

'But he's dead,' Emily continued, the tears now freely rolling down her face, 'so I feel horrible when I think that. I hate him *and* I miss him.' Her tears mixed into her mouth as it screwed up with her final words.

Ash got up with such a start that her chair fell backwards as she went to Em and kneeled by her chair.

'It's okay, Em,' she said, pulling her into her arms. 'It's okay to feel like that.'

Ash's voice cracked, while the rest of them sat around the fire as stunned onlookers, unable to glance away.

No one was game to speak as Ash and Em cried in each other's arms.

'I'm sorry, Mum,' Em sobbed.

'Don't be sorry. I understand. Sh.' Ash was stroking her hair amid tears and sniffles.

Nikki didn't know what she should do. Leave? Help? But she didn't have to decide, because Ash stood up and pulled Emily with her.

'Come on.'

Without a word she steered them towards their hut, shoulders slouched and Em's guitar hanging from her limp hand. No one spoke until the door was closed and the night went back to a silence only interrupted by the crackle and pop of the fire.

'Is Em okay, Mum?' Chloe's concerned voice broke the stillness.

'I'm not sure, honey. They might need some time alone for a bit.'

'Is this to do with his suicide? Or something else?' Chloe whispered.

Nikki hesitated. She could understand Em dealing with the ongoing trauma of losing her dad, but this seemed different. It was as if she were glad he wasn't here, relieved, and that made her feel guilty. Like mother like daughter with the guilt.

'I'm not sure, Chloe,' she said finally. 'Possibly. Suicide leaves them with a lot of unanswered questions.'

Chloe nodded; she probably had many of her own.

Nikki met Chris's eyes over the fire and knew that similar questions were running through his mind – but they were questions no one wanted to ask in front of the kids. They shared a confused shrug and for the moment their issues were forgotten.

No one seemed to know what they should be doing next, and soon a sense of melancholy settled over the group.

'I might go have a shower and then hang out in the tent,' said Josh. 'Micky's gonna camp with me,' he added.

'Yep. But if you snore or fart, that's it, I'm going back to my own bed,' said Micky, but no one laughed.

It seemed enough to break the seriousness. Luke and Chris started talking about the finishing touches to their project at the beach as the boys left.

Chloe's face was still pale in the firelight and she kept glancing toward Ashley's hut. Nikki put her hand on her daughter's knee. 'She'll be okay. She has her mum. But tomorrow she may need a hug and maybe a friendly ear.'

Chloe nodded, her face glum.

'But don't push. She'll talk when she's ready. Or she may never be ready,' Nikki added and suddenly thought about her own circumstances. She would have to take her own advice with Ash, who had never confided any issues about Owen. Nothing but the usual husband banter . . . he won't clean up after himself, doesn't like this, doesn't like that. It didn't seem anything out of the ordinary. They never saw much of Owen; his fly-in–fly-out roster meant he was mainly absent from school events and get-togethers, and when he was home but didn't join them, Ash would usually say he was worn out, was busy with appointments or simply didn't like crowds. Nikki had never questioned it. Owen was just a busy man who liked to keep to himself, or so she thought.

Nikki sighed and stared into the red-hot coals.

Was *everyone* hiding some sort of secret?

23

Ashley – The Past

IT HAPPENED WHILE ASH WAS ADVISING A CUSTOMER ON THE best strapping for her son's ankle injury. The woman was talking about her child's brilliant sporting ability when suddenly Ash was struck by a random bout of nerves. Not the excited sort, more a strange, foreboding sense that something wasn't right.

She guided the customer to the till. 'Tim will help you,' she said, giving Tim a smile and heading back to the aisle where she was loading up the new shampoo arrivals. Her watch said it was six o'clock, an hour until home time. She glanced out into the shopping centre, and the thrum of late-night shoppers jangled her nerves. It always did. This was the only night she worked late and Owen picked up Em from school. When he was back on shift she would then swap with her colleague Anna, which meant they got to share in the overtime.

'I love late-night shopping,' said Tim as he appeared beside her. 'There's something about shopping at night – people seem happier, or maybe it's just that I like night-time events,' he said with a wiggle of his eyebrows.

Ash forced her face into a smile she didn't feel, wishing she could share his enthusiasm. Today she especially felt the need to get home.

That feeling grew worse when she pulled into their driveway and saw the house in total blackness. She would have thought the power was out, but the rest of the houses in the street were lit up.

What was going on here? Had Owen taken Em somewhere? A random visit to the zoo or a night-time walk in Kings Park? A call would have been nice just to let her know. But he didn't tend to do that, she realised.

And then she spotted Owen's ute through the small shed window.

'What the . . .'

The hairs on the back of her neck rose as she grappled through her bag for the house keys and cursed when she took three attempts to get the right one.

The door eventually opened into the darkness. It was dead quiet, too quiet. She swallowed as she reached for the light switch, pulse racing as she considered what she might find when the lights came on.

Ash closed her eyes and flicked the switch. It took a moment before she had the courage to open them. Her eyes darted around the lounge room but nothing seemed out of place. She let out a breath.

That's when she smelled it. A strange musty scent, like an unaired house and something else she couldn't quite put her finger on.

On instinct she headed straight for Emily's room, glancing in the kitchen for her schoolbag, but it wasn't in its usual spot.

By feel she turned on Emily's light, but her room was empty and was the same as it had been that morning. Her guitar in the corner, her green doona thrown into place quickly and her smiling purple Furby in the centre.

'Where are you, my girl?' Her words were just a whisper.

She glanced to Owen's music room, took tentative steps towards it. His door was shut. Did she dare open it? She knew she had to.

Ash said a silent prayer and gritted her teeth as she turned the knob as quietly as she could, afraid to wake whatever ghosts might be lurking behind it.

That smell hit her again but much stronger. The scent of stale whiskey and alcohol oozing from pores.

She turned on the light, and Owen's figure appeared on the floor, like in a crime scene: his body face down on the carpet, his arms splayed and his face to the side. Drool, or maybe vomit, gathered at the corner of his lips. An empty glass was tipped over beside him and the bottle of Jim Beam sitting on the desk was empty.

She felt his pulse in his neck, making sure he was alive. His skin was clammy, to the point she wiped her fingers on her skirt.

Ash felt like a trespasser. His room felt cold and strange. Grey walls, grey carpet, a black sofa that doubled as a bed, all his guitars lined up along the wall, sheet music on stands, and at his table were notebooks with songs scribbled onto the pages. The blinds were down on the window and looked like they hadn't been opened in years, judging by the dust and spider webs at the top. Around the desk on the floor and near his bin were scrunched-up pages, and Ash almost wanted to open one just to see what thoughts he was throwing away. But her missing daughter was foremost in her mind.

'Emily?' she suddenly called out and began to run through the house, checking each room. She checked out the back and she checked Owen's ute. When she'd exhausted all options she ran back to Owen, where she flopped down beside him and slapped his face.

'Did you even pick her up from school?' she shrieked.

Owen didn't move.

'Owen, wake up! Where is she? *Where is Emily*, you bastard!'

She wanted to scream at him, hit him, shake him until he told her where Emily was, but equally she didn't want to wake the sleeping bear. A drunk Owen with whatever medication he had in his system was one she had to tiptoe around.

'Damn you, Owen. Where is she?' Ash choked out and started to cry. '*Where is she?*'

She sat back on her heels, Owen hardly stirring while she was going into meltdown mode. Ash couldn't think what to do. Her daughter was missing. Was she still at school? Why had they not called? Had she been abducted trying to walk home?

Killing Owen seemed like a plausible option right now. If she was hurt . . .

'Hello?' a woman's voice called out.

And then another. 'Mum, are you home?'

Ash jumped up and ran towards it. 'Emily? Emily?' she yelled as she ran to the front door, meeting her daughter in the hallway and scooping her up. At nearly twelve she was far too old to be carried, but Ash didn't care. She hugged and kissed her, holding her so tightly.

'Mum, I can't breathe,' Em said eventually.

That's when Ash realised another woman was standing not far from them.

She put Emily down but kept hold of her hand, keeping her close.

'Hi, I'm Jill. I live across the road, in the brick house.' Jill looked to be in her eighties, and reminded Ash of her own grandmother with the flowery blouse and grey clipped curls.

'Did you find her?'

Jill nodded. 'I was walking my dog Oscar when I saw this little poppet crying her eyes out and banging on the front door. She was so worked up.'

Ash saw Jill's face flash with concern and sensed she was eyeing off Ash and deciding if she needed to call child welfare.

Ash looked at Emily. 'Did you walk home from school?'

Em nodded. 'Dad didn't turn up and then I got home and no one was here. I got scared,' she admitted, looking at her feet.

'It's okay, Emily. I'm glad you're safe,' she reassured her and tucked her hair back around her ear.

This made her look up. 'Jill said I could wait at her house until you got home from work. We had cups of tea and biscuits,' Em said with a big grin.

'Oh, thank you, Jill, for looking out for her. Her dad was supposed to pick her up but something must have happened. I need to give him a call. Em, say goodbye and thank you to Jill and go pop your stuff in the kitchen.'

To her surprise, Em went and hugged Jill. 'Thank you. Can I come and play with Oscar again one day?'

'Of course,' the woman replied before Em left.

'I'm so sorry to disrupt your afternoon,' Ash said as she ushered Jill to the door, 'but thank you so much for watching over Emily. I was so worried when I couldn't find her.'

'She was no trouble. Just distraught, but my little Oscar cheered her up. If you ever need help, or someone to watch Emily for a while, just ask. We would love the company again. Only Oscar and me in that big old house,' she said with sad eyes that had seen a lifetime.

'I can't thank you enough. And I might just take you up on that, Jill. It's been lovely to meet you. I know it's late now, and I better see to Emily.'

Ash was herding the old lady out her door, desperate to make sure Emily didn't stumble across Owen.

'I understand. We would love the visit,' Jill replied with a last wave.

'Are you okay, Em?' Ash said as she entered the kitchen and hugged her again.

'I'm fine, Mum. I actually had a nice time with Jill and Oscar.'

'Good, I'm glad. I might have to give you some numbers you can give Jill to call if ever Dad can't pick you up again,' she said, her mind ticking over things she needed to put in place so this would never happen again.

'Mum. Why did Dad forget me?'

Her heart ached at Em's confused words. Again she found herself thinking up a lie; she was adept at it by now. 'He got stuck at work, honey. He tried to call me but the message didn't get through. Just a communication mix-up. But you're okay and that's the main thing. It will never happen again, I promise.' Or she would die trying.

Emily smiled. 'That's okay. I *was* scared,' she admitted, 'being all alone and locked out of the house, but it got better. Can we have dinner now, I'm hungry.'

And just like that her brave girl had moved on from her ordeal, happy to be home and continue as though nothing had happened. *How did she get to be so strong when I'm anything but?*

'Sure. How about you choose your favourite and I'll go wash up,' she said.

Leaving Emily in the kitchen, she went to Owen's room. He was still sleeping it off, his cheek red and showing finger marks. *Good.* Silently willing him not to wake up until tomorrow, she closed the door firmly and headed back to Em.

When he was capable of hearing every word, she would give him a serve, and probably march him back to the doctor. He knew full well he wasn't supposed to drink while on his medication. She hated these days, these moments of Owen's actions that affected Emily. Living with mental illness was no fun for Owen, she understood that, but when it affected their child, her understanding faltered. It didn't happen often, but every time it did Ash wondered about the next time. She kept hoping there never would be a next time, but life was never that black and white. It was grey and fuzzy and frightening.

Putting on a brave face, she joined Emily and pretended nothing unusual had happened. Like she always did.

24

Ashley

'*I HATE HIM.*'

Emily's shock admission last night had twisted Ash's heart, squeezing all the blood from it as if it were a soggy dishcloth. At that point she'd forgotten everyone else around the fire; all she saw was her daughter in pain. Em hadn't had an outburst like that, ever. The thing that had stunned Ash the most was that Em had said some of the things Ash felt herself. *Guilt.*

She glanced across to see her daughter sleeping, her rugs twisted about her like a python.

When she'd got Em back to the hut last night they'd sat side by side on her bed, not speaking for a moment. Then Em had asked between her tears, 'Why do you paint Dad in such a good way? Why don't you talk about the bad times? Or how it really was? How come we don't talk about him at all?'

Her words had hit like a blunt stick to Ash's heart. 'I'm so sorry, Em. I was trying to do the right thing by you. And

226

maybe, if I'm honest, I was trying to make a situation better than it was.'

'Because you were embarrassed about what people would say?' Em had probed. 'About Dad being . . . different?'

Ash had shrugged. 'I don't know, maybe. I didn't want your dad's mental health to be anyone else's business but ours. Your dad was a very private person. He didn't like people to know. And I thought I was protecting you.'

'But you couldn't completely. I knew when to run and hide, to read Dad's moods, but you bore the brunt of it all. And yet you still talk about Dad as if he was perfect like Chris.'

Ash had almost smirked. *Chris isn't as perfect as we all thought.*

'Your dad had his good days too,' she'd said. 'It wasn't all doom and gloom. Dad was only like that when his medication wasn't working or he'd gone off it. He didn't ask to have mental health problems, honey. He didn't want to be depressed.'

Emily's cheeks were stained with tears and her eyes red; her hands were scrunched together on her lap as she leaned desperately towards Ash.

'I know, Mum, but his good days were few and far between. I think you grip on to the good bits so much that you believe that's what it was like. Weren't you just as scared as I was?' She paused, watching Ash, then looked down, hanging her head. 'I actually have moments where I'm glad he's not here, relieved almost. It's like I can finally breathe and not be worried about him. But I hate myself for thinking those thoughts, Mum. I loved Dad, it was just hard at times.' A heartbeat had passed. 'Mum, Dad killed himself. Why would he leave us like that?'

Ash hadn't been able to stop the onslaught of tears. And she didn't have an answer.

Even now as she put on her shoes and headed out of the hut she felt tears prickle her eyes. She blinked rapidly to keep them at bay. Outside, as she walked from the quiet camp in the faint morning light towards the beach, the cool breeze helped dry them. The call of the ocean had her moving, but with each step along the grey sandy track last night's conversation repeated in her head like a scratched CD.

'Why wouldn't you talk to me about it? Didn't you think I'd cope?'

Ash had sniffed back her tears and wiped her eyes. 'I'm sorry, Em. I was trying to protect you, and in the end I wasn't sure what to say. What words can make it better?'

Em had shaken her head. 'I don't know. Maybe there are none but at least we could have talked about it more. Like, why did he do it? Was I not good enough? The shrink lady at school said it wasn't because of us.'

'No, Emily, no way.' Ash had squeezed her closer. They sat huddled together in their own little agonised cocoon. 'And she's right. He took his life because ... well, because he had demons that we couldn't see. He loved us very much but it got to a point that he couldn't bear it. Don't ever blame yourself, honey. Dad wouldn't want you to feel that way. We'll never know what your dad was thinking that night, and we can't churn ourselves up about it. Do you understand?'

Em had nodded.

Ash stopped and leaned against a small tree on the side of the track. She felt weak and out of breath. Her tears refused to stop, but somehow she managed to walk on and took the left path up to the lookout. She'd been here only once before on one of her long walks but she hadn't taken much time to sit and enjoy the view.

And what a view it was, although as she sat there staring out over the ocean she wasn't really taking it in. The clouds filled the sky like wet tea bags coating the earth in a damp grey, and a cold breeze blustered up the headland to dry her tears. She heard the waves crashing over the rocks and was tempted to walk to the edge to see if she could see any water spray but thought that in her vague state standing near a cliff wasn't the best idea.

'Can we talk about Dad more often, the real Dad?' Em had asked last night. Her eyes had been large and pleading.

'Of course, if it's what you want. Maybe it's what we both need.' Ash had thought for a moment. 'You're right. I don't think dealing with it alone served us any good. From now on let's promise to speak more openly, no hiding the real stuff.' And they'd hugged on it.

Ash thought now about what she'd said. It was true. She'd spent so long tiptoeing around Owen, making sure everything was as he wanted it to be so it wouldn't trigger a outburst or a shift in his emotions, trying to shield Em from what he was dealing with, trying to help Owen manage his illness. The build-up would start when she knew Owen was flying back from work, making sure the house was shipshape and then living on the edge while he was home. She felt like an egg on a peak, trying to balance, not sure which way she might fall. Trying to keep Owen's mood swings from Emily, trying to protect her. Trying to protect Owen from himself, watching for signs he wasn't taking his medication or that it wasn't working. It was all exhausting. She'd been trying to cope for so long she wasn't sure how to get back to normal. What was normal? Ash couldn't even remember the person she was before Owen.

She'd loved the outdoors, camping with her family. She'd thought about going to university and becoming a journalist or a nurse. But she would never be that girl again; she'd seen too much, changed too much. What she needed was to figure out who she was now.

'Hey you, thought I might find you here.'

Ash jumped at Luke's words.

'Mind if I join you?' he asked.

He stood squinting into the wind, his handsome face covered with stubble and a gentle smile, one he would probably give the cows when he didn't want to spook them. She was drawn into his eyes, a liquid silver that reflected the sky. His eyebrows raised and she realised he was still waiting for an answer.

'Oh, yes, sorry. I'm miles away.'

He sat beside her on the chair, not too close but not like she had a contagious disease either.

'Are you both okay?'

His voice was soft, and her 'We're fine' reply was automatically on her lips before she clamped them shut. She'd promised Em no more lies, no more secrets, no more pretending. She might as well start now.

'No, not really,' she said with a sigh, tucking her hands into the end of her sleeves. She started to pick at the worn threads on her jeans by her knee. 'I've been a pretty crap mum.'

Luke's jeans looked as worn but were a light blue against her darker pair. He pulled at the sleeves on his blue checked shirt but didn't look as cold as she felt. He was probably acclimatised.

'Don't be so hard on yourself, Ash. Being a parent isn't easy. We try to do what we think is best at the time and there are no guidelines. You shouldn't worry, Emily's a great kid.'

'Yeah, I know. She's amazing.' Ash's nose prickled as the tears appeared, blurring her vision.

Luke sat quietly, his expression sympathetic, as if he were here to listen but only when she was ready.

It took probably five minutes of wave watching before Ash was ready and blurted what was on her mind.

'Em is upset because I don't talk about Owen, the real Owen. I didn't realise how much I was hurting her by omitting the truth.'

Luke reached over and held her hand. He just took it and brought it back to his lap and closed both his hands over hers. It was warm and comforting. And a little sweet. Was it wrong that her heart should skip a beat while she was talking about her husband? Ex-husband. Former husband? Late?

'Who was the real Owen?' he asked softly.

Ash shrugged. 'I don't really know. I was so young when we started going out. Then I fell pregnant with Em and our whole world changed. Cue a quick marriage and a new direction in life. Back then Owen was fun and happy, but I hadn't known him long. Well, not long enough to realise he suffered depression and later was diagnosed with bipolar disorder.'

'Pretty heavy stuff.'

Ash nodded. 'His father died when Owen was twelve, and his Uncle Trevor stepped in and played a big part. That was until he committed suicide when Owen was nearly sixteen.'

'Man, that's tough.' Luke grimaced as if he was in physical pain but his fingers kept up the rhythmic stroking on her hand.

'I know. Owen started off all right. He was on depression medication when I met him; he was twenty and I was eighteen. But it wasn't until I was nearly due to have Em that I noticed the changes in his moods. At first I put it down to being an expectant dad – I mean, it was a shock but we decided together that we would make it work. He proposed two months after Em was born. He told me he had his two girls and life was complete. It was a hard adjustment – you know what it's like having a baby – and my parents helped a lot. Some days Owen was amazing, some days he couldn't cope. But I kept waving his behaviour away.'

Ash swallowed. Why was it so easy to blurt this out to Luke? She hadn't even confided this much to her mum.

The small circles Luke was rubbing on her hand were like an energy boost when she felt depleted.

'The bipolar?' Luke asked.

'Yep.' Ash nodded and licked the salt from her lips. 'It took many years before he got it diagnosed, though. I started to manage his ups and downs, figuring out what set him off and what kept him calm. Finally one day I came home after work and Emily was missing. She was twelve and had walked home by herself after Owen had forgotten to pick her up. I found him inside passed out. He'd been drinking all day. I demanded he see a doctor to sort out his medication. Sometimes he took himself off his depression meds when he felt good.' Ash sighed. There had been some rollercoaster times. But that was the worst.

'How does Em feel about it all?'

'That's the horrible bit. I didn't talk to her about it. I thought I was protecting her. I thought she was too young to know the details. But all I did was leave her to deal with it on her own, to try to figure out reasons herself instead of explaining it. She's one tough kid and I underestimated how much she could handle. If only I could go back . . .'

Luke tugged her hand slightly to get her attention. 'No, Ash. We can't live in "if only" land. Believe me, you just tear yourself up over something you can't change. Nothing will ever change, the past is in the past. All we can do is keep moving forward, learn from our mistakes and try to be a better person.' He shrugged. 'Well, that's my philosophy.'

Ash hunched over as she sighed. 'I know, you're right.'

She watched him as he gazed out to sea. No, he wasn't looking at the water, he was staring at the area in front of them as if he were watching a scene play out in his mind's eye. His lips curled slightly; had she not been studying him she might have missed it. Those amazing eyes of his glossed over for a moment before he blinked rapidly and cleared his throat.

'Of course I'm right.'

He shot her a smile. A real, bright one. She couldn't help but return it.

'Thanks, Luke. Thanks for checking in.'

'I had a few people there for me when I needed it. It's nice to share the love. If you ever want to talk, I'm here. And you *are* in the best spot for it.'

He held her face captive with his gaze. Ash had a feeling she forgot to breathe, but then he withdrew his hand and stood up. 'I better head back and feed the girls. As in sheep,' he clarified.

Ash's hand felt cold and she moved to tuck it under her legs as she watched Luke turn to leave.

That's when she spotted the plaque on the chair. *Rebecca – Always in our hearts.*

'Hey, Luke?'

He stopped his long strides and turned back. 'Yeah?'

'Who was Rebecca?' she asked.

Luke didn't reply straightaway, as if he were lost in memories. 'Rebecca was my grandmother. The strongest woman I knew. She loved this spot and made the best sponge cakes. She also wasn't afraid to give me a clip around the ears for being cheeky,' he said.

He smiled, then continued on his way, leaving Ash to the view, and to her thoughts.

25

Nikki

NIKKI WAS GETTING SOME EGGS OUT OF THE FRIDGE IN THE
camp kitchen when she saw Luke stride past, his tall body
visible through the mismatched wall of windows and doors.

'Hey, Luke, have you seen Ash in your travels?' she asked
after running out to meet him.

'Yeah, she's at Rebecca's spot.' He raised his hand as if
shooing a fly. 'She's fine, we had a chat. I'm sure she'll be back
for breakfast.'

And with that he continued on his way, past Chris, who
was heading to the kitchen from Luke's place. His head was
low and his hair unbrushed.

'You about to do breakfast? Want a hand?' Chris asked
cautiously.

In reply she just shrugged and walked back into the kitchen
area. Chris followed at a safe distance and together they started
making toast, taking out eggs and plates.

'Last night was a bit different,' he said as he opened the bacon packet and put strips onto the pan.

Nikki had just cracked her first egg into another pan. 'Yeah. Do you know what's going on?'

'Not really. I mean, I didn't really know Owen but maybe Em's just upset about how he died?' Chris whispered his words.

'I was wondering the same.' Their shared concern for Ash and Em made their issues take a back seat for the moment.

Josh crawled out of his tent, oblivious to the kangaroo right beside it eating grass as he staggered towards food, his hair stuck up like a white sail on a yacht. Micky was close behind but looking more awake. He stopped and called out to the kangaroo before stepping closer to give it a pat.

'Bacon wafts through a tent better than the hut, hey, mate,' said Chris, rubbing his son's head.

'Something like that,' he mumbled as he took a plate and loaded up with two eggs and enough bacon to sink a ship.

Nikki could see Micky hesitate. 'Dig in, Micky. Plenty to go around. Is that your pet kangaroo?' she asked.

'Thanks, Aunty Nik.' He smiled and grabbed a plate. 'Yeah, she'll come to me but she's wary of others, and her joey's still scared of us.'

'Hey, look what I found in the hut. It's a little game.'

All eyes turned to Chloe, who took a seat at the table, moving the game around in her hands. Her hair was brushed and styled but her face was clear of make-up.

Nikki caught a glimpse of Ashley coming back down the track before she headed for the hut. Then five minutes later she emerged with Emily, who walked timidly beside her like a toddler who has just woken up.

'Morning,' Ash called brightly, but there was nothing cheery in her anxious gaze.

'Morning. Would you both like bacon and eggs? It's still warm,' said Nikki as she pointed to the leftovers. The rest of them sat around the wooden table, just about scraping their plates clean.

'Thank you. That would be great. How hungry are you, Emily? Grab a plate and dig in,' Ash said exuberantly.

Em looked a bit shy, a bit embarrassed as she hid behind her hair and clung to Ash's side as if she were stuck on with double-sided tape.

'Em, hurry up. I want to show you this game I found,' said Chloe, raising the hand-held plastic game in the air.

Emily lifted her head, hair falling back as her large eyes peered at Chloe. 'What is it?' she replied, clearly intrigued.

'It has these tiny balls and you have to get them into these little holes but the moment you get one and go for another it falls back out. I've been at it all morning,' said Chloe.

Ash shot Nikki a grateful smile, but it was all Chloe's doing and it made Nikki proud.

'Not fair, I wanted a go next,' said Josh with a pout.

'Don't worry, mate. We can go get the bikes filled up with fuel. Then we can use them to drag some wood to our cubby. I have the perfect spot picked out.' Micky stood up and motioned for Josh to follow.

Josh copied Micky, putting his dishes in the sink. But on his way past he leaned over the table for another bit of bacon.

'He must be about to have a growth spurt,' muttered Chris.

'He can't be far off one,' agreed Ash.

'Oh, nearly.' Chloe leaned over Emily's shoulder as she moved the small box to get the balls into their designated spots. 'It's so tricky.'

Nikki was about to put her plate away when she heard Chloe mutter to Emily: 'Are you okay, Em?'

The adults at the table had gone quiet, all holding their breath.

Em shrugged, keeping her eyes on the small balls in the game. 'I think so.' Then she stopped to look at Chloe. 'But thanks for asking.'

'I don't really know what to say, especially about your dad,' Chloe admitted. 'Was he really sad?' she asked softly.

Em glanced to Ash and they shared a look Nikki couldn't interpret. It was Ash who spoke first, sitting down beside Em. 'Yeah, Chloe. Owen struggled with depression and was quite sad at times. He was on medication, which helped with his mental illness.'

Em gave a weak smile but she seemed a little more relaxed, relieved almost.

'Oh, I didn't know.' Chloe screwed up her face and put her hand on Em's arm.

'I didn't realise either, Ash, I'm sorry,' said Chris, putting a hand on her shoulder.

'It's not your fault, it's not anyone's fault,' Ash admitted. 'Owen struggled with it his whole life. When he stayed on his medication he was fine. But then he started at the mine and was later diagnosed with bipolar disorder and things got a lot harder. And it ended tragically for us all.'

Nikki opened her mouth to speak but then closed it.

'Is that why we never saw much of him?' Chloe said. 'Your dad didn't come to our house much. I think I only saw him a few times.'

'Yeah.' This time Em replied. The game was resting on the table between her hands. A finger rubbed up and down along the edge of the plastic square. 'He didn't like going out much unless he was in a good mood, then he'd want to do a family trip and end up climbing trees. Literally,' she said with a smile as if a memory had taken form. 'Those were the days you probably saw him, when he felt great.'

'That would have been hard on you guys too?' Nikki said, staring at her friend and wondering how she never knew any of this. She had assumed Owen was antisocial or just didn't really like them.

'Yeah, it wasn't easy at times,' replied Ash. 'We tiptoed around him a bit. He was much worse when he started his mine job. He hated it there but he wouldn't leave. I tried to convince him to quit and find another job but he refused, said the money was too good. His health deteriorated and he drank more. My nerves were always on edge, wondering what he'd do next and making sure everything was perfect for him so he wouldn't worry.' Ash sighed then continued. 'He had it hard when his dad died when he was young and then his uncle committed suicide. I think it affected Owen more than anyone realised.'

'Dad often said he was a burden on us,' said Em. 'He told me once that he wished he could be a better dad, a stronger dad.' Her face contorted as if fighting off tears. 'But he *was* a good dad, especially when he was well. I do miss him, and I don't hate him,' she added as she glanced at Chloe. 'We did have some great times, playing guitar together or when we went on our fun adventures.'

Nikki remained by Ash's side, unable to finish her breakfast, while her mind processed this information. It was all a bit surreal, hearing about Owen in this way. A whole side of him and this family she'd had no idea about. The silent struggles they had endured together. The things Emily and Ash must have seen. It made Nikki suddenly appreciate the carefree life she'd had with Chris. Up until now. But even then . . . was it even in the same realm?

Was this why Emily seemed so much more mature than Chloe, even though they were the same age?

'Mum, do you think Luke would mind us going around the sheep to check for lambs?' Em asked suddenly.

Ash shrugged. 'You'd have to go find him and ask.' Then she stood up. 'I'll come with you.'

'I think it's my turn on dishes.' Nikki got up and started to collect plates, Chris moving alongside her like he had for years, the two of them like synchronised swimmers. She took comfort in the familiarity, the fact that no one knew her like he did and vice versa. Mandy wouldn't know how Chris liked his steak or that he loved it when she massaged his shoulders or that his favourite dessert was her salted-caramel cheesecake. She wouldn't know that he cried when both his children were born and that he cut their cords, nor would she know how he looked after all three of them with so much tenderness and without complaint when they shared a vomiting bug. Would she know that he cried his heart out every time he watched *Red Dog* and that onions burned his stomach?

But it wasn't just what she knew about Chris, it was the things only he knew about her. At times over the years she felt as if he knew her better than she knew herself. He'd bring chocolate home just as she was craving it, maybe keeping note of her cycle better than she did. Or there would be flowers on the table after a hard day at work. Foot rubs and hugs at the perfect time.

She didn't want to give all that up. So, why had Chris? Why had he threatened their strong foundation?

'That was pretty full-on,' said Chris as he took the plate she'd just washed.

'Yeah. I think it was good for them to speak about it. Em looked like she needed it. Poor kid.'

'I know. A father is supposed to be someone you can count on, someone you can turn to at all times,' said Chris.

'It wasn't Owen's fault he suffered depression,' she replied. 'But I get what you mean. It's sad for all of them. I'm sure he wished things were different too.'

'It really makes you appreciate your own life more; well, I have.'

Nikki plunged another plate into the soapy water, washed it then handed it to Chris. It was almost therapeutic washing dishes with him.

'Nik, I'm really sorry.' Chris held her hand instead of the plate, forcing her to look at him. 'Please let me explain? To make this right?'

'You should have thought about that sooner,' she said frowning and removing her hand from his. She dropped the plate on the edge of the sink to dry and pulled the plug as if she were pulling a stuck weed from the ground, and watched as the water drained away, making sucking noises as it went. Then she turned to Chris. 'How long would it have gone on if I hadn't found out? Tell me that? After you got her pregnant and then decided you wanted to leave me, us?'

His mouth dropped, horrified. 'I would never leave you. You and the kids are my life!'

His words were said with such force that Nikki took a step back. But she didn't let it shake her. 'Then what the hell were you doing with Mandy?'

His mouth moved in all directions as if trying to formulate the right words, but nothing came. Nikki huffed and spun on her heels, stomping from the kitchen and heading for the sheds.

'Nikki, wait. I don't want to say something to make things worse.'

She didn't stop.

'I love you!' he shouted. 'Will you stop being so pig-headed and let me explain.'

She kept walking and her thoughts whirred to match her pace. She could tell it was killing him to not be able to explain his side but a tiny part of her enjoyed making him hurt, drawing out the pain to try to compensate for her suffering. She didn't want to make it easy for him but at the same time she wasn't making it easier on herself.

Besides, it was too hard. Too hard to hear his words when all she saw was Mandy's lingerie-clad body.

The mental picture was never far from her mind. How was she supposed to move on from that? How could she compare? Her self-esteem had never been as low as it was now; any lower and she'd be burning up in the Earth's core.

She continued her walk around the farm and eventually her mind settled a bit as she returned to the camp, to find Ash trying to befriend Micky's kangaroo.

'Have you seen any kids?' she asked. 'It's so quiet.'

'No, it's rather strange not hearing "I'm bored" on repeat,' said Ash.

Right on cue, a motorbike came roaring around the house and up to the camp kitchen. Chloe was driving and Em was hanging onto her waist. Both girls had smiles from ear to ear and hair all tangled and knotted.

'Oh my *god*, Mum,' said Chloe as she turned off the bike and they ran over to them.

'It was sooooo amazing,' said Em.

'We birthed a baby,' Chloe was almost yelling, slightly breathless. She glanced at Em. 'We were awesome.'

They had practically spoken over the top of each other in their excitement, and Nikki found herself smiling, their happiness contagious.

'Slow down, what happened?'

'Well, we went to check the sheep,' said Em.

'And we saw one lying down and went over to check,' added Chloe. 'She wasn't moving and we could see two little feet.'

'We waited a bit to watch but nothing was happening,' said Em. 'Then we realised the lamb needed help.'

'So, then Em goes, "Grab the legs, Chloe, we have to help it." And I'm, like, screwing up my nose, but Em grabbed them and started pulling.'

'But it was hard. So then Chloe helped me and together we pulled that lamb free.'

'Yeah and we fell over,' said Chloe, showing the grass stain on her jeans. 'And our hands were all gooey but, Mum, that lamb started moving and the mum got up and it was sooooo amazing!' Chloe wiped her hands on her jeans at the memory.

Em put her arm around Chloe and beamed. 'We are parents. We decided to call the lamb Lucky.'

'Yeah, Lucky we were there.' Chloe turned to Em. 'Let's go find Luke and tell him.'

'Um, do you want to wash your hands first?' asked Nikki.

'Oh, yeah, great idea,' said Em as the girls rushed off to the toilets. Their excited voices could be heard as they washed, chatting about their life-saving moment.

Ash cupped her face with her hands as she listened to the kids. 'That is so cute, they're so happy.'

Nikki dropped her voice. 'I don't think I've seen Chloe that animated in ages. And without her phone.'

The girls came out, skipping with their arms linked. This time Em drove the bike and Chloe jumped on the back and wrapped her arms around Em, resting her chin on her shoulder.

'To infinity and beyond!' Chloe yelled as they headed towards the sheds.

Nikki sat in a chair, watching the girls disappear. 'I hope we don't end up with a pet lamb,' she said with a chuckle. But if getting a lamb meant seeing Chloe – this Chloe, with life and light – then she'd take home a bloody trailer load of lambs.

26

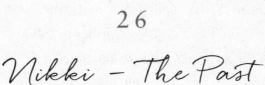

Nikki – The Past

'IT'LL BE OKAY, NIKKI. I'LL BE HERE THE WHOLE TIME.'

Chris gripped her hands just a fraction too firmly, almost a panicked hold like a toddler on their first day at kindy. And yet his face remained calm, a pillar of strength and support for her to rely on. After his moment in the car after her diagnosis he'd been determined to be the rock she needed. Just like he'd been with the birth of their children – a little scared but mostly in awe of how she'd managed it. This time would be no different.

'I know it will. I'm doing the right thing,' she said, reassuring him. 'It's only a couple of hours.' She wanted to thank him, to tell him just how amazing he'd been through the lead-up to this moment, but her mouth went dry and she could only gaze at him with tears in her eyes and a massive lump in her throat.

He nodded and kissed her before letting her get changed into her hospital gown. Then they sat quietly in the preoperative holding area before her nurse appeared.

'Ready?'

'I guess so,' Nikki replied and got to her feet, suddenly feeling light-headed.

Chris jumped up and lifted her hand to his lips, kissing it before bending over to kiss her lips. 'I love you,' he whispered.

'I love you too,' she replied automatically.

The nurse smiled and gestured for her to follow, then nodded to Chris. 'We'll have her back in no time.'

Chris waved, an encouraging smile on his lips.

'This way, Mrs Summerson. That gown looks very fetching on you,' the nurse added with a wink as she led Nikki to a small narrow room that could have been a hospital storage cupboard.

'The surgeon will be in soon,' the nurse said before leaving.

They must have passed each other in the hall, because he walked in seconds later.

'All right, Nikki. Please would you mind dropping the top of the gown and I'll quickly mark up where the incisions will be made.'

Nikki felt a sudden sense of déjà vu; it was the same process for her breast augmentation only this time it was to have bits taken out. In a way it calmed her a little because she knew what to expect.

Nikki and Chris had only met this surgeon a few days ago when he explained the operation procedure. He was younger than the doctor who gave her the diagnosis and she liked the steadiness of his hands. As he wielded the felt-tip marker she could see how his smooth hands would be with a scalpel and she felt reassured.

'Okay, all done. I'll take you through to the anaesthesia room. It will be all over soon,' he said with a warm smile.

As she lay on the table watching the nurses set up and the surgeon go about his pre-op routine, she tried not to think about what he was about to do. Nikki would rather think about her children. Josh and Chloe would be in school right now. Her mother had dropped them off and would no doubt spoil them rotten for the next few weeks during the school holidays, making their favourite meals, letting them stay up late and giving them money to splurge on toys and treats. Just this once Nikki wasn't concerned about them being pampered. Life was too short not to enjoy it.

It gave her comfort to know her kids would be blissfully happy and unaware of what was going on now. This would all be over soon and she'd be rid of the awful cancer.

As she floated into nothingness she pictured Chris and that smile he'd given her.

―

'How are you feeling, love?'

Nikki blinked. It was a woman's voice. She tried to focus on the glowing dark skin of the nurse smiling at her.

'You're in the hospital recovery room, and we're just going to keep an eye on you before we shift you to your room where your husband is waiting.'

She smiled, bright white teeth, and then Nikki faded back into sleep.

When she woke again she was in the same room. It felt like she'd been asleep for an age, yet the same nurse was watching her. As time moved on and the drugs wore off, her mind cleared more and more. The nurses monitored her blood pressure and body temperature, and before too long she was moved into a room where, just as the nurse had said, Chris was waiting for her. The moment the door opened she could see him pacing along the window wall. He skidded to a halt when he saw movement and his body went from rigid to relaxed in a millisecond.

'Hi you,' he said, stepping closer but not approaching until the nurses had her moved into place.

'She's all yours,' one said before they left the room.

That's when Chris went to her bedside and took her hand in his. 'How do you feel?'

Nikki smiled. 'Sleepy. It's okay, I'm not going to break,' she said and was relieved when he bent over and kissed her forehead.

'I missed you.'

'I've been on a long sleep,' she said, still enjoying the after effects of the medication. She knew soon the pain would appear and maybe the nausea the nurses had warned her about. But so far she felt okay.

Her eyes roamed down to her chest. The white sheet lay flat over her, a few bumps from the dressing was all that remained of any shape. Nikki tore her eyes away and focused on Chris. She'd done the right thing.

⌐

'What's this?' Nikki said as Chris helped her to their bedroom on the day she was finally released from hospital.

The small TV was set up by the bed with the DVD player in reach along with her favourite collection of rom-coms. *Pride and Prejudice* sat on the top. Netflix was also available but Chris knew some of her favourite feel-good movies weren't on there.

'You heard what the discharge nurse said: all rest and no work. I can't have you getting bored and wandering around the house cleaning. This way everything is at your fingertips. If you need to reach anything else, just call me or text me and I'll come straightaway.'

He pulled back the bed cover and held out a steadying arm for her. 'Is it better lying down or sitting up? I can get more pillows?' he asked and then ran to the cupboard.

Nikki smiled as she let him do his hero work, fluffing up the pillows. 'Thanks, honey. I could get used to this.' She moved her arm and flinched as the action sent pain across her chest. Some parts felt numb and strange, but under her arm at the incision point was where it hurt the most.

'Right. It's nearly time for some pills,' said Chris as he watched her and then looked at his watch. 'I'll go get you some water.'

He took off before she could thank him.

They still had another week at home before the kids were due back. The term holidays started on Friday, and her parents were taking Chloe and Josh on a caravanning trip down south, which meant no surprise visits from them to pick up more clothes or a phone charger or something else they had left behind and desperately needed at Nan's. Meanwhile, as far as they knew, Chris and Nikki were off on a romantic getaway.

That night Chris helped her with her shower. The waterproof dressing was in place, so they couldn't see much. Not that there was much else to see except for a red wound.

Mirrors she avoided, not wanting to see the full extent of her surgery. It was as if the universe had decided that because she wasn't happy with her lopsided breasts it would just take them away.

'At least with your prosthesis you'll have two breasts the same without having to modify bras,' Chris had said.

'Trust you to find the silver lining,' she'd replied.

Until she had her prosthesis fitted Nikki had two Knitted Knockers, which she had found from a website, www.knitted-knockersaustralia.com. The testimonials from women who'd had mastectomies preferred the knitted breasts to their actual prosthesis so she'd put in an order for a free pair made by the wonderful volunteers. She hadn't decided about the reconstructive surgery – taking from other parts of her body to make new breasts – and the long operation wasn't very appealing, but nor was the thought of having no breasts at all.

It was still early days, and she didn't want to think too hard on it yet. She just wanted to rest. She needed time to accept and digest the past six months.

So, rest she would.

27

Ashley

'IT'S COOL ISN'T IT, MUM?'

Ashley nodded as she watched Emily brush the ground with a big branch at the entry to Josh's cubby in the bush.

'I love what you've done with the place,' she said, admiring the walls that had been made by weaving sticks and branches together. There was a more structured roof put together into a peak and held together with nails. They'd even built a sitting area off the ground with wood spanning two trees.

'It's looking good,' said Chloe, who adjusted some logs to use as chairs. She had dirt smeared across her face and a leaf stuck in her hair.

The boys were up on the raised floor hammering in the last nails on the boards they'd found in Luke's old shearing shed. Micky was certainly going to take after Luke in the handyman department. 'It looks amazing, you guys, well done. So, you'll be sleeping out here tonight?' she asked them.

'For sure,' said Josh, through his mouthful of nails. 'Might make a ladder next,' he added as he leaned back on his heels and admired his work.

'Ah, not us,' said Chloe. 'Luke said Em and I can have the spare hut to sleep in, so we're going to get that ready next.'

'Yeah, just a quick clean then it's all ours,' agreed Em.

It took Ash back to being a child, playing chasey on the lawn and building tepees with her cousins in the bush by her grandparents' house. They were the lasting, wonderful memories of her childhood that she hoped these kids were now making. She was pretty sure Josh wasn't going to look back on his youth and think, *Oh, remember that day I sat inside playing Minecraft all day and we built a ship.* Special memories need people and connection; those were the things that really counted. Her own father worked hard and was never home but that's not what she remembered. It was the holidays they spent at the beach, or driving the go-kart they built together, or the times he carried her on his shoulders as they ate ice-cream. Her dad had shown her that it was possible to be a busy parent, a hard-working one who supported the family, and still make the little moments count. Two weeks a year was all she needed to know that she was loved and to make awesome memories with her dad.

'Well, in about an hour we're packing up and taking lunch down to the beach.'

'Oh cool,' said Josh. 'I'm starving.'

Go figure. All Josh did was eat.

'Are we taking the utes?' asked Em.

'Yeah, why?'

Em shot Micky a cheesy grin. 'Micky said he'd teach us to drive.'

Micky laughed. 'I'll teach you around the farm first before we let you loose on the track.'

'Really? That would be cool. Can we start after lunch, please?' asked Em.

'And me!' said Chloe.

'Me too,' added Josh.

Micky laughed again and put his hands up. 'Sure, if it's okay with all the parents and Dad, we can make a start when we get back.'

The kids cheered and Ash let them finish pottering in the cubby. She followed the short narrow track back to the clearing, past the two motorbikes and to the camp kitchen.

Nikki was loading up an esky while Chris was checking the portable gas stove worked.

'Have you guys seen the kids' cubby? It's amazing. Makes me want to join them,' said Ash, holding open the esky so Nikki could put the buttered buns inside.

'I had a look yesterday,' said Chris. 'Great to see Josh enjoying a bit of nature.'

'I must go and have a look.'

'Go now, Nikki, I'll finish packing up,' said Ash.

'Um, okay. Sure, thanks.' Nikki put her hand against her head as she checked over what was to be packed.

'We've got this. Just head down to the bikes and follow their track into the bush.'

Nikki nodded and headed off.

'It will do her good to go and spend a bit of time with the kids,' said Chris. 'I hope she takes her time there,' he said longingly in her direction.

'Um, yeah.' Ash shrugged and started packing the burgers and sauce.

'Has Nikki said anything to you, Ash?'

She paused, the barbecue sauce in her hand hovering over the esky. She turned to Chris and realised her mistake. Looking into his big golden, pleading eyes, she felt a conflict: did she help Chris or remain loyal to Nikki?

But she couldn't lie.

'A few things.' It was all she would offer. Surely that wasn't betraying her friend.

Chris sucked in a deep breath, his chest expanding like a balloon before he let it out slowly.

Ash prepared herself for the next question, more probing or maybe an attempt to excuse his behaviour.

'I'm glad she has someone to talk to. She needs it more than she realises.'

Ash's mouth dropped open slightly as she frowned. Suddenly she got a feeling there was more to this fight than just Chris. Like all things, there were two sides to the story.

'I'm here if she needs me. Always,' she reassured him.

He nodded and seemed satisfied. Which just confused her even more.

They were all packed up when Luke arrived with his ute and together they transferred all the food and cooking gear onto the back as well as their chairs.

'Perfect day for it. Sun's out and the wind has dropped. Almost feels like a warm spring day,' said Luke.

'Anyone would think it was summer with you in shorts,' said Ash with a grin. Luke's lean tanned legs were just as appealing as his muscled arms. As far as she was concerned, he should wear shorts with white T-shirts more often. It also made Ash feel like she'd just got off the plane from Ireland with skin that hadn't seen sun.

'Feels like summer today,' he replied. 'Where are all the kids?'

'In the cubby,' said Chris. 'I'll go get the other ute and bring them all if you two want to get a head start and set up?'

Ash raised her eyebrow. 'Are you getting out of cooking duty again, Chris?' she teased him.

'Wouldn't put it past him,' agreed Luke. 'He never was a very good cook.'

'Hey, I got better.'

'You eat your baked beans out of a bowl now?' Luke laughed at his own joke.

Chris rolled his eyes. 'I cook a mean salmon and roast potatoes if you must know, as well as a curry. Just to prove it, I'll cook us all a curry tomorrow night if you catch some fish today. That's if you can fish, Luke?'

'Yeah, I've got better at that too,' Luke said with a smirk.

Ash was smiling watching the cousins tease each other.

'I think there's more to this fishing story,' she said to him a minute later as he drove them to the beach. They had the windows down and the coastal air was filling the cab.

He laughed, then shook his head. 'We were fishing down here with my dad when we were little and I accidently let go of my rod when casting in. Which was totally embarrassing as I was supposed to be the better fisherman, not Chris the city boy. I got all wet trying to retrieve it while Chris lost it laughing and reeled in a small herring. Then the second time Dad took us into Bremer Bay to fish off the jetty at the marina and I got seaweed and lost my hook on some rocks while Chris pulled in a decent-sized herring.' Luke glanced across to Ash and smiled. 'I don't think I've lived it down since.'

'So, you're going to go fishing this afternoon, then? What's there to catch?'

'Yeah, I'll throw a line in and see if the kids want a go. Sometimes we catch big salmon off our beach.'

He slowed down as the track turned sharply and the sound of a tree branch scraping the side of the ute made Ash cringe.

'Sometimes from up at the headland I can see the schools of salmon come in like a big black moving ink spot.'

'Do you see sharks?' she asked.

Luke shrugged. 'A few, but not up close. It's their home and that's their lunch swimming around, so I'm always aware that I'm in their territory.'

'But doesn't that scare you when you go swimming or surfing?'

As they reached the top of the small hill Luke stopped the ute and they gazed out over the now visible ocean.

He turned to Ash, the ute idling and one hand still on the gear stick.

'We take risks every day. Getting in a car and driving some-where is just as dangerous as surfing. Any idiot could hit you any time. It all depends on when your time is up, and when it's up there's usually not a damn thing you can do about it. Even the safest non-risk-taker can still die. I think it's best not to dwell on death; instead we need to live. If anything, we need to live for those who can't. But,' he cleared his throat, 'getting back to your question, yes sometimes I get scared when a shape lurks below me in the water,' he admitted quietly. 'Or when dolphins appear by my side, I may have a very brief moment of panic.'

Ash couldn't take her eyes away from him as she let his words soak in. Luke was big and strong, and she found his confession a little unnerving. 'Well, it's nice to know you're human,' she said with a smirk.

'How about we start tomorrow?' said Luke as he started the descent to the beach.

'Huh?'

She noticed his lips curl into a smile.

'Your first surf lesson.'

Her mouth fell open. Luke saw her face and chuckled.

'We've just been talking about sharks and you want me to go surfing? Um, you need to work on your timing,' she said shaking her head.

'Seize the day, Ash. Seize the day.'

He threw her a challenging look. One that dared her to step outside her comfort zone. One that made the hair on the back of her neck stand up. One that made her courage roar up in her chest and want to prove to him that she could and would give it a go.

'Fine,' she replied, giving him a steely gaze. 'You just want me to be the shark bait so you can surf.'

His eyebrows shot up. 'Never. Besides, sharks don't like redheads.'

Ash rolled her eyes. 'No one likes redheads.'

Luke pulled up next to the new lean-to and opened his door. 'I like redheads.'

The clang of his door shutting shook her from his words. It wasn't so much the words but the husky way he said them. It had reverberated down her spine and sent shockwaves over her skin.

She opened her door to join him unloading and tried to work out if he'd been flirting or if she had imagined it. It had been such a long time since anyone had flirted with her, she wasn't sure if she could tell the difference.

Grabbing the esky off the back she trudged through the soft sand in her thongs to the shelter and then paused. 'Wow, it looks even better up close. Great job, it's perfect.'

'I had help. And you helped with the idea.' He clapped her on the shoulder on the way past to get the chairs.

It was made from old pine logs and the top clad with old tin but the effect was rural and rustic, which blended perfectly into the surroundings. Something new wouldn't have worked at all.

'Maybe a long drop out the back would be handy too?' she said when he came back and set down his armful.

'I've never really thought about one, but it would make sense if we were to get the camp off the ground again. It's quite a walk back if you're busting to go.'

Ash kicked off her thongs and rolled up her khaki cargo pants to her knees before she opened the plastic table they'd brought.

'Any other great ideas you'd like to share with me before you leave?'

'Um, not at the moment but there's still time,' she said with a smile.

Just as Ash was thinking how nice it was to spend time alone with Luke she heard the roar of the other ute as it made its way over the crest towards the beach.

Chris, why couldn't you have taken just a little bit longer?
Even as she thought it she felt the guilt roll around her body
like an automatic reaction.

'Ah, there goes the peace and quiet,' said Luke.

He shot her a smile that made her feel like she needed to take
her jumper off. Maybe it was just hotter under the tin roof. Ash
watched him head back to the ute and her gaze dropped from his
arms to his backside. God, who was she kidding? It was Luke.
He was making a winter's day feel like a scorching summer.

Stop drooling, Ash! She cursed under her breath as she
moved to get back to the task at hand and crashed into the
table like a fool.

'You all right?' Luke called out.

He was on the way back, arms bulging with the weight of
more chairs.

'I'm fine, just a klutz.'

He put the chairs down while watching her and she had
the distinct feeling he knew damn well why she'd crashed
into the table. His little smirk was making her even more
flustered.

'I'm starving!'

Josh's catchcry was a welcome distraction from the intensity
of Luke's gaze.

'Best I get cooking, then,' she said, turning away to open
the portable gas burner.

Now was the time she wished the cold breeze was blowing
in off the ocean. Anything to cool her burning cheeks.

2 8

Nikki

'WINE?'

Nikki was going to say no, just because it was Chris offering, but then changed her mind. It was too nice a day not to enjoy it with a glass of wine. 'Sure, why not.'

Chris pulled the bottle from the ice esky and poured some into a plastic wine cup.

'Thank you.' She took the drink and sipped it while watching him fetch a beer for himself. The sausages were all eaten and the kids were off climbing the rocks and hunting for crabs for Luke so he could try to catch an elusive groper out at sea. Micky had shown Josh his three fishing rods and then made some lures for this afternoon's fishing session. Apparently they were going to try to catch some big salmon off the beach. Josh's eyes had bulged when Micky had shown him the average-size salmon he normally caught here. To Josh, who had only ever caught small skippy or herring, it seemed massive and his enthusiasm was infectious. Nikki had never seen him so animated, and they hadn't even got to the fishing part yet.

'I don't think Luke will need a beer just this minute,' Chris said before closing the esky lid and sitting beside Nikki.

The sun was glorious and there were no clouds to halter the warmth but they still sat their chairs in the sun, a metre out from the shelter the boys had built, to get the full heat.

Nikki had kicked off her thongs before lunch and now dug her toes into the white sand, burying them until the last of her pink nail polish was gone. She had braved shorts today, as had Chris and Luke. Luke's golden sun-kissed skin made him look like a surfer, whereas Chris was pale from all those days at work in long pants and shirts.

They sat in silence, while in front of them Luke gave Ash a surf lesson.

'I don't have my bathers,' Ash had said when Luke suggested it after lunch.

He'd chuckled and assured her she wouldn't need them. That had raised her eyebrows and they'd all laughed at her expression.

'I remember Luke teaching me that once too,' said Chris. 'I would do it perfectly on the beach then get out in the water and forget to drag my foot up into position.'

They watched Luke lying in the sand beside Ash, showing her how to paddle and then pop up on their imaginary boards. Ash's hair was coming out of her loose top knot and red strands glistened with flecks of gold in the light. She was smiling, and Nikki could see the banter between the serious moments of learning.

'Hm, they certainly do get on well,' Nikki surmised. 'It's nice to see her laughing. I don't think I've seen her this relaxed ever.'

'I'd say living with Owen would have had its moments.'

Nikki looked at her husband. The cold glass of his beer reached his lips as he sipped, and she found she missed those lips. 'I feel rather lucky that life with you has been pretty good. Up until recently,' she added.

Chris smiled and then it faded upon her last words. His eyes latched onto her.

'What about second chances, Nik? I'm only human. I have moments of weakness like everyone else. Of stupidity. Lack of judgment. Loneliness that's too painful to bear at times.'

Nikki frowned. 'Lonely?' Why would Chris feel lonely? Nikki was the one who felt alone in her cancer turmoil.

'Yes, I feel alone because you push me away. Nikki, I've been trying hard to be there for you and help but you fob me off and try to deal with it alone. You shut me out. I know I haven't been through what you have and I can't possibly know how you feel but I wish you'd talk to someone about it. It's ripping us apart,' he said softly. 'It's ripping me apart.'

Her mouth felt dry, so she sipped her wine. She didn't know what to say. Chris took her moment of silence and used it to his advantage.

'I love you, I always will. This thing with Mandy . . . it's nothing.'

She squinted at the mention of *her* name and focused on the waves, back and forth, frothing onto the sand like a spilled fizzy drink.

'We went to school together in Katanning and got connected through our reunion page on Facebook. She lives in New

South Wales now because she married a man over there and has three kids.'

Nikki didn't want to hear this but she couldn't find her voice. Maybe some part of her did want to know the sordid details? The fact that Mandy lived in another state had her feeling a little better. She wouldn't be stuck wanting to drive by her house waiting for the courage to confront her, possibly with some form of weapon. She sighed. Who was she kidding? That would never happen. But the imagery of it in her mind was thrilling. Was a cricket bat too much?

'It started out as just normal catch-up messages, and then it got to photos of each other to see what we looked like. She's recently separated, and I think she was lonesome too. Anyway, she said I was still good looking and I guess the comments went to my head. It touched the lonely part of me that was craving some attention. Attention you wouldn't give me.'

Nikki shot him a frown.

Quickly Chris put up his hands. 'It's no excuse, I know, I'm just trying to explain how I was feeling at the time. We were so close, Nik, and then the surgery happened and it's been you on your own ever since. I can't even touch you without you cowering. Do you know how that makes me feel, every time?'

His words were thick with emotion. He paused, regaining some composure before clearing his throat. 'Anyway, Mandy just made me feel needed, I guess. I've not seen her in person, it's just been messages. She asks me how my day was when you're not interested. And it's only just got to the underwear photo, I swear. Nothing past that.' He shoved his hand in his hair and tugged on it before sliding it away.

'Would it have progressed further had I not found out?'
Nikki mumbled.

She was staring at Luke and Ash now but not really seeing
them; there was too much internal turmoil for her to focus.
She was conflicted, confused, angry, disappointed, jealous and
even slightly relieved. Images of Chris with someone else had
been her torture these past few days. It was amazing what the
mind could conjure up; like a movie it all played out over and
over again. She imagined what they might have said to each
other, how they would have undressed each other and the way
they might have made love. Such relief that he'd not got to that
point. And yet she still felt angry and betrayed. Yet his words
had also made her consider just how much she'd shut him out.
It wasn't like she'd meant to.

She felt his eyes on her as he spoke. 'Honestly, I don't know.
It felt wrong when it got to that stage and yet I liked having
someone interested in me. This is the first time you've ever shut
me out, Nikki. I don't know how to cope without you. I feel
like I'm just floating through each day waiting and hoping
that you'll come back to me. I just wish there was something
I could do to fix all this,' he finished with a sigh.

It felt like the longest few seconds as she downed the last
of her wine and placed it in the chair's cupholder.

'I'm not sure I'm fixable,' she said quietly, then she got up
and walked off up the beach without looking back.

With each step into the squeaky sand she tossed her thoughts
around like popcorn in a pan. The reality was that she didn't
feel whole, and she didn't know if she ever would again. Even
though Chris may not have technically cheated on her, in a

way he still had. The fact that he'd been finding comfort with another woman, even through messages, tore something inside her, leaving her somewhere between jealousy and shame. If she could have sorted herself out, then Chris wouldn't have been tempted by Mandy.

And then there was the real question: why couldn't she bear to have Chris touch her?

She knew there was a physiological explanation, and she could seek professional help to get her through it, but Nikki had been so sure she would get through it eventually, by herself. She thought that being alive to be with her family would be a strong enough pull to get her out of this feeling . . . and yet here she was, still feeling like she wasn't a complete woman. And if she didn't feel like a real woman, then how could Chris love her? Why would he want to touch her? She didn't like what she saw, so why would her husband?

Was she also keeping Chris at arm's length in case she got sick again? The cancer scare was the hardest thing she had ever had to face – deep down was she worried it might come back? She kept walking, powering through the sand with painful determination. Maybe Chris was right, maybe she did need to talk to someone. There were helplines and support groups; maybe there was some local support she could find?

'Mum, Mum, wait up!' called Chloe.

Nikki didn't hear her the first time but eventually her daughter's words penetrated and she turned just as Chloe almost slammed into her, wrapping an arm around her waist. The intrusion on her thoughts was a welcome distraction and she found herself smiling.

'Hello, my girl.' Nikki put her arm around her shoulder and together they walked arm in arm along the beach. She glanced back to see Chris looking sad and utterly alone. 'Finished looking for crabs?'

'Yeah, Josh caught three. Why do boys find that so exciting?'

Chloe looked up at her, eyes bright and blonde hair a little wild. Nikki loved this version of Chloe, a girl without a care or a dot of make-up. She looked just like a fifteen year old should.

'Well, I'm sure Josh says the same about you with clothes and make-up,' she replied.

Chloe sighed. 'Yeah, true.'

'So, are you having fun? Or still wishing you could Snapchat all five hundred friends a gazillion times a day?'

'Mum,' said Chloe rolling her eyes.

They took a few matching steps along the beach, close enough to the water that the sand was damp and cold.

'Well, it's okay,' Chloe eventually admitted. 'At first it was hard, but I kind of like not needing my phone. At times it feels like a relief. The pressure to make sure I keep up with everyone and comment on every photo so they don't think I hate them. It feels like I'll be left behind if I'm not on it or I'll miss something. I don't feel that stress here. I wake up in the morning and I don't have to reach for my phone. And it's been fun doing different things with Em. Riding bikes and building the cubby. Saving our baby lamb. And I like our nights by the fire and the jokes.'

Nikki tried to keep her smile hidden.

'Can we do this every year? But maybe in summer so we can swim and sunbake?' she added.

'I'd like that very much. I'm pretty sure Uncle Luke would too.'

'I can't wait to drive the ute. It's going to be so cool. Em and I were thinking of making some pancakes for breakfast tomorrow. And she also said she knows how to make honey joys. We haven't had them since my sixth birthday. We think tomorrow will be a good cooking day. Is that okay?'

'Sure, honey. We can help if you need it.'

'Nah, we should be all right. I think we have all the ingredients. If not, I'm sure Uncle Luke won't mind us raiding his supplies. Em said she'll teach me a few songs on her guitar tonight when we're set up in our hut. Oh, and we found a little lizard and have named him Steve.'

As Chloe prattled on beside her Nikki felt her heart swell. This was what she'd missed. Suddenly she could see a part of what Chris was missing.

She stopped walking and kissed Chloe's forehead. 'I would love to meet Steve.'

'What do we feed him?' she asked, but before Nikki could answer, a cold wave suddenly hit their feet and they both screamed as the water splashed up their legs and they ran backwards laughing.

'Mum, you should have seen your face. So funny.'

'Oh, my pants,' said Nikki between chuckles.

Nikki looked at the dark wet patch up between her legs.

'Looks like you wet yourself,' Chloe said with a snort.

'Why you . . .' Nikki launched at her daughter, causing her to squeal and take off running and laughing. Sand flicked up from her feet and Chloe giggled like a little girl as she tried to evade Nikki's grasping fingers.

In that moment Nikki felt the most alive she'd been in ages. And it was glorious.

29

Nikki — The Past

'DON'T LIFT THAT. HERE, I'VE GOT IT,' SAID CHRIS AS HE swooped in and stole the washing basket right from her grasp.

Nikki gritted her teeth and tried to control the build-up of steam like a kettle about to boil. Chris had been amazing . . . in the beginning, but now he was just irritating.

She was fully fit, able to get back to normal, or at least she was trying to, but Chris was still treating her with kid gloves. Going above and beyond in the supportive husband department.

Nikki headed into Chloe's room. Normally she wouldn't attempt it but she desperately wanted to clean something. The soft blue doona cover was screwed up at the end of her bed as if Chloe had kicked it there before getting out. Nikki made the bed and then began to collect the clothes on the floor; some were clean and some weren't, so she just took them all.

She reached down and grimaced, half expecting the movement to hurt, but relaxed when there was no pain. It was strange – sometimes she felt like her breasts were still there. It was almost like the sensation following her breast augmentation, but instead of having to get used to suddenly having breasts, now there was nothing.

'Here, I'll pop them in the wash,' said Chris appearing from nowhere like a genie.

Nikki sighed. 'I can put a load of washing on, Chris.'

'I know,' he said with a smile and took a step back. 'I'm just trying to help.'

He put his hand on her shoulder and she flinched, from habit. 'Sorry. It still feels like it will hurt,' she said before shrugging and heading to the laundry. She couldn't handle the apologetic sadness she saw in his eyes. It wasn't even his fault and yet she kept hurting him, without meaning to.

That night she stood in the bathroom, undressed to shower, and stared at herself in the mirror. The doctor had confirmed they'd removed the small tumour successfully, it was all clear and she was cancer-free. Cancer-free. Those two words bounced around in her head far too often, as if she needed to remind herself of what they actually meant. And could they really be trusted?

Nikki moved her body in the light, but no matter how she stood the scars reminded her of eyebrows on a cartoon character. She traced the red marks, over the fine bumps. Every time she undressed she found herself staring at them, maybe trying to remember what her previous breasts looked like or maybe just trying to adjust to this new version. She had been scared to show Chris the first time. To the point she looked away so she couldn't read his expression. If he was disappointed or upset, she couldn't have that image stuck in her mind forever.

'Not much different from my one small boob,' she'd half joked when the silence had become unbearable.

'It is what it is, babe. Doesn't mean I love you any less. If anything I love you so much more for being so brave and strong. For doing the best thing to keep you around for me and our kids.'

He'd taken her chin and turned her face to him and he'd waited for her to open her eyes.

When she did, all she'd seen was the love he'd spoken about, brimming in his eyes as he gazed at her.

'I miss my breasts,' she'd said softly.

'When you're ready you can have reconstructive surgery,' he'd reminded her.

She knew that. They'd talked about it and decided to wait; the reconstructive surgery would take longer to heal and Nikki didn't want anything to disrupt their lives any longer than necessary. Nor did she want to risk her family finding out. She knew her parents would have a pink fit at hearing 'breast cancer', and their worry and stress would go through the roof. It had been Nikki's decision to just get the mastectomy done, get the cancer out and get home and back to the kids as soon as possible without making too much fuss.

The bathroom door rattled behind her.

'Nikki?'

Chris tried the door again.

'I'm just going to have a shower. Be out in a minute.' Nikki quickly turned the tap on, causing the water to hit the tiles with a splash.

'Kids aren't home yet,' he said.

'Sorry, habit,' she said again and stepped into the warm water.

She'd started locking the door just in case the kids came in. It wasn't uncommon for Chloe to wander in while she was having a shower to get more toothpaste or steal her fake tan or moisturiser. And it was because of this that Chris understood her reasoning.

But that was a lie.

It wasn't just the kids she didn't want to see her naked.

She was scared enough of her own feelings, she couldn't handle seeing his too. It was okay during the day when she could wear her prosthesis – though her Knitted Knockers were lighter and didn't rub against her scars – and pretend she was normal, but at shower time it was real. As real as a face slap hard enough to rattle teeth.

Then there was bedtime. Waiting. Wondering. Knowing Chris was counting down until she was ready for sex. How long could she put it off?

By the time she was out of the shower and dressed and had tidied the bathroom she heard the kids bang through the front door. Rushing towards the kitchen, their usual port of call, she hoped to catch them before they vanished into their rooms.

'Hey kids, how was school?' she asked.

'All right,' said Josh as he dropped his bag in its usual spot by the side wall and then immersed his head in the fridge like he'd just come in from a long run in the sun.

Chloe was opening the cupboard where the biscuits were kept, two white cords dangling from her ears like long noodles. Nikki had to tap her on the shoulder.

'Good day?' she asked.

'Huh?' Chloe mumbled and then pulled out one ear piece as if it pained her to do so.

'How was your day?' Nikki motioned to the stove. 'Would you like some pancakes?'

'Nah, thanks,' Chloe said loudly. 'I'll just have a muesli bar.'

Then she shoved the ear bud back in and headed to her room.

Nikki sighed. 'What about you, Josh? Pancakes?'

Josh had since removed himself from the fridge and had just lined some bread with a wedge of butter, then slapped another bit on top before taking a big bite.

'I'm good.'

She watched him head to his room, the butter and knife where he'd left them. When they were little, Nikki had been the centre of their universe. She couldn't leave the room without them wanting to go with her, and know what she was doing every second and why.

This morphing into independent little humans was hard to take.

'Seen the kids?' asked Chris as he paused beside her.

'I did, briefly.'

'I'll go see if I can get Josh to help me with the lawns,' he said and then headed towards the bedrooms.

Nikki went and tidied up the lounge room before making a start on dinner. Chris came in later, slightly sweaty in his singlet and smelling like cut grass.

'So much for Josh helping?' she queried.

'Josh couldn't start it and then went AWOL.' He rolled his eyes. 'I'll just have a quick shower and then help you with dinner.'

Nikki prepared dinner as fast as she could so that when Chris came back she was serving it up onto plates.

'I'll get the kids,' he said when he saw she was sorted.

Dinner was quiet. Chris tried to talk to the kids, engaging them about news events and what was happening at school, but in the end it felt like just the adults talking while the kids scoffed their dinner so they could leave the table and get back to whatever it was they were doing before food interrupted. With everything that had been going on before and after Nikki's surgery she and Chris had let the phone rules lapse a bit. Nikki knew it was time to get a handle on things, get back to a good routine.

'I think we just manage food-disposal units now,' said Chris as he collected the empty plates. 'I can't wait until Josh starts playing soccer again so at least we can discuss that.'

'I might take Chloe shopping on the weekend. Maybe we could all go to the movies?' she suggested.

The clear-up didn't take long with Chris loading the dishwasher and Nikki wiping down the table. With each minute bedtime was drawing closer.

Nikki had learned how comfortable it could be to sleep without breasts. Quickly she undid her bra, the Knitted Knockers falling onto the bed, and pulled on her black singlet. It was firm and fitting around the chest so no chance of her top gaping and revealing her scars. She pulled on her full-length blue striped cotton flannel pyjamas before scooping up her wool breasts and shoving them in her bedside bottom drawer.

She was reading *The Testaments* when Chris finally joined her in bed.

Putting her purple bookmark in between the pages, she placed it on the bedside table next to her phone and flicked off the light.

'Don't let me stop you reading,' said Chris as he got comfortable under the blankets.

'It's okay, I've read enough.'

She rolled onto her side away from Chris but she felt him move closer. His legs brushed against hers, which was fine because he was warm and toasty. Then his hard chest pressed against her back. She could smell his deodorant and feel his breath against her neck.

His hand touched her hip before moving up to pull her closer. But when his hand landed inches from her chest she jumped. It was more like a spasm, the kind she couldn't control and made her whole body kick out, causing Chris to pull back.

'Sorry,' he said quickly. 'I didn't think . . .'

His words fell away. Nikki didn't know what he was going to say but figured he didn't either. They lay there for long agonising moments just listening to each other breathe.

'I'm so sorry,' he murmured, and she felt sick. A coldsweat sick full of guilt and exhaustion. Without warning tears sprang from her eyes and within seconds she was sobbing uncontrollably.

She reached her hand back, searching for Chris, unable to tell him how she felt for the gasping sobs that stole her breath. But he found her hand and held it in his, squeezing firmly. He stayed away, only their hands touching, until she started to calm down. Her reaction had scared her, so god knows what it would have done to Chris.

The last time they'd had sex was two nights before her surgery. Nikki had loved every minute of the hot, passionate lovemaking. Now the very thought of getting intimate made her break out in a sweat.

She wiped her face on her pyjama top.

'I'm sorry,' she muttered.

'Oh, honey, it's okay. Look at me,' he pleaded.

Nikki rolled over to face him, even though she could only just make out his face from the faint light from their ensuite.

'I need more time,' she'd whispered to him. She couldn't wash away the fear of being intimate with Chris. It had nothing to do with him and all to do with herself. Her scars were mental and physical.

'We could go and talk to someone,' Chris said quietly.

Shaking her head she replied, 'No. I'll be okay. Just time.' She reached out and caressed his face. 'It's just taking a bit to get used to. I'll be all be good soon.'

That's what she kept telling herself.

Soon she would feel better.

'Okay, well, you just let me know when you're ready. I don't want to pressure you. But know that I'm not scared by your scars.'

No, but I am.

And as the weeks went by Chris remained patient and diligent as ever. She knew he was waiting for a sign, a small nod, anything to welcome him in but the longer she waited the harder it got. She was getting used to her safe space, used it like a cocoon she could hide inside.

Only, she was so busy hiding from herself that she didn't notice the change in Chris. She didn't see the sadness in his eyes or the loneliness. All she saw was her own suffering.

30

Ashley

'HERE, THIS SHOULD FIT YOU.'

Luke passed her a black wobbly wetsuit that felt like a seal skin and watched as she held it against her. He was right, it should fit.

'Did this belong to your wife?' she asked without thinking and then mentally cursed.

Luke was loading surfboards onto the back of his ute. He was in shorts, even though it was very chilly in the early morning, and a black hoodie that made his eyes look like silver moons in the night sky. Ash snuggled further into her blue knit jumper and tugged the beanie down over her ears. Everyone else was still asleep except for the birds that chatted excitedly in the trees around them. Luke glanced at her over his shoulder, his expression inscrutable. Was he almost smiling or was that a grimace?

'No, it's a second-hand one I picked up in town. I thought

having a few extras of different sizes would be handy for guests. They haven't been used in years but they still do the job.'

'Have they been checked for spiders?' she said, tilting her head to the side and holding the wetsuit away from her.

Luke laughed. 'They're kept in a sealed container. All good.' He tied a knot in the rope that secured the boards and then threw their towels and wetsuits on the back. 'Let's get going.'

Ash felt a nervousness ripple through her body as she climbed into the ute beside him. Maybe it was his fresh-scented clothes or his recently deodorant-sprayed body, or the thought of sharks or the cold water. Or the huge possibility of making a fool of herself. Again.

Chewing the inside of her cheek she watched Luke as he drove with relaxed ease. It was mesmerising, his movements natural, as if he could drive this track blindfolded and knew he wouldn't get bogged. She liked the ruggedness of his stubble. He was so different to Owen. Owen didn't touch power tools, didn't do home repairs unless it was the computer. His job at the mine had involved sitting in an office managing safety protocols, and before that job he worked in an office for a computer-repair company. But Luke was someone who reminded her of her own father who loved to tinker in his shed, making toys for his kids and fixing stuff around the house. If Ash ever had a dodgy door or a broken panel in her fence her dad would often come over to fix it. Maybe that's why she found Luke so appealing – she could see her dad, a man she'd idolised growing up, reflected in the man beside her.

It doesn't hurt that Luke is gorgeous either.

Ash sighed. What was she in for this morning? 'You will make sure I don't get sucked out to sea in a rip or drown?

Or become shark food? Is there some form you can sign that guarantees I'll survive this?' she said.

He glanced at her, frowning.

Ash smiled, letting him know she was just teasing.

'Sorry, no guarantees here but I can pretty much vouch that no shark will swim into the white wash where we will be.'

'That's reassuring . . . I think.'

The ute ducked and weaved around the shrubs and bushes. Her belly lifted as they started the descent.

'Do you ever get sick of this view?' she asked. 'Has it become less amazing over the years?' The rugged, craggy coastline was something she couldn't imagine growing tired of, especially the baby blue almost turquoise water that morphed into a sapphire and midnight blue out deep. Shark territory. Shark blue, she would call it. Even now she scanned the ocean, looking for pointed fins and hoping she saw a whale instead, or dolphins.

'No, never. One of the reasons I can't leave. I just couldn't bear not being able to drive down here when I want. It's like my own meditation retreat. Good for the soul.'

They pulled up on the beach and Luke turned off the ute and then smiled at her.

'What?' she said, with a frown.

'Blue looks good on you,' he eventually said.

'Thanks. It also happens to be my favourite colour,' she said, pretty sure her face now matched the colour of her hair.

Ash helped Luke get the surfboards off and then he placed a small tarp on the ground.

'It makes it easier to get the wetsuit on and off if you're not standing in sand,' he said and then proceeded to take off his shirt.

Ash clung to the wetsuit like a safety blanket as her eyes bulged and her tongue stuck to the roof of her mouth. *Good lord.*

'Wow, do you work out?' she blurted.

You idiot! Stop staring.

But she couldn't.

To her surprise, Luke chuckled.

In her haste to do something other than stare she started to rip off her clothes too.

'Interesting bathers,' he said.

Ash rolled her eyes. 'Underwear is practically bathers. Besides, I didn't think I'd be swimming, it's winter!' She felt a little self-conscious about standing in her underwear but hoped he was too busy to notice much.

She soon realised getting into wetsuits wasn't as quick or easy as she had imagined, and Luke had plenty of time to see her black cotton briefs and crop top against her pale skin. It would have been completely embarrassing except for the fact that Luke had dropped his shorts and was wrestling into his own wetsuit. She had time to inspect his black trunks with a white Bonds band, and smiled.

'You're one to talk,' she said.

He shrugged. 'Bathers are a waste of time for blokes. In summer I usually surf in my shorts.'

Maybe this surfing thing wouldn't be so bad after all. It had been a long time since she'd seen a man nearly naked, and the only ones that looked like Luke had been on TV the last time she'd binge-watched *Hart of Dixie* and anything with Jason Momoa or Chris Hemsworth.

'Did you used to surf with your wife?' she asked.

Luke motioned for her to turn around so he could zip her up. 'Do you always just say what's on your mind?'

Ash turned when he was done, sucking on her bottom lip, and nodded. 'Sorry. Only when I'm nervous,' she added and then cursed herself. Which was pretty much most of the time.

Luke grinned and zipped up his own wetsuit from the front. 'There's nothing to be nervous about. I'll be right beside you the whole time.'

That's what Ash was hoping but it was also what was making her so jittery.

'Right, let's start with some beach practice popping up on the board first.'

As Luke set up their boards she quickly braided her hair; she wasn't the best swimmer and didn't need to be drowned by her own locks. Her long strands were like red pythons trying to strangle her if not contained.

'How do you do that?' Luke asked.

'Practice. Lots of practice.'

'Good, I might make a surfer out of you yet.'

Then he put her through her paces on the board. He'd given her a long board that was a bit thicker than the normal ones she'd seen, better for beginners.

'Okay, now let's get into the water.' He picked up his board, tied the strap to his ankle and headed down to the waves.

Ash followed suit and squeaked when the freezing water hit her feet. But to her relief as she walked further into the waves nothing else was cold, thanks to the wetsuit.

She staggered against the current as the waves crashed through her on their way out. The salty water felt silky against her skin, a little cold but only on her feet and hands. She bounced off from the bottom and felt the wonderful natural buoyancy along with the extra flotation from her wetsuit. 'Gosh, I haven't been in the ocean for years.' She was ashamed to say just how long. The ebb and flow moved her body as if she were doing Tai Chi.

'It's my religion,' said Luke. 'Being in the water is cleansing. It's also a bit addictive. Right, hop on your board and let's try to catch a small wave.'

Ash climbed onto her board and felt like a seal at a zoo show, beaching itself on the side of the pool for a treat. All thoughts of trying to look graceful died.

'Now I'm going to give you a little push into this next wave so you can focus on popping up.'

She glanced back, saw a small wave peaking along with her nerves. Quickly she faced forward as she felt the board scoot forward and the swell of the wave gather behind her. She tried to get up and made it to almost standing before the surfboard went out from under her.

Being under the water felt safe and quiet, and for a moment she moved with the swell before coming up for air. Luke was smiling and clapping.

'Good job. Again,' he said encouragingly.

Luke kept pushing her board into some of the smaller waves and shouting encouraging commands.

'Now, pop, that's it. Wider stance. Keep your hands flat on the board, don't hang onto the edge.'

'Look where you want to go, not at your feet.'

'Keep your knees bent, that's it.'

On her third go she got up and rode the white wash for a little way, starting to get the feel of the board and her balance before falling off with a splash.

She shot him a look. 'It's harder than it looks,' she said as she made her way back to him. It was a good workout, moving against the current, and she was puffing slightly.

'Yeah, but you're going great. You have good balance, considering,' he said with a smirk.

'Considering what?'

'Considering walking on land is . . . um . . .'

'Challenging?' she offered.

He laughed and she couldn't help but laugh with him. She enjoyed his good-hearted teasing.

Luke glanced behind them as a wave further out rolled in.

'Are they good waves?' she asked. He nodded. 'Well, you go. I think I'm good here to keep practising and I can touch the bottom, so I'm unlikely to drown.'

'You sure?'

'Yep.'

'Okay, just remember to paddle hard so you're moving when the wave reaches you.'

After a few attempts Ash could see why he was pushing her into waves – paddling was harder than it looked, and if she left her run too late she would miss her chance. Luke made it all look effortless, he seemed to glide across the water like he had fins on his hands and feet. While taking a rest, lying on the board, she found herself floating and just watching Luke. There was a synchronicity between his body and the wave, like a symphony it was a blended piece of magical music. It brought back her schoolgirl crush on Kelly Slater.

'You're not doing much practice,' said Luke as he paddled over after his last wave.

'I'm studying the master,' she said with a smile. 'It looks so cool. I wouldn't mind getting that good.'

Luke straddled his board like a horse. He seemed exhilarated and peaceful at the same time. She was drawn to the energy he was radiating.

'There's nothing to say you can't get a board and surf back in Perth. Where do you live? I can tell you the nearest beaches for good surfing and what kind of board to get.'

Ash tried to imagine strapping a board to the roof of her car and heading out to catch waves as the sun came up. It seemed magical. Was it possible to do? It could be her new thing just for herself. She did have a lot of free time now with no work.

'Thanks, Luke. I might actually do that. You may regret offering to help,' she said with a chuckle. But the idea of calling him after this holiday ended was very appealing.

'Never,' he said with a grin. 'I could talk surfing and boards until the cows come home. You're always welcome to come back here for a surf, any time.'

'Cheers. I must say I'm having a ball. I don't think I've felt so relaxed in ages. I think it's been great to try to figure out who I am now.'

'It's a bit like that after huge changes. I understand, I think, how you're feeling.'

Water dripped from his damp hair and his long eyelashes. They stared at each other as they bobbed over the waves and their boards drew closer.

'Maybe that's why I feel so comfortable with you,' she said, though there was nothing comfortable about the way her heart was starting to race under his entrancing gaze.

'Come on,' he said, eventually breaking the silence. 'I want to show you something.' He lay down on his board. 'It's a bit of a paddle, and we have to get out over the waves. Think you can do it?' he said, shooting her a challenging smile.

'If you can do it, so can I,' she replied, more bravely than she felt. But at this moment she would probably follow him to the ends of the earth.

His eyes sparkled before he turned and began to paddle out to sea.

She squeezed her eyes shut and blinked as sea spray coated her face but she paddled on, not as gracefully as Luke but she tried to remember the technique he'd shown her and soon was gliding over the waves behind him.

He took her into the sapphire waters, but she didn't dare look down, just kept paddling out past the rocky headland and then Luke headed right as they skirted around the rocks. 'We won't get caught up in the waves that crash against the rocks here,' he called, then he glanced back. 'How ya going?'

She could only nod. *Don't look down. Don't look for sharks. Head up.*

'We're nearly there,' he said, pointing.

That's when she noticed a tiny, well-hidden patch of sand as they edged further around the rocks. It was like a baby beach, maybe ten metres wide. A semi-circular patch of sand nestled between rocky headlands that almost hid it.

As Ash got off her board and walked up the beach she noticed a little translucent pool off to the left, and a rock ledge that hung out, creating a cave.

'Wow, this place is gorgeous. What's it called?'

Luke, lying on his side, was on the sand beside his board and Ash joined him as they got their breath back. She just wanted to be next to him, to keep this dreamy exhilaration that she felt in his company.

'I call it Secret Beach. I don't think anyone knows it's here. There's no track to it.'

'Are you going to make one?'

He shook his head slowly. 'I like keeping it a secret. You're the first person I've brought here.'

Ash opened her mouth, making a silent O.

Sand covered his black wetsuit and water lapped at their legs. He laid his head down on his outstretched arm, silver eyes stuck on her.

'It was after Denise left that I found this spot.' His lashes moved like silent waves as he blinked slowly. 'I was lost. Hurting. Struggling to breathe. So angry. I finally got on my board and just spent ages in the water.' He paused and looked down as he drew circles in the damp sand. 'Maybe I was waiting for a shark, or for the current to draw me way out to sea, I don't know. It was a dark time and I was so bitter. Anyway, I found myself way out there,' he said, pointing out to sea. 'Something made me look back and that's when I saw the tiny bit of white. It drew me.' Luke's voice dropped, raw and gravelly. 'I felt like this place showed me that life was still beautiful, you know?'

Ash nodded. 'It's nice to be reminded.' She waited a moment, then ventured softly, 'So . . . Denise?'

He sighed. 'She wasn't happy. I think she felt trapped in our marriage, in her role as a wife and mother. She was always a creative free spirit and I guess I knew that when I asked her to marry me. I thought we could make it work. And then Micky came along and as I grew happy to be a father, Denise seemed to struggle. Probably a bit of post-natal depression; well, that's what I used to tell myself in order to understand why she could just leave. I thought after a break she might come back but she never did and then I learned she'd met some hippy, who I assume she's still with.'

He rolled onto his back, and Ash leaned over so she could look down at him.

'It took me a long time to let go of Denise, and the anger and resentment I felt towards her leaving us both. But in the end I wouldn't change a thing because I have Micky.'

Ash was so moved by his honesty, without thinking she moved her hand to caress his face, running her thumb across his stubbly chin. She didn't know what to say. Instead she bent down and gently kissed his lips. It was just a peck and yet she still felt the lasting pressure of them against hers. She itched to lick her lips but he was staring at her, a little surprised. He wasn't the only one. The kiss had come from nowhere, an impulse.

'Sorry. I couldn't think of what to say,' she admitted as her face flared with heat. 'I can't imagine how hard that time was for you and Micky.'

Luke reached up and tugged on her plait, his lips curving slightly, before weaving his hand behind her head and drawing her closer. Ash didn't have time to think before he'd crushed his lips against hers. This was no peck. The salty taste of his lips as they met hers was exhilarating and at some point she had to gasp for breath and in the next moment Luke's tongue was deepening the kiss. Moist and electrifying, tasting like the sea and setting her skin alight. She'd not been kissed like this in a very long time. She'd forgotten how roller-coaster, hang-onto-your-hat, ride-of-your-life it could be.

'Wow,' she mumbled as they pulled apart, gasping for air.

'Sorry, I couldn't help it. You're just too bloody irresistible with your damp red hair and sparkling blue eyes.'

'You must be the only person I know who thinks that,' she said with a shy smile.

'Oh, I'd bet I'm not.' He reached up and touched her cheek, tracing her skin as if he were connecting her freckles with his finger.

'You know, you're the first person I've kissed since Owen . . .' Her words faded away. She didn't know how she should feel. Guilty? Normally she would but in this moment she felt alive, and like Luke said, you can't live in the past. Owen wasn't here; he wasn't coming back. She was allowed to kiss other people. 'It still feels a little strange, thinking I'm allowed to kiss another man. I still feel married to Owen.'

'I understand,' he said quietly. 'I'm sorry if I've gone too far. This is my first too,' he admitted. 'It's been years. I hope I wasn't too bad?' he added, trying to lighten the mood.

Ash's heart was still pounding in her ears like the crash of the waves over the nearby rocks. Luke was looking at her like he wanted to devour her and it made her body tingle all over.

'No, you haven't.' She gave him a reassuring smile. 'At some point I do need to move on, I get that. It's just . . . strange. It's new,' she muttered, while trying to hide her grin. 'I might have to try it again just to see if it gets any better.'

She'd barely got her words out before he kissed her again. Scooping her up in his arms he rolled her over, crushing her against the wet sand and opening the kiss. Ash clutched his wetsuit-clad body, revelling in the weight and hardness of him. Her tongue searched for his as their lips crashed together and a big wave splashed over them, which only made the whole thing feel hotter.

'Better?' he managed to huff out against her lips.

'You're getting there,' she replied, grinning like a fool.

He lifted himself up on his hands. 'Come on, I want to show you the pool.' He did a push-up so he could give her one last quick kiss before standing up. He reached out a hand and she took it, relieved that he'd ended the moment and yet her body craved more.

'Thank you,' she said, knowing he'd stopped so they didn't rush into anything, that it was new territory for both of them.

It was the right choice, even if the taste of his lips still burned on hers and the weight of his body still lingered.

31

Nikki

NIKKI HEARD ASH LAUGH BEFORE SHE GLANCED OVER THE
top of her book to see her friend walk past with Luke. Ever
since the surf lesson yesterday she'd noticed a slight change in
them both. Maybe it was the fact that they walked a few inches
closer together or when they shared a look it wasn't fleeting.

Was she watching the beginning of a blossoming friendship
or a new romance? Either way it made her feel a little excited
for them, because they both deserved some fun. Ash seemed
so much more confident and relaxed in a way that made Nikki
wonder if she was finally seeing her friend for the first time.
Even just talking about Owen so openly had changed both
Ash and Emily. And the changes were spreading. At breakfast
Josh had dropped a piece of bacon in the sand and then chased
Chloe around the campsite threatening to put it in her mouth
or her hair, both of them screaming and laughing.

'Dad would have had a pink fit if we'd done this at home,'
Emily had said to Ash.

'I know,' she said, and they shared a smile. 'Owen couldn't deal with loud noises,' she explained to Nikki. 'His stress levels would go through the roof, so we always tried to keep a quiet, calm house.'

'Quiet? With kids? I can't imagine what that must have been like. Is there such a thing?' Nikki replied gently.

Even Emily seemed more open, sharing the things she loved doing with Owen. How most nights he would sing her to sleep with some nineties tunes or songs he'd written just for her.

'He used to sing Pearl Jam's "Better Man" but changed it to "Better Girl",' she'd said and played it the night before by the fire with tears glistening in her eyes.

'Is it just me or are those two getting on like a house on fire?' said Chris, gesturing to Ash and Luke. He sat down beside Nikki with a book in his hand.

It was early afternoon and it felt like rain wasn't far away, with the scent of it on the breeze. Everyone was rugged up in jumpers, and Nikki had donned her ugg boots and pulled her chair as close to the fire as she could safely get. Luke kept the wood well stocked so the flames were always warm and inviting.

'Do them both good,' she replied. 'What are the girls doing?' she asked, her eyes still on her book but not reading.

'Um, they're in their hut working on some dance moves or something for a TikTok thing? I'm not even sure if I have that right but it's an app, apparently.'

Nikki recalled Chloe mentioning it once after she asked what she was doing dancing in her cupboard filming herself.

'I think they plan on posting them when they get their phone signal back,' Chris added. 'Apparently I might have to make a cameo appearance one day.'

She nodded and tried to focus on her book again, *Diamonds and Dust*. What a fascinating life this woman had, the hardships and tragedy. It certainly made her think about her own life, which seemed rather easy in comparison.

'Nik . . . um, would it be okay if I moved back into the hut? Our hut?'

Chris's words had taken a moment to register. She put her book down and glanced at him, his eyes as big as dish plates and his face slightly red as if he were holding his breath.

Nikki closed her eyes and thought for a moment.

'It's just that Josh saw me coming out of the house this morning and I don't want to worry the kids. I can sleep in the bunk,' he added.

He made sense, and Nikki didn't want the kids to find out either. They didn't need to worry about their parents. So, she nodded her agreement while Chris breathed out. He opened his mouth to say something else but then closed it. With a sigh he picked up his book and began to read.

They stayed quite amicable for the rest of the afternoon, mainly because Nikki was so engrossed in her book. It wasn't until after dinner, when the rain had come down in a steady shower, that things started to go pear-shaped. Chairs were hurriedly dragged back into the camp kitchen while the fire hissed and spat with each drop that landed on the red-hot coals.

'It doesn't look like it's going to stop,' said Ash snuggling further into her jumper.

'I'm going back to our hut before we need gumboots,' said Em.

'Good plan.' Chloe grabbed her hand and together they

took off, squealing as they splashed through small puddles that were beginning to grow.

Josh and Micky were already up at the house engrossed in a darts competition, and Nikki couldn't imagine them voluntarily coming back outside.

'Nice. It's just the adults. Shall we break out the wine and board games?' asked Ash.

'I'm in,' said Luke as he pulled out a chair and sat at the table in the middle of the camp kitchen. He turned to watch the rain splash down from the large opening, then, just as Nikki was thinking that it was a little chilly, he jumped up to light the gas heater in the far corner and drag it over to the table.

'What game?' said Chris as he pulled out Sequence and a deck of cards from the cupboard.

'How about we start with some easy card games,' said Nikki. 'Like Fish and Poker.'

'Oh yes, I haven't played cards in ages. Em and I used to play Fish when she was five.' Ash sat at the table after retrieving glasses and a bottle of wine from the back of the fridge. She poured everyone a generous amount.

'That's like two standard drinks,' said Nikki with a chuckle.

Ash shrugged. 'Why do they make the glasses so big, then? Seems like such a waste.'

As she filled Luke's glass her eyes flicked to his and they shared the sort of smile that made Nikki look away; it was so intense she felt like she was intruding.

'Right, I'll shuffle,' Chris said, sitting down next to Luke and oblivious to the sexual energy.

By the end of their second game of Fish their wine glasses were empty. Nikki got up to refill them while they discussed what to play next.

'Strip poker,' joked Chris.

'It's too bloody cold,' said Ash but her face was flushed pink and her gaze on Luke more often than not.

'No!' Nikki cringed and sipped more of her wine. The rain had eased up to just a light shower but the smell was invigorating and she welcomed it against her flushed, alcohol-warm body.

But that all changed when Chris put his hand on hers. It felt warm but threatening, like a bee about to sting. She pulled her hand away in anger and shot him a look that could curdle milk.

'Come on, Nikki,' he said softly. 'I miss you.'

The look on his face churned her up inside and she felt the emotion take over, bubbling to the surface and ready to cause pain that she couldn't contain. He didn't get to say something like that and make her feel like the bad guy. She didn't want to be cruel, but her response was automatic.

'Well,' she spat, 'you should have thought of that before *Mandy.*'

He sat back in his chair and threw his cards down as if she'd slapped him. 'Why don't you just tell everyone,' he said sarcastically.

Luke and Ash both toyed with the cards in their hands, but the tension around the table was undeniable.

Nikki knew the alcohol was fuelling her choice of words but couldn't stop them. 'They already know parts of it. Why hide the truth? Why shouldn't they know that you've been texting another woman?'

Poor Luke didn't know where to look, he just squirmed in his chair like a kid strapped into a stroller, along for the ride whether he wanted to be or not.

'Because they don't know the whole story,' Chris said, a hint of bitterness in his voice. His eyes darted from Nikki to Ash. 'You want us to tell the truth? Then why don't you tell them about your surgery? About why you've been so distant and closed off?'

Nikki felt something smack her, cold and wet like a fish, but it was just Chris's powerful words that woke her from her cosy wine cocoon. Her mouth fell open as she stared at him in disbelief. 'How dare you share that,' she whispered with venom.

'*Why hide the truth* – they were your words! And besides, we're among friends and family,' he stated.

Nikki sat frozen, her hand on her wine glass as she stared at the liquid, waiting for it to drown her. It seemed an easier option than facing the truth, to talk about what she'd been through.

Ash looked at her with concern. Luke was still staring at his hands and in that moment Nikki realised that this was probably the best time to tell her, while she was half drunk.

'Want me to fill them in?' Chris said, his tone suddenly subdued.

Nikki leaned forward and put her face in her hands and breathed out slowly, her head feeling a little fuzzy.

'Nikki? Are you okay?' Ash put her hand on her shoulder.

She kept it there, the gentle movement making Nikki feel better. She wanted Chris to tell them, but this was her journey, her demons to fight, and maybe this was a step in the right direction. She inhaled deeply and dropped her hands, clutching them together in front of her. She couldn't look at Ash or Luke or even Chris, she just focused on her hands as she mustered up the courage to say the words she feared.

'I found a cancer lump in my breast,' she said with a shaky breath.

Ash's hand kept up its rhythmic movement in a way that gave her strength. Ash hadn't shouted with shock, or inhaled loudly or even stopped moving her hand. All these things kept Nikki steady.

'I underwent surgery not long ago to have it removed . . . along with my breasts.'

'You had a mastectomy?' Ash asked.

Nikki nodded. She could hear the shock in Ash's voice, even though she tried hard to hide it.

'Yes, a double mastectomy.'

'Why didn't you tell me?' Ash said. 'I could have been there to help. Even if it was looking after the kids. You daft woman,' she said with love.

Nikki was so shocked by Ash's comment that she turned to face her friend. The smile on Ash's face wasn't the pity-filled expression she was expecting.

'I'm sorry, I didn't want to tell anyone. I haven't told my parents or the kids. I just don't want anyone to worry.'

'Is there anything to worry about?' Ash asked seriously. She wore a black beanie with her hoodie over the top but a few red strands had escaped and framed her face.

'No, I got the all clear.'

'Good, then I won't worry,' she said matter-of-factly. 'I just wish you'd shared this so I could have been there for you.'

Nikki sighed. 'I thought I was doing the right thing. I didn't want to upset the kids or worry my parents after Dad's cancer scare. I guess maybe I was trying to downplay the whole thing, and by telling even you, I was admitting it. I didn't want to become a *cancer* person. I just wanted life to stay normal.'

'But it hasn't been normal, has it, honey?' said Chris softly.

Nikki could only shake her head. Chris was right, even though she didn't want him to be. All the anger and fight seemed to seep from her body. Now she just felt tired.

'How long ago was this? Are you still sore?' Ash asked, concerned.

Luke reached for the wine bottle and topped up Nikki's glass, shooting her a supportive smile while Chris remained quiet but attentive.

'It's been nearly six months.'

'Shit, you know how to keep a secret,' said Ash taking a sip of her wine. 'How did you manage that?'

'Same as you, I guess,' said Chris. 'Lots of white lies.'

'Touché,' replied Ash, nodding.

Nikki continued when she realised Chris hadn't upset Ash by pointing out their similarities. 'I had the operation during school holidays and my parents had the kids so I could recover at home. We told them we were sneaking off on a romantic getaway.'

'Are you going to tell them? Your parents and the kids?' asked Ash, glancing to the girls' hut.

Nikki shrugged. 'I don't know. I don't really want to. I don't want them to worry, but I hate lying to them. I'm worried they'll just get anxious about it, and worry the cancer might come back. I want them to be happy, carefree kids. If the results had been bad and I had to undergo chemo, then I would have told them; I wouldn't have been able to hide it. But this?' She shrugged again.

Ash screwed up her face. 'Hm, I don't know. What I *have* learned though is that our kids are quite capable and they don't like being left out or lied to.'

Nikki nodded. She met Chris's eyes, large and golden like honey, and she realised that there was no way she could have got through this without him. He had been amazing. But he had faltered because she had struggled to find herself.

'How are the scars?' asked Ash.

'They're as expected, I guess.' She forced a smile. 'It is a bit weird having no breasts.'

'You know, I hadn't even noticed,' Ash said gently.

Nikki gave a small smile. 'You wouldn't. I wear a prosthesis; it helps me feel a little normal,' she admitted. 'And I can have reconstructive surgery. But I'm not sure I want to go through surgery again.'

'I can't imagine what all this has been like for you, Nikki, but I think you are incredibly brave. Just know I'm always here, for whatever you need.' Ash gripped Nikki's hand. 'You're my best friend.'

Nikki smiled. The alcohol was probably doing a lot of talking in this conversation but she no longer cared. 'Thanks, Ash, that means a lot.' She blinked as the sudden onslaught of tears prickled in her eyes.

Ash saw them and scooped her up in a hug.

It was a warm, tight hug and the feelings it brought were ones she had missed and hadn't realised she'd been craving for a while. She'd been too scared to hug Chris in case he got the wrong idea and she didn't want to lead him on . . . but, oh how she'd missed being hugged.

'Thank you,' she whispered again against Ash's ear.

This holiday was supposed to be about the kids and getting them to reconnect. Nikki hadn't realised that she would need some reconnecting too.

32
Ashley

ASH WAS UP EARLY. SHE HAD ALWAYS BEEN AN EARLY RISER, taking solace in the quiet before dealing with the day.

There was a skip in Ash's step as she carefully dodged puddles on her way to the bathroom to brush her teeth and freshen up before walking over to the sheds. Her heart was racing and she felt like a nervous teenager off to meet her new boyfriend. Not that Luke was her boyfriend; she didn't know what he was just yet.

Luke was leaning against his red ute, waiting. Long legs clad in light denim jeans with a tear at the knee and a long-sleeved red checked shirt that looked warm and cosy. He lifted his head and his eyes sparkled when he saw her. Butterflies launched in her belly as she realised she wasn't the only excited person.

'Morning,' she said grinning as if she were in a toothpaste commercial.

'Hey, you,' he replied in his sexy deep voice.

She stopped in front of him and silently they drank each other in. His lips curved into a smile and in that moment she wanted nothing more than to kiss him.

As if reading her mind he leaned forward and pressed one to her lips.

'Shall we go check the sheep?' he said, gesturing to the ute.

'Sounds great.' Ash ran to the other side and got in while glancing around for any early risers, but the farm was eerily still.

The quiet between them was easy, and their need to not rush hadn't been stated but was innately understood. Ash had Em to think about and Luke had Micky, plus the fact that he was still married. But she didn't want to think too hard on that right now. It was just nice being swept up in this indulgent, giddy feeling.

'How did you sleep?' he asked as he drove away from the sheds towards the paddocks.

'Out like a log after all that wine. Probably a good thing too, otherwise I think I would have been up all night thinking about Nikki.' Ash frowned. 'I still can't believe what she's been through.'

Luke nodded. 'I know. She's very lucky she got it early.'

He tapped the seat beside him and Ash slid across towards him.

'That's better. Hey, you.' He took his eyes off the road for a second while he planted a kiss on her head.

'Do you think Nikki and Chris will sort this out?' she asked, snuggling against his side, the warmth from his body delicious against the cold.

'I think so. Chris has been so lonely and it makes sense why now. They've both been dealing with a lot but I'm sure they'll get through this. It's clear they love each other very much.

Unlike Denise and me. It was probably doomed from the start. We were so different but we both tried hard up to a certain point. I guess Denise just wanted more than I could give her. I don't know. I still can't understand how she could leave her son. She hadn't been that keen on having kids, except I didn't realise how blind I was to it all until I look back. The signs were there, she even told me so when we married. I guess I thought she'd change after she had a baby. But she wasn't happy until she met the new guy.'

'Do you hate her? Or have you forgiven her?'

Luke blew out a breath. 'Tricky questions for this time of day. You don't pull any punches, do you?' He smiled. 'I detest what she's done to Micky, leaving him like that, but I don't hate her. I can understand why she left me and I have forgiven her, if just to be able to move on with my life, you know? She made her choice and she has to live with it.' He was silent for a moment, then said: 'Do you miss your husband?'

Ash paused to think. 'I do, but he's not coming back. I'm still learning to move forward.'

'I can see that.' Luke pulled over near a big tree off the side of the track and shut off the ute. He adjusted his body to face Ash and stroked her cheek. 'I see the sadness in these blue eyes, the guilt you feel when you're with me sometimes. You strike me as someone who's always putting others first, even if it's to your own detriment.'

Ash closed her eyes; his fingers playing over her skin were hypnotic, as well as his breath that caressed her like a minty breeze.

'I think you have the wrong person,' she mumbled, opening her eyes.

His silver eyes hit her with such heat and benevolence that she almost forgot to breathe.

'No, I'm pretty sure I have the right woman.' His eyes dropped to her lips. 'I've been dying to kiss you properly since the moment I saw you this morning.'

His hand snaked behind her neck and tilted her head back so her mouth was ripe for the taking. When he finally did she almost whimpered from the intense build-up.

Her body felt like it was on fire, every touch sent her nerves into a frenzy and she'd never felt so alive.

'We're fogging up the windows,' she said breathlessly when they finally drew apart for air. 'At least no one can see us,' she added.

'We should be careful, but I find it very hard to think straight when I'm near you,' said Luke as he played with a long curly strand of her hair.

'I'm pretty sure Nikki knows. She's given me a few looks.'

'She hasn't said anything?' he asked.

'No. But I'd say she has enough on her mind already. Although she did mention when we arrived that we would be great together. I laughed her off, thinking she was nuts. I haven't even thought of other men since Owen. You took me by surprise,' she admitted, dropping her eyes.

Luke put a finger under her chin, lifting her head until she glanced at him.

'You took me more than by surprise – you knocked my socks off from the moment I saw you when you landed at my feet,' he said with a grin.

'Hm, not my finest moment.' Ash tucked her head against his chest, hiding her face.

'It just made me like you even more. You seemed so vulnerable and yet you shook it off as if it was nothing. You were
fascinating. *Are* fascinating,' he clarified.

He claimed her lips again and with strong hands and arms
and a little shuffle she found herself straddling his lap on the
bench seat. Things heated up quickly as his hands went up
her jumper along her spine and she arched back while pressing
down against him.

She didn't think she would ever feel this hungry again.

Luke kissed down her neck and along her collarbone, while
she hummed with pleasure. His hands went to her backside
and pulled her closer, which began a slow rocking motion. Her
hands were clasped around his neck and she leaned down to
kiss and nibble his ear.

Ash could feel how tightly strung his body was and how
her kisses sent ripples through him. It was so powerful, this
heady mix of passion and power.

'My god, I feel like I'm eighteen and want to rip your clothes
off, but I'd be a bumbling mess,' he admitted. His hands rested
on her thighs as he sucked in breaths.

'I know. I don't want to get carried away either,' said Ash.
She could feel her lips were slightly swollen and her breasts
were tight and aching to be held. She rested her head against
his as they focused on breathing.

'It's been a long time,' said Luke. 'I want better for you than
a clumsy one in my ute.'

Right now Ash didn't care, she'd have him this instant. But
she knew what he meant. She slid off his lap and snuggled up
to his side. She tried not to look at his tight, straining-at-the-
zipper jeans.

'We can be sensible grown-ups,' she agreed. The thought of a quick fling sounded nice but there were always repercussions. The fact that he was Chris's cousin. The fact that she had to head back to Perth soon. There were kids to think about. Responsibilities. Adult stuff.

'Let's go check some sheep. That will help.' Luke moved across to the steering wheel, adjusted his jeans and started the ute.

He reached out for her hand and they drove like that for a while in silence, just admiring the morning.

'They've just about finished lambing,' said Luke, breaking the silence when he reached the end of the paddock. 'I only noticed two pregnant ones.'

'It beats what I do. What I *did* do,' she clarified. 'Listening to people describe their ailments as if I'm a doctor and then getting something completely different to what I suggest. Or sometimes I get the same few oldies in, which makes me a little sad because I think one of them might have Alzheimer's.'

'Did you enjoy working at the pharmacy? Was it your dream job?'

'Pftt. No. I spent a lot of time in there with Owen's medications, and when I saw a job vacancy and applied I was already on a first-name basis with the staff. My dream job was to be a journalist or a vet.'

'You like animals?'

'Yeah, you wouldn't think so, right? Owen wasn't big on animals, so we never had pets. But when I was young I wanted to have my own sanctuary where I could help injured wildlife. I was a bit of a Steve Irwin fan,' she admitted.

'Crikey.'

Ash laughed. 'I guess I don't need to ask you what your dream job was. I can see how much you love it here. And I'm rather jealous. You have a farm and a beach, animals and your own ocean lookout.'

'Yeah, it is pretty great and I love sharing it with Micky. But at times I do get lonely. I sit at Bec's chair and imagine how great it would be to sit there with a soul mate.' He chuckled. 'Well, maybe not a soul mate – I'm sure they're as rare as hen's teeth – but to have someone special who gets me. A companion.'

Ash could picture it. The serenity. The beauty. 'You're a bit of a romantic, Mr Summerson.'

He grimaced. 'Don't tell anyone.'

She smiled and leaned over to kiss him. 'Your secret's safe with me.'

Ash found herself suddenly aware of how few days they had left of their holiday. It was an unsettling feeling that sat in the bottom of her stomach like water in a fuel tank.

One day at a time, she reminded herself again and again. *You can do this; keep it easy, casual, fun.* But was this another tiny white lie? Already she had a feeling this was the most amazing thing that had happened to her and she didn't want to let it go.

The truth was, it was going to hurt.

33

Nikki

NIKKI GLANCED OVER AT CHRIS AS THE MORNING LIGHT glowed through the lace curtains. He was asleep on his side in the bottom bunk. This had been his third night in the hut with her and she had to admit she found it comforting.

Taking her moment, she slipped from the covers and reached under the bed for her prosthesis. Facing away from Chris, she slipped it on and quietly dressed.

'You don't have to hide from me.'

His voice made her jump as it echoed around the still room. She didn't reply, hoping he would go back to sleep or at least leave her be.

'I don't know what you're afraid of,' he said. 'Are you scared of how I'll react?'

Still she didn't reply.

'Because I can tell you that it won't shock me or disappoint me. Nikki, you're the love of my life.'

She remained sitting on the bed with her back to him and could hear the bed sheets rustle as he moved to sit up.

'You turn me on by the way you move your head and I see a glimpse of your collarbone or the soft milky part behind your ear. You make me hard when you bend over to pick something up and you have no idea what you've done. And there's something so goddamn hot when you wear those tiny shorts and walk around barefoot or when you look at me with those eyes and flutter your sexy eyelashes. Honey, you don't need breasts to turn me on, so if that's what you're worried about, then don't. All those things I mentioned, plus more, turn me on every time.'

His voice was filled with a thick passion and it drew her around to face him. Tears were starting to pool in her eyes.

'We can take it as slow as you want, but please don't cut me out. I need a smile or two, hold my hand on occasion, and if you're up to it a hug would be nice. I miss touching you. I miss being a breath's whisper from you. I miss the way you used to look at me. I promise none of it will go further unless you want it to.'

Chris was looking a little rough around the edges, wayward hair and stubble across his chin and his eyes were glassy as if on the verge of tears. He looked rather sexy in a ruggedly handsome way.

'I miss you,' he said again softly.

Nikki shuffled over to the bunk and sat next to him. She let her knee press against his as she lifted her hand to caress his face, feeling the stubble against her hand.

'I miss you too,' she admitted and was delighted with the sparkle of relief in his eyes.

'Good. I was a little worried you didn't want me.'

A smile tugged on her lips. 'I'm a woman, we never know what we want. But I'll always want you, Chris. I love you.'

She was hoping he would smile but instead he let out a deep sigh and bent his head until it touched hers.

'I've been so worried.'

Nikki stayed close, didn't pull away, but before she could think of a response, the door flew open and slammed into the wall with a bang. They both jumped. Chloe stood before them. Nikki stood up, a sick feeling in her stomach.

'Is it Josh?' she asked quickly. She expected a motorbike crash, or a fall from the treehouse and subsequent broken bone.

Chloe frowned. 'No,' she said screwing her nose up in confusion. 'It's Luke. He said there are whales and if we get to the lookout now we should be able to see them.'

'Whales?' Nikki was a little slow to process Chloe's words as images of Josh covered in blood or with strangely angled limbs were still filtering through her mind.

'Well, let's go,' said Chris, standing up and reaching for his jumper and pants.

'Oh Dad, gross,' said Chloe as she turned around and left.

'Come on, Nik. Put some shoes on.'

Nikki snapped to it and found her runners, pulling them on as fast as she could and grabbing her jumper off the corner of the bed as she followed Chris to the door.

'Hurry up!' Josh yelled.

He was standing on the back of the ute and Micky was at the wheel, with Emily and Chloe in the front. Josh looked like he'd just been dragged out of bed, which Nikki would bet a million bucks was exactly what had happened moments earlier, but his face was alive and excited. Even with sleep caked in the corners of his eyes and a crease across his face from where he'd been sleeping on the pillow.

'Guess we're on the back,' said Chris as he climbed up and then held out his hand for Nikki.

When she was on, Josh banged on the roof. 'Go, go, go!'

Micky revved the ute and took off up the track. Nikki let out a yelp and then a laugh as she clung to the bar. Chris put his arm around her and held the bar so she was safely cushioned by him. She felt instantly warmer, and for the first time in a long time she didn't mind the closeness of him.

'How many are there?' Chris asked Josh.

'Uncle Luke said there were two and a baby,' said Josh before he ducked as a low branch flew past. 'He called Micky up on the two-way and he came and got us.'

The moment Micky hit the top of the hill they all scanned the ocean trying to spot the whales. He parked the ute over by Luke's and they all climbed out and set off jogging along the track to the top.

'Can anyone see anything yet?' called Chloe.

She ran in front of Nikki, huffing and puffing while her thongs threw up sand. Parts of the track grew firmer, and more and more rock jutted out beneath the thin layer of dirt and even the shrubs grew sparse until the top, where there was nothing over knee height.

'You sound like a train chugging up a hill,' said Ash as they all reached the summit.

She was sitting on Rebecca's chair. Luke stood nearby but Nikki had a feeling he'd only just vacated the spot beside her.

His hands were nervously in his pockets then out of them to rest on his hips.

'They're just out there,' he said, pointing to the blue expanse.

Josh, much to Nikki's horror, practically skipped to the cliff edge for a better look.

'Josh, get back,' she warned.

'It's okay,' said Micky as he joined Josh's side. 'We stand here all the time.'

'What if it gives way?' She turned to Chris, shooting him a loaded stare.

Chris understood and took a few steps towards them.

'It won't,' said Luke. 'It's all solid rock and there's no over-hang that can break.'

None of that reassured Nikki, whose heart rate only increased further as Chloe joined the boys, looking over the edge.

'Wow, that's so cool.'

Nikki felt giddy, as if she were peering over the edge herself. 'Oh my god, can you all just step away from the edge, you're freaking me out.' Nikki hated to sound like the over-protective mother and she could imagine Josh's eye roll, but she couldn't help herself.

'There's a whale!' screamed Chloe.

Everyone turned to the water, frantically scanning and all saying, 'Where? Where?' But they didn't need a reply – seconds later they all watched as a whale breached and splashed back down.

'Wow,' said Josh and Chloe together.

'I think it's a southern right whale,' said Micky. 'They usually have newborn calves with them.'

'What else can you see here?' quizzed Josh.

'Well, last year we went on the Naturaliste Charter out to the Bremer Canyon and we saw around a hundred pilot whales and orcas. We noticed some birds going crazy and spotted around sixty orcas that were attacking a pygmy blue whale. It was so incredible,' said Micky, beaming.

'They were killing it?' asked Josh in disbelief.

'Yeah, the water was red with blood. They kept chasing it and attacking. I've never seen anything like it.'

Josh, big-eyed like a black moor goldfish, turned to Chris. 'Dad, can we do that tour too?'

'They operate from January during the school holidays,' said Luke. 'They head out from the marina.'

Chris glanced to Nikki and smiled. 'We could come down for a summer holiday,' he said with a shrug.

Nikki thought about coming back in summer, getting around in shorts and a singlet, warm breeze and refreshing swims in the ocean. Sunglasses and wine and books. Kids playing, phones forgotten. Yes, coming back here would be wonderful. If just to see that look of awe on her kids' faces from seeing the whales.

'Mum, come closer,' said Josh, 'this is so cool.' He started jumping up and down like a dog expecting a treat.

Nikki was shaking her head when movement caught her eye. Before she could react, though, Chloe's scream rang out.

'Snake!' Chloe lunged back, charging into Josh, who was flung toward Micky and the edge of the cliff.

Ice ran through Nikki's veins. Her hand shot out and she screamed Josh's name as he crashed into Micky and slowly – so slowly – she watched them both go over as arms flailed about. They were going to fall and there wasn't anything she could do to stop it. Visions of their bodies crashing against the rocky edge as they plummeted down to the thrashing waves below assaulted her mind.

Chris reached out, snatching Josh's shirt and yanking him backwards as the material ripped but held. But Micky had taken a few steps back and the last step had been over the edge and he was now waving his arms like windmills to stay upright. Chris threw out his other hand and somehow Micky managed to latch on as he fell.

Nikki screamed again. She screamed so hard she wasn't sure if she was even making a sound.

They say your life can flash before you before your death, but Nikki didn't have to die to feel it all rush past as she watched the love of her life heading over the cliff. It was silly little stuff that ran through her mind as the scene moved in horrifying slow motion before her. How much she wished she'd hugged Chris this morning. How she would give anything to hold him again. *Please god, don't take him from me!* How would she survive without him? How would Luke survive without Micky?

Nikki felt the blood drain from her body, her legs turn to jelly and the edge of her vision blacken like dark ink swirling in a pool of water.

The last thing that went through her mind was an awareness that life was about to change forever.

34

Ashley

ONE MINUTE THEY WERE HAVING A BEAUTIFUL MOMENT AND in the next it was mayhem. *Oohs* and *ahh*s changed to shrieks and screams, blood-curling screams.

Ash had seen the snake when Chloe screamed, and she watched it slither away to a shrub, but Nikki's cries pulled her eyes back to the unbelievable scene before her. She shot up off Rebecca's seat as Josh hurtled towards the edge. Somehow Chris dived forward and yanked him back just as Micky was losing his footing.

Beside her the low, guttural moan of a man about to lose his world ripped her to shreds and there was nothing she could do about it. Ash saw Luke move in her peripheral vision but knew he was too far away to save his son or Chris. They were all too far away, helpless but to watch the events unfold in gut-wrenching fashion. Josh hit the dirt and embraced it like a giant safety blanket and remained there breathing heavily, puffs of dust churning with each breath. Chloe was now frozen in horror, her face distorted in a way that showed internal destruction as she watched what she'd caused.

'*Micky!*'

Luke's cry was earth-shattering, enough to move the ground beneath her feet like a quake. He threw himself forward, arms outstretched as Micky fell into the open air.

Chris had reached out his hand and grabbed Micky but doing so would pull him over too. Ash didn't want to watch yet her eyes remained unblinking, her mouth open and a sick, sick feeling in her stomach that she never wanted to feel again.

Beside her Nikki crashed down, hitting the ground hard, arms splayed beside her at uncomfortable angles. Ash bent to reach her but didn't take her eyes off the scene, in particular Micky. Em was on Nikki's other side and helped move her until her head was resting on her lap.

Micky's eyes were huge. In them Ash saw his fear. It was a calm fear, as if he knew there was nothing he could do to save himself, he knew what was coming and had accepted it. But mixed with that fear was a sadness, deep and raw. He was looking at his dad, and Ash knew Micky was thinking how much this would hurt Luke.

Tears blurred her vision.

Then, it all happened at the same time, seemingly in slow motion.

Chris hit the ground with a sickening crunch, half his body going over the cliff face with Micky just as Luke, still flying through the air, reached out and latched onto Chris's feet as they dragged along the ground towards the cliff. Luke's weight was enough to hold Chris and stop him from going any further, while Micky continued to drop until he had vanished from view.

There was a moment of suspended movement: Luke held Chris, while Chris reached out, his arm bent tightly over the cliff so she could tell he still held Micky.

'Hold on, Micky,' Chris grunted.

He was physically in pain, the rocks cutting into his arm. A moment to catch their breath. A moment where everything was still okay. But it was no moment at all, it was the milliseconds before Micky crashed against the cliff and Chris grunted in pain.

'*Argh.*'

Micky's cry as he hit the rock face echoed up towards them and the force on Chris's arm intensified.

'I'm slipping!' cried Micky.

'Hold on, Micky!' Luke yelled as he tried to pull Chris backwards but it was awkward and they were both too heavy.

'I can't. Dad!'

Ash covered her mouth. Micky's call to his father was so heavy with emotion and despair.

'Micky, noooooo!' Chris screamed and then his arm went slack.

Luke roared and Ash fell to the ground beside Nikki, her hand on her still body. Ash was momentarily jealous that Nikki wasn't able to feel this moment. Chris didn't have to say anything, his gut-wrenching tone told them everything.

Micky had slipped away. He was no longer on the end of Chris's grasp.

'Chris?' Luke pleaded.

'I'm sorry, Luke, I couldn't hold him.' Chris shimmied back until he was safe but his hands gripped the edge as he looked over.

Luke crawled to the edge beside him and almost threw himself over in his eagerness to spot Micky.

Ash had a frightful moment thinking Luke was about to jump, to join his child.

'Micky, Micky can you hear me?'

Ash felt Nikki stir and helped her sit up.

'Can you see him?' said Josh, his voice shaky and desperate. Tears filled his eyes as he sat up. Chloe threw her arms around him, gripping him tightly, with tears streaming down her face.

'Yeah, he's on a small ledge,' said Chris looking back over his shoulder.

'Oh my god,' mumbled Ash. 'Is he okay?'

Nikki blinked as realisation dawned on her. 'Did I pass out?' she said but no one paid her any notice. All eyes were on Chris and Luke as they lay on the ground, the top half of their bodies leaning over the edge to get a better look at Micky.

'He's not moving,' said Luke. 'Micky?' he called out, his voice carried by the breeze. 'He might have knocked himself out,' he said.

'His leg doesn't look good,' Chris said as he turned to Luke. Blood dripped from his nose and there was more blood on his arms from rock cuts. 'We might not be able to winch him up.'

'I'll go get help,' said Luke, shimmying back from the edge before standing up.

Ash felt the need to reach for her phone, to call for help – but there was no signal and no phones.

Chris moved back but didn't get up, instead he rolled over then sat up with his knees bent and his bloodied arms resting against them while he let his nose drip. 'I'll go,' he offered.

But Luke shook his head. 'I know where everything is, I'll be faster. You stay here and try to wake him. Be there for him.'

The cousins shared a look that said more than words and time would allow. Chris nodded and Luke turned and ran down the track to the ute.

Ash glanced to Em, who was still by Nikki's side holding her hand.

'I'll go with Luke. You help Nikki and Chris.'

'Yep. We'll be okay,' Em assured her but her face was white.

Ash gave her a nod before running after Luke.

She had to run fast to keep up with him, dodging rocks and jumping shrubs, and managed to climb into the ute just as he was backing it up to turn down the home track. Ash didn't speak; what was there to say that would comfort Luke in this moment? His face was set and focused as he drove the track like he was at Bathurst in a V8 supercar. Branches slapped the ute so hard she thought the glass window might shatter but it held firm and the campsite came into view.

'I'll get some water sorted, food and blankets. We could lower it down to him?' she said as Luke parked.

Luke nodded. 'I'll get a rope after I've called for help.' He disappeared inside the house to call, so Ash went straight for her hut.

She grabbed her water bottle, some muesli bars and chocolate, and rolled up a rug and tied it with a belt so it was easy to transport down the side of a cliff. Well, she hoped. She grabbed the first-aid box and paper towel from the kitchen.

Ash was putting the last of it on the back of the ute when Luke joined her with ropes and straps.

'There are no trees to use, so I might have to try to drive the ute up to the lookout,' he said as he flung them on the back. He took in all her items and nodded. 'Thanks.'

Ash wanted to hug him but now wasn't the time; instead they got in the ute and began the frantic drive back along the track. Ash reached across and put her hand on his leg.

Without taking his eyes off the track he moved his hand to briefly cover hers for a moment, as if drawing some strength from it before putting it back on the steering wheel.

'How soon can help get here?' she asked.

'They're sending out the RAC Rescue chopper, it might be a while but an ambulance is on its way to try to assess Micky, and the SES.'

'Do they know where to come?' she said, a little concerned. 'Should I wait at the house for them?'

'I know the local ambos, so Greg's going to come out in his ute to get up here and they'll leave the ambulance at the house. There's enough room for the chopper to land there too,' he said in a nervous rush.

'Oh, good.' A little further along the track she added, 'He'll be okay.'

'I hope you're right,' he replied. 'I'm not sure I would survive losing him.' His voice went thick and gravelly on the last bit and she felt a lump the size of her shoe lodge itself in her throat.

'But he's a strong kid.' Luke nodded as if to prove his words were truth.

'Do you think you can get the ute up to the top?' she queried.

'I don't know. They don't want me to go over to him, it's not safe and they don't want to have two to rescue,' he said dryly.

'But you can't just leave him there, can you?' What parent could just sit back and wait? Not Luke. He was a man who would move a mountain to get to his kid, no matter the risk.

He shook his head. 'No. I can't let him go, Ash.'

'There's enough of us, we can work together to make sure he gets through this.' Ash wished she could put a money-back guarantee on that but there was no such thing. She hadn't looked over the cliff, she had no idea if Micky was hanging on by his pants or if the ledge was big enough for two. Maybe it wouldn't hold?

When they reached the end of the track Luke kept driving, swerving to miss the bigger shrubs and up over rocks. Ash gripped the door as the ute launched forward and she hit her head on the roof.

'Sorry,' Luke muttered between clenched teeth.

At one point the ute nearly got stuck but with some rocking motion between reverse and first Luke got them out.

'I'd thought about putting a proper track up to the lookout but I didn't want to take away from the beauty of the walk and serenity. Now I'm regretting that decision.'

Ash remained silent. She liked his reasons for keeping it a walking track. Who would know the events that would unfold today? You couldn't plan for that. Ash had been trying most of her life to pre-empt things, from how Owen would react to any given thing on any given day, to making sure every situation went to plan. And in the end none of it had worked. Sometimes there was no rhyme or reason to why things happened. The universe put that snake there, which started the domino effect that resulted in Micky going over. You could also blame the whales for being there or the fact that they went on holidays to Bremer Bay. You could make yourself go mad trying to find something or someone to blame.

In that moment of epiphany she knew she couldn't blame herself for Owen's death. She was not responsible. It was his choice and she couldn't take on the guilt. It was a strange time to suddenly come to that conclusion but seeing what Luke was faced with put so much into perspective. Life was short. Make the most of it. Don't live with regret. Don't live with guilt. Live with passion and love.

The ute stopped suddenly.

'Think this is as far as we can go,' said Luke.

Ash could see the lookout, she could see Nikki and the girls on Rebecca's chair and Chris leaning over the edge with Josh sitting on his legs. But in front of them was a rock ledge that was too steep for the ute to climb.

Luke was out and gathering armfuls of rope and straps and the rug while Ash got the rest and followed him the last leg of the track. Nikki met them and helped Ash carry a few things.

'You okay?' Ash asked.

'Yeah, fine. Just feeling stupid for passing out.' Nikki turned to Luke. 'Chris said Micky was moving, so he must be coming to.'

'Oh good.' Ash breathed out a sigh of relief as Luke ran up to the top, dropped the ropes and crawled along the rock beside Chris.

'How's he going? Help coming?' whispered Nikki.

'Yeah, the RAC chopper is on its way and the ambos and SES. How are the kids?'

'Traumatised like the rest of us. I thought I was going to lose Chris. I've never felt so awful.'

They stopped at the top and put all the bits on the ground, then Ash drew Nikki into a hug. Before they knew it Chloe and Em had joined their hug and fresh tears fell all around.

'I'm so sorry,' cried Chloe. Her face was red and eyes puffy. 'It's all my fault.'

Ash hugged Emily to her side as Nikki wiped away her daughter's tears before pulling her into a tight embrace.

'He'll be okay. Sh . . . it's okay, Chlo. It was an accident.' Her words were calm and soft.

'He's alive!' shouted Josh. 'He's talking.'

The girls turned towards the cliff but Ash and Nikki held them back.

'Stay here. You don't need to look, just be happy he's awake,' Nikki warned. 'I know it's hard, but we have to do what's best for Micky.'

Chris slid back to safety and joined them. His cuts had stopped bleeding and the blood had dried along his arms like paint runs. His face was smeared red but his nose had dried up too.

'Oh, honey.' Nikki touched his chin near the chunk of skin that had been scraped off when he'd hit the rock edge.

Chris shrugged it off. 'He seems okay. He knows where he is and who he is, so there doesn't seem to be any concussion yet.'

Chris swayed a bit and Nikki gripped his side.

'Wow, blood to my head,' he said.

'Chris has been there this whole time you've been away,' Nikki told Ash. 'He didn't want Micky to wake up and move and cause himself to fall off the ledge.' Nikki grabbed his arm. 'Maybe take a seat, Chris?'

Horrific images plunged into Ash's mind as the scenario took hold. 'I'm glad you were here, Chris. It must be terrifying for Micky down there.'

'No, I'll get back to Micky,' he said but took the water Ash offered. 'It was lucky his leg is hurt, it stopped him from moving too much and allowed him to get his bearings. Tough kid,' he said shaking his head in awe.

Ash watched as Nikki clung to Chris, not just to help hold him up but with a protectiveness she hadn't seen since they'd been on holidays. That same feeling made her step towards Luke and listen to him talk to Micky.

'I'm right here, mate. We've got a chopper coming to help get you up. Try not to move. We'll get some water down to you.'

His voice was so thick with emotion Ash felt that lump in her throat again and tears sprang forth. She sucked in salty air and tried to gain some control. She couldn't start crying now; if she did she wouldn't be able to stop. Tears, shock and all the other emotions could come after they had Micky safe.

Luke turned around and saw Ash watching and he gave her a smile. In that one moment she felt his relief and joy that Micky was still with him.

She returned his smile and felt her muscles unclench.

For the first time in what felt like a long time she allowed herself to breathe properly.

35

Nikki

'LET ME PATCH YOU UP,' SAID NIKKI AS SHE INSPECTED HER husband's cuts.

'It's okay, we'll sort it out after Micky's safe. I'll just rig up some water on the rope for him.'

Chris pulled away and Nikki felt the hole he left; she had never missed him so much. As he worked to tie up the water bottle with the ropes Nikki watched in awe of the way he was taking charge and making things happen. That was the kind of man he was, always reliable and always putting others first. It was a high pedestal she'd put him on, and when he faltered she hadn't cut him any slack. But no one was perfect. And for that she needed to forgive Chris and she needed to forgive herself. She was not perfect, but that was okay.

They all stayed at the lookout until, after what seemed an age, the ambulance officers arrived, their green uniforms blending into the shrubs as they came up the track along with a bloke Nikki later learned was the neighbour. He'd come when he heard the sirens.

There wasn't much Nikki or Ash could do but keep the kids back and out of the way as the officers chatted to Micky and tried to assess him. Not long after, the SES ute roared up the hillside and parked next to Luke's ute. Then, one by one, orange-uniformed men climbed out, five in total, and started carrying equipment to the top.

'He's about ten metres down on a ledge that might be big enough to hold two of you,' Luke told them.

They all appeared to know Luke and Micky, and they listened carefully before the head SES officer went to the ledge to look over for himself. He came back and gave orders to the rest of his crew, who went about setting up harnesses and ropes for a vertical descent.

'What's going on, Chris, can they get him?' Nikki asked. It was hard sitting back and watching all the action but not really knowing what was happening. Chris had become their information gatherer.

'They'll go down and see how bad his leg is; it might need to be braced before they move him. I think they'll use the chopper to winch the stretcher up because there are too many jagged edges and overhangs to pull it up this way.'

They sat, the four of them squished on Rebecca's seat with Josh sitting on the ground leaning back against Nikki's legs while green and orange bodies moved around the cliff top.

The neighbour's wife, Beth, came with a big basket full of food and drinks for everyone and slowly the small lookout began to feel crowded. All the while, Luke remained as close to Micky as he could get.

'The first bloke is going over now,' Chris said.

They watched in silence, breathing shallowly as the man in orange slowly leaned back over the edge, his harness pulling tight.

'Careful!' Luke called out as loose debris fell from his foot holds, raining it down onto Micky.

'Micky, cover your face if you can,' he yelled down.

The SES leader gave his man the nod to continue and this time he went slower, watching his steps as he disappeared down and out of sight.

'He's halfway there,' Luke called out to them.

Nikki felt her heart flop in her throat every time Luke looked over the edge to see how Micky was going.

'He's down.'

Chris got up and joined Luke. They chatted for a bit before he came back with a relieved smile on his face. 'Micky apparently asked them what took so long.'

Only Josh smiled at this; Nikki instead felt tears of relief fall down her face.

'Do they think his leg is broken?' asked Ash.

He nodded. 'And there's a nasty bump on his head, so they're watching for concussion. They want to take him straight to Albany.'

Nikki licked her dry, cracked lips and realised she needed to drink some water.

'Mum, I need to go to the toilet,' Chloe whispered. 'But I don't want to leave.'

'Just go down by the ute.'

'What if there's more snakes,' she said wide-eyed.

'With all this noise I doubt there will be any for miles. You'll be fine.'

'I need to go too,' said Em.

The girls headed off together. Nikki hadn't drunk enough water to need a toilet break. She hadn't even had a morning coffee yet and it was now well after lunch.

'Look, the whales are still there,' said Josh pointing them out. 'Maybe they know Micky's hurt.'

Nikki ruffled Josh's hair.

'They've sent a second man down and then they'll lower the stretcher ready for him to be airlifted,' said Chris.

It was a relief to have Chris relay everything that was happening. 'Thank you,' she whispered to him, touching his hand gently. He squeezed her fingers before heading back to the scene.

'Is that the helicopter?' asked Emily as the girls returned.

Nikki looked around as she too heard something in the distance.

'There it is!' yelled Josh excitedly as he pointed to the sky.

A yellow blob could be seen against the blue sky as the *whomp whomp* of the rotor blades grew louder. It was like watching a scene from a rescue show, but this was real and she couldn't just turn it off and walk away.

The helicopter hovered just off the cliff edge and lowered a winch down. The downward force blew dust and dirt around the top of the cliff, causing them all to shield their eyes.

'Aw, I can't see!' yelled Josh over the sound.

Nikki squinted through her fingers and saw the helicopter try to swing in closer to the cliff face.

Luke was lying down, watching over the edge. The SES leader had tried to get him to move away but Luke refused to go. 'I'll stay with my son!' he'd growled.

'He's in the stretcher,' Luke yelled but his voice was muffled by the noise of the helicopter. 'He's hooked on.'

Heads tilted skyward as the helicopter rose and then finally they saw the stretcher that carried Micky.

The crew cheered and clapped but Nikki was too exhausted, she just closed her eyes and offered a silent prayer of thanks. This day could have ended up so much worse.

'Let's get back,' said Luke, heading for his ute.

Quickly they scrambled, collecting some of the gear and jumping on the back of the ute, leaving the rescue crew to pack up. The ambulance officers and a rescue bloke followed, jumping into Greg's ute. Luke let them go first but followed closely; a little too closely for Nikki's liking.

Chris put his arm around her to hold her safe as they clung to the back of the ute, their eyes all skyward as they watched the chopper and the tiny stretcher floating through the air towards camp. Micky was a yellow line against the big blue sky and sometimes, if she blinked, he would vanish until she found the chopper and looked below it. Nikki felt giddy thinking how high Micky was, swinging over the land.

'Is the chopper coming down?' asked Josh.

'They'll put Micky down first and then put the chopper down in a paddock where there's room, and then they can give Micky a good check over before loading him up in the chopper and taking him to the hospital,' replied Chris.

'Can we see him?' he asked, his face hopeful.

'Sorry, mate. Best if just Uncle Luke sees him for now.'

Nikki rubbed his shoulder. 'He's going to be fine. We can go see him later at the hospital maybe,' she reassured him.

As it turned out they all got to say a quick hello to Micky just before the ambos carted him to the helicopter.

His face was scratched and bloody, but he held up his hand and gave a thumbs up.

'See you soon, Micky,' said Nikki, giving his hand a squeeze.

They had put a drip in and were working on pain relief while immobilising his broken leg. It had been a long ordeal for Micky, whose energy had waned, his face pale and his eyes heavy.

Luke had his hand on Micky's shoulder and it didn't leave even as he climbed into the ambulance with him.

'Don't worry about the farm, we'll keep it running,' said Chris.

'And I'll sort some clothes for your both,' added Nikki. 'Don't worry about a thing,' she reassured him.

Luke nodded and gave them a short smile before turning back to Micky as the doors were closed and the ambulance drove off towards the paddock with the waiting helicopter.

'I don't know what to do now,' said Nikki as they all stood in the clearing not far from the camp kitchen.

'Me either,' said Ash. 'I feel lost.'

They stood together, facing the chopper in the paddock until they saw it rise up and fly towards Albany.

Nikki realised she was gripping Chris's arm, but she didn't let go.

'Why don't you two go pack up some stuff for them,' he said, running his hand through his stubble, flinching when he brushed over his cut chin.

'I'll stay here with the kids and we can see off the crew, give them our thanks.'

'Sounds like a good plan. Get them to look over your cuts please!' Nikki demanded and they started to head for the house. But she turned back and threw her arms around Chris, hugging him tightly.

He was rigid for a moment, caught by the surprise but soon melted into her arms and held her just as tightly. Tears pooled as she felt so much relief drown her. 'You were amazing. Saving Josh and Micky. And for not dying,' she added softly against his ear.

He pulled back, tears in his eyes. 'What a day,' he mumbled. 'God, I love you.'

'I love you too,' she said before reaching up to kiss him.

36

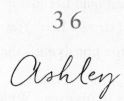

'RIGHT, WHAT SHALL WE PACK? TOILETRIES, UNDERWEAR, a few sets of clothes,' muttered Nikki as they entered Luke's house.

Ash got as far as the hallway when she saw a family portrait. It was up on a canvas print, bright against the dark rammed-earth wall. The photo had been taken at the beach with bright blue sky and water against the white of the sand and in the middle a family of three wearing T-shirts and shorts and smiling faces.

'They look happy,' she said, her eyes finding Luke's handsome face and his arms lovingly around Micky. Micky looked like a young Josh, still short and baby faced. Then her eyes settled on Denise.

'Is she what you imagined?' asked Nikki, coming to stand beside her.

'Not really. I kind of pictured more of a hippy but she seems like any other woman.'

In fact Denise could have been half the mums Ash had met at Em's school. Her shirt might have been bright and decorative but nothing shouted 'child abandoner'.

'She was a hippy, but it's hard to see the finer things in a photograph of one tiny moment. Come on, Luke's room is down here.'

Ash followed her to the corner room. There were photos of Micky on the walls; his bedside table held an old alarm clock radio and a watch; his bed cover was dark blue; and his wetsuit hung over a chair in the corner. There were no feminine touches, no leftover jewellery, no large mirror or make-up area. It smelled like him and she automatically reached for the check shirt that had been discarded on the end of the bed.

'What's going on with you two?'

'Huh?' Ash blinked away her tears before glancing at Nikki, who stood with her hands on her hips.

Nikki gave her an expression that said she didn't come down in the last shower.

'I'm not sure what it is yet, but it's very nice,' she said truthfully.

'It doesn't have to be anything. I think you both probably needed some companionship. I like seeing you both happy.'

'Thanks, Nik.'

She turned to open his cupboard and Ash quickly pressed Luke's shirt against her face.

'I think you should take this stuff to Luke at the hospital,' Nik said as she threw out a few shirts onto the bed.

Ash spotted a black bag under the chair and retrieved it to put the things Nikki was pulling out into it. 'Why?'

'I think he would prefer your company to ours,' she said with a grin. 'Besides, we can manage here and it will give you two some time together, and I need some time with Chris.'

'That sounds promising?'

'Yeah, today has really shaken me up. I seriously thought I was going to lose him. Never felt so devastated. I know he loves me, I love him. I want to fix this, I want to fix myself. I'm the problem. I need to face my self-image. I need to face my fears.' Nikki blurted out her words in quick succession.

Ash placed three pairs of jocks in the bag before turning to Nikki. 'I'm proud of you. I know you can overcome this. I never had what you two have, Owen and I were never that close, nowhere near soul mates and I think you'd be silly to give up on it. And for what it's worth I still think you have a rocking bod, and who needs tits – you still have the bits that matter.'

Nikki smiled. 'Thanks, Ash. I can always count on you to tell it like it is.'

Ash grimaced but Nikki pulled her into a hug.

'I don't know what I'd do without you. I'm glad we ended up friends.'

'Oh shit, stop. I'll be a blubbering mess. It's been an emotional day and I'm barely keeping a lid on it.'

'Same here.' Nikki wiped at her eyes. 'Let's get this finished. Don't forget to take your phone so you can call us. We'll try to stay close to the house so we hear the phone ring.'

It was strange being in Luke's room without him, a visitor amid his private stuff, yet she felt comfortable, almost at home in his space.

Inside his bathroom she collected his toothbrush, toothpaste and deodorant, and when she stepped back into the hallway Nikki was ending a call on the landline.

'Right, I have you booked in a hotel that's close to the hospital. You okay with one room? I figured he'd probably stay at the hospital most of the time and only stop in to shower and change, unless . . .' she said, wiggling her eyebrows.

'No, we haven't slept together. We're trying to avoid that, didn't want to complicate things too much.'

'Well, it's a queen-size bed if you change your mind.'

Nikki crushed a bit of paper into Ash's hand. 'Here's the address, and I wrote Luke's number at the bottom so you can call us.'

'Thanks. I better go and have a chat to Em. We're practising being honest with each other, so I want to explain why I'm going.'

'She'll be fine with us. Chloe could use the company; poor kid feels so bad.'

They carried the two bags outside to Ash's car. 'I'll make sure to tell Em to keep an eye on her.'

A horn honked as the emergency vehicle drove past full of orange-covered bodies. Ash and Nikki waved affectionately at them, calling out their thanks as they passed.

'I better go pack some stuff for myself and get my purse,' Ash said as they headed back to the camp kitchen.

Emily was sitting with Chloe and Josh and Chris but got up and followed her to the cabin.

'I'm going to drive to Albany and take Luke and Micky some things,' she said, shutting the door and reaching for Em.

'Yeah, that's cool.'

'Are you right to stay here and keep Chloe company? I think she's feeling bad about today and could use a friend.'

'Yeah, I know. I'll stay.' Em brushed her hair back, her blue eyes searching.

Ash took a steadying breath. 'Luke and I . . . we've been getting on well just recently . . . and, um, it's nothing serious but I just wanted to let you know.'

Em smiled and almost chuckled. 'You're so funny when you're embarrassed.'

'Hey, don't pick on me. That was hard to admit I've been . . .' Ash didn't know how to finish what she was going to say.

'Kissing a boy?' Em offered.

Ash frowned. 'You're not upset?'

She shrugged like teenagers love to do. 'No. I like you when you're around him. You smile and laugh. Plus, I like Luke. He's cool.'

Ash let out a breath she didn't realise she'd been holding. 'It's not like we're dating or anything serious. It just sort of happened and it's been nice.'

'A holiday romance? I could write a song about it,' Em teased.

Ash laughed. 'Please don't. Oh, and while I'm being honest . . . I lost my job.'

Emily's eyes grew wide and her mouth dropped open. '*What?* How could they do that? Was it Margie? She's so mean.' When she finished the questions she changed her tone. 'What will you do?'

'I don't know. I guess I'll start looking for a job when we get home. But don't worry about it. I'll find another one.' She pulled her in for a tight hug. Em didn't need to know about how Owen's life insurance wouldn't pay out; she just needed to know that her mum would find a job and they'd be fine.

'That's okay, Mum. I know you will. I hope it didn't make you too sad.'

'No, not really,' she said lying a little. 'It's been a big day, though. How are you feeling?' Ash rested her chin on Em's shoulder, not letting her pull away.

'I don't know. Exhausted. So happy that Micky's okay. It was scary, though. So scary.'

'I know. I felt so helpless.'

'Me too.'

'I love you, so much.'

'I love you too, Mum.'

Ash had never driven to Albany from Bremer Bay, and she enjoyed the quiet drive. It gave her time to collect her thoughts and wonder about seeing Luke outside his farm. Would things feel different?

At the hospital, with its splash of orange and bright yellow poles, she found a park and headed inside with just Micky's bag. She felt a flutter of nerves when she asked the woman at the desk for Micky Summerson's room number. It had been more than two hours since they'd left the camp in the helicopter, so he could have even gone into surgery in that time.

'Thank you.'

Clutching the bag as if it were a precious newborn baby, she headed up a floor. Each step was like the pounding of her heart, wondering what Luke would think when he saw it was her and not Chris or Nikki who had come.

The room number appeared and she slowed, suddenly feeling anxious. The first thing she saw was an empty bed, white sheets, white walls and blue curtains.

A blur of colour caught her eye as she found Luke sitting in a chair. He looked just like he had when she'd last seen him, wearing his checked blue shirt and jeans but looking tired. She thought he was sleeping until she stepped into the room and his eyes shot open.

'Ash!' he said with surprise.

'Hey.'

He stood up as she stepped closer and then suddenly she was in his arms and he was holding her like she'd just arrived back from the moon.

Micky's bag dropped to the ground and she threw herself into the hug. It felt so good to hold him.

'I'm so glad you're here. Thank you for coming.'

'You don't mind that it's just me?' she said as she leaned back to read his face.

He shook his head and to prove his point he dipped his head a little to kiss her softly.

'I brought your phone, and the others are waiting for updates. Nikki booked a hotel room for me, so you have somewhere to go and have a shower.' Ash retrieved his phone from her back pocket and handed it to him. 'How is Micky?'

'He's in surgery now.' Luke grabbed a chair from the other side of the two-bed room and motioned for her to sit. When they were both comfortable he filled her in. 'We flew in and they took him off to X-ray, which confirmed he has a tibia fracture. It's a displaced fracture, so they needed to align it through surgery. His concussion was mild and so all in all he's pretty lucky, considering. He'll need four to six months to recover from the break.'

'How are *you*?' she asked when he'd finished.

His quicksilver eyes watched her carefully. 'Better now you're here.' He reached for her hand. 'I'll survive. I'm worn out, feeling depleted, but none the less I'm happy that I still have Micky. I've been scared enough today to fill an ocean.'

'It was very traumatic.' She studied him, from his long stubble to the tired creases around his eyes. And yet he was still gorgeous. 'Have you had anything to eat yet?'

'I grabbed a chocolate bar from the vending machine.'

'That doesn't count. I'll go get you something decent. Why don't you call Chris and fill everyone in?'

She stood up to leave, but Luke followed and pulled her closer. Cupping her face he watched her for a moment and she felt her knees lose feeling. The way he looked at her made her insides heat up and pop all over the place like popcorn over a flame. Her lips parted slightly as his came closer and pressed against hers. It was a slow, purposeful kiss that filled her with a joyful calm that made her forget the world.

'Thank you,' he whispered against her lips.

When she returned with a chicken wrap and a Coke, plus a piece of caramel slice, Micky was asleep in the bed and Luke was sitting at his side.

'Oh, how is he?' she asked.

'All good. Leg's in plaster and he's sleeping it off still.'

Micky, who was almost an adult and usually looked like one, today resembled a little boy as he slept beneath the white sheets in the sterile-looking room.

'Here, why don't you eat before he wakes up?'

'Good plan. Thanks again,' he said after she'd handed the food over.

Micky woke when Luke ducked out to the toilet, so Ash went to his side.

'Hey, mate, how are you feeling?' she said brushing back his hair from his forehead.

'Ash?' he said frowning.

'Your dad's here, he just went to the loo. He's been here the whole time,' she said softly giving him a smile.

He closed his eyes for a moment and Ash realised she was still stroking him like she used to with Emily when trying to get her to sleep.

'Is he awake?' said Luke.

'Yes, just,' she replied as Micky opened his eyes again. She took her hand from his forehead. 'Sorry, Micky, automatic mothering tendencies kicked in.'

'It's nice,' he replied.

And then it hit her – he probably hadn't had anyone stroke his hair in a long time, and that saddened her greatly. So, to compensate she rested her hand on his arm after giving him a pat. Luke went to his other side, his face beaming.

'Hey, son. Looks like no farm duties for you for a while.'

'Sorry, Dad.'

'Ah, I'm just stirring,' he said, ruffling up his hair affectionately. 'I'm just relieved you're okay.'

The room was still for a moment, just the three of them huddled together.

'How are the others?' Micky asked when he was more alert.

Ash filled them both in with what had happened after they flew out and how everyone was eager to know he was okay. 'There was no point them all coming up here, you'll be back home soon.'

'Mum?' Micky mumbled the word.

Ash frowned and glanced to Luke, suddenly wondering if Micky's concussion had taken a turn for the worse. Luke shrugged but then followed Micky's gaze to the door and froze. Shock splashed all over his face and he quietly cursed. Ash didn't have to turn around to know who was standing at the door.

Denise.

But she turned anyway and recognised the woman from the family photo, except this one had a grave expression on her face and more lines. Her hair was cut short now and she wore a long flowing patterned skirt, white shirt and lots of leather bands and bangles on her wrists and around her neck.

'What are you doing here?' Luke almost rumbled.

'I . . . I saw it on the news,' she stuttered. 'The video of the helicopter, and they said they took him here. I had to come.'

Luke frowned.

'I still have friends that live in Bremer Bay, they made sure I knew.'

Luke looked like he was ready to kill these so-called friends.

Denise had briefly flicked her eyes to Luke but the majority of the time they were glued to Micky.

'Wow, you've got so big,' she said softly. She didn't move, just hovered near the door.

'You gave up your right to be his mother,' Luke growled as he stepped towards her.

'Luke, please. I still care about him.'

Luke grabbed her arm and walked her back outside the door into the corridor but Ash could still hear them, which meant Micky could too.

'Why do adults do that,' he said, his voice squeaking like his voice was breaking all over again.

'What do you mean?' she asked, trying not to listen to their conversation.

'You have no right to just show up here,' Luke snapped.

Ash could feel his anger and hurt, his desperate need to protect Micky.

'Parents go outside to "talk" but you can still hear every word,' said Micky, rolling his eyes. 'They may as well have just stayed where they were.'

'He's still my son. I love him.'

'You have a funny way of showing it.'

Ash turned and saw Luke throw his hands up in despair through the window, but she couldn't see Denise.

'I know that he's loved and looked after with you. We both know it's better this way. Would you rather I visit all the time?'

'It's not up to me, that's up to Micky. Did you ever ask him if he'd like to see you more? No, you just vanished and started a new life, one that you preferred. I hope you're happy.'

He meant the words to hurt.

'I *am* happy, very much so. I was dying inside, depressed. I had to live my best life, Luke, and I'm sorry that wasn't with you. I hope you're happy too? We weren't suited. I know I'm not the best mum, but I still love Micky very much. Please let me talk to him.'

Ash realised she was holding Micky's hand, as if that would shield him from whatever pain this would cause him. He hadn't pulled away, but now he tugged on her hand.

'Ash, can you please ask Dad to let me see her?' Micky's eyes were pleading; he knew it was a big ask.

'Sure, kiddo.' She let his hand go and walked to the door, feeling a surge of terror at having to butt into their private, not so private, moment.

Ash cleared her throat as she approached them. 'Um, sorry to interrupt,' she said before turning to Luke. 'Micky would like to speak to her.'

Luke stared as he processed her words. She could tell he was upset but he sighed and nodded. It was what Micky wanted. He gestured for Denise to go in, and she pounced on the chance, her eyes lingering on Ash as she passed.

They followed her inside and Ash wondered what Luke was thinking. Micky was his world and to have her abandon him and then come back must have filled him with fear.

'Hi Michael,' said Denise.

It was strange hearing his full name, and even Micky winced. 'I prefer Micky,' he informed her.

Ash saw Luke's lips twitch.

Micky glanced at his dad. They shared a silent conversation before he spoke to Denise.

'You can stay with him while I go shower,' Luke said to Denise but it sounded like each word was painful.

'Thanks, Dad.'

'I'll be back soon,' he reassured Micky.

Luke stepped towards the door and held out his hand. 'Ash?'

'Oh yes, right,' she said. 'Be back soon,' she told Micky giving him one last pat then setting off to take Luke's hand, all the while aware of Denise's eyes following her as they left.

Ash didn't have a chance to talk to Luke as he stomped his way through the hospital. It wasn't until he got outside that he realised he didn't know where to go. He stopped abruptly, saw Ash still clinging to him and sighed heavily.

'Sorry. That was all a bit of a shock.'

The cold coastal breeze was in, and Ash moved closer to Luke's warmth. 'I bet it was. You okay?'

He looked skywards and didn't reply.

'She can't take him away from you, if that's what you're worried about. Micky's life is with you on the farm. He'll just be curious to see her, maybe ask her some questions.' She tugged his arm so he would look at her.

He sighed out again but smiled grimly. 'Yeah, I know. Thanks.'

'At least she made the effort to come and see him. At least Micky will see that she does care. I don't think she's here to take him away.'

Luke didn't reply until they were in the car, sitting in the warmth that had been building in the late afternoon sun.

'Are you sure? What if he's so curious he wants to spend time with her? She's his mother.'

'He's old enough now to have a say in how he lives his life. I don't think you'd have to worry about him moving with her. I do think what you did back there was very brave.' Ash wasn't so sure she'd have done the same. Even so she could tell his decision was twisting him up. 'Come on, the sooner we go, the sooner you can get back.'

—

While Luke showered in the hotel bathroom, Ash lay on the bed and tried to go through her phone but found she couldn't concentrate. From seeing Denise or knowing Luke was a wall away, naked in the shower, she couldn't pick what had her mind so scattered. Probably both.

He came out wearing just his jeans, his shirt in his hands.

She squinted at him as he started to put it on. 'Did you do that on purpose?' she asked, slack-jawed and positively salivating at the view.

He winked. 'Maybe. Did it work?' He finished pulling on the shirt and flopped onto the bed beside her.

Ash had to steel herself as her senses were assaulted by Luke's clean-scented body.

Her phone fell to the bed as he pulled her against him.

'Do you want to come back with me?'

'Hm, I might stay here. You take my car and take all the time you need. I think I'm best left out of any family reunions.'

'I'm sorry you had to witness that.' His face grew dark. 'I don't love her anymore but the pain she caused still flares up when I see her. Like a kneejerk reaction.'

Ash touched his face gently. 'It's all right, I understand. I just think you might like the space to chat with Micky too.'

Luke nodded. He kissed her softly. 'Is it okay to come back here to sleep?'

She was trying to read his interpretation of 'sleep' and found herself smiling like an idiot.

'For sure.' Oh, she was asking for trouble.

Luke played with her hair, brushed a strand across his face
and then groaned.

'I better go or I'll never leave.' He pressed a kiss to her cheek
and moved off the bed. 'See you later.'

'Bye, Luke. Good luck.'

'Thanks, I might need it.'

Then she watched his firm denim backside walk out the
door, and instantly missed him.

37

Nikki

'GOD, I'M EXHAUSTED.' CHRIS PUT ANOTHER LOG INTO THE pot belly in the corner of the hut. 'It's nice the girls are letting Josh camp with them. I don't think he wanted to be alone.'

Nikki put her towel on the hook by the fire and headed to the bed, pulling her hair from its top knot. There were still wet strands by her neck. She padded over barefoot and in her black track pants and one of Chris's old Led Zeppelin T-shirts.

'He's not the only one,' she said, jumping in and patting the empty section beside her.

His eyebrows shot up. 'Are you sure?'

Nikki nodded. 'I need another hug,' she replied.

Chris pulled off his shirt as he walked to his side of the bed, his lean body and slightly hairy chest making her feel a little giddy. He was going to take off his track pants but changed his mind and got into bed.

He waited, letting her be the one to move towards him before he gently caressed her back. Nikki snuggled against his chest and closed her eyes, the feel of his heartbeat rhythmic and soothing. It put all her nerves to rest and felt like she was finally home.

'I hope that's our excitement over for a long time. I don't think my heart could take any more action,' mumbled Chris against her hair.

'I think today has changed us all. I don't think you can go through something like that and not have it affect you. Even the kids seem different,' she mused.

'I certainly feel very blessed right now. I just want to hug everyone forever,' he said with a chuckle and then groaned when he bumped his sore chin against her head.

'Oh, my poor husband.' Nikki raised her head to look at him. 'I'm sorry for making the last few months hard. And you're right, I think we should tell the kids and my mum when we get home. Today has taught me just how much we all need each other through the good and the bad.'

Chris brushed her cheek with his finger, tucking some strands behind her ear as his eyes burned with pride and glistened with tears.

Emotions from the day still bounced around them and Nikki felt that maybe they all needed a good cry to release some of it. Feeling brave she reached for his hand and held it for a moment before slowly moving it down towards her chest.

She saw the concern and panic in his eyes. The fear of how she would cope. Nikki didn't know the answer to that either but she was learning that she couldn't keep guessing how things would turn out. She had to trust. Trust in Chris and trust in herself.

Gently she pressed his hand to the centre of her chest, holding it there over her shirt, waiting for something . . . anything . . . but nothing drastic happened. Just their heavy breathing and Chris's loving gaze locked onto her. Feeling braver she slowly moved his hand across to her heart side, where her breast used to be. She felt her heart pound harder, as if it wanted to touch his hand.

It was strange how calm she felt in this moment. As if the fear that had once consumed her had fled like disturbed butterflies. She felt strong, Chris's hand a pillar of strength that flowed into her. He smiled and she returned it.

'I don't think it's possible to love you any more than I do right now,' he said with tears falling down his face even though he was still smiling.

Nikki's flood gates opened and she cried as Chris slipped his hand around to her back and pulled her back into a hug.

Nikki cried; she cried for her missing breasts, she cried for Micky, she cried for Luke, she cried for her children and she cried for Chris. And Chris held her through it all. They fell asleep snuggled together and it was her best night's sleep in months.

38

Ashley

ASH HAD CRASHED EARLY, THE DAY'S EVENTS TAKING THEIR
toll, and she only woke when Luke pressed a kiss to her cheek.
It took a moment to get her bearings but Luke's body warmth
drew her in and she snuggled against his naked chest.

'Sorry, I didn't want to wake you,' he said.

The smile on his face said otherwise. But she instantly
forgave him. 'That's okay. How was it,' she mumbled, trying to
wake up if he needed to talk about it. 'You decided not to stay?'

'No, Micky said he was quite capable of sleeping by himself
and that I'm too old to sleep in a chair.'

Luke chuckled and she felt it reverberate down his chest.
She could tell he was gathering himself for the next bit, his
muscles tensed as he sucked in a breath.

'She was still there when I got back. I was a little surprised,
to tell you the truth. We didn't talk much but she gave us her
number. She said she wouldn't try to barge her way back into

our life but she would be available if we needed anything.
I guess that's nice. It was kind of a relief.'

Ash started tracing her finger over Luke's skin, revelling in
the firmness of it. 'How was Micky about it all?'

'He didn't say much, not sure if that's good or bad, but he
was joking with me and it was like she'd never been there. He
did say he just wants to go home and have everything back
to normal. I think that's his way of saying things aren't going to
change. I don't know, I didn't want to pressure him about his
mum. I figured he'll talk about it when he's ready.'

'How soon can he come home? Tomorrow?'

'Yeah, they'll do some more obs but he should be right to
go. Seems all clear on the concussion front. Just a broken leg
to contend with now.'

'Who's going to help you on the farm now?' She meant
it more as a joke but realised the seriousness of her question
when Luke sighed heavily.

'I've been thinking about that.'

Silence.

Whatever he'd been thinking had her a little cautious.

'And?' she finally prompted.

He propped himself up on one elbow and she could see his
unease in the light from the bathroom.

This was serious. Ash followed suit, sitting up, and then
watched Luke's eyes drop to her singlet, which only just covered
enough flesh.

He cleared his throat and glanced away. Ash pulled up the
sheet to help him concentrate but she smiled nonetheless.

'I was thinking . . . Any chance you'd be keen on a new job?

One that comes with sea views, country air and lots of space and an easy-going boss. A real job, to start when you can.'

His eyes darted back to her as he waited for her answer.

It took Ash a moment to realise what he was actually offering.

'Me! A job? With you?' She hadn't meant for it to sound so ridiculous.

'Look, I know we've only known each other a few weeks and that you have a life in Perth and a daughter set at school but on the off-chance you're thinking of a sea change . . . would you think about it? I need someone around here I can trust to help with the farm and Micky while he's stuck with one leg, and to get the campsite set up and running again. I would happily pay Em if she wanted to help out too and she could go to school with Micky.' He touched her arm. 'Look, I know what I'm asking seems huge but please think it over. It's a job, but also I'd like to see where we could go.'

Ash stared dumbly at him. She'd been caught off guard but could feel a little niggle of possibility as the idea began to grow.

'I love having you around, Ash. The thought of you going back to Perth . . . I don't like it. It's like having a night sky with no stars. I'm already thinking about how much I'll miss seeing this red hair and those freckles,' he said playing with her hair.

'Oh, Luke.'

What he was offering sounded amazing. Being with him felt right, but it was like a dream, a lotto win that surely couldn't be possible. And she had Em to think about too. Maybe Em would be happy to leave her school bullying behind? But their life was in Perth. Could she really just up-end it?

'Don't answer me yet. Think about it. Talk to Em. That's all I ask.'

'Okay. You might need to talk it over with Micky as well.'

'Yeah, I will. After we've settled in back home.' He yawned.

'Get some sleep, you're dead tired,' she said brushing a thumb across his stubbled jaw.

He burrowed back into bed and tucked her into his side.

'Not sure I can sleep with you lying next to me,' he said with a cheeky grin.

Ash was thinking the same thing but before long he was breathing heavily as he settled into a deep sleep. Content that he was resting, Ash relaxed and nodded off as well.

39

Ashley

OVER THE NEXT FEW DAYS THEY GOT MICKY HOME AND KEPT
things low-key. They gave him plenty of time to rest. No
yahooing on motorbikes or big fishing trips that he would
miss out on. On the last day of the holiday they left Luke and
Micky and took a trip into Bremer Bay to show the kids the
local beaches. All six of them crammed into Nikki's Prado.
Chris took great delight in being their tour guide, showing them
John Cove where he did his swimming lessons as a kid, then
out to Blossoms and Native Dog Beach where Luke sometimes
surfed. Little Boat Harbour was Ash's favourite, a little beach
tucked away in the rocks.

'These are just a few. There's plenty more out towards Point
Ann, Peppermint Beach and then out Luke's way is Fosters
and Reef Beach where you can catch some massive waves and
big salmon.'

'You'd never be bored,' said Ash. 'It must be magic in
summer.'

'It sure is,' said Chris excitedly. 'It's not uncommon for Blossoms to be packed with four-wheel drives from one end to the other.' He parked at the lookout, but no one was keen to brave the cold and get out of the warm car. 'Nikki and I are thinking of coming back for summer. Maybe you should too,' he said turning in his seat.

'Yes, you must!' agreed Nikki.

'Oh yay, that would be so awesome,' said Josh, his head popping up over the back seat.

'I could wear my new bathers,' Chloe piped in.

'Could we please come back too?' asked Emily. 'Please? We could do the whale tour?'

She turned her big puppy-dog eyes onto Ash and pouted.

Ash just smiled. The fact that Luke hadn't said anything since that night about his job offer made her wonder if she'd imagined it. Or if he'd changed his mind. A moment of weakness, perhaps? Confused by the arrival of his wife? Ash wasn't going to bring it up in case she ended up looking like a fool so she'd pushed it to the back of her mind and focused on enjoying their last moments here.

'Summer in Bremer would be awesome,' Ash eventually replied to Em and the whole car erupted in squeals of delight.

'Let's celebrate,' said Chris and turned the car around and headed back out of town and past a caravan park nestled in peppermint trees on the way to Fishery Beach.

'Wellstead Museum and Cafe,' said Chloe trying to read the sign that flashed past.

Ash was in love. Six kangaroos stood in a lush green area before old stone buildings. 'It's so beautiful.'

'The old museum's worth a look, and Luke says the coffee and cake here is pretty good.'

And Chris was right; a treasure trove of old farm equipment, vehicles, medical equipment and other memorabilia kept them all entertained for hours.

'Oh Mum, I should have thought to bring my phone. They have internet here,' said Chloe as they sat at a table having hot chocolates and cheesecake after their adventures. She was watching another girl using her mobile phone.

As they headed back to the car Ash looped her arm around Nikki. 'You look happy, Nik. Carefree,' Ash commented.

'Thanks. I am. It's been an amazing few days, and Chris and I have come along in leaps and bounds.'

Her grin was proof and Ash squeezed her arm. 'Oh Nik, that's so great. I've noticed the change and I'm glad you two are back on track. You're my favourite couple, besides Ryan Reynolds and Blake Lively.'

'Ha, funny.' Nik leaned in close to Ash's ear. 'I um . . . showed him my chest, and it wasn't scary, a little hard at first but I think soon we'll both be comfortable with it and he's teaching me how to love myself again. That helps.' Her face blushed slightly. 'But what about you and Luke? Chris told me he saw Denise at the hospital.'

Ash's eye bugged out. 'Oh my god, I'm so glad you know.'

'You saw her?'

'Yep.'

'What happened? Did he yell?'

'A little. But he let her have time with Micky and they managed to talk without screaming.' Ash chewed on her fingernail, suddenly anxious.

'Are you two still . . .' Nikki gestured with her fingers, tapping two fingers together in a kiss scenario.

'Yeah, but he's with Micky a lot and busier with the farm now, so I understand. But I meet him in the mornings for a chat.'

'And a kiss,' Nikki supplied.

Ash felt her face flame up and glanced to where the kids were chasing each other around the sheds. Chris was also on his way back and rounding up the kids as he went, so Ash hurried out her reply. 'Maybe a few.'

'You going to miss him? Is that why you'll come back for summer?' Nikki had dropped her voice to a rushed hush.

'Yes and maybe.'

Their last night at Hakea Hollow was spent sitting around a big bonfire talking and singing. Minus Luke, because he had to attend a town progress meeting. He was going to cancel but Chris told him to go and they would look after Micky. Ash could have killed Chris. It was her last night around the fire and she wanted to be making googly eyes with Luke through the flames and imagining holding him one last time.

Looking around the fire, it seemed she wasn't the only one feeling melancholy. Despite the upbeat singing everyone looked a little sad, staring into the flames with faraway expressions.

Even Em put her guitar down. 'At least we'll be coming back soon,' she said.

Everyone nodded and smiled. Life was about to go back to normal. Back to work, back to school.

'I just hope those mean girls have forgotten me,' she added.

'It won't matter, Em. I'll have your back. We'll just do what we talked about,' Chloe said, giving her a wink.

Ash wondered what plans the girls had cooked up but also felt relief that Em now had someone willing to stand up for her. She still had the option of moving Em to another school if things didn't improve.

'I think I'll head off to bed,' said Micky, yawning.

'Here, I'll help,' said Ash, jumping up and grabbing a torch. 'I'll light your way.'

Micky was getting quite good on his crutches, though Luke had confided that shower time wasn't much fun.

'Do you need a hand with anything else?' Ash asked when they'd reached the house. 'I can get you some water?'

Micky grinned. 'I'm right thanks, Ash. I'll just go crash into bed.'

Ash turned off the torch, realising she didn't need it in the lit house. They stood in the hallway, right near the family photo, which he glanced at now.

'You look so much like your dad there,' she said, suddenly struck by just how much.

Micky grinned. 'He's the best.' He began to hobble away but turned back. 'He likes you a lot, I can tell. And so do I,' he added as he continued to his room.

Ash smiled as she saw herself out and stood leaning against one of the bush poles on the verandah. Lights were coming down the driveway, Luke was coming home. It felt nice waiting and watching him pull up by the house as if this were her home too.

He didn't say anything, just got out of his ute and stepped towards her with purpose. His hands went straight to her face, cupping it gently, and he leaned down to kiss her lips.

'I've been thinking about doing that all night,' he mumbled into her mouth. He pulled back a fraction. 'You been waiting here for me?'

She could see desire swirling in his eyes from the light coming from his kitchen window. It sent her body temp into the red.

'I helped Micky come to bed,' she said. 'And I saw your lights as I came out and thought I'd wait.' She smiled and he kissed her again.

'I've been thinking,' he murmured against her ear.

'Thinking what?' she pushed when he didn't elaborate.

His breath was heavy as it caressed her sensitive skin.

'I've been thinking how badly I want to make love to you.'

Her body shivered as she arched towards his warmth.

'But,' he sighed. 'I'm scared that once we take that step I won't want to stop and it will just make tomorrow a million times harder.'

Ash nodded. 'You're reading my thoughts.' What if sex with Luke was the tipping point – how was she supposed to go back to Perth? They could try a long-distance relationship, but it was, what, a six-hour drive?

'As much as I want to, I don't want it to cloud our judgment,' he said while playing with her hair.

Ash looked into his eyes, wondering if he was talking about the job offer, or something more. She was about to ask when a crash of glass broke through the night. Luke jumped.

'Micky?' he called out. 'I better go.' He kissed her one last time before heading inside.

'Micky, you okay?' Ash heard them inside, their voices muffled and then laughter. She smiled and started the lonely walk back to camp, her heart extra heavy while her lips still tingled.

The next morning the camp was a hive of activity as they packed up the cars.

'Just as well we're heading home. We'd have to start eating out,' joked Chris as he took the last empty esky to his car.

Ash had been feeling off all morning and kept herself focused on last-minute cleaning to fight off the trepidation that was building. She collected all their sheets and started putting them through the washing machine in the laundry area at the end of the bathrooms.

'Hey, you don't need to do that,' said Luke.

'I don't mind,' she said as he entered.

'Unless you've taken up my offer of a job?' he said slowly. He tilted his head, waiting hopefully.

She stared. 'You still want me to?'

He frowned and stepped into her personal space. 'Of course I do. I wouldn't have asked otherwise.'

'Oh. It's just that you haven't mentioned it again, so I thought . . . you'd changed your mind.' Ash felt like a teenage girl hoping the popular boy was really asking her out.

'Never. I was just giving you the space to think about it. I don't want to pressure you into it. It has to be your decision and I understand how huge it is. It's like asking me to move to the city, it can't be done lightly.'

'I see.'

'So, I take it you haven't spoken to Em about it yet, then?'

She shook her head and felt her neck prickle with heat. 'Have you talked to Micky?'

He grinned like he'd won a bet. 'Sure have. He said it sounds cool. You know he's mad keen to see the camp restored to its former glory and he'd like to have someone to ride the bus to school with. Win–win in his book.'

Ash couldn't quite match his flippant take on the situation and shot him a look.

'Okay,' Luke admitted. 'He was concerned I might get my heart broken again, and I think he's worried about his own as well. But I told him, what's life without risks. You need to love to live.'

'Wise words, Mr Summerson,' she said, trying not to smile.

'Probably read it on a tea packet. Anyway. The choice is yours. Please think on it and get back to me.' He paused for a moment, his face turning a little pink. 'Also, I called Denise and asked for a divorce.'

Now that caught Ash off guard. 'Really?' A little bit of her hoped he'd done that for her, even just a tiny smidge.

'Yep. It was time. It's long been over and I want to start fresh.' He bent down and dropped a kiss on her forehead. 'I'm afraid if I kiss you I won't want to stop.' He sighed and stepped back and pointed a finger at her. 'And everyone is waiting by the cars for you.'

'Oh, are they?' Ash looked at her watch. 'Crap.'

She followed him out to where everyone was indeed waiting. Then the hugs and goodbyes started and Ash had to work hard to keep a lid on it.

'Bye Luke, thanks for everything,' said Em as she threw her arms around him. 'We'll be back in January, that's a promise,' she said before stepping back so Chloe could hug him.

Ash hugged Micky, who was leaning against her car so he didn't have to balance on his crutches. 'Thanks for teaching Em to drive. You're a remarkable young man,' she said with a smile as she gripped his shoulders. 'Your dad is very proud, and rightly so,' she added in a whisper.

'Thanks. I hope you come back soon,' he said with a knowing smile. His words implied more than just summertime, and she couldn't help but return his smile.

Suddenly she was facing Luke and her throat closed up.

'Hey, you. Gonna miss ya,' he said pulling her in and kissing her passionately.

Ash forgot that everyone was watching. She forgot everything. All she could think about was Luke's strong arms and his melting kiss. When he pulled away she realised everyone was cheering and whistling. Except for Josh, who was making gagging gestures.

'Couldn't resist.' Luke smiled at her unashamedly. 'Please, think about the job. If not, please come back and visit. Call me. Often.'

'I will. Bye Luke, thanks for everything.' She reached up to kiss him one last time. To drink in the salty scent of him and hardness of his body. Holiday romance be dammed, this felt like so much more.

They all piled into the cars. Chloe and Em had commandeered the back seat of her car and would swap over closer to home. Ash waved out the window, unable to open her mouth for fear of a cry escaping. Chris led the way and Ash kept watching in her rear-view mirror until Luke's tall waving form disappeared from view.

The drive to Boxwood Hill was nonstop chat in the back, the girls singing and discussing everything under the sun. It wasn't until Williams that Chloe got back in her own car so she could get home. The peaceful quiet in their car now was nice. At the edge of the city Emily finally spoke. 'Mum, what did Luke mean by the job?'

Ash's eyebrows shot up as she glanced at Em. 'Oh, yeah, he offered me a job. Well, us actually. Working at Hakea Hollow to get the camp back up and running and to help around the farm, especially while Micky is out of action. Sorry I forgot to mention it. I'd been a bit consumed by leaving,' she said pulling a sad face.

'Ah, okay. Wow. So, we could move to Bremer Bay and I'd go to Micky's school and stuff?'

'Well, yeah, if that's what we want to do. It would mean a lot of changes.'

'Hm.' Em nodded and they lapsed back into silence before she connected her phone to the car and started to play some loud music. Her thinking music, she called it.

It was well into the afternoon when they arrived home.

'Home sweet home,' said Ash as they stepped through the front door, but it felt anything but. She scratched her arm as she looked about. There were so many memories here, some good and some bad. If only she could focus on the good.

'Mum?'

Em stood by her side, glancing around the house.

'Yeah?'

'I want to go back to Bremer Bay.'

Ash looked at her daughter and smiled. 'So do I.'

40

Nikki

'HOW GOOD IS THIS, HEY?' CHRIS LEANED OVER AND KISSED her before jumping up and running towards the water. 'Come on, Nik, dip time,' he said beckoning her.

Nikki was just about at that unbearably hot stage where a swim was called for. Chloe and Em were lying side by side under the shade of the lean-to but their legs were in the sun. The two had been inseparable since arriving yesterday.

'Don't you two get burned! Chloe, we're here all summer, remember.' Nikki got up and checked where Josh was. He was boogie boarding on some waves with Micky, and further out Ash and Luke were surfing. She'd got quite good in the short time they'd been away.

'Are you sick of all this yet, Em?'

Em rolled onto her side and peered up at her over her sunglasses. 'Not for one minute,' she beamed. 'It's been so good. The small school is different but in a way that's cool because

I know everyone and we all have to get on. And Mum is so happy. I actually live in paradise,' she said gesturing around.

'Bitch,' mumbled Chloe.

Em laughed. 'Even if there is sucky internet and I have to work, but I kind of like those things too. Just don't tell Mum,' she added quickly and nestled back onto her towel. 'Chloe, you just need to come and visit more often.'

'Oh, you wait until I get my licence. I'll visit all the time.'

'Nikki, come on!' yelled Chris, waving her on.

'I'm coming.' Nikki stood up and reapplied zinc to her face and took off her hat and T-shirt.

'Oh, I love those bathers, Nikki, green is your colour,' said Em.

Nikki smiled and looked down at her suit. It was a one-piece with high-cuts and black strips up the sides. Alice, of course, had helped her pick it out. The top was quite full with just a black zip down the front. Since starting a bit of a health kick, hoping to ward off any future cancer, Nikki had lost some weight and got quite fit after joining a gym. Chris said she looked like a runway model, all willowy and toned. And she had the flat chest to boot. It was funny how it didn't worry her; she felt healthier in herself, which made her mentally stronger. And she had the love of a good man. Life was good. The only down side was that Ash was no longer around the corner and they had to resort to long phone calls. She missed her friend dearly but Alice had recently got engaged and was expecting a baby, so Nikki was finding the void being taken up by a new close friend. And there would always be summer holidays to Hakea Hollow.

Breaking the news of her cancer to her mum had been hard but being able to reassure her that it was gone had helped. Of course her mum worried, she could tell because she dropped round more and called to check up, but Nikki didn't mind. She was trying to embrace family time.

The kids took it better than expected too. They had hugged her for ages after she told them, and Josh had remained a little clingy. At times she would be in the kitchen and he would wander in, pull up a chair and start talking to her while she made dinner, rather than coming in just to raid the fridge. He had changed a bit since Bremer Bay; he still loved his games but when they got home Chris had helped Nikki enforce a curfew for devices and they had stuck to it. The kids were well adjusted now and no one bucked the rules. It probably helped after having no internet, to be able to implement change. Their family life felt better. Meal times were a no-phone zone and they actually talked. It was her favourite time of day, along with the weekend lunches in the backyard. She still had to fight Chloe on her make-up use from time to time but it was only at school. On weekends she didn't bother.

One Saturday Chloe had asked to do Nikki's make-up because she wanted to practise some new styles. Nikki had agreed and they'd chatted as she worked. Chloe finally asked the questions Nikki had been waiting for.

'So, Mum, with your boobs gone, does it feel weird?'

'It did at the start, honey. But I'm used to it now. I don't even wear my prosthesis much anymore.'

'Can I see your scars?' she'd asked timidly.

Nikki had taken her shirt off for her and Chloe had stared at her scars, silent tears rolling down her face.

'Oh, Chloe. It's okay. They don't hurt, they just look funny.'

Chloe had sniffed before throwing herself into her arms. 'They don't look bad, Mum. It's just the reminder of how close cancer came,' she'd said, hugging her tightly. 'I don't know what I'd do without you.'

Nikki had never felt so close to her daughter as she had in that moment. Telling her had been the right thing. Life was hard. Life had challenges. She couldn't protect them from that. This way she was creating stronger children who would have the ability to face future hardships. At least that's what she hoped.

'Hurry up, Nik.'

She took her time walking to the water's edge, each step purposeful, with a sway of her hips and arms in rhythm. The sand was cool and moist underfoot.

'God, you are so sexy,' Chris crooned as he came to meet her, unable to wait. He took her hands and pulled her towards the water. 'Come on, I need some cold water to hide the woody you've just given me,' he said with a naughty grin.

Nikki rolled her eyes but laughed as they splashed into the water. He pulled her towards him as a wave crashed over them, causing her to squeal with the shock of it.

Chris's body was warm, she clung to him and found the cold water was not helping his cause.

He was looking over at something, and she followed his gaze to the cliff face.

'Funny how that day almost changed our lives,' he said soberly.

'It did change our life, babe. For the better.' Then she took his face in her hands, drawing his eyes away from the events of that day and kissed him as another wave soaked them.

'Get a room, you two!' shouted Luke.

Ash and Luke were nearby on their boards; she hadn't noticed them paddling in, too preoccupied by her handsome, horny husband.

'Getting better, Ash. You'll have to give me lessons soon,' said Chris.

'Any time,' she beamed back. Her red hair spilled out over her wetsuit as she pulled the elastic band from it. Luke's eyes watched every second and she smiled.

It had only taken Ash a week to sort out moving back to Luke's and changing Em's school. And as of last week she'd put her house up for sale.

'Barbie on the beach tonight?' asked Luke.

'Hell, yeah,' replied Chris, trying to pull Nikki back against his chest just in case they could see through the water.

'We'll have to show you the blow hole Ash found too. We've made a track to it and added more tracks to this side of the hill,' he said proudly.

'A blow hole? Cool,' said Chris.

'I was walking up around the lookout, trying to see how many floral species I could find, when I heard this sound, a rush of air. I found this little dip in the earth, like a rock crevice and with each wave up would come a whoosh of air. It's so cool. It blew Micky's hat right off his head,' said Ash. 'The campers love it.'

As they all bobbed about in the water, Nikki drank in her surroundings, her friends, the sparkling water and the bright sun in a clear sky.

Life was pretty darn good.

41

Ashley

'HOW DID I KNOW I'D FIND YOU HERE,' SAID LUKE AS HE came and sat beside her on Rebecca's chair.

The sun was just about to pop its head up, filling the pale blue sky with rays of yellows and pink. The air was at its best this time in the morning.

'I read that book *Buddhism for Busy People*, it was the last book club pick and it said we should try to find time to meditate. Quieten our minds.'

Book club was a relatively new thing. She'd joined to meet more local people and it was turning out to be a fabulous idea. She'd made some new friendships and enjoyed the monthly outing.

'I see. So, this is going to be a regular event up here?' he asked sliding in beside her.

Ash nodded. 'Maybe. I do enjoy it. More now you're here.'

As if taking that as an invitation Luke bent across to kiss the spot below her ear.

'Mm, not sure if I would call that meditating, though,' she said with a smile.

He sat up but reached for her hand. 'It's nice having the crew back again, hey.'

'Yeah,' she agreed. 'Brings back memories of all this, though,' she said motioning to the cliff.

'Yep.'

They settled in silence for a while as the sun rose higher, until it was all exposed.

'I don't regret how it all turned out. Not one bit,' he said in his deep gravelly voice.

'Me either,' said Ash truthfully. Em was thriving in this environment and so happy to be herself and was learning so much from Luke and Micky that her confidence had soared. She mixed with the campers and did song nights for them. In fact, she wasn't the only one. Ash was now helping Luke build trails and little huts and her nails had grown long and she hadn't needed her oils in months.

It was happiness. Pure contentment.

'I love you, Ashley.'

Luke's eyes were shining in the light, almost taking on gold hues that made him look more like Chris. He reached for her hair, like a moth to a flame, playing with the curl.

'And I love you, Luke.'

She loved him more than she ever thought possible. At times she thought of Owen, maybe when she saw him in Emily, but it no longer came with sadness or anxiety. He had given her the most precious gift and for that she would always be thankful.

'What are you thinking about?' Luke probed.

'Just how lucky I am to have Emily.'

'And me?'

'Oh, of course,' she teased.

He took her face in his hands and kissed her in a way that showed her she would never forget how lucky she was to have him too.

Acknowledgements

FIRSTLY I HAVE TO THANK MY TEENAGE CHILDREN, BORN IN the age of technology and the fear it brings for a parent. I'm so glad social media wasn't around when I was a teenager!! You guys have inspired this story, along with our many wonderful trips to Bremer Bay. There is something about the beach that can invigorate and relax. I hope my readers get to experience that through this book. To the Bremer crew, you guys are what make Bremer that next level of awesome. (I'd go see the whales if boats didn't make me queasy!)

As always, my family have been amazing, so supportive. Huge shout out to my cousin/sister Julene Cronin, my stand-in author and proofreader, thank you! Love you long time. My family are very close and I'm truly myself when I'm with them (and they still love me!). To Mum and Dad, thank you for all that you do for me. I am the favourite, at least that's what I tell my brother. And to my bro, for the surf lessons and giving me a new favourite pastime/addiction. I look forward to hitting the waves with you again soon. (Just not where the sharks are!)

To the Hachette family, Kelly, Bella, Karen and everyone who has helped with this book in any way, THANK YOU. Also Claire for the wonderful edits. I left the best for last: Rebecca, thank you so much for believing in me and for being the most amazing publisher.

To Dr Sam Cunneen, thank you. A wonderful professional, approachable, and generous with your time. Thank you for the information and playing a starring role in the book. You and Jo have been fabulous.

Lots of love to my amazing author friends, Rach and Anthea especially, who help me through the good and bad times. You guys are my sanity and my saviours. Massive hugs to all the fabulous readers who make this possible. I continue to be here because of you, thank you.

Also by Top Ten bestselling author Fiona Palmer

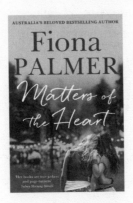

Western Australia, 2019: The **Bennets** are a farming family struggling to make ends meet. **Lizzy**, passionate about working the land, has little patience for her mother's focus on finding a suitable man for each of her five daughters.

When the dashing **Charles Bingley** buys the neighbouring property of Netherfield Park, Mrs Bennet and the entire district are atwitter with gossip and speculation. Charles and Lizzy's sister Jane form an instant connection, but it is Charlie's best friend, farming magnate **Will Darcy**, who leaves a lasting impression when he slights Lizzy, setting her against him.

Can Lizzy and Will put judgements and pride aside to each see the other for who they really are?

Australia's bestselling storyteller Fiona Palmer reimagines Jane Austen's enduring love story in this very twenty-first-century novel about family, female empowerment and matters of the heart.

'Ideal for those who love stories about romance, family dynamics and the value of friendship' – *Family Circle*

hachette
AUSTRALIA

If you would like to find out more about Hachette Australia,
our authors, upcoming events and new releases you can visit
our website or our social media channels:

hachette.com.au

 HachetteAustralia

 HachetteAus

J7